FO[...]

Behind Gudhsaerk, standing in the same place she had been when she slit the man's throat, was a vision of impossible, inhuman beauty and savagery, a sinuous, supple shape of smooth, curved limbs, nude except for the scantiest suggestion of raiment and armour. The witch elf smiled at Biaerghsven, Gudhsaerk's blood still dripping from her long-bladed daggers.

'Animal, I am named Beblieth,' she told Biaerghsven, her voice giving the Baersonling language a curious, melodious menace. 'I am going to cut your heart from your breast and present it to my lord Khaine. You may beg for mercy now.'

A WARHAMMER NOVEL

FORGED BY CHAOS

C. L. WERNER

*For Vic and Earl for their enthusiastic appreciation of my
previous work.*

A BLACK LIBRARY PUBLICATION

First published in Great Britain in 2009 by
BL Publishing,
Games Workshop Ltd.,
Willow Road, Nottingham,
NG7 2WS, UK

10 9 8 7 6 5 4 3 2 1

Cover illustration by Andrea Uderzo.
Map by Nuala Kinrade.

With thanks to EA and Mythic Entertainment.

A CIP record for this book is available from the British Library.

ISBN 13: 978 1 84416 781 4

See the Black Library on the Internet at
www.blacklibrary.com

Find out more about Games Workshop
and the world of Warhammer at
www.games-workshop.com

Find out more about Warhammer Online - Age of Reckoning at
www.warhammeronline.com

Printed and bound in the US.

THIS IS A DARK age, a bloody age, an age of daemons and of sorcery. It is an age of battle and death, and of the world's ending. Amidst all of the fire, flame and fury it is a time, too, of mighty heroes, of bold deeds and great courage.

AT THE HEART of the Old World sprawls the Empire, the largest and most powerful of the human realms. Known for its engineers, sorcerers, traders and soldiers, it is a land of great mountains, mighty rivers, dark forests and vast cities. And from his throne in Altdorf reigns the Emperor Karl Franz, sacred descendant of the founder of these lands, Sigmar, and wielder of his magical warhammer.

BUT THESE ARE far from civilised times. Across the length and breadth of the Old World, from the knightly palaces of Bretonnia to ice-bound Kislev in the far north, come rumblings of war. In the towering Worlds Edge Mountains, the orc tribes are gathering for another assault. Bandits and renegades harry the wild southern lands of the Border Princes. There are rumours of rat-things, the skaven, emerging from the sewers and swamps across the land. And from the northern wildernesses there is the ever-present threat of Chaos, of daemons and beastmen corrupted by the foul powers of the Dark Gods.
As the time of battle draws ever nearer,
the Empire needs heroes
like never before.

CHAPTER ONE

BLOOD EXPLODED FROM the Kurgan's nose as a leathery fist splattered it across the dark-haired barbarian's face. The Kurgan gave a wail of agony as pain roared through his body. In that moment of suffering, he forgot to bring his club chopping down into the slave's skull. It was an opportunity that would not come again.

Kormak ripped the heavy iron chain from the slaver's numbed fingers, then brought it whipping back, slashing open the man's face from brow to cheek. Blue-black blood dribbled from the wound with syrupy slowness as the slaver staggered back.

'Kill him!' the Kurgan roared even as Kormak's fist smacked a second time into his face, spilling him onto the rough paving of the street like a poleaxed ox.

Kormak spun around, glaring at the knot of black-faced slavers converging on him. He lashed the iron chain at them, cracking it like a whip. 'Who dies first?' he growled.

The slavers hesitated. Kormak was an imposing foe, a brawny brute of a Norscan, his limbs bulging with muscle, his skin peppered with tiny growths of bone. From either side of his head, ram-like horns thrust out from his skull. The features they framed were bestial, the nose pointed and flared like the beak of a bird of prey, the eyes little glowing embers burning from the shadow of his heavy brow. Sharpened fangs swarmed in his mouth, pushing against his cheeks and lips to further disfigure his face. Iron fetters hung in shattered disarray from his wrists and ankles and the collar about his throat was warped and broken, cracked by nothing more than the force of the muscles in his neck.

A hulking Kurgan wearing a battered kettle helm and armour flayed from the hide of some immense reptile spat curses on the defiant slave and rushed the Norscan, a grimy axe lifted high. Kormak dove beneath the furious attack, smashing bone-studded shoulder into the slaver's chest. The armour split beneath the impact and the Kurgan was bowled through the ranks of his fellows. Kormak snarled in his enemy's face, using the impetus of his momentum to drive the slaver into the steely mass of the iron wagon in which the Kurgans transported their wares. Ugly, thorn-like spikes jutted from the curled bars of the cage that rose from the bed of the wagon, sharp fangs of rusty metal from which the slavers had hung the decaying tatters of those too weak to endure the hard trek across the Wastes.

Kormak's victim shrieked as he was smashed into the side of the cage, spikes punching through breast and belly.

Kormak seized the slaver's face, twisting it and pounding it against the bars, impaling the Kurgan's skull on a spike with such force that the disembodied rib cage already spitted upon it was crushed into splinters. The Kurgan's entire body shivered and writhed, twitching like a beetle on a pin. Kormak was quick to tear the rusty axe from the dying slaver's nerveless fingers, giving a bestial grunt of murderous pleasure as he felt the reassuring weight of steel in his hand.

'Now let's give him some company on his way to meet the Crow God,' Kormak growled, hefting his stolen blade and fixing the other slavers with his malignant gaze.

The street upon which the fray was unfolding erupted into shouts and jeers. Pressed between the cyclopean walls that formed the bastion of the Inevitable City, the streets were a maze of winding lanes and passages, like the tunnels of a rat run, cast in perpetual shadow by the gigantic walls. Huge flagstones formed the base of the street, ancient blocks of granite that had been worn down by time and elements, stained and pitted by the violence and evil that had unfolded upon them down through millennia. Stakes of iron and bronze rose from between the blocks, supporting tattered banners daubed in the profane symbols of the northern tribes or the rotting wreckage of one of the city's many victims. Braziers smouldered from poles of ivory and copper, casting strange, sickly lights through the eternal twilight of the city, sending weird clouds of noxious smoke crawling through the blackness. Huddled against the steel-banded walls that towered hundreds of feet into the purple sky, like vagabonds seeking refuge in the bizarre angles of the bastion, hundreds of huts of leather and hide had been raised on supports of ivory, bone and bamboo. Here were the yurts of the Hung alongside the tents of Kurgan and the huts of Norscans, even the crude shelters of beastkin and still more savage creatures could be found squashed against the walls. Over all, glowing with spectral blue vapours, were the eyes of the bastion itself, eerie witch-lights dozens of yards across set high upon the battlements. Trapped within settings crafted from silver and engraved with swirling runes, the daemon-lights gnawed and gibbered, forever trying to break free of their bondage and slaughter the mortal things upon which their light fell.

This was the Inevitable City, a place of infamy and horror, held as a dark legend in civilised lands, told as a grim fable around the cook-fires of the northern tribes. Built by daemons or by the madness of some nameless god, it was said that no man found the Inevitable City, but rather that the city would find him when it decided he was ready. All roads in the Wastes, legend maintained, led from and to the Inevitable City, just as none of them did. One man might tread the same path for his entire life and never find the place while another might step from the familiar game trails of his own hunting grounds only to find the Inevitable City looming before him.

The city found who it would in its own time and none who stepped into the shadow of its mighty walls could leave before the city was finished with him. Such it had always been. So it would always be.

The crowd of onlookers were as motley as the cluster of tents and huts nestled against the walls. Sallow-faced Hung horsetraders eagerly cast bets with one another while Norscan reavers, still stinking of brine, howled encouragement to Kormak, but their voices were all but drowned out by the masses of dark-haired Kurgans roaring their own support of the slavers. Kormak glared at the jeering watchers, promising himself that after he killed his captors, he would wrest a tithe of wergild from the battered carcass of each and every one.

As Kormak's furious gaze swept over the crowd, he was brought up short by the smouldering eyes of one of the spectators. Like faceted gemstones, the weird eyes gleamed from a pale face darkened by the spiral of a writhing tattoo. It was a face steeped in wickedness, pinched and withered by pursuit of secrets obscene and arcane. The hook-like nose drooped beneath the loop of the enormous gold ring stabbed into one nostril and from which a tiny runestone depended. Silvery studs spitted the arching brow of a sloping forehead, shining alternately from the pale skin and the black of the tattoo in a strangely compelling pattern that made Kormak's thoughts feel fuzzy and pained. The Kurgan's colourful robes were a riotous assemblage of feathers torn from the wings of more breeds of bird than the Norscan believed could exist. A frilled collar, like the scruff of a vulture, engulfed the man's shoulders and about his waist was a girdle of flayed manflesh, the stretched face staring in mute agony from the Kurgan's midriff.

The Kurgan noticed Kormak's scrutiny and gave the Norscan a gruesome smile of blackened teeth and dripping fangs. There was condescension and scorn in the look, but also an air of avaricious interest, like a man studying a boat or a horse he was interested in. Kormak scowled back, then spun around to deal with the bold slaver who had worked up the courage to brave his axe.

Gore spurted from the maimed stump of the slaver's arm, his bronze sword clattering on the flagstones while a mongrel hound darted out from the crowd to snatch up the severed limb itself. Kormak's arm closed about the shrieking man's neck, snapping it with a savage twist. He turned and flung the twitching corpse into another pair of slavers.

'Kill him!' the slave master roared anew, still wiping blood from his mangled face. 'I want that animal dead!'

The slavelord's commands did nothing to spur his fighters. Caught between the wrath of their master and the fury of their foe, they were quickly realising that Jun the Whip was the lesser threat.

Jun saw their hesitance, kicking one warrior forward, heedless of the way the unbalanced man was quickly dropped by the Norscan's axe.

'Kill him or I'll put you all on the block and sell you to the Slaaneshi of Khard!' Jun raged.

The threat urged his warriors to a new effort. They circled Kormak like a pack of wolves, snapping and jabbing at his flanks, trying to use their numbers to offset the Norscan's greater skill. Kormak was not deceived. As one Kurgan thrust at his side with a barbed spear, the Norscan spun to cleave the collarbone of a man rushing him from the other side.

Jun watched his men being butchered, new anger boiling behind his eyes. It was not the death of his men that worried him, but the expense of replacing them. He might be able to sell their carrion to the city's beastmen or some of the lower Hung tribesmen, but it would do little to offset his losses. The cursed Norscan was costing him a small fortune! First there had been the other slaves the Norscan had strangled in the cage so that he might take their ration of water, then there had been Jun's brother-in-law, who made the mistake of stumbling too close to the bars one icy night while they were still in the Shadowlands. Jun was not enjoying the idea of telling his wife about that.

Now the filthy barbarian was chopping through Jun's most experienced man-catchers. Finding men of their experience and calibre was not going to be easy, much less after word got around how he had lost his old warband. Jun could feel that looming expense almost like a physical pain. Damn that Norscan and whatever fiends spawned him! And a curse on whatever mad impulse had made Jun seek out the Inevitable City to dispose of his wares rather than making the journey to Khard as he had intended! A chill went up the slaver's spine as he wondered if the idea had been his own, or if it had been the will of the city itself drawing him to it.

Reflexively he fingered the talisman of Tzeentch hanging around his neck and banished the superstitious thought. The Inevitable City was just a place, a settlement lost in the Wastes like so many others. It had not been built by daemons. It did not have a mind and soul of its own.

'A pity you cannot take him alive.'

Jun spun around at the throaty voice, then checked his anger when he saw the feathered robe of the speaker. He could read the meaning of the weird tattoos that covered the robed man's face. This was one who served the Raven God and was infused with the strange magics of the Changer, one of his sacred zealots. It was taboo to strike down one of the god's divine healers, a crime which even the blood-crazed servants of Khorne were loath to contemplate. The chill returned to Jun's spine as he found his eyes drawn to the bleached skull hanging from the zealot's girdle, little drops of glowing fire falling from its sockets to blaze and writhe on the ground.

'He must be a considerably valuable slave,' the zealot continued.

'He is a mad cur that will be put down and sold for meat!' Jun snapped, anger working its way past any deference common sense demanded he show the sinister priest.

'A pity,' the zealot shook his shaven head. 'I should think he would bring a mighty price, especially after such a gripping spectacle as this street-show.'

Jun's face contorted with annoyance. He gestured to the battle. One slaver was on hands and knees before Kormak, trying to push slimy loops of entrail back into his body while the Norscan held a second man by his neck a full foot off the ground. 'My men are having enough problems killing him, much less recapturing him. I'll be lucky to have a half-dozen left by the time this farce is finished!'

A black-toothed smile spread on the zealot's face. 'I could make it easier... for the right price.'

Jun eyed the feather-clad sorcerer with new suspicion. 'Why... how would you...?'

'The why is three talents of silver,' the zealot answered, holding out his hand. 'The how would turn your brain into soup if I explained it to you. Being that we are not in a sealed circle, it would not be healthy for myself either.'

Jun looked back at the swirling melee, watching Kormak bury his axe in the breastbone of an attacker, then wrench the weapon free in a spray of splintered ribs and torn flesh. 'All right,' the slave master agreed. He reached to one of his burly arms and began snapping off thin bands of silver. With a last, regretful look at the broken arm-rings, he handed them to the zealot.

The priest's hand closed about the slaver's silver. He reached to his girdle, the stretched mouth of the flayed skin opening to accept the money, snapping closed again with a wet smack when the zealot withdrew his fingers. Next, the zealot removed the skull from where it dangled from his girdle. He lifted the desiccated head, staring into its dripping sockets. Faintly, Jun could hear words escaping the zealot's lips, each syllable seeming to leave a stain in his ears. He knew this was the Dark Tongue, the sacred language of Chaos itself, and was thankful that the zealot had not shared the secret of his magic.

Coils of dark energy swirled around the skull, pouring out of its mouth in a cloud of glowing mist. Across the street, a similar cloud began to form around the horned head of the Norscan. Kormak yelled, trying to swat away the fell magic with his axe. He glared through the press of his foes, fixing his eyes on the zealot. With another bellow of fury, Kormak charged through the slavers, rushing past them to confront the magician. Jun blanched as he saw the fearsome Norscan coming, but the sinister zealot just kept whispering to the skull.

Kormak was almost upon the feathered zealot when a great booming report, like the crack of thunder, rolled through the street. The glowing mist around the heads of both Norscan and skull swept into their chosen sanctuaries, seeping into living man and dead bone like water soaking into a sponge. Three steps away from the zealot, his axe raised high, Kormak gave a final shout and toppled senseless at the sorcerer's feet.

'He is not dead,' the zealot assured Jun when the slave master prodded Kormak's body with his foot. The black-toothed grin was back as the priest nodded to his recent patron. 'I think you will find him easier to sell this way.'

Jun grinned back. 'When he gets where I'm taking him, he will wish he was dead!'

THE INEVITABLE CITY sat poised upon the lip of a mammoth crater, a pit stretching between the physical world and the eternal Void of Chaos. Swirling energies, coruscating tempests of black lightning and glowing fog rose from the nothingness of the Void, tearing away at the crumbling lip of reality that sought to bind and contain it.

The searing essence of raw madness, the Void chewed incessantly at the city, corroding its foundations with the tireless labour of an eroding tide. The broken stumps of buildings and walls hung precariously over the bottomless insanity of the pit, bits and pieces of themselves levitating as they broke away, clinging to the emptiness of the Void for hours or centuries until at last sucked down into the Realm of Chaos.

Over this vacuity, this hole in the fabric of reality, great clods of earth and stone floated upon the aethyr. Thick chains of iron stretched from each chunk of ground, tethering them one to another until finally forming an unbroken line back to the crumbling lip of the crater. The combined essence of physicality of each fragment was stronger than they were alone, strong enough even to defy the devouring hunger of the Void. Upon the largest of these floating islands, surrounded on all sides by tethered satellites of stone, sprawled the Eternal Citadel, the poisonous heart of the Inevitable City.

Huge beyond the work of human hands, the Eternal Citadel hovered above the Void, lightning crackling about its spires and battlements, tentacles of darkness and glowing fog crashing about its walls of scarlet stone, consumed and drawn down into floating gargoyle heads to be trapped within the purple light shining from mouth and eye. The central spire of the citadel stabbed upward, twisting round and round upon itself like the horn of some titanic unicorn. The top of the tower was formed into the melting half-moon and unblinking eye, the most potent of Tzeentch's profane symbols. Purple light glowed from behind the stained glass of the eye, betokening the power chained within.

It was here, within the central spire that the mortal soul of the Inevitable City reigned. The Prince of Tzeentch, Warlord of the Raven Host, mightiest of the Changer's living pawns, Tchar'zanek was the only man of sufficient cunning and power to bend the daemon spirit of the Inevitable City to his will. Lesser men would walk blindly into the fires of the Soul Forge or have both face and identity consumed by the Lyceum, to serve the spectral forces forever more as one of the Timeworn. These and even greater perils Tchar'zanek had mastered. He had stared into the Void, gazed into the abyss, felt the coruscating nothingness of the beyond stare back at him and he had not been driven mad by the experience. Chosen of the Raven God, Tchar'zanek had endured, endured to become the living instrument, the agent of the Changer upon the mortal plane. Field Marshal of the armies of Tzeentch, perhaps the last herald of the End Times.

The Chaos lord's throne room was a thing of insanity, like a great maw, needle-like fangs jutting from ceiling and floor, forming an unbroken lattice of malachite teeth. They were not constant, these fangs of stone, but subtly changed in size and shape whenever only the corner of an eye was watching them. Their weird mutters, like the babble of tiny children, formed a strange harmony with the crack of lightning outside the citadel walls. Those who concentrated too long upon the sounds could not shake the impression that the walls of the throne room and the lightning of the Void spoke to each other. Sometimes, Tchar'zanek would tilt his head and mutter back to the eerie sounds, seeming to converse with the daemonic essence of his domain.

It was within this chamber that Urbaal the Corruptor knelt upon armoured knee. Faintly, some dim part of Urbaal's mind rebelled at the otherworldly horror of this place, recoiling into the shadows of his soul. The warrior pondered the strange sensation, wondering what forgotten mystery it might reflect. Long had Urbaal been in the service of the Raven God, longer than a sane man would believe. He had forgotten much in his long quest for power and knowledge. Somehow he knew that he had once been something, someone other than Urbaal and it was the sward of some kindlier land he had walked in the long ago. The warrior dismissed the simpering nostalgia. Had there been a woman, children even? A fragment, an image tried to form itself from tattered shreds of thought, but there was too little left for his memory to reclaim. It was unimportant anyway. Nothing was important except serving mighty Tzeentch, pleasing the capricious Changer of Ways and gaining the great rewards only a god could grant.

Urbaal had served the Raven God well in the long ages of his life. He bore the mark of his god upon his flesh, the sign of Tzeentch's Chosen. The armour that encased him, the skull-faced helm of gilded horns and slit visor, the blade of burnished bronze and shining sapphire, these were gifts from his god. The armour was forged from the souls of sacrificed daemons, the blade had been grown from a shimmering pool of crystal. They were things alive, more a part of Urbaal than his own forgotten memories. They sustained the champion through his many battles, preserved him through the long war waged between gods and mortals. They had become more real to him than his own flesh, so much so that Urbaal realised what it was his mind had tried to piece from tatters of memory; the image of his own face.

The Chosen rose, straightening his tall body of sapphire plates and golden adornment. There was a suggestion of raw physical might beneath the gilded vambraces and spiked pauldrons. From the shadows of his helm, Urbaal's eyes simmered like live coals, two points of smouldering light within a nest of shadow.

The figure beside Urbaal likewise rose from the floor. He was the antithesis of the Chosen in size and appearance, presenting a short, gaunt apparition of a man, swathed in light airy robes of powder blue and soft grey, a kilt of silvery scales draped about his waist and a thick cloak of what might have been beams of moonlight billowing about his shoulders. Like that of Urbaal, the countenance of Vakaan was hidden behind the mask of his all-enclosing helm. Like the beaked face of a falcon, the silver helm stabbed forwards, great wings sweeping up and back to join into a peak above the sorcerer's skull. Vakaan was a magus, one of the warlocks of the Kurgan tribes, a villain steeped in the black arts of the Changer, able to draw daemons from the aethyr and into the physical world. It was Vakaan who spoke, and even the voice of this man who pitted his will against that of unearthly daemons shivered with awe. 'We come, Great Lord Tchar'zanek, that through your command we may better serve the Changer.'

Urbaal watched the magus bow again, the silver helm brushing against the polished floor of the throne room. Some trick of light made it seem the sorcerer's head passed through his own reflection in the glistening obsidian tiles. The babble of the walls lessened, as though the citadel itself were waiting and listening.

The thing upon the throne stirred. Taller than Urbaal, more like an ogre than a man, Tchar'zanek rose from his seat, descending from his dais on feet that were the paws of some reptilian beast rather than anything of human shape or form. The warlord's blue armour was warped and twisted around his mutated frame, all semblance of symmetry erased by the physical rewards his god had bestowed upon him. From his left side, only a single powerful arm hung from the Chaos lord's horned shoulder, but from his right side, a scythe-like insect-like limb sprouted beneath the human limb like some parasitic growth. As Tchar'zanek moved, the noxious member flexed and quivered, as though eager to lash out and rip into flesh.

The warlord's head was like his shoulders, festooned with horns. The left horn was noticeably thicker and larger than the right and its calcified substance had bled downward, spreading to engulf the better part of Tchar'zanek's face, hardening it into an armoured, unmoving carapace. The rest of Tchar'zanek's face was pale, of the colour and consistency of a fish's belly. The features were harsh, steeped in eternal evil and obscene secrets. The eyes of Tchar'zanek gleamed with the feral keenness of a panther and from each corner of his face, a thin membrane flickered to protect and moisten that indomitable gaze.

'You are here because it is the will of Tchar,' the warlord said, his voice betraying an inner power that was elemental in magnitude, like the bellow of angry storm gods. 'The names of Urbaal the Corruptor and Vakaan Daemontongue. Of all my pawns, it was your names the Changer sent to me.' Tchar'zanek stretched a clawed hand, indicating the thin figure of the sorcerer standing at the foot of his throne. The scrawny man was lost beneath the black folds of his robes, only his thorny helm serving to give the shadowy shape any distinction in the black-walled chamber.

The robed sorcerer opened a gigantic tome clutched in his wormy fingers. Sheets of wafer-thin steel turned beneath the gentlest sweep of those fingers. Urbaal could see glowing characters speeding from one page to the next, as though each steel page were writing itself as the sorcerer gazed upon it.

'Once there was made a weapon, a blade to tempt the rage of the Blood God,' the sorcerer's reedy voice crackled like kindling in a hearth. 'It was surrendered into the hands of unbelievers, those who in their foolishness would defy the true gods and who in their same foolishness still play their part in the Changer's plan. In time the weapon became a sacred relic, made sacred to one of the petty gods of the faithless lands. Its true purpose was hidden and its true name forgotten, and so was Great Tchar content for many ages of men.'

The sorcerer paused, the eyes behind his mask of thorns blazing with avarice. 'But it did not suit the plan of the Raven God to abandon the bane of his rival. A great warrior set upon the decaying towers of the elf-folk, bringing a mighty fleet to ravage the shores of their enchanted island. The fleet was broken, the warhost shattered and the warrior's bones sank into the sea, and still he had served the Changer. One of the warlord's minions, a powerful magus, fell prisoner to the elves. By spell and torture they broke his spirit and from his bleeding tongue the loremasters of the elf-folk learned many things, things they imprisoned within their books and hid away lest they be tempted by the power of such secrets.

'What is hidden may be found. A magician of the elf-folk when casting the most minor of spells, felt the touch of Tzeentch upon his spirit. He was destroyed by the unleashed might of his magic, and with him many chambers and halls were ravaged. In that destruction, things that had been hidden escaped into the light to be found once more. One of the elf loremasters discovered again the knowledge of the long-dead magus and this time it was not hidden from the elf-folk the meaning of the sorcerer's words.'

'The Changer moves our enemies,' Tchar'zanek intoned. 'The decadent elves of Ulthuan seek alliance with the unbeliever southlanders that together they might bear the holy weapon into the lands of the true gods. They seek the Bastion Stair, the gateway into the realm of Khorne. They think to cut off the Winds of Chaos by using the weapon to destroy the portal between worlds.' The warlord clenched his fist, knuckles cracking as his fingers curled against his scaly palm. 'This I will not allow.'

'But how can they know how to find the Bastion Stair?' Urbaal dared to ask his warlord. The Bastion Stair was even more of a myth to the people of the northern tribes than the Inevitable City. The gate between the world of men and that of the Blood God, it was a place from which no man had ever returned. If it existed at all.

'The Bastion Stair is a deceit made real,' the sorcerer explained. 'A dream given substance, a phantasm become physical. It does not exist as we exist, but extends in the spaces between the mortal and the eternal. It is different things at different times, moved by the murderous whims of the Blood God…'

'But solid enough now to serve the will of Tzeentch,' Tchar'zanek growled. 'My scouts have found the Bastion Stair, I have moved an entire warherd of the beastfolk to wrest it from the debased followers of Khorne. We shall await the coming of the elves and their allies. When they bring the weapon, we shall take it from them. We shall use it to cut asunder the gate between worlds and unleash the Lord of Change!'

'Too long has mighty Kakra the Timeless been the prisoner of Var'Ithrok the Skull Lord!' the sorcerer shouted. 'Chained within the Portal of Rage, his immortal power bound to the petty schemes of the Blood God! The Spear will end Kakra's enslavement. It will shatter the chains that bind him, will remove the hold of the Blood God upon the Portal of Rage! The gate between worlds will be restored to the dominion of the Raven God!

'The Winds of Chaos shall sweep over the Raven Host,' the sorcerer cackled. 'They shall fuel our spells and call down legions of daemons upon our foes! Nothing shall stand against the glory of Prince Tchar'zanek! All the world shall bow before his might!' The sorcerer's glare focused on Vakaan, then turned towards Urbaal. 'It is a sacred honour for such lowly creatures to be the instruments of Tchar'zanek's triumph.'

Urbaal felt a cold hate seep into his heart as he heard the sorcerer's sneering words. He took a step towards the robed magus. 'Yet we were chosen.'

The sorcerer gave a reluctant bow of his head. 'There was a page… a page of this tome, the *Mirror of Eternity* that related to the prophecy. To unleash the might of Change, to break the chains that bind it, would take those chosen by the Raven God. We… I could not find this page… with the last of the prophecy. Great Lord Tchar'zanek sent the beastfolk to secure the Bastion Stair, to prepare the way for his champions. Then… then the page upon which were written your names returned to us, crawling across the floor like a living thing to rejoin itself to the book!'

'Others seek the weapon,' Tchar'zanek told Urbaal. 'Do not make the mistake of assuming shared enemies mean shared purposes. Use such tools as Tzeentch presents them, but never trust them.'

'Anything that stands against the might of Tchar'zanek will feed its soul to my sword,' Urbaal replied. A hungry moan of eagerness rasped from the blade sheathed at his side, a spectral note of unearthly bloodlust.

'You are marked for great things, Urbaal,' Tchar'zanek warned. 'The finger of destiny points at you this day. Do not fail the Raven God. Do not fail me. There is nowhere in this world or the next you can hide if you do.'

CHAPTER TWO

MORNING SNOW SHIMMERED upon the pines as Freya skipped through the narrow stretch of woods that separated the village of Angvold from the icy shore of the Sea of Claws. The Baersonlings had set their village some distance from the fjord as a protective measure, to hide the settlement from the attention of raiders from the sea. Every autumn, the men of the tribe would beach their longships and drag them inland over log rollers, settling in for the chill of winter and the long twilight of the Dark Time. It had been many generations since the old Angvold had been razed to the ground by the Southlander fleet of a terrible red-haired ogress the sagas called Katrin Kindersbane. Why she had come, not even the wisest skalds could say. Many held that she had been touched by the Blood God Khorne and came to slaughter for sheer love of destruction. Others said she had entered a profane pact with Mermedus, the terrible god of the deeps to fill his sunken temples with the bloated bodies of the dead. Whatever the reason, she had left an impression upon those Baersonlings who had escaped her wrath and endured to restore the numbers of their tribe. Angvold was rebuilt far away from the sea and watchtowers placed to warn if ever death again rode the waves.

Freya did not think about such grim things, however. She was intent upon reaching one of the isolated, lonely sentry posts hidden among the trees, her tiny arms laden with a woven basket. Her father, Venyar, was serving in one of the towers, keeping his eyes peeled upon the sea. He was no thrall of Angvold's jarl, but a freeholder with a farm and a longhouse and thirty slaves of his own. But freeholder or bondsman, every able-bodied man of Angvold did his turn watching the sea. As recently as the days of Freya's grandfather there had been a terrible battle when Aesling sea-wolves had followed a longship as it was returning to the fjord and thereby discovered the secreted village. The blond-haired Aeslings had been vanquished by the dusky Baersonlings, but only at terrible cost. It was a grim lesson from wily Tchar the Trickster that it was never safe to be lax in one's vigilance, but always watching for the Hand of Change.

The little girl tensed as she heard a rustling among the snow-covered trees. Her eyes quickly scanned the boughs, looking for the telltale sign of disturbed snow and falling ice. She breathed a little easier when her study went unrewarded. Wolves and bears,

prowling ice-tigers and man-eating ymir were only a
few of the dangers that were wont to descend from
the jagged Norscan mountains to stalk the glacier-
carved valleys beside the sea. Her own father had
killed a troll in these very woods, a battle so fierce he
still bore the scars from it upon his face. Jarl Svanirs-
son had made Venyar a freeholder for his bravery and
strength, knowing that Angvold was fortunate to
have such a warrior among its people.

Freya smiled as she thought of the respect even the
jarl showed her father and she dug a mittened hand
beneath her goatskin tunic to feel the scrimshaw
dragon he had given her and which she wore about
her neck. None of his other children, even Venyar's
sons, had ever been given such a treasure, something
created with his own hands. It was a token, a silent
talisman of the bond between father and daughter.

The other children resented Freya, and she was
hated by Venyar's wife, the woman only cruelty and
pain could force her to call mother. Her real mother
had been a princess of the Graelings taken captive
when the Baersonlings raided the lands of her tribe.
Venyar had taken the woman as a war prize, but Freya
knew it was because he had loved her. Soon he raised
her from mere household thrall to become his wife –
an act that had deeply upset his first wife. It was her
constant complaining to Venyar that made him trade
Freya's mother to a huscarl from Vinnskor when
Freya was still in swaddling. Freya knew that was why
her father looked upon her with such affection,
because in her he had something of her mother that
could never be taken away from him.

Freya glanced up at the sky, watching the way the mist twinkled in the star-ridden half-night. Even at the height of day, the sun was not so strong as to make the stars hide their light. The child looked at the purple tapestry above her and picked out some of the runes her father had shown her how to find. She could see the Crow God with his crown of bone and the Old Dragon with his forked tongue. There was the Berserker, his axe lifted high and beside him Ulfscar, the hungry wolf. Venyar had told her how to find her way by looking for the sky-runes, but had also warned her that sometimes they would lie to those who trusted them too far, or if she had done something to upset Tchar the Terrible then the Changer would move the stars so that she would never find her way.

The girl shivered and made the crooked finger gesture that was said to honour the Raven, most capricious of the gods of the Baersonlings.

Again she froze as a faint, indistinguishable sound reached her ears. She peered through the snow-covered brush, trying to find any trace of what had made the sound. Perhaps it was one of her brothers trying to scare her. Freya shook her head. No, that was a foolish hope. Venyar's wife would never let *them* go into the forest alone, not *her* precious children. It had to be some beast, and the realization made the girl's blood turn cold. She glanced guiltily at the basket in her hands, thinking of the bread and cheese and mutton inside. Any winter predator would linger over such a bounty if she abandoned it; at least, unless it were one of the Forest-kin who liked the flesh of man better than anything.

Freya bit her lip as she pouted at the cowardly thought. Her father was waiting for his dinner, depending on her to bring it to him. Would a shield maiden of the sagas betray her trust simply because she heard a noise in the woods that frightened her?

With a last wary look around, Freya resumed her journey, a quicker pace in her step than before. Now she could hear the faint rustlings and stirrings more frequently, sometimes the knock of something tapping against the frozen trunk of a tree. She stopped, almost tripping over at her own momentum and spun about, trying to catch even the most fleeting glimpse of the thing she was certain was now stalking her. Always her efforts to catch it were thwarted, the sounds always coming from someplace just out of sight, their source vanishing before she could turn. Cold horror gnawed at Freya now, her imagination now thinking of wights and ghosts rather than beasts and trolls.

Now the girl was dashing through the pines, no longer daring to linger over each sound, terrified that she might see what was making them. Familiar landmarks rose from the snow: a lightning-blackened tree, a grey boulder that looked like a scowling dwarf digging out of the snow. The watchtower was close. A hundred yards, then fifty. The spectral noises came more rapidly now, filling the silence between each pulse of her pounding heart. Freya begged the Wolfhound for some of his fierce courage, the Serpent for some of its sinuous speed and the Raven for the craft to escape whatever was chasing her.

Perhaps Freya's grim gods did hear her pleas. Ahead she could see the timber struts that supported the tower, then through the trees she could see the tower itself, its thatch roof groaning beneath its shroud of snow. The girl gave a cry, squealing for her father like a frightened lamb. She fairly dove for the rough ladder that rose amid the nest of support timbers to open in the tower's trapdoor.

Freya pulled back her hand in shock, finding it covered in warm, wet crimson. Her terrified eyes stared at the rungs of the ladder and the blood that continued to drip down them in lethargic streamers. She looked with new horror at the tower, then back at the sinister forest around her. Fear finally decided her. Despite the blood on the ladder, the tower offered the only refuge from the thing in the forest. Her father would protect her. Venyar would not allow anything to get her.

Shivering, Freya climbed into the tower, her tiny body struggling to throw back the ironbound trap. The room she lifted herself into was dark, filled with shadow, the only light coming in from the long window staring out to sea. She was struck by the sinister glimmer of the sea, the play of starlight upon the crashing waves. Faintly, through the fog, she could make out a ship anchored in the fjord. It was not like the longships of Angvold, though. It was a lean, rakish thing with sharp, cruel sails and evil, wicked angles to its hull. It looked to Freya more like some barbed dagger floating on the water than a vessel. Her breath caught in her throat and she dropped the basket of provisions as she realised what it must be.

The skalds sometimes related legends, old fables about the terrible elf-folk of the sea, fiends with the souls of daemons and hearts of pitiless malice. It was better, the skalds said, for a man to cut his own throat and curse the gods than fall alive into the hands of the elves.

The trembling girl backed away from the window, recoiling from sight of the sinister ship. She felt something sticky and cloying tug at her shoes, then felt something push against her back. Freya spun around and screamed as her eyes discerned the shape that loomed over her from the shadows.

It had been Venyar, once. Now it was a mass of butchered meat, almost unrecognizable as human. Only her father's face resembled what it once had been; though horribly mutilated, Freya could not mistake him. The old grey scars, the marks of a troll's claws from the warrior's youth stood livid upon the leathery skin of his face. Painstakingly and with tortuous patience, each scar had been cut open anew, the old grey tissue saturated in fresh blood.

Freya shrieked again as the dead thing lurched at her, rolling off as she pushed at it to crash leadenly on the floor. Evil, gash-like letters had been carved into her father's bared back, some so fresh that blood was still rising to fill the wounds.

A footfall tore the girl's eyes from her father. A slender shape detached itself from the darkness, resolving before Freya's gaze into a lean figure of exquisite beauty, a faerie vision of perfection of limb and carriage. Milky white skin, like polished alabaster, shone from the shadows, broken only by the sharp, bladed blackness of armoured shoulder guards and high leather boots studded with silvery spikes of steel. The curve of the apparition's legs rose to a chain belt from which clung a brief loin-clout of translucent gossamer threaded with little strings of ruby and gold. The trim body was bare except for the compact curves of a metal bustier that trapped the swell of firm breasts beneath their clawed, blade-like steel fingers. The face of the figure was surrounded by a wild mass of black hair bound by a sort of jewelled crown or circlet, its rubies seeming to twinkle beneath the dark tresses like hungry eyes. The face itself was one of awful beauty, of such perfection of symmetry and aesthetics that it made the soul quiver with shame, desire and repulsion.

There was a chilling smile on the woman's face, a smile of sardonic amusement and perverse appetite. Slowly, with a delicate grace Freya knew no human could match, the woman lifted a hand towards her face. Blood dripped from the fang-like dagger she held in her slender, gloved fingers, blood that Freya knew belonged to her father. A pink tongue darted from between the woman's pursed lips, rolling along the bloodied steel, wiping it clean with languorous indulgence. The woman's dark eyes closed as an expression of almost ecstatic pleasure throbbed through her features. Freya could only watch in mesmerised fascination as the sinister creature repeated her perverse display with a second dagger held in her other hand.

When the last drop had been licked clean, the witch elf opened her eyes and fixed her gaze upon the little girl, as though seeing Freya for the first time. A cruel, hungry smile pulled at her mouth. She took a step towards Freya, leaning down. The thorny daggers in the elf's hands gleamed in the darkness. Freya felt her heart hammering against her chest, threatening to burst with the enormity of her fear, but still she could not force her eyes away from the sinister gaze of the elf.

The witch elf leaned in close, Freya could smell the exotic powders and perfumes that had been rubbed into the elf's pallid skin, could feel the reek of her father's blood in her nose. The black stain of the elf's lips brushed against the girl's ear.

'Boo!' the whispered word shuddered through Freya's senses.

The spell of paralysed fright was broken. The girl shrieked, darting to the trap, half jumping half falling to the ground below. As she ran back into the forest, a light melodious hiss pursued her, the harsh, musical laughter of her father's red-handed murderess.

FIRE RAGED THROUGH Angvold, tendrils of flame leaping high into the darkened sky, thick black smoke boiling through the wide lanes of the village. Shouting Norscans were everywhere, scrambling from homes, struggling to release livestock from endangered pens and stables. Amid the confusion, Jarl Biaerghsven roared commands even as his grandchildren swarmed around him, fastening the straps and catches of his armour. The jarl took his broadaxe from the crippled clutch of his youngest son, maimed during a shipwreck on the Sea of Claws. The chieftain smiled beneath his bushy black beard when he saw the mix of pride and envy in his son's eye.

'Put down those fires!' Biaerghsven growled, gesturing with his axe at a knot of thralls who had just come stumbling from one burning home. The slaves nodded hastily, scrambling to join the bondsmen and freeholders already shovelling snow onto the burning roof and wall.

Biaerghsven scowled at the sight. The fires were no natural thing, they had not leapt from any ill-tended hearth. It was no normal flame that clawed so readily and so greedily at half-frozen timber. Hrokr, Angvold's seer, would have blamed the fires on the wrath of Tchar or the curse of a witch. Biaerghsven was more pragmatic. Gods and hags did not leave faint footprints in the snow when they worked their magic.

Distinct beside a burning storehouse, the snow unmarred by fire fighters, Biaerghsven could see the narrow marks of slender boots. They were dainty marks, those that might have been left by a woman or a boy. The jarl's scowl grew. It would be like the honourless Aeslings to send children to work their mischief! They had little stomach for a proper fight, more like Kurgans in their ways than proper Norscans.

Out of the corner of his eye, the jarl saw a black-cloaked figure dart between two buildings. Suddenly, a fire leapt from the wall of the nearest home. Biaerghsven howled in rage as he spotted the saboteur, his fury drawing the armoured bulks of his huscarls to him. The chieftain gestured angrily at the fire, then at a second flame which had started on the other side of the village.

'Sneaking scum!' the jarl raged. 'Burn my village, will they. After them! I'll stretch their skins to make tents for those they've ruined this day!'

Gudhsaerk, the captain of the huscarls, lifted his gold-trimmed horn to his lips and blew a trumpeting note that rose above the crackle of flames and the shouts of frightened children. At his call, warriors detached themselves from the little knots of fire fighters, some dodging back into burning dwellings to fetch swords and axes. Soon a muster of powerful, soot-faced men was forming around Biaerghsven's huscarls, racing after the chieftain as he pursued the fire starters.

The cloaked figures had kept to the shadows, using stealth to conceal their activities, but now they broke from cover, converging upon the lane and fleeing from the village. The sight of their terror emboldened the wrathful Norscans and they bounded after the slight, womanish shapes with all the fierce passion of hunting hounds. One of the cloaked shapes stumbled and fell, cursing its comrades as they left him behind in a shrill, lilting voice. The other fugitives turned and mocked their comrade, their cruel contempt impressing Biaerghsven even through the strange, musical flavour of their weird language.

The fallen man tried to rise and Biaerghsven could see now why he had slipped. An arrow or dart was lodged in his knee, jutting from it like an accusing finger. More prominently, the jarl could see the man's face, finding that it belonged to no man at all. The skin was too fair, too pallid, too fine, the bone structure too precise and sharp, the features too perfect for anything human. There was an eerie, alien quality, a terrible sense of age and eternity, of horrible malice and malignance in that face. Biaerghsven recalled stories told him about the awful elf-folk across the seas and their loathsome habits. It made him feel a burst of deeper satisfaction when he lifted his axe and brought it chopping down, cleaving through the elf's upraised swordarm and into the hateful visage it had tried to defend.

The axe caught in the elf's skull, forcing Biaerghsven to linger over the body so that he might free it. A few of his huscarls stayed behind with him, but the rest continued their frenzied pursuit of the elven shades. Because he had fallen behind, the jarl had a perfect view of what happened next. The elves allowed the Norscans to nearly close with them, then, with a burst of speed and agility that Biaerghsven found difficult to follow, they pulled ahead. It came to the jarl that the creatures had just been playing with his warriors, allowing them to get only so close before tiring of the game. A terrible presentiment gripped the jarl as he saw the snow banks towards which the elves were now fleeing. He turned to order Gudhsaerk to sound the recall, but it was already too late.

From behind the snow banks rose a line of elves, but these wore blackened suits of armour and high, narrow helms. In their hands were bulky contraptions of steel. Sickness bubbled in Biaerghsven's throat as he recognised the similarity of the devices to the crossbows employed by guards on Tilean merchantmen. Some of his warriors must have recognised them too, for they cried out warning to their comrades and threw themselves flat. The warning was far too late. In a single volley, the elves loosed their bolts, sending steel shafts skewering into the bodies of the Norscans. The burly warriors toppled into the snow, each man spitted by shafts in belly, breast and knee. None of the men were killed outright, but lay upon the snow in screaming, bleeding piles.

The survivors of the volley and those who had thrown themselves flat now rose and charged the line. The veterans among them knew it took precious time to reload a crossbow, time in which a purposeful warrior could strike the head from the defenceless archer.

The elves stood silent and still, making no move to fit shafts to their weapons or crank back the string. They allowed the Norscans to close the distance to them, then lifted their weapons once more. Some fiendish invention enabled the crossbows to loose another volley, a repeating mechanism strange and horrible. Full into the very faces of the warriors the bolts flew, smashing through bone and flesh with terrible force. The elves did not play further games with their foes, but targeted the backs of the routed survivors of the second volley, loosing again and again with their awful crossbows.

Now, from behind the snow banks rose a third company of elves, armoured like the crossbowmen but with great scaly cloaks draped over their shoulders. They moved with the rolling prance of seamen as they charged down from their position behind the line of crossbows and began to butcher the men crippled in the volley. Biaerghsven could liken their malicious glee in the activity only to the petty cruelty of a child tormenting a wounded animal. He knew, from the way the scale-backed elves laughed, that it was with the same capricious disregard that they fell upon their prey.

Outrage swelled within Biaerghsven's heart, his loathing for these dancing fiends overwhelming his pride. 'We must abandon Angvold. Send messengers to the other villages, rouse the entire tribe, yes even send to the Sarls and Aeslings! We'll drive these devils back into the sea and send their corpses to rot in the chains of Mermedus. Sound the retreat, Gudhsaerk!'

But as the jarl turned to face the captain, he saw the huscarl's whitening face staring incredulously at the spurting stump of his right hand. In the snow at his feet, still gripping the horn, was the huscarl's severed hand. Even as Gudhsaerk opened his mouth to cry out, there was a flash of metal and a thin slit appeared across his throat. Gudhsaerk's eyes became glassy and his head slid forwards, dangling obscenely from a nearly severed neck. The dying Norscan slumped to his knees, then crashed face-first into the snow.

Behind Gudhsaerk, standing in the same place she had been when she slit the man's throat, was a vision of impossible, inhuman beauty and savagery, a sinuous, supple shape of smooth, curved limbs, nude except for the scantiest suggestion of raiment and armour. The witch elf smiled at Biaerghsven, Gudhsaerk's blood still dripping from her long-bladed daggers.

'Animal, I am named Beblieth,' she told Biaerghsven, her voice giving the Baersonling language a curious, melodious menace. 'I am going to cut your heart from your breast and present it to my lord Khaine. You may beg for mercy now.'

PRINCE INHIN BONEBAT watched the Norscan village burn, wrinkling his patrician nose at the odour of dung and animal flesh borne by the hot breeze. He clenched his gloved hands together, his fingers stroking the gemstones set into each knuckle. It was a habit that had become familiar to the crew and passengers of the *Bloodshark*, a sign that the prince was irritated. Things usually died when Inhin was irritated, often in interesting and outlandish ways.

The elf turned away from the sight, a look of utter boredom on his pale features. His gloved hands slipped from each other to caress the thorny hilts of the swords thrust beneath the sash of purple thread that circled the noble's waist above his suit of armoured plate. Inhin fixed his disapproving gaze on the grim features of Abhar Thornstrike, captain of the *Bloodshark*. The elf corsair was taller than the prince, the body beneath the heavy cloak of sea-dragon scales was thick and muscular, almost freakishly so for a race as lithe as the druchii. Even so, it was the corsair who looked away in deference.

'The beasts might have put up a bit of a fight,' Inhin observed with all the emotion of a yawn behind his tone. 'After two months at sea, this sorry spectacle is hardly enough to break the tedium.'

'They did kill two of my crew,' Abhar replied, his voice subservient in a way it had never been while the *Bloodshark* was at sea. 'And one of your shades fell to them.'

'The shade was a spy and attended to as such,' Inhin said. 'As for your crew, a few bumbling ship-rats being set upon by barbarians playing dead is hardly what I'd call entertainment. You bore me, Abhar. I think you should go now.' The prince gave a dismissive wave of his hand.

A flash of stung pride flickered in the captain's eyes, but he quickly recovered, bowing and excusing himself from the noble's presence.

Inhin watched him skulk off. Abhar would spend the next few hours working out his frustrations torturing whatever prisoners his corsairs had taken. The filthy pirate was singularly unimaginative. Fortunately his usefulness to Inhin was at an end.

'Even Abhar is not such a fool as to think you made the journey from Naggaroth simply for what sport these hairy animals can provide.'

Inhin turned, regarding the person who spoke to him. Pyra Nightblade was a striking sight in her purple gown and jewelled girdle. The hem of her dress was slit up the sides, nearly to the hip, exposing every luxurious curve of her slender legs; her bodice was parted almost to her navel, displaying the plump swell of her breasts and the shadowed valley of her cleavage.

A tall headdress, tipped with blade-like rays of silver rose from the rich thick tresses of her hair. Her face was beautiful even by the jaded tastes of her people, the sort of face that had sent men to the executioners and their families to the slavepens. Prince Inhin knew, because he had sent many of them there himself.

Pyra was a sorceress, a creation of the Convents where the arcane arts of dark magic were taught to the chosen daughters of Naggaroth's elite. They were wedded to the Witch King himself, Malekith, lord and master of the druchii. To violate the vows of a sorceress was a crime punishable by the most excruciating death; even the murderous rites of the witch elves were desirable by comparison. For a creature like Pyra, however, Inhin knew the danger was worth it. A lascivious smile graced his face as his eyes drank in her scantily clad beauty. Malekith would not be master of Naggaroth forever, Lord Uthorin was going to see to that. Then Inhin would be free to openly flaunt his possession of Pyra and her charms.

'He will believe what he is told,' Inhin said, then shrugged his shoulders. 'If he doesn't, it is of small concern. Even if he suspected our purpose here, he will never tell Malekith. He is being paid too well to betray me.'

'There is always the question of loyalty.' The objection came from the elf who stood beside Pyra, a tall, powerfully built warrior encased in elaborately gilded and engraved armour, his face hidden behind the smooth polished gleam of his horned helmet. 'There are many among our folk who still feel a sense of obligation to the Witch King.'

'Are you one of them, Sardiss?' Inhin quipped, suspicion and challenge mixing with the levity of his
tone. The prince shook his head. 'No, if Malekith
can't even maintain the loyalty of his Black Guard, he
won't have anyone's much longer. That fool and his
bitch mother are on their last legs. Soon it will be
their heads spitted on the walls of Naggarond!'

'Uthorin will need the barbarians,' Pyra pointed
out. 'He will need this warlord, this Tchar'zanek, to
wield as a weapon against the Witch King. To do that,
he will need to control the animal, make its dull
mind tractable.'

'That is what you have promised Lord Uthorin,'
Inhin said, stepping in close to the sorceress, reaching out and stroking her arm. He saw the way Sardiss
bristled inside his armour at the familiar, possessive
way he treated the woman. 'A way to control the savages and use them against both Malekith and the
decadent mongrels of Ulthuan.'

'Used properly, Tchar'zanek's Raven Host is a
weapon that will cut down all our enemies, be they
deranged tyrants or the last pathetic remnants of the
foolish asur.' Pyra slowly brushed Inhin's fingers
from her arm, as though his hand were some crawling vermin. 'Lord Uthorin will not bleed our strength
against these "high" elf traitors, he will use the animals to fight for us. Whichever side prevails, the
fleets of Naggaroth will wipe the exhausted victor
from the shores of Ulthuan and we shall again
reclaim our homeland and our birthright.'

'This relic,' Inhin asked. 'You are certain it will give
us power over the barbarians?'

'We have sailed half way across the world in pursuit of it, tortured hundreds of captives to learn of its powers. Have I not called upon the nameless powers of Old Night in pursuit of it?' Pyra shook her head. 'No, my prince, I do not risk my life and soul following a fool's errand.'

Inhin's expression became wistful, covetous. 'The Spear of Myrmidia. That fool Dolchir thinks he can use it to close the portal between worlds, to stop the flow of the Winds of Magic! He would pit himself against both gods and daemons! How like the pathetic, grandiose delusions of the asur, so supreme in their self-righteous prattle! The truly wise do not fight gods and daemons, they bend them to their will, use them to achieve their own purposes!'

'And what is your purpose, my prince?' There was just a suggestion of amusement in Pyra's voice. 'Do you support Lord Uthorin or do you return to the safer path and grovel at the feet of Malekith?'

The noble's hand shot out, curling about Pyra's jaw like a vice, twisting her head so that she was forced to look up at him. 'Do not bait me, strumpet! If I tire of you, how do you think the Witch King will receive his unfaithful bride?'

'If I *have* been unfaithful,' Pyra hissed through clenched teeth. The words caused Inhin to relent. For the first time he noticed the way Sardiss' hand had closed about the Black Guard's monstrous sword, inching it from its scabbard.

Inhin favoured Pyra with a thin, withering smile. 'You forget your place. Even in jest, such things are in ill taste.' The noble looked away, glancing back at the village, watching Abhar make sport with one of the captives. 'I will gather my warriors. It is time we were leaving this place. Abhar and his corsairs can stay behind with the ship. It would be unfortunate if anything were to befall the *Bloodshark* and her crew.' His face broke in another sardonic smile. 'Most unfortunate indeed. Lord Uthorin might never know if we ever reached Norsca.' The prince let his words linger in the chill air, then stalked off to gather his minions.

Pyra watched her patron walk away, then turned to glare at Sardiss. 'Idiot!' she spat. 'He already suspects you are a spy sent by the Witch King to watch him. The only reason he hasn't killed you is because I have convinced him that if he did then Malekith would only send someone else, someone better at the job! If he even thinks about what other activities you have been occupying yourself with…'

Sardiss bowed his armoured head. 'The cur is a traitor. His skin should already be hanging on the walls of Naggarond!'

Pyra patted the Black Guard's shoulder, as though comforting an upset dog. 'If you kill him, how will you ever bring the Spear to Malekith? We need him Sardiss.'

'But if he brings the Spear to Uthorin!' protested the warrior.

The sorceress laughed. 'Inhin will never bring the Spear to Uthorin. He wants that power for himself.' She let her hand slide down the cold surface of the Black Guard's breastplate. 'Sometimes I question why Malekith sent you. Then I remember that loyalty and intelligence are not the same thing.'

Sardiss stiffened at the jibe, then pushed Pyra from him. The Black Guard was looking past the sorceress, at the trees beyond her. Pyra turned to follow his gaze, watching as a sinister scarlet shape emerged from the trees. The red-robed, almost skeletal figure of Naagan crept towards the two elves like a jackal sniffing for carrion.

Naagan was an unsettling sight. A belt of tiny skulls, the silvered heads of sacrificed infants, circled his waist and from it swung the ugly knob of a flanged mace of elfin steel. A jewelled pectoral drooped from around his thin neck, a bronze pendant in the shape of a cauldron. Daggers and skulls were embroidered throughout his robe, forming a shifting tapestry of murder and death. His face was gaunt, cadaverous, with a pallor that was sickly even for a druchii. His iron-grey hair was streaked with lines of crimson where he had dyed it with blood.

Naagan was a disciple of the Cult of Khaine, the gruesome god of murder worshipped to the exclusion of all other gods by the dark elves of Naggaroth. The order of Khaine was unusual in its practices, its priesthood almost entirely female, with the blood-thirsty witch elves, the handmaidens of Khaine, as the bulk of their initiates. Some few men were allowed to devote themselves to the rites of Khaine; the babes who were stolen in the dead of night to be raised as the cult's assassins. Naagan was different, an outsider whose tireless devotion and fanaticism for Khaine had drawn the attention of the cult. Because the Hag Queen considered him useful, he was allowed to become one of Khaine's disciples, taught the profane rituals of the Lord of Murder.

The priest nodded his head in deference to Pyra. 'Your plan has proceeded flawlessly, mistress.' He told her, his voice like the discord of a cracked bell. 'Beblieth swam ashore and silenced the watchers before ever our ship came in sight of land. I thank you on behalf of Khaine for so many offerings, even if they were only animals.'

'What of the other thing?' Pyra asked.

Naagan's eyes sparkled with malice. He threw back the folds of his robe, exposing the trembling little girl he had concealed beneath the tapering sleeve of his raiment. 'I found it in the trees, running from one of the watch posts. I apologise, but it was the best I could find.'

Pyra stared down at Freya. The girl tried to look up at the elf, but the awful beauty of the sorceress was too terrible to her frightened mind.

'Can you find your way to other humans?' Pyra's voice was stern as she interrogated the girl, struggling with the crude human words. Freya nodded, too terrified to speak. 'That is well. You will go to them and tell them what happened here. Tell them the ship is staying here, that we are staying here.' Pyra waved her hand at the forest. 'Now go, before we kill you.'

Freya bit down on her lip to keep from crying out. Dodging away from Naagan's skeleton figure, she darted for the trees, vanishing into the snow with all the fright of a fleeing rabbit.

'The barbarians will descend on this place en masse,' stated Sardiss.

'When that happens, we will be long gone from here,' Pyra assured him. 'A pity Captain Abhar will not be able to say the same.'

A dry croak rattled from Naagan's throat. 'I only wish we could stay to see his face when the salt plugs in the hull of his ship melt and he watches his only chance for escape sink beneath the waves.' The priest shook his head with mock sadness. 'He really should have watched what I was doing down there. A more pious elf should know it does not take so long to offer the hearts of slaves to Khaine!'

CHAPTER THREE

THE SMELL OF burning flesh wafted through the soot-blackened hallway, whipping through it on a sweltering breeze. Cowering behind the heavy oak door, Ilsa could smell the stench oozing up from the tiny crack between portal and floor. The foul stink brought stinging tears to the girl's eyes and fresh sobs of despair from her trembling body.

If only she had listened to her mother. If only she had listened to Father Bottcher, the grizzled old priest of Sigmar who made the journey down from Richterberg each month to minister to the spiritual needs of the village. She should never have accepted a position at the tower, never have taken on the job of chambermaid for *him*. The pay was good, more than even the village hetman Steiner might see in a year. That was what had seduced Ilsa and the other servants away from the security and normalcy of the village for the sinister isolation of Char Peak and its macabre inhabitant. Father Bottcher had warned that they were jeopardising their immortal souls by accepting service under a wizard, but the lure of money had made them deaf to his words.

Now, too late, Ilsa understood the menace of sorcery. It was not meant for man to delve into such awful, obscene powers. Even with the noblest and most selfless intentions, only evil could come from trafficking in magic. Magister Kabus was a good man, a decent man, kind in his way and always considerate of his servants. Ilsa had never seen him call upon daemons or curdle the milk of an honest man's cow, as her mother warned her wizards were wont to do. But she had seen the effects of his spells, felt the unnatural aura that pervaded the man and even the stones of his dwelling. The tower on Char Peak was never cold in winter, no matter how deep the snow and she had seen rain sizzle as it fell upon the wizard's shoulders when he stood upon the battlements to watch an autumn storm. Such displays had made her frightened, but she had quieted her fears by reminding herself that nothing bad had happened. Nothing really bad. And there was the wizard's gold…

Ilsa's breath caught in her throat as she heard movement in the hallway outside the little closet that had become her refuge. Terror in her eyes, she shoved her hand into her mouth and bit down to stifle her sobbing. The salty taste of blood rolled across her tongue. Somewhere, in the distance, she heard a scream followed by coarse, brutal laughter. From nearer, she thought she could hear a rough, slobbery noise, like a sickly dog snuffling at the floor. Wet, squishy steps, the sound a gigantic toad might make, slapped against the flagstones as something scurried down the corridor. Despite the hand clenched between her teeth, a little moan of horror wheezed past her lips.

The evil had come! Drawn out from the darkness by Magister Kabus's reckless pursuit of forbidden, profane things. It had descended upon Char Peak like a tempest, savage and ghastly, without warning or mercy.

The snuffling noise came again, this time much louder and closer. The oak door shivered as something brushed against it, the light showing beneath it was broken by shadow. Ilsa bit down on a scream, but the effort was wasted. Whatever was outside knew she was there.

The thing pressing against the door pulled away and for a moment the door was still. A moist, barking croak, halfway between a growl and a hiss, rumbled from the hallway. Suddenly the oak door shook violently in its frame as a powerful force smashed against it. Ilsa drew her hand away and screamed, crying out to Sigmar and Shallya to preserve her from the monster outside.

If the gods heard her plea, they did not listen. The portal shuddered again, this time the thick wood splintering. Ilsa fought through her terror, pushing her legs out, setting her slippers against the rough panel, trying to bolster it against its attacker. Her effort was far too little. As the thing in the corridor

slammed against the door for a third time, Ilsa felt
the impact shiver through her bones. Daring to look
at the growing hole in the middle of the door, the
maid saw a pair of immense black eyes regarding her
hungrily. She shrieked, pulling her legs back, curling
herself into a little ball of fear in the corner of the
closet.

The black-eyed monster uttered another croak-
growl and pulled away again. It threw itself against
the oak door once, twice. On the third impact, there
was a terrible cracking sound as iron fastenings were
bent and the door beneath them ruptured. Jagged
splinters of wood stabbed out at weird angles from
the gaping hole that had been bashed through the
door.

Ilsa could see the monster now, trying to squirm its
bloated body through the opening. It was unspeak-
ably hideous, a great ball of scabby flesh with a pair
of short fat legs beneath it. Its colour was somewhere
between that of a scab and a bruise, its tough hide
peppered with ugly nodules of horn. Thick black
claws, each the size of Ilsa's hand, tipped its powerful
legs. Saucer-shaped eyes, dull and witless, stared at
her ravenously. All this, the maid noted only fleet-
ingly, for her attention was soon fixed upon the main
feature of the monster's anatomy: the gigantic mouth
that stretched from one side of its head to the other.
The beast seemed to be all mouth, so grotesquely did
its gaping maw dominate its physiognomy. Yellowed
fangs, each the size of a dagger and serrated like the
edge of a saw, jutted from the monster's mouth,
snapping and gnashing as it fought to push its way

into the closet. Ilsa had seen a wolf-trap once, but she doubted if even the trap's steely teeth could match the havoc the creature's yellow fangs could work upon flesh and bone.

Scrabbling furiously at the door, the monster pushed and wheezed its way inch by inch into the closet. Sometimes it would stretch itself, snapping at Ilsa, testing its reach. She could smell its vile breath, could see the gristle and fat from old meals trapped between its fangs. The maid gave a wail of horror, crying out to her gods again for deliverance from this devouring monstrosity.

From outside, in the hallway, Ilsa heard a shrill, whispery voice call out. She could not make out words, if indeed the grunts and snarls were words, but she saw some element of awareness intrude into the monster's eyes. The shrill voice snapped out again, then there was the meaty smack of something cracking against the monster's backside. A sullen, almost comically contrite expression came into the monster's hideous face; even in her horror, Ilsa could think only of a scolded puppy as she watched the change come over the creature. Awkwardly, with ill grace, the monster squirmed its way back out the hole and into the corridor.

It was on her tongue to give thanks to Shallya for her deliverance, when Ilsa's eyes were drawn to a new shadow blotting out the light beyond the door. Her body went cold as she saw a figure pushing itself through the hole in the door. It was like a little man, no bigger than a nine-year-old boy and with a stringy, wiry build. It wore crude garments, rough leather tunic and trousers stitched together from spongy, greasy hides. Stiff boots, little spike-like nails jutting from its toes and dagger-like thorns embedded along the inside of its calves, protected the little creature's feet while stiff gauntlets of the same spongy hide as its tunic encased its hands. Ilsa was horrified to see the dried face of a fang-creature staring at her from the back of one of the gloves, its teeth spread across the fingers of the one who wore it.

The creature's face was more horrible still, a cruel lean visage with a long slender nose and a knife-gash of a mouth filled with needle-like fangs. Beady red eyes gleamed maliciously from the leathery green skin of the creature's face. Upon its head, the dried husk of another monster formed a weird hat, the monster's withered legs dangling like the liliripes of a jester's cap. Ilsa had never seen such a creature before, but she knew it for what it was just the same and that knowledge set her heart quivering with utter terror.

The thing in the doorway was a goblin. It grinned at her, like a mischievous child, displaying those wickedly horrible teeth. Its tiny fingers pulled an ugly-looking knife from its belt. Ilsa screamed as she saw the dull, rusty blade. The goblin's grin grew wider.

'Wot dis?' the goblin cackled in its shrill whisper, its degenerate command of Reikspiel almost unintelligible. 'Ya 'fraid soft lil' humie? 'fraid ol' Zagbob gonna hurt ya?'

The goblin crept forwards, running a leathery thumb along the back of its knife. Ilsa screamed again.

'Dat gud!' Zagbob laughed. 'Make da pretty noise! Ya an' ol' Zagbob gotz plenty o' time ta play!'

GORGUT FOECHEWER STOMPED through the blood-stained halls of the tower, absently chewing on a sheep's leg, spitting clumps of wool from the side of his mouth. A massive hulk of swollen muscle and scarred flesh, the black orc stood nearly eight feet tall at the shoulder. His leathery skin was a deep shade of green where it was not marred by puckered grey scar tissue or stained white with fungus-pigment tattoos. The orc wore a crude vest of rusty chain, battered plate and polished bone, all held together with a lunatic confusion of rivets, tethers and staples. A simple grinning face, its smile twisted by grotesque fangs, was painted across the largest scrap of armour lashed over the brute's chest. Above the monster's broad, ape-like shoulders, a low-browed head jutted forwards, piggish eyes glaring from above a smashed slit of a nose and a wide gash of a mouth. Massive tusks stabbed from the orc's lower jaw, crushing his cheeks beneath their carved enamel.

Gorgut closed his beady red eyes, letting himself savour the screams and roars that echoed through the tower. His entire body quivered, throbbing with excitement, the urge to charge, to rend and rip and tear. His ham-like fist tightened about the heft of the huge cleaver-like weapon he carried, the leather grip crackling beneath the pressure. The black orc fought down the almost overwhelming impulse, forcing his steps to remain slow and unhurried. He was the boss, and he had to act like it. The boss didn't go running

around throwing himself into every scrap like some
wet-bottomed tusker cutting his first stuntie. The
boss had to be above that kind of thing, had to use
his head and stick to the plan. That was what made
him the boss. That and the ability to thrash any orc
that thought otherwise.

The warboss shouldered his way through a
smashed doorway, kicking a pile of mangled meat
that might once have been a footman out of his way.
His nostrils flared as he drank in the smell of fresh
blood and excited goblin and his stomach growled.
He stared at the sheep's leg in his hand, tossing it
aside, tired of digging wool from between his fangs.
There was enough fresh meat lying around that he
didn't want to ruin his appetite. Nagdnuf, his goblin
cook, had a variety of clever ways to prepare human.
Of course, the goblin wasn't always careful. If Gorgut
was a suspicious orc, he might have suspected the
grimy little weasel had tried to poison him with that
plump saddle merchant they'd caught on the road to
Brass Keep. He didn't think Nagdnuf would try that
again, not after Gorgut had taken the goblin's leg to
replace his spoiled supper. The black orc licked his
lips at that memory.

Growls and grunts broke the warboss from his
reverie. The room he had entered might once have
been some sort of parlour, something that had been
far too flowery and petite for any orc's tastes. It was a
shambles now, smashed furniture strewn pell mell
throughout, the burning tatters of a tapestry crumbling against the wall. A pair of orcs, thick-skulled
brutes a head shorter than Gorgut and with much

lighter coloured skins, were roaring at one another while a small clutch of goblins circled them, giggling like idiots and making whispered wagers on which of the brutes would pound the other into the ground.

'I want 'em!' snarled one orc, a scar-faced warrior with a horned helmet crushed down around his head. 'I saw 'em first and they're mine!'

'Snotling-fondling swine!' barked the other, a thick-necked reaver with an old pistol ball lodged in the bone above his eye. 'You were busy cutting up the dead human! That means they're mine!'

The helmeted orc snorted his contempt and reached down to the jumble of shattered wood piled between the two belligerents. Once, the shattered mahogany had been a richly etched cabinet, a work of uncompromised craftsmanship that would have fetched a fortune in Nuln or Altdorf. Now it was so much kindling, only its shiny brass knobs offering any interest to the raiders.

Bullet-face shoved the scarred orc away as he reached for the knobs. 'I need 'em!' the orc bellowed. 'They'll make good buttons to hold up me trousers!' He tugged at the waist of the confusion of stitched furs and hides he wore.

'And I want 'em for my ear!' snarled the other orc, tugging at the lobe of an ear already sagging from the weight of the many rings and studs embedded in it.

Bullet-face snapped a brass knob from the wreckage and bounced it off the nose of his antagonist. 'There you go, git! Have one on me!'

Spittle dripped from the scarred orc's mouth. 'I ain't wearin' nothin' that's holdin' up your trousers!'

Gorgut seized both orcs by their necks as the two warriors pounced at one another. The warboss brought both of their heads smacking together with a loud crack, then dropped the two dazed monsters to the floor. 'Find something to kill that isn't green or I'll feed you both to the squigs,' Gorgut threatened as he strode by the stunned warriors, scattering goblins as he marched past and out the other side of the parlour.

The black orc clenched his fist. He hadn't been able to take his pick when he'd left Mount Bloodhorn. Indeed, it had been pretty much any warriors and goblins greedy enough, crazy enough, or stupid enough to think scheming against Warlord Grumlok was a healthy idea. Even so, there were times when Gorgut was tempted to gut the whole lot of them. If he didn't need the slack-jawed morons. But he did need them, and not killing something when it was still useful was another thing that made him boss.

Gorgut had seen what magic had done for Grumlok, making the preening git the most powerful warlord in the Badlands. Without those magic amulets, Grumlok would be nothing, not even fit to wrangle snotlings out of holes. But with them, he was warlord and everybody bowed and scraped before him if they knew what was good for them.

Gorgut spat a blob of phlegm onto the marble tiles beneath his feet. Grumlok! He was every bit as tough and strong and clever as that swaggering stooge! He didn't need some little goblin whispering in his ear to make him cunning! All that set Grumlok over everybody was his magic. Well, Gorgut would find his own magic! Then he'd return to the Badlands, build his own horde and show Grumlok who's who and what's what!

A feral grin spread over Gorgut's face, but it quickly faded. First he had to find some magic, then he could start thinking about what he was going to do to Grumlok.

Gorgut's warband had ransacked a small village two days ago. The humans had put up a pathetic fight, which made his mob even less inclined to take any of them alive. Still, there had been a few who survived the orcs' frustrated lust for a good scrap and the goblins' penchant for torturing helpless things. Gorgut had interrogated them at length, trying to learn if they knew where he could lay his hands on some magic. They had pointed him to an isolated tower some distance from their village, telling him some sort of witch-man lived there. In gratitude, Gorgut had ordered the prisoners killed clean instead of letting the goblins play with them first.

Assaulting the tower, however, had been no easy task. The human spell-chucker had been waiting for them, making Gorgut wonder if letting his mob burn down the village had been such a smart thing. He knew smoke could be seen from a good distance.

He'd lost a fair number of his orcs trying to break into the tower. The witch-man, his scrawny body wrapped in flowing red robes embroidered with weird drawings that made Gorgut's eyes hurt, had stood upon the balcony of his tower, watching the orc vanguard rush towards his home. Then the wizard gave a terrible cry and stretched out his hand.

Five of Gorgut's biggest warriors were enveloped in flame, shrieking as the skin melted off their bones. Gorgut had brained a few goblins for laughing at the sight of his best boys running around like living torches.

The second attack went as badly as the first, but Gorgut was out of patience when he ordered the third assault on the tower. The whole mob had charged out from the woods, Gorgut and his bodyguards lingering at the back to make sure none of the goblins tried to pull a fast one and sneak back into the forest. The wizard was laughing as he continued to set Gorgut's warriors on fire, but his laughter slackened a bit when he tried to incinerate Pondsucker.

Pondsucker was Gorgut's troll, a huge smelly beast dredged up from some nameless swamp his warband had encountered after crossing the Black Mountains. The troll's warty, slimy hide was just too icky for the wizard's spells to burn. It took everything the witch-man had to finally ignite Pondsucker's scalp, but by then it was too late. The troll had reached the gates of the tower and was battering them down with his fists before his dull wits realised the top of his skull was on fire, and he was in the courtyard before his body accepted the fact that it couldn't keep walking around with everything above its shoulders burned off.

It was the loss of the troll that really upset Gorgut. He'd make the human spell-chucker pay for that, and no mistake. He was still somewhere in the tower, hiding from the orcs, trying to sneak away like some slinking goblin. Well, it wasn't going to work! Gorgut had sent his most trusted henchman to track the wizard down. Dregruk wasn't the brightest orc in his mob, but that was what made him so trustworthy; he was too stupid to do anything except exactly what he was told. Dregruk had been told to find the wizard, so that was what he would do. But to make doubly certain, Gorgut had Oddgit looking for him too. Oddgit was the most important of Gorgut's followers, a shaman from Iron Rock, an orc who had been touched by Gork and Mork, the gods of havoc and trickery. Oddgit was able to cast his own spells and see weird visions when the winds blew right. Gorgut was trusting that Oddgit would be able to sniff out another spell-chucker, even if it was a human one.

Gorgut scratched his tusk and chuckled darkly. Once they found the wizard, then it would be up to him to make the puny human talk and give up whatever magic gewgaws he had hidden in his tower. The black orc wasn't worried about that. Anything that could bleed he could make talk.

The warboss smiled as he heard the sounds of battle ringing down the corridor ahead. The wizard's retinue was putting up a better fight than that miserable little village, he had to give them credit for that. As he loped down the hall, he saw a burly orc bouncing an armoured human's head against the wall. The way the helmet was dented and the wall was stained, Gorgut was pretty sure his minion's plaything was dead. He cuffed the orc's ear, feeling cartilage crumble beneath his fist. The orc spun around, dropping his bloodied toy and started to snarl. One look at Gorgut's glowering face made him think better of it, however, and the warrior hastily retrieved his axe from where he had dropped it on the floor and scurried off before Gorgut could hit him again.

Witless scum! Gorgut spat as he watched his warrior leg it down the hall. They'd forget their own names if the chance to bash something came along. Well, if they forgot what they were here for, Gorgut would make sure there were some green bodies joining those of the humans when Nagdnuf made his stew!

The black orc pondered vengeful thoughts for a time before he remembered the sounds of battle that had lured him down the hall. He could still hear them, and among the cries he thought he could hear Oddgit calling out to the orc gods as the shaman worked his magic. There was something strained, almost desperate in the shaman's voice, something that made Gorgut's belly clench. Anything that could defy the shaman's spells wasn't something he really wanted to meet.

Unless it was the human spell-chucker!

Gorgut started running down the hall like a mad bull. If Oddgit killed the wizard, he'd wring the gory old tusker's neck!

THE COWLED ORC shaman stood among the ashes of its minders and guards, soot-blackened sweat dripping down its sloping face. It stared through eyes that were foggy with smoke and hacked cinders from its throat. Its wolfskin garb was hanging from its emaciated, withered frame in charred strips, its bone-adorned staff nothing but a blackened stick crumbling beneath its meaty paw.

Kastern Kabus, Magister of the Bright Order, Pyromancer of Char Peak, glared down at the monster. The fire wizard stood at the top of a flight of stairs that led up into the inner sanctum of the tower. It was here he had decided to make his stand and it was here that the orc shaman and its warriors had found him.

The wizard curled his lip in a sneer as he saw the greenskin drawing power into itself with his witch-sight. The crude magic of the savage monster was pathetic, a rough patchwork of primitive sorcery that only skimmed the power of the aethyr, drawing scraps and bits from all the colours of magic in its desperate need for power. Kastern could even see the spell taking shape in the shaman's brain. A giant green foot smashing down on the wizard! The magister sighed. It was the third time the monster had tried that particular incantation. If the beast's magic was poor, its imagination was outright pathetic. Kastern focused upon the orc's spell, dissipating it before it could even begin to form.

The shaman staggered as its magic was dispelled, some of the severed energies snapping back into its body with the violence of a cracking whip. The charred staff fell from its fist, sending a little puff of orc ash rising as it hit the floor.

Kastern threw back his shoulders, his crimson robes billowing about him as though they were living flames. The wizard's eyes were little embers that quickly blazed into life, burning from the depths of his lean face, little fingers of fire singeing his red eyebrows. Kastern extended a hand clothed in a scarlet

gauntlet and focused the power of Aqshy, the Red
Wind of Magic, into his mind and fingers.

The orc below howled as its remaining rags began
to smoke. It slapped desperately at the burning garments, then shrieked as its leathery green hide began
to smoulder as well. Panic gripped the monster, and
panic was all that its enemy had been waiting for.

Kastern leaned forward with his other hand, the
one holding a staff of fire-blackened wood bound
in copper and tipped with an enormous fire opal.
Writhing dragons of gold held the gemstone in
place and as the wizard's lips began to form strange
words, the mouths of the dragons began to smoke.
The pyromancer glared down at the shaman one
last time, then pictured the monster vanishing
within a sphere of fire. From the head of the staff, a
blast of withering heat exploded, sending a ball of
crackling, shimmering flame straight into the reeling shaman.

The wizard did not revel in his adversary's destruction, but was instantly locked in a battle with the
powers he had drawn upon, forcing them back into
the aethyr only by an effort of will. The fires of Aqshy
were not the most servile of forces and given the
chance, they would destroy his home every bit as
quickly as the orcs.

It was only an instant that Kastern was distracted by
the truculence of his magic, but it was enough. When
he again focused upon the physical world around
him, he saw a mob of snarling beasts gathered at the
foot of the stairs. A second group of orcs had come
and judging by the way their black-skinned leader

was looking at him, they weren't too happy about the loss of their shaman.

GORGUT REACHED THE stairway just in time to see the human wizard's spell immolate Oddgit. He watched as the shaman's smoking skeleton wilted into the floor, crashing in a cloud of dust that the black orc knew was all that remained of the shaman's guards.

The warboss fingered his axe, glaring murder at the scrawny human with the red beard and gloved hands. He'd take the human's beard out by its roots, hair by hair, and make the spell-chucker eat it! He'd take those gloves and make him eat them too! He'd take that pretty staff and...

Gorgut snapped around, attention drawn to the sound of feet behind him. He found himself face-to-tusk with a burly, broad-shouldered orc wearing a vest of steel plates and a look of confused rage beneath a spiky bronze helm. The warboss fixed his gaze on the beady eyes of his lieutenant.

'Where were you idiots?'

'Looking for the spell-chucker, boss,' Somehow, even from a hulking brute like Dregruk, the words came out in a sort of desperate whine.

'Well, I found him!' Gorgut snarled. 'He just done for Oddgit and if you don't want to end the same, you'll get him!'

Dregruk growled, hefting the massive choppas he carried, huge scraps of sharpened steel that were equal parts sword and meat cleaver. The orc's savage bloodlust spread to the rest of his mob and they surged past Gorgut, eager to wreak havoc.

'Alive!' Gorgut raged. 'I want the spell-chucker alive! I want his magic!'

Kicking a few of the rear guard, Gorgut realised that they were too far-gone to listen to orders. When they were like this, they knew neither fear nor common sense. And the warboss didn't have time to kill a few to remind them what a command was. Cursing, Gorgut smashed his way through the throng, embracing the oldest maxim of warlords throughout the Badlands.

If you need something done right, you'd better do it yourself.

Gorgut managed to head off his mob of warriors before they reached the stairs. Amazingly, the human wizard didn't seem to notice them. Gorgut felt a momentary chill as he saw the little fires burning where the human's eyes should be, then remembered his warriors were watching him and shook off his fear. It wasn't good to show weakness around the lads, it gave them funny ideas.

'All right you scum!' Gorgut snapped at his warriors. 'I'll get him, you just make sure he doesn't get away!' He slammed the head of his axe into the foot of the foremost warrior, sending the orc hopping back with a howl of agony and a few severed toes. 'And remember: don't kill nothing!' Coupled with the visual aid of their mangled friend, Gorgut hoped they might remember that last bit.

The black orc surged up the stairs, Dregruk and the others at his heels. They hadn't taken more than a few steps before the wizard's eyes became black pits of hostility. For a moment the man stared down at them, then fires swelled once more in the depths of his eyes. He stretched his hand, gestured with his staff and the stench of brimstone filled the air. Gorgut yelped in pain as bars of writhing flame leapt into life all around him, penning himself and Dregruk's mob in a fiery cage of searing magic.

Dregruk raged at the fiery bars, yelling at them as though they were some jeering enemy. He slashed at them with his choppas, only relenting when he saw blobs of molten metal dripping down from the pitted steel.

The wizard was smiling beneath his crimson beard, a smile filled with malice and madness. He stretched his fingers again and Gorgut felt a blast of heat wash over him, could smell his clothes and armour beginning to smoulder as little fingers of fire began to ooze up from within his own body. The black orc howled, rushing at the bars of flame, but even his rage was not enough to overcome the withering heat and he recoiled in agony.

THE WIZARD CLUTCHED at his breast, feeling his heart hammering against his ribs. The strain, the ordeal of drawing the fires of magic into his body was wearing on him, draining his strength, devouring his vitality, consuming his very essence. Kastern knew he could not draw upon such forces much longer. Not without help.

Kastern glared down at the orcs in their cage of fire. Grimly, he reached a decision. Raising a trembling hand, he tore a tiny lead locket from around his neck. Summoning the tiniest flicker of energy, his hand became white-hot, the lead melting through his fingers, exposing what it had imprisoned. The ugly black stone gleamed from his palm, its corrupt energies already flooding through him as it melted through his skin. Warpstone was a substance accursed and outlawed throughout the Empire, mere possession of it grounds for the owner to be burned as a witch. It was an ironic sort of fate for a fire wizard to fear, Kastern considered. A bitter smile came to him as he fought to control the invigorating flow of energy. If he didn't destroy the orcs he was a dead man anyway.

Kastern Kabus began to whisper, hot words singeing his lips as he evoked the dire power of Aqshy. He could feel his blood burning beneath his skin as he drew the magic down inside himself, gathering it for one blast of fire that would annihilate the foul invaders of his home. The flames would purge his sanctum of the monsters, leaving only soot and ash. His beard began to curl as the heated whisper grew into a chanted snarl, as the fires of Kastern's body began to rise.

Stabbing pain in his side snapped the wizard's concentration. Kastern staggered, hands reflexively closing about a black-feathered shaft protruding from his hip. He could feel the venom of the arrow sizzling into his body. Quickly he ripped it free, slapping his hand against the wound, invoking his magic to cauterise the injury. Flame burst all around his hand, reducing his scarlet gauntlet to burned tatters. Beneath his palm, the pyromancer's flesh sizzled and blackened.

Kastern raised his staff just as a horrible bounding thing came capering towards him, a fungoid horror of claws and fangs. The wizard sent a blast of force through the staff, rendering it white-hot as it struck the monster. The squig squealed like a gutted pig, horns and flesh wilting beneath the touch of the super-heated staff. It started to retreat, but the wizard opened his mouth, releasing more of the magic he had drawn into himself in a fiery gout of dragon's breath. The squealing monster crumbled into cinders even as it fled.

An arrow hissed through the air, but this time the wizard was ready for it, unleashing a withering pulse of magic that turned it to ash before it could strike him. Kastern's eyes narrowed as he saw the archer, a wiry little goblin wearing leathery hides. He pointed a still blazing finger at the goblin, glaring death at the back-shooting villain. Even as he pointed, a tinge of horror raced through Kastern's mind.

Why was the goblin laughing at him?

The answer roared at him when Kastern spun around. Distracted by the squig and the goblin, he had not concentrated on the cage of fire that penned in the orcs below! He turned, finding the last of the fiery bars flickering out and the largest of the orcs, the black-skinned brute who was their leader, lunging up the stairs towards him.

Hastily, the wizard drew power back into his body, frantically summoning a conjuration with power enough to destroy the charging black orc. Forcing himself to concentrate, trying to blot out everything to work his spell, Kastern was struck dumb when the warlord roared at him in debased Reikspiel.

'I'z gonna feed ya that stick, spell-chucka!'

GORGUT CHUCKLED AS he saw the human shut his mouth in the middle of his spell, stunned by the coarse barbarity of the warlord's threat. It was only a momentary lapse of concentration, but it was enough to get the black orc ten steps closer. He watched as the wizard did something with his hands, blinking his eyes shut as a glaring light flashed before him. When he opened them again, a flaming sword had erupted from the pyromancer's hand. The black orc grunted appreciatively. He'd been afraid it was going to be easy.

The warlord brought his axe smashing down at the wizard, but Kastern's flaming sword blocked the blow, resisting the orc's bulk and strength with a force that went far beyond the wizard's frail physique. Gorgut's nostrils flared as the smell of burning steel reached him. He reared back, roaring in fury as he saw the notch the wizard's fiery sword had melted in the edge of his axe. Forgetting his own orders, he brought the axe chopping down in a brutal arc aimed at the man's face.

Again the flaming sword was there to intercept, again Gorgut could smell his favourite weapon being ruined by the human's cursed magic. The black orc snarled, spitting a blob of phlegm at the wizard's eyes. The spittle sizzled as it hit the super-heated air that billowed around the magister. Kastern sneered at the orc, pressing the attack. Gorgut felt the fiery sword slash across his armour, felt it singe his skin as it swept past. He felt himself being driven down, forced back by the dazzling flash of the wizard's sword. He retreated one step, then two. Up above, he could see Zagbob the goblin scout watching the duel, snickering his weasely laugh.

Gorgut's face contorted into a scowl. *He* was warboss! Not some crippled thing dancing to amuse goblins! The black orc stared into the human's fiery eyes, then brought his steel-shod boot crashing up between the wizard's legs. The fires winked out in the man's eyes as though cold water had been thrown on them. They were black and wide and filled with pain. The flaming sword fell from the wizard's hands as he clutched at his groin, the spectral weapon evaporating as it floated to the floor.

Gorgut brought the heft of his axe cracking into the top of the stunned wizard's skull, spilling him onto the stairs at his feet. He gave the man a good kick in the ribs just to make sure he was out, then set a foot on the wizard's back. Puffing out his chest, Gorgut looked down at Dregruk and his warriors.

'That's how you do a spell-chucker,' Gorgut told them, the posturing only slightly spoiled when his half-melted breastplate decided at that moment to fall off and clatter down the stairs. Gorgut wrinkled his face in annoyance and gave the wizard another kick.

'WAKE UP, YA zoogin' grot-fondlin' spook-calla!'

Kastern tried to open his eyes, but the left one was swollen shut. As the swirling mix of colours in the right one assembled themselves into an image, he found himself wishing the right one was swollen too. He was sitting in what had once been his library. The orcs had turned it into a rough bivouac because of the large fireplace that dominated the western wall. Entire shelves of books had been gutted, the priceless tomes they had held now acting as kindling for the upholstered Westerland furniture the greenskins were burning in the hearth. He could see a couple of goblins trying to pry gilded letters off the binding of a volume of Teradasch while a one-eyed orc was flipping through a first-edition Sierck and ripping out the illustrations. Another orc was using a poker for a spit and cooking something with fingers. Kastern closed his good eye then, not wanting to see any more.

'Da boss talkin' ta ya!'

Kastern felt a sharp pain in his side. He gasped, trying to lash out at his tormentor. It was that stinking goblin, the one that shot the arrow into him. The little fiend was more than back-shooter and scout to these monsters, he was also their resident sadist and torturer. He had an endless array of daggers and needles crafted from the fangs and claws of squigs and a loathsomely inventive mind for using them. He regretted now that he hadn't seared the little fiend's brain when he had the chance.

All chance was gone now. His tower was a shambles, his servants murdered, his treasures sacked and looted by monsters too stupid to recognise their worth. He struggled in the chains that held him and as he did so, Kastern reflected on the worst the orcs had done to him. Fearing his magic, they had made him safe to keep prisoner.

They had cut off his hands.

Even if he survived, even if somehow he escaped, Kastern knew he would never again wield the power of Aqshy. If he lived, he would do so as a mundane, maimed cripple. He would never feel the fires of magic burning through him again, never again feel the might of sorcery. It was better to be dead.

'We'z gonna play dis game all da day.' It was the orc speaking, the big black-skinned devil who had captured him on the stairs. The brute had been hovering near throughout Kastern's ordeal, slapping around the goblins whenever they got too enthusiastic with their torture.

The monster had made repeated demands for 'da powa'. It had taken three of Kastern's teeth before he understood the orc was looking for magic. The stupid, dim-witted brute seemed to think he could just collect magic like he could sheep or swine! He thought Kastern had a hoard of artefacts locked away in his tower, like some miser with a pile of gold. It didn't do any good to explain that the monsters had burned most of his treasures when they violated his library. What few charms and talismans he did have were things the orcs were singularly too thick to appreciate: a necklace to keep rain off your head was hardly going to impress a monster whose idea of hygiene was to wipe his bloodstained hands on another orc's trousers instead of his own!

'Where'z yer magic!' the black orc growled. Kastern flinched as Gorgut flicked one of his stubby fingers against the tip of his already broken nose. 'I knowz ya gotz lotz, spell-chucka! Now, where'z da swag!'

'Yeah, da swag!' chimed in Zagbob, twisting one of the needles in Kastern's arm.

Gorgut backhanded the goblin, sending him flying. 'I'z doin' da talkin' squig-sucka!'

Kastern coughed, blood oozing down his lip. He fought down the urge to laugh. 'There's... there's nothing... here,' Kastern managed. He winced as Gorgut clenched his fist. The last time the orc had hit him, it had broken his jaw. 'But... I know... where there's lots... of... power!'

Gorgut leaned in close to listen, oblivious to the smile twisting the wizard's battered face.

'Go... go north... past the lands of ice... past the places of snow,' Kastern licked his lips, feeling the taste of blood on his tongue. 'Keep going north... keep north until the land turns purple and the sky becomes green... keep north until the sun is like a ball of blood and the clouds whisper to you.' Kastern spit a broken tooth from his mouth. 'That's where you... you will find... power!'

Gorgut slapped the human's face in what would have been an almost appreciative gesture if there had been less force behind it. 'Dat's more like it, spell-chucka!' the black orc grunted. He patted his belly and turned about. 'One you lot go an' fetch dat lazy gimp Nagdnuf! I'z gotz some meat fer da stew!' The warboss looked again at Kastern and chuckled darkly. 'Betta tell 'im ta pick up some o' Oddgit's bones too! Might need 'em fer texture!'

Kastern was too resigned to death already to feel any horror at the end the orc planned for him. The only thing he could think of was how much worse it would be for the greenskins when they got where he was sending them. The Chaos Wastes beyond the borders of Kislev were lands of madness and mutation, a place that had swallowed up entire armies without a trace, where daemons and monsters reigned and the very land itself was cursed with insanity. Oh yes, Gorgut would find his magic, and then the filthy beast would choke on it!

'Oi!' Gorgut bellowed as he stomped among the lounging bulks of his warriors. 'Any youse lot know where'z north?'

CHAPTER FOUR

THE FEAST HALL of Hafn Hundred-eyes was a din of boisterous shouts, drunken boasts and caustic laughter. The reek of spilled mead, human sweat, vomit and the noxious fumes of ox-dung fires rose lazily up into the folded ceiling of the immense mammoth-hide tent far overhead. A brutish chandelier, crafted from nine intertwined skeletons, candles of human fat dripping from their skeletal claws, hung above the misshapen throng crowded about the long timber tables that stretched across the hall. Burly warriors clad in scraps of fur and leather, hulking knights encased in blackened armour of steel and bronze, even the robed figures of sorcerers and seers crowded about the hall, draining ivory flagons and leather jacks, jesting, cursing and carousing.

Hafn Hundred-eyes watched the activity filling his hall with a greedy smile. Many had been drawn to the Inevitable City by the promise of glory and the favour of the Changer. Not Hafn. He had made the journey out of baser concerns. Wherever a body of warriors gathered, wherever an army such as the Raven Host assembled, there would be a place for men like him. The warriors would need places to drink and feast, places to entertain them when they were not campaigning in the name of the Raven God. Hafn provided such a place, and for a little silver, a little gold, any man in the Raven Host was welcome beneath the roof of his tent.

The Baersonling chuckled as he watched one of the lissom serving wenches dart away from the drunken grasp of a Kurgan, then slide back into the man's embrace when he set a bracelet of gold and emeralds down on the table. Hafn had taught his daughters well. Any warrior so deep in his cups already would make easy pickings in one of the back rooms once they were alone. He rubbed the eye set in his chin, causing it to water and moisten the thin black beard to either side of it. When the girl was done, he hoped she had sense to send the kitchen thralls in to clean up. The patrons would be hungry and there was no sense letting all that meat go to waste.

'You agree on the price then?'

Hafn didn't bother to turn around. The dozen eyes staring from the back of his shaven head could see Jun well enough already. 'Five talents of silver for a pit-slave? The gods may have seen fit to render you mad or stupid, but Hafn still has his wits.' The Baersonling touched a clawed finger to the temple of his head. 'Two, and at that I am being generous!'

Jun sulked at the rebuke, thrusting his thumbs beneath his belt and puffing himself out. 'You know he's worth ten times that. Every man in this place has heard about how he tried to escape, the mess he made out of my warriors. You'll make a fortune on the bets alone!'

Hafn shifted the gaze of several clusters of eyes to stare at the Norscan chained between two of Jun's slavers. The Baersonling had to admit the man was an impressive specimen. He'd bought worse slaves for his hall's fighting pit. There was a look of such homicidal rage in the prisoner's eyes that Hafn felt nervous just being around him. If he had that effect on a man like himself, Hafn knew the effect the slave would have on his patrons. Jun was right, there was money to be made from such a spectacle. Still, the slaver was much too anxious to dispose of the Norscan, and that made Hafn suspicious.

'You think so!' Hafn said. 'You tell me to buy this slave and put him in the pit with Noeyes! Who's going to wager on that?' The Baersonling laughed cruelly. 'Noeyes has torn bigger men to ribbons without trying. Pox of Nurgle! I set ten ungors against Noeyes just last night and they didn't even scratch it! No one is going to bet on this… this Kormak!'

'They will if they heard about what he did to my men,' Jun's voice dripped bitterness.

Hafn's eyes, those with lids at least, narrowed dangerously. 'If he's really that dangerous, then I certainly don't want him. They come here to see Noeyes rip things apart. What if this idiot manages to hurt Noeyes, or even kill it?'

Jun turned and looked into Kormak's glowering face. Every ounce of spite in the slaver's body spread across his visage. 'I said you should put him in the pit with Noeyes,' Jun said, rubbing the scar across his face where Kormak's chain had gouged his flesh. 'I didn't say to give him anything to fight it with.'

Hafn chortled at the villainous idea and began counting out the slaver's silver.

KORMAK'S THICK FINGERS carefully kneaded the cramped muscles of his arms after Jun's slavers removed his shackles. The two Kurgans quickly scrambled for the guide ropes that would haul them out of the pit, as eager to be away from the powerful Norscan as the thing he would soon face. Kormak ignored the fleeing men, instead scrutinizing his new surroundings. The fighting pit in Hafn's feast hall was a roughly cylindrical gouge in the bare rock of the floor, twenty-five feet deep and nearly twice as wide in diameter. Above him, Kormak could see the long feast tables with their covers of flayed skin and their benches of unworked timber. The face of each of the revelling warriors was turned toward the pit, raucous calls for fresh drink drowned out by eager wagering between the tables.

The pit itself was floored in great flagstones of green-veined limestone. The walls were studded with spears, their points jutting out from the bare earth in a crazed pattern of iron spikes. On several, Kormak could see the decayed remains of men and half-men dangling like rotten fruit. At the far side of the pit was a great iron gate and from it came the foulest stink to

ever assault the Norscan's nose. It was the reek of
death itself, magnified and compounded into a terrible aggregate of horror. A low warbling groan
sounded from the darkness behind the gate and
sometimes a furtive snuffling sound like a sickly dog
sniffing for scraps.

'Friends and celebrants!' the booming voice of Hafn
Hundred-eyes roared over the din of the feast hall.
'Warriors of the Raven Host! Huscarls of Great
Tchar'zanek the Mighty! Tonight I present you an
experience unlike any other! Tonight I offer you the
sensation of sensations! From the frozen wastes of
Norsca, at great expense and danger, I bring you Kormak the Troll-eater, Scourge of the Sarls and Sorrow
of the Aeslings! Killer of men and women and daemons all! Twenty warriors lost their lives bringing this
barbarian atavism from the wilds of the Shadowlands
to set him here, before your eyes. Some of you may
have seen him try to break free in the very streets of
the Inevitable City itself.' Hafn paused and waited
while murmurs of conversation crawled through the
hall as those who had seen the street fight related it
for the benefit of those who had not. After a time,
Hafn raised his arms high, motioning for silence.

'Yes, here he stands,' Hafn declared. 'Kormak,
whose father was one of the Blood God's hounds
and whose mother was the most debased she-devil
ever born of the Tong. What foe, what adversary can
we pit against this human monster that would be
worthy of his terrible might? What antagonist can we
loose against Kormak Giant-smasher that would be
worthy of this audience?'

Hafn folded his arms and waited. It did not take long. First a few voices, then the voices spread into a chant, from a chant into a howl. 'Noeyes! Noeyes! NOEYES!'

The Baersonling raised his hand and nodded his head. 'You have spoken, friends. You have asked for it, you shall be given it. Tonight, Kormak of the Skull Land shall face Noeyes!'

The announcement brought a roar of approval from the crowded hall. Wagers passed quickly among the tables.

Kormak stared straight up from the pit, into the smirking face of Jun the slaver. The Norscan gestured with his thumb at the gate in the far wall. The sounds behind it had grown into a moaning growl and the iron bars trembled in their settings as something huge and powerful smashed against them.

'Noeyes?' Kormak asked. Jun's smile grew. 'How do you expect me to fight without a weapon?'

The Kurgan slaver spit onto the floor at Kormak's feet. 'I don't expect you to fight. I expect you to die. Slowly. In great pain. Noeyes doesn't like to eat things that aren't still moving.'

Kormak made a lunge at the laughing slaver, but his leap was not enough to carry him past the ring of spears set into the wall of the pit. He fell back, his shoulder and side gashed by the iron points. The smell of blood excited the thing behind the gate. The moaning growl became a whine, eager and hungry. Dust and pebbles trickled from the gate's settings.

Kormak turned and faced the gate, glaring at the darkness beyond. They wanted a spectacle, he would give them a spectacle. And then he would climb out of this pit and kill every last one of them!

Hafn gave a signal and a knot of burly thralls bent their backs to an immense wheel. As the wheel turned, chains lifted the iron gate, removing the barrier between pit and shadow.

Before the gate was more than a few feet off the ground, a great clawed hand was groping beneath it, trying to stretch itself far enough to reach Kormak. It was a monstrous hand, bigger than a man's chest, each finger longer than Kormak's forearm and tipped by a black talon as large as his entire hand. The apparition was covered in leprous, mouldy skin that was almost transparent where it clung tightly to the bones underneath. Ugly, fungoid growths and black tumours mottled the pallid hide, adding to its charnel stink.

After a time, the scrabbling claw relented and was pulled back into the shadows. The hungry whine and snuffling noises rose as the thing in the darkness resigned itself to wait for the gate to finish its ascent. Kormak waited as well, watching as the iron barrier slowly groaned along on its rusty chains.

The instant that groan ended, a gigantic figure sprang from the black cave. Kormak had judged that it would be immense from the size of its claw, but he had not prepared himself for the awful sight of its full form. It towered over the mouth of its cave, twelve-feet tall despite its curved and hunched back. Its shape was roughly the approximation of a man's, but monstrously immense and hideous. There was some suggestion of an ogre about the broad, thick bone-structure and heavy features of the face, but there was none of the prodigious power and glutto-nous exuberance of an ogre in its withered flesh and scrawny frame. In his youth, Kormak had helped his father destroy a pack of ghouls that had dug their way into the funeral barrows of their ancestors. This was something of the same sort, a ghoulish debasement of ogre.

The gangrel thing snuffled and snarled at the crowd above, displaying its crooked maw filled with cracked yellow tusks. The monster's face was twisted with the most abominable depravity, an almost idiot malig-nance that was all the more horrible for the primitive instinct behind it. Kormak raised his head to stare defiantly in the monster's eyes but shrank back from it in loathing instead. True to its name, the monster had none for the Norscan to stare into. To either side of its squashed, bulbous nose there was only an empty socket, a crusty residue of decaying tissue clinging stubbornly to the skull. A troglodyte night-mare from the black depths of the earth, the monster had been unable to endure even the dim light filter-ing down to the fighting pit and, so, it had clawed out its own eyes to stop the pain.

The gorger spent a moment roaring and mewing at the crowd above, making a few feeble efforts to leap at them until the stabbing pain of the spears drove it back. It patted the ugly wounds its blind efforts had produced, licking its own treacly blood from its claws. Then, as though the taste of blood had aroused some dim memory in its simple brain, the beast spun about, its nose snuffling at the air. It made a drooling cry of unnameable hunger and lunged towards Kormak.

Kormak did not wait for the gorger's rending claws to strike. The Norscan drove at the monster even as it rushed him, sinking his fist into its belly. His other hand scythed across the beast's bicep. Noeyes squealed in pain, its claw slashing across Kormak, hurling the Norscan across the pit, smashing him into the far wall.

A hush fell upon the shouting spectators. They stared in wonder at the ugly gash across the arm of Noeyes, its thin blood spurting from the grisly wound. The gorger licked at the injury, confused by its wound. It snuffled loudly, its insane half-witted brain incapable of understanding. There was no smell of steel or iron about the prey it had attacked. Therefore it was impossible the human could have hurt it.

Slowly, painfully, Kormak rose from the bloodied floor of the pit, clutching at bruised ribs with his right hand. The other he lifted high, shaking blood from the bony, serrated cleaver-like appendage that had replaced his left hand. The crowd above roared their approval. The Norscan was a marauder, a mutant warrior of the Wastes, capable of twisting his flesh and bone at will into new shapes. The slaughter arranged by Jun and Hafn was not so one-sided as they had imagined. Kormak bore the mark of Tzeentch upon him!

Noeyes shook its head, lank strips of filthy black hair streaming about its hideous face. The brute bellowed, snorted, and then charged the little man who had hurt it. Like an avalanche the gorger came, its enormity threatening to break Kormak like a twig. The monster's very mass and momentum betrayed it. As Noeyes charged, Kormak dove from its path, rolling along the ground. He let the brute smash against the wall of the pit, then rushed upon the dazed gorger, his axe-blade hand hacking through its knee.

The gorger wailed as its leg folded beneath it. The degenerate ogre struck out blindly with its claws, the sweep of its talons slashing so near its foe that they scraped along Kormak's left horn. The Norscan was swift to retaliate, his axe-hand chopping down on the descending claw, severing three of its dagger-like fingers.

Shouts of 'Kormak!' rained down upon the pit as man and monster circled one another warily. Frightened, pained by the hurt already done it, the terrible hunger of Noeyes would not let the gorger retreat. Kormak did not even consider the prospect. He knew the only way out of the pit was over the beast's corpse.

'Kill that mutant bastard!' Hafn snarled. The hundred-eyed Baersonling seized the shoulder of one of the feast hall's bouncers, pushing the man into the pit. The man landed with a crash, sprawled upon the floor of the pit. Before his battered head could even start to make sense of the abrupt change in his own fortunes, the guard was set upon by the enraged Noeyes. Drawn by the sound of the man's fall, the gorger pounced upon him, crushing his ribcage beneath its prodigious mass while it ripped great slivers of meat from his body with its remaining claw.

Kormak seized upon the gorger's distraction, leaping upon the monster's back. His axe-hand bit down, slashing into the brute's neck. The gorger rose, shrieking, trying to buck off the Norscan straddling its curled spine. The bleeding stump of its hand slapped wetly at Kormak. The marauder ducked beneath the mad swipe of its claw, the black talons ripping into the gorger's hide as they missed the man.

The marauder roared with bloodlust. He stabbed his axe-like limb into the gorger's neck, sending an ugly spray of blood jetting from the wound. Kormak leaned back, the bony blade of his hand changing, shifting before the eyes of the spectators. A serrated mouth spread across the middle of the axe-head, forming a reptilian maw that gaped and snapped at the gorger's spurting arteries.

'He's killing Noeyes!' raged Hafn. The Baersonling seized a spear from one of his guards, hurling it at the man straddling his monster's back. The shaft sank into Kormak's shoulder, the pain staggering him long enough that one of the gorger's clumsy strikes connected and sent him sprawling.

Angrily, Kormak snapped the spear shaft protruding from his body, casting the splintered end full into the face of the crippled gorger. 'Here, monster!' he snapped. 'Give your cringing master a bit of sport before I kill you!'

Noeyes charged at the Norscan, narrowly missing him as he sidestepped the lunge.

A sly smile worked its way onto the marauder's harsh features. He sprinted across the pit, flinging himself at the ring of spear shafts, grabbing hold of the lowest blades. He ignored the biting pain in his hand, fought to control the snapping teeth of the axe-mouth that had replaced the other. Exerting every ounce of strength in his powerful frame, he pulled himself as high on the spears as he could. He was still well short of the lip of the pit, but the opportunity for escape would present itself soon enough.

'Ho, you pig-suckled runt of a whoreson whelp!' Kormak shouted at the blind, snuffling beast. 'I'm over here now, you walking midden heap!'

Noeyes bellowed, thundering across the pit towards the voice of its enemy. Kormak waited until the beast leapt at him, then released his hold on the spears. The Norscan dropped to the floor of the pit while the gorger smacked full force into the spear-studded wall.

The monster's heels scrabbled against the earthen wall as its final breath wheezed out of it. Impaled upon a half-dozen spears, the gorger was pinned to the wall like a moth in an alchemist's collection case.

A shocked silence spread through the feast hall. Kormak did not allow the shock to pass. Once more he lunged at the wall, this time using the gorger's body to climb above the ring of spears. Bracing himself upon the leprous shoulders of the monster, he threw himself at the lip of the pit. The marauder's axe-hand changed, melting and contorting into a great crustacean claw. Kormak stabbed the spiny tip of his new appendage into the stone floor of the hall like a mountaineer's piton. Secured, the barbarian pulled himself the last few feet. He was greeted by a clutch of Hafn's guards.

They did not delay him long.

Hafn Hundred-eyes was the last to die.

Kormak lifted the squealing, blubbering Baersonling over his head, then up-ended him into the fighting pit. Hafn's skull cracked like an egg upon the solid stone floor, eyes bursting from the gory wreck like seeds from a shattered melon.

Jun the Whip cowered as the hulking Norscan approached him. The other surviving slavers had deserted Jun as soon as they saw Kormak break free. The slave master had been too overcome by awe and terror to move. Now he wilted before the marauder's advance. Kormak's mutant limb melted and shifted between an array of loathsome and murderous implements. Jun fumbled at the sword in his belt, but a snake-like tendril shot from Kormak's mutant fist, sending the blade clattering across the floor.

'I don't expect you to fight,' Kormak growled, edging ever closer. 'I expect you to die. Slowly. In great pain.'

Jun screwed his eyes shut, waiting for Kormak's revenge. It took some time for him to realise that he wasn't dead, that his flesh had not been gouged and butchered by the marauder. When he opened his eyes, he could see the Norscan looming over him, his axe-hand raised for a murderous blow. A weird yellow glow filled Kormak's eyes and he was as still as a statue.

'Our paths cross again, Jun of the Chains.'

The slaver turned to see a familiar figure stalking through the feast hall, warriors and mutants scattering before him in frightened deference. There was no mistaking the robes and the pallid, tattooed visage of the zealot who had cowed the marauder once before with his magic. This time the mystic held a different skull in his pale hand, a grotesquely painted thing with amber set into its empty sockets and a sinister yellow glow swirling about it.

'Tolkku Skullkeeper, at your command,' the zealot said with mock courtesy and a jeering bow. 'I think I might take the mutant from you. How much?'

'Thr… no… two talents of silver,' Jun sputtered. For a moment, just an instant, the yellow light flickered in Kormak's eyes and the axe-hand descended several inches closer to the slaver. Jun squealed in fright.

Tolkku smiled beneath his stained skin. 'No, I think you should give me more to take him. Shall we say seven talents of silver? Or would you prefer I freed him from my spell now? Think about it. I am sure you will make the right choice.'

Urbaal's retinue of warriors rode through the cluttered streets of the Inevitable City, watching the spiked battlements and the hovering bulk of the monolith that hung suspended above the city fade away behind them. The Chosen could feel the envious eyes of knights and warleaders, champions of every shape and form regarding him with hate. Each resented the honour Tchar'zanek had shown him, each despised the caprice of fortune that had smiled upon Urbaal and not themselves. Each, he knew, would try to stop him if they but dared. Only fear of opposing Tchar'zanek made it safe for Urbaal and his followers to walk the streets. Beyond those streets, beyond the menacing threat of Tchar'zanek's displeasure…

'When we are past the walls of the city, we must watch for treachery,' Urbaal said, his voice echoing within the steel of his helm.

Vakaan the magus nodded in agreement, a gesture that caused his own steed to dip as it levitated over the flagstones. Unlike the rest of his retinue, Urbaal's sorcerer did not depend upon the strength of a horse to bear him. The magus had bound one of the almost formless predators known to daemonologists as 'screamers' to his terrible will. The thing had been given shape and substance by the craft of the Raven Host's armourers, trapping the daemon within a great ring of bronze, forcing it into the flattened form of a discus. Such daemon platforms were capable of carrying a sorcerer powerful enough to command them, and the same runes that bound their spectral essence also sustained them in the physical plane. Discs of Tzeentch the loathsome constructs were called, and they were a sign of prestige and pride among the thousand cabals of the Changer.

'Treachery is Tzeentch's way of choosing those who are worthy… and those who are unfit to serve as instruments of Change,' Vakaan pronounced. The sorcerer's familiar, a vile thing that looked like the foetal stage of some dwarfish bat-ape, chattered into the magus's ear. 'Nastrith says one who watches for betrayal must keep one eye upon himself. As always, the imp clouds his words in half-truths, but there is wisdom for one who would find it.'

'I have no time for crooked words,' Urbaal said, his eyes narrowing behind the visor of his helm. 'I ask if your powers have shown a threat to my mission, you answer in vagaries and the mutterings of daemons.'

Vakaan laughed at the warlord's petulance. 'You are mighty, Urbaal and well-favoured among the warriors of the Changer, but you fail to appreciate the nuances of plot and counter-plot, weaving the strands of fate so that they become as much your servant as your sword or your steed.' Vakaan stamped his boot upon the back of the fleshy horror he stood upon. The disc slavered and gibbered its displeasure, little dribbles of burning light trickling from the jaws set into its underside. 'You are too much the warrior, not enough the schemer.'

'What need have I for schemes when I have you?' Urbaal challenged. 'There are some among your cabal whom you did not destroy and whose power you did not steal.'

'Petty warlocks unworthy of my attention,' Vakaan waved aside the threat, but the smile had dropped from his face and his familiar had withdrawn into the sanctuary of one of his sleeves. 'I do not need your protection.'

Urbaal leaned back in his saddle and stared hard at the magus. 'Indeed. I wonder Vakaan, who needs whom more. The sword or the sorcerer?' He patted the weapon sheathed at his side, his gauntlet ringing against the scabbard. 'If I do not think you useful to me, perhaps we will find out. I have other magicians I can call upon.'

'That skull-collecting fanatic, Tolkku?' scoffed Vakaan. 'Ask him to heal your wounds and he might manage. Ask him to slaughter your enemies, to call down the daemons of the aethyr, ask him to crumble the walls of a fortress or turn a forest into a sea of flame and see how far you get!'

The Chosen turned about in his saddle, watching the ranks of his warriors, looking over their armoured bulks. He could see Tolkku astride the back of an almost skeletal horse sporting crooked antlers and the multi-faceted eyes of a spider. The zealot was holding one of his skulls in his hand, muttering to it like an indulgent mother soothing an uneasy child. Urbaal looked past the shaman-priest, glancing at the hulking brute who followed close behind Tolkku's horse. Alone of Urbaal's retinue, this man went on foot, his hands bound before him, a great iron collar about his neck and chains securing his bonds to Tolkku's saddle. Urbaal saw the huge marauder swing his horned head in his direction, their eyes locking for an instant. It was the Chosen who at last broke the gaze, turning back to Vakaan.

'Tolkku has a new toy,' Urbaal said.

'Some idiot whose peculiar skull has intrigued him,' Vakaan observed. 'In a few days Tolkku will take out his flaying knife and that will be the end of him.'

Urbaal shook his head. 'He'd better not try it with this one. I hear the Norscan killed Noeyes and Hafn Hundred-eyes all by himself.' Urbaal raised his armoured gloves. 'With nothing but his bare hands and the gifts Great Tzeentch has bestowed upon him.'

'All the more reason Tolkku will add his skull to the collection,' Vakaan said. 'There is a great deal of power to be gained by killing such people. I should know.'

The warleader again shook his head. 'I hope he does not try it. I can't afford to lose Tolkku. My other magician has proven less reliable of late.'

Vakaan glowered at Urbaal, then cast an anxious look at the streets around them. 'Foresight only goes so far before it becomes unreliable, too susceptible to the Changer's shifting moods.' The magus lowered his voice to a whisper. 'And when it is reliable, it is unwise to discuss it where there are too many ears.'

Urbaal nodded, spurring his horse forwards, waving his arm to hasten the rest of his retinue. The great gates of the city were still some distance away and he would be far from the Inevitable City before they lost what little light the shimmering sky allowed them.

As they rode, they were watched by a pair of particularly envious eyes. The watcher waited until the last of Urbaal's men had passed from sight, then turned and strode to the mammoth wall of the city. The skulking man drew a heavy clay jar from beneath his black robes. Raspy words crawled from the throat hidden beneath the folds of his hood and his thorny helm leaned close to the mouth of the jar. A ghastly azure light began to rise from the jar and with it a clacking host of crawling things. The sorcerer stepped back, allowing the legion of daemon insects to creep free of their prison. He stabbed a scrawny finger at the wall of the city. In response, a scarlet rune imposed itself upon the stonework, glowing evilly in the shadows.

The crawling army turned and marched towards the wall, setting upon the glowing rune with the rapacity of termites. Stone crumbled beneath their daemonic mandibles, falling in clumps of dust as they worked their havoc. The sorcerer waited until the hole was large enough to suit his purposes. He lifted a fat-bladed dagger of cold-wrought iron and brought the athame crashing against the jar. The vessel shattered and with it was broken the spell of azure light. The tiny daemons that had been bound within the jar flickered and faded back into their spectral world.

The sorcerer snapped his gloved fingers. Armoured warriors detached themselves from the shadows around him. He pointed at the hole his daemons had gnawed through the wall of the city. Silently, leading their horses by the reins, the warriors began to steal into the growing night beyond the walls.

The sorcerer smiled within the darkness of his hood. Tchar'zanek would learn his mistake in choosing scum like Urbaal and Vakaan to undertake such a vital quest. He would make certain the warlord understood that, when he sent him their heads in a silver box and claimed the artefact they had been sent to capture for himself.

CHAPTER FIVE

THE ICY GRIP of Norsca pawed at Pyra's loose robes, caressing her pallid skin with frosty fingers. Whipping through the narrow, snow-covered valley between the frosty mountains, the wind was like a ravenous beast prowling the desolation. The sorceress smiled at the invigorating sensation. There was a subtle energy, a power in the very air of these northern lands. She could just see it if she concentrated and focused her witch-sight, a shimmering gleam crawling in the breeze. It was the raw element of magic itself, the primordial force ignorant cowards called Chaos and damned in their fear.

Pyra was neither ignorant nor a coward. If she were either, she would have been dead long ago. She was playing the most dangerous of games, pitting the malignance of the Witch King against the ambitions of Lord Uthorin. Each of her patrons ultimately believed she was acting as their double agent, spying and sabotaging the schemes of the other. She was content to allow them such fantasies. In the end, she did not overly care which sort of tyranny ruled Naggaroth. She was more practical than that. Idealism was for idiots clinging to outdated fancies like honour and morality. The asur were steeped in such archaic delusions, allowing them to bleed away the vibrancy of their race. Every day, the elves of Ulthuan grew weaker while the druchii grew stronger.

She would be part of that strength, whether at the right hand of Malekith or Uthorin, she would be there. With the horde of Tchar'zanek as their plaything, the dark elves would stretch their hand across the oceans and reclaim ownership of their homeland. And from the enchanted shores of Ulthuan, they would remake the world itself in their image. Brutish humans, muddle-headed dwarfs, all would be bent to the will of their rightful masters. Nothing would stand against them. Not even the gods!

Pyra closed her eyes, pressing her fingers against her forehead. She tried to will the intoxicating influence of magical power from her mind. She cursed her own carelessness. She should have expected the effect the raw energies of Chaos would have upon her. Attuned to the magical winds, Pyra was more open to their baleful touch, more susceptible to their empathic influences. Those who wielded the might of Dark Magic, the most elemental and powerful shape of sorcery, had to be ever wary. It had a seductive lure, easing the wielder into a false sense of might while it corroded their very essence from within. It would be a bitter irony if all her grand ambitions led only to her body being overcome by Chaos and she ended her days as some degenerate thing feeding off squirrels and carrion!

'You are ill?'

Pyra opened her eyes to find Prince Inhin leaning over the side of her palanquin, a hint of concern in his sharp features. She knew his concern had less to do with her welfare than for his own. Without her sorcery, he would be unable to tap into the magic of the megaliths. Without the standing circles, Inhin's small force of elves would be forced to march across Norsca and the Troll Country to reach their objective. Even a noble as arrogant and prideful as Inhin Bonebat knew his chances of accomplishing such a feat.

The sorceress gave her lover a reassuring stroke of her fingers along the back of his hand. 'I will endure,' she told him. 'The winds of magic are strong here. They will grow stronger the closer we draw to the Wastes. It is an invigorating sensation, so much power at my beck and call.'

Inhin licked his lips with a nervous flutter. Pyra enjoyed watching him squirm under her enigmatic gaze. The prince enjoyed her being dependent and subservient to him. However, he was never really certain of his dominance; no despot really could be where sorcery was concerned. That was probably why she continued to fascinate Inhin, why he had not brought a string of concubines along with him on his long sea voyage. Still, he didn't like to be reminded of the fact, much less of the possibility that Pyra's powers were growing stronger the farther north they travelled.

'The rearguard has spotted something,' Inhin said, quickly changing the subject to more secure ground. He snapped his fingers and a pair of his shades drew close to the palanquin, bowing their heads as they met Pyra's expectant gaze.

'Barbarians follow us, my lady,' one of the cloaked elves said. 'Only twenty, but they may be scouts for a larger force.'

'They were lead by a druchii,' added the other scout. 'One of those pirate bastards from the *Bloodshark*!'

Pyra nodded her head, dark tresses flowing about her face as they snaked out from beneath the band of her circlet. 'Such ingratitude after Prince Inhin's generosity. Obviously the corsair thinks to have his petty revenge by setting the animals on our track. Knowing our numbers, he would certainly have pressed the barbarians to come in force. You are doubtlessly correct when you say the ones you saw were an advance party.'

'We should leave a rearguard to delay them,' Naagan interrupted. 'Every moment we tarry, the faithless asur and their allies have time to undo our plans.'

'My plans,' Pyra corrected the disciple.

Naagan bowed his head in deference to the withering authority in her voice, then cast a sideways glance at Prince Inhin. The noble kept quiet, making no issue of the assumed dominance of the sorceress. 'You had someone in mind for this rearguard?'

'If it pleases your lady, I think that Sardiss would be an ideal choice,' Naagan answered. Unlike Inhin, he made no effort to keep challenge out of his voice. 'As one of the Witch King's Black Guard, his martial prowess is unquestioned. As one of the Witch King's Black Guard, his loyalty to the cause of Lord Uthorin is less certain. That uncertainty makes him the most disposable of the assets at Prince Inhin's disposal.'

Pyra turned her head, bristling at the smug smile that wormed its way onto Inhin's features. Naagan would never have dared speak in such fashion about Sardiss if the Black Guard had been present. Inhin had placed his hated rival for the favours of his lover at the head of the column where he would be the first to encounter any danger. Pyra knew how keenly this treacherous plot of Naagan's would appeal to her patron. She also knew that Sardiss's usefulness to her made such a plan repugnant.

'And what of the loyalty of the Temple of Khaine?' the sorceress snarled. 'Can we truly be certain that your loyalty is to Lord Uthorin? Perhaps you speak out against Sardiss so openly because you think to cloak your own perfidy behind such a transparent display of fealty.'

Naagan's hand closed tight about the hilt of his sword, his eyes glowing like embers of rage. 'You would dare!'

'Convince me my fears are misplaced, Naagan,' Pyra taunted. She turned back to Prince Inhin. 'I suggest a compromise, my lord. We can ill spare many warriors to delay the animals on our trail. Naagan is correct when he says what we need is a lone fighter of incomparable martial prowess. But I do not think it is wise to send Sardiss. If he is loyal, we lose a valuable servant. If he is truly a spy of Malekith, we cannot afford to allow him out of our sight.' Pyra watched as her word of warning wiped the smug expression off the noble's face. 'I propose that we test the loyalty of Naagan as representative of the Temple of Khaine. He can leave behind his witch elf. She can linger and confront the barbarians. If she is quick about it, she might even be able to rejoin us before we reach the standing stones.'

The sorceress grinned coyly at Naagan. 'Either way, such a gesture would bolster my confidence in the Temple of Khaine. And its representatives.'

THE LANDSCAPE KORMAK saw as the warband left the Inevitable City was not the same he had travelled through in the cage-wagon of Jun and his slavers. Where before he had seen snow-swept tundra, now the terrain was a blasted plain of splintered rock and grisly, thorn-like growths taller than a full-grown pine and as imposing as a field of claws. A sickly pink mist rippled around the thorn-stalks, writhing between and around them like a living thing. The sky overhead seemed to pulse and gyrate in sympathy to the ugly fog. Kormak could not shake the impression of a beating heart and wondered if he was gazing upon the very essence of his Dark Gods. Crazed seers sometimes spoke of a being beyond the gods, something they called the Great Beast. The thought made even the marauder's blood turn cold.

The warriors of Urbaal's retinue went into the wasteland with trepidation. Those who entered the Inevitable City could never be certain if they would

ever leave. Those who left could never be certain
where their exodus would take them. Just by looking
at the warriors around him, Kormak could tell that
this plain of thorn-stalks and pink fog was as strange
to them as it was to him. Like the chained thrall, they
were at the mercy of the primordial powers that
moulded and shaped the Chaos Wastes with their
lunatic thoughts and idiot whims.

Kormak tested his chains for the hundredth time.
The blackened steel was eerily flexible, warm beneath
his touch as though it were a living thing. The ugly
Kurgan runes etched into each link glowed with a
putrid light. The marauder glared at the tattooed
zealot who had presumed to take ownership of him.
The shaman would need all of his magic if Kormak
broke free of his chains. He'd stuff the zealot's own
head into the sack of skulls he carried.

There was hope of escape. Kormak had been exerting his mutant limb, twisting and reshaping his arm.
At first the enchanted chains were able to match the
shifting flesh, but the longer Kormak persisted in his
efforts, the slower his bonds were to reshape themselves. It was an almost crippling effort, sending
knives of agony lancing through Kormak's body. The
Norscan's lip bled where his teeth had gnashed
together against the pain. Lesser men would have
resigned themselves to bondage rather than endure
such suffering. Kormak despised such chattel. The
gods had no use for cowards and weaklings, Kormak
would not fail beneath their merciless gaze. He
would make an offering of Tolkku's soul to the Raven
God before he snapped the preening zealot's spine.

The Norscan shifted his gaze from the robes and tattoos of Tolkku, studying again the sombre warriors who surrounded them. They were massive brutes encased in armour of steel and bronze, their horned helmets obliterating their faces, scalp locks and other gruesome trophies dangling from their breastplates. Each bore a monstrous axe or murderous flail and the steeds they rode were fanged, savage giants, each horse displaying the mutating touch of the Wastes upon its powerful frame. Here was an animal with four eyes, there a steed with reptilian claws and hooves the colour of crushed rubies. Together, warrior and steed made a sight seldom seen even in Norsca, and then only as heralds of bloodshed and destruction. Knights of Chaos, riders of the Northern Wastes, these were the kind of warriors every man in Norsca openly envied and secretly feared.

At their head was a figure of blackness and glistening sapphire. Kormak could feel the power of the armoured rider as keenly as he could the hot breath of a forge. He did not need to be told that the man was one of the champions of the gods, one of their Chosen, favoured by the Ruinous Powers in ways far beyond the simple mutant gifts of Kormak or even Tolkku's sinister magic. The Chosen sat atop his fanged black warhorse like a scaly leviathan brooding upon the waves, its awesome power slumbering, waiting, hungry and eager, for the call of battle. Urbaal, Kormak had heard the dark champion called, and the marauder did not doubt that here was a man who had long served the Raven God by sowing the ultimate change: the change from life to death.

Man? Perhaps there was nothing left inside the spiked carapace of sapphire and steel that could still be called human.

Beside Urbaal, a shape no less unsettling rode upon a sinister contrivance of spectral flesh and blazing bronze. Kormak had seen the Discs of Tzeentch before and knew that only the most powerful and wicked sorcerers could bend such daemons to their will. Vakaan was a Kurgan, if the twisted features of the magus's physiognomy were any measure of his breeding. All those who dwelled in the shadow of the gods respected and feared their power. Even the seers and shamans, men blessed with magical powers by the Dark Gods, grovelled and trembled before them. Sorcerers were different. They sought to make pacts with the gods, to treat with them as princes seeking audience with a king. The arrogance and hubris of such men was second only to their awful power, for the gods often rewarded the bold. At least until their mood shifted and the pride of the magus was no longer amusing to them. The sagas were filled with tales of the horrors visited upon sorcerers who lost the favour of Tchar.

Vakaan's beaked helm turned, Kormak could feel the magus's fiery eyes study him. His body shuddered as the sorcerer's gaze gripped him, bony growths pimpling his arms, tiny horns sprouting from his face. His mutated limbs moved in rebellion to his mind, oozing like mud around the underlying bones. An instant, Kormak felt his corrupted body exult in the fiery light of the magus, then the instant passed and the marauder felt his mutant flesh reform, lapse once more into the familiar patterns of humanity. The marauder dared raise his head and look again into the bird-like mask of Vakaan's helm. Now the eyes of the magus were clear and blue, filled with a haunted emptiness. No, not empty. There was something in there, deep within the azure pools. Kormak could not be certain, but he thought he could see envy in the sorcerer's eyes.

A FOETAL GARGOYLE thing scrabbled up Vakaan's robe, climbing until it was upon the magus's shoulder. It gibbered and drooled into Vakaan's ear, whispering and whining. Vakaan bent his head, listening to the insane muttering bubbling from his familiar's mouth. He closed his eyes, willing his sight into the daemon world of his familiar. Vakaan opened them quickly, the daemon disc upon which he rode rotating at some unspoken command to face Urbaal.

'Tzar Urbaal, we are attacked!' Vakaan gasped.

The words were unneeded, however. A circle of purple light exploded into life upon the broken ground ahead of the warband. Strange glowing runes shimmered upon the periphery of the circle, dancing with infernal volition. A deadening chill raced through the warband, exciting even the fearsome horses upon which they rode. It was a chill beyond physical cold, the parasitic clutch of something pawing at their very souls.

The warmth leeched from them gathered within the glowing circle, the stolen scraps of life force allowing something to breach the barrier between worlds. Like a foulness, the thing burst out from the void, billowing forth from nothingness like smoke from a flame. It was vile and hideous, shifting and burning with coruscating bands of light and fire. From a few inches it expanded into a towering nightmare of glistening flesh and gyrating vapour. Its pulpy, stalk-like body was like that of a mushroom and it swelled rapidly into horrible life. Ropy limbs separated from the pulpy trunk, a mass of black tendrils burst from the truncated cap, rivalled only by the wiry coils that oozed from its base and seared the dead ground with blazing ichor.

The daemon whirled within its circle of light. Little eyes, like the eyes of a thousand spiders, crawled up the trunk-like body, settling between the tendrils of the cap, finding little pock-mark perches from which to stare at the panicking horses and horrified men. A beak-like blade of bone pushed its way out from the stalk just below the level of the spider-eyes and smiled. Malicious, merciless, and utterly inhuman.

'Back!' Vakaan shrieked, his hands already moving in the gestures of a spell.

There was no time for the magus's warning to have any effect. The daemon's ropy arms expanded like the petals of a flower, exposing thick oily veins. As the limbs opened, from each of the rope-like veins a gout of luminous purple fire exploded. Three of the riders were caught in the first blast of daemonic flame; men, beasts and armour melting into a waxy mash as they were utterly consumed.

A ghastly shriek, like a vulture's giggle, thundered from the daemon's beak. As if in response, war cries roared from behind the pink mists. Through the forest of thorn-like growths, warriors in blackened armour and horned helms came charging, axes and flails clenched in their pounding fists. Soldiers of the Raven Host, but their advent did not mean relief for Urbaal's beset warband. Their arrival meant betrayal.

Urbaal glared through the smoke rising from his slaughtered knights. He saw the cloaked sorcerer commanding both warriors and daemon. There was no mistaking the thorn-crown of Odvaha, court sorcerer of Tchar'zanek himself.

Urbaal did not know how deep Odvaha's treachery ran, nor how mighty the magus's sorcery might be. The entire landscape they had entered upon leaving the Inevitable City might be Odvaha's creation, the flamer that attacked them but the most minor of his minions. This did not matter to Urbaal. By betraying them, Odvaha had defied the command of Tchar'zanek. To defy the will of the Prince of Tzeentch was to defy the Changer himself!

The Chosen roared, a sound magnified into metal thunder by his helm. 'Kill the faithless traitors my sons of ruin!' Urbaal drew his sword, staring into the spidery eyes of the daemon. 'I shall deal with their noisy puppet!'

HULKING, BRUTISH SHAPES clad in strips of mail and heavy furs, the Baersonlings maintained a relentless pace through the frozen landscape of their barren homeland. Rage and revenge were etched into each man's fierce heart, twisting hard faces into harder scowls. They had seen firsthand the massacre the dark elves had made of their kinsmen, the degenerate sport the inhuman fiends had taken as they slaughtered helpless children and women. Death and cruelty were common enough in Norsca, but the elves had displayed a depth of malevolence and sadism that offended even the jaded hearts of the northmen.

The revenge of the Baersonlings had fallen like the fist of a titan upon the elf corsairs. Some had been cut down before they could reach their ship, most had died in the waters of the fjord when that same ship had mysteriously sunk beneath the waves, as though the decaying hand of Mermedus had reached up from the depths to drag it down into his watery domain. The waterlogged survivors had been pulled from the surf, dealt with in such fashion as they had treated their own victims. The thin, piercing screams of the elves still echoed in the ears of the Norscan warriors, haunting wails of agony that each man knew he would never forget.

The wretch ahead of them was the only one they had spared, buying his life only by promising to lead the Norscans to more of his kin that had set out for the mountainous interior. The elf was kept leashed like a dog, a grizzled Norscan whaler following close behind him, stabbing his flanks with the barbed tip of a harpoon whenever the elf displayed signs of reluctance or fatigue. They would let this lithe fiend believe he could save himself by betraying his own to them. It would gain him the honour of being the last to die. The seers would be happy to offer his soul to the Raven God. Nothing pleased Great Tchar so

much as the heart of a traitor, fresh and bloody upon
his altar stone.

Rafn Sharkstabber pulled the whetstone from the
pocket of his bearskin cloak and ground it against
the edge of his axe for the umpteenth time. Blue
sparks danced from the stone as it rubbed against the
metal. He wanted the blade keen enough to shave a
vulture's beard when they found the elves. There
would be gory work for his weapon then and he
wanted it to be equal to the task.

The brawny warrior turned his head to boast of
some of the havoc he would visit upon the elves. The
boast never left Rafn's bearded lips. He stared in confusion, trying to understand where the man beside
him had gone. Melkolfr had been there only a
moment before. Rafn studied the terrain, looking for
bushes or outcroppings the warrior might have withdrawn behind to relieve himself. There was nothing,
only the howl of the wind and the line of their own
footprints behind them.

Rafn tucked the whetstone back in his pocket and
took a wary step back down the valley. He watched
the jagged crags of the mountains, studying them
with a practised eye. There were many things in the
mountains of Norsca that could set upon a lone man
and snatch him away without a trace. The ice-tiger,
the ymir, even an exceptionally cunning troll. But the
Baersonling did not think what had gotten Melkolfr
was a simple predator. Anything quiet enough to
grab a man from the midst of comrades was also
smart enough not to risk attacking such a large
group.

The warrior turned his head as something caught his eye. A small crimson stain in the snow, its very smallness unsettling to him. He bent, dipping his finger into the dark patch. He put the icy muck to his mouth, tasting its bitter saltiness. The familiar taste told Rafn it was human. He stared even harder at the ground, but could find only the marks of Melkolfr's boots in the snow. Even an ice-tiger would have left paw marks behind if this had been the work of a beast.

Rafn spun about, cupping his hand to shout to his fellows. Now that he was aware of the menace, he could see that others were missing. Nefbjorn Half-Sarl, Olfun Red Spear and Faksi Shieldbreaker. All three men were gone, vanished as completely as Melkolfr! Rafn's mind whirled with images of daemons and the restless dead, spectral horrors that struck from their invisible world beyond the understanding of men.

A wet gargle was all that came from Rafn's mouth as he tried to shout warning to his fellows. So sharp was the blade that had transfixed his throat that he hadn't even felt its touch. Slender fingers twisted the weapon then pulled it free with a savage tug. Rafn's axe fell from his hands as he clapped his fingers about the spurting wreckage just below his chin. Through pain-wracked eyes, he saw a lithe shape slowly circle him, licking blood from one of the silvery daggers she held. Rafn felt his pulse quicken as he saw his attacker, the seductive twist of limb and carriage that melded into her every motion. There was horror mingled into the ethereal beauty, a malicious taint that was inhuman and alluring. The warrior felt his body throb and his gorge rise as the elf leaned towards him.

'Why do they even think beasts like you can be useful?' Beblieth mused. Faster than Rafn's eye could follow, the witch elf's blades flashed at him, slashing through both of his knees. The Norscan tumbled into the snow, crashing on his face.

'Crawl, little worm,' Beblieth told him, slicing one of her wickedly sharp daggers along his spine. 'Warn your little friends that they are all going to die. It might make them more challenging.'

Rafn's mutilated body heaved as he tried to go after his oblivious kinsmen, a wretched rattle of despair bubbling from his throat.

Trying to staunch the blood dribbling from his throat, Rafn used his elbows to pull himself through the snow. Each foot was an agony of frozen suffering, each yard an impossible effort. Always he could see the backs of the other Norscans marching farther and farther away, oblivious to the fiendish menace stalking them.

Rafn prayed to his gods for strength, for the endurance to go on. He could not feel his lower body now, blood loss had rendered his legs into icy lumps of meat dragging at him. His entire body shivered as warmth continued to drain from between his fingers. He slumped into the snow, his face crashing into the icy powder. How easy it would be just to accept, just to let death steal over him. Then he remembered the mocking seductive lure of the witch elf, the unspeakable way the druchii had massacred the village. He thought of his comrades, butchered, murdered without chance to die deaths the gods would smile upon.

The warrior forced his body up from the snow. Like a bleeding slug, he slithered through the ice. He could only just make out the cloaks of the Norscans ahead of him, with every second they seemed to march a league further into the valley. He tried to squeeze the ruin of his throat together, to muster the voice for one shout of warning. Nothing came of his effort except a rasping cough.

The witch elf stepped before him, pinning him to the frozen ground with one of her knee-length leather boots. Unseen, unheard, she had followed Rafn during his wretched attempt to reach his comrades, never more than a few paces behind. Beblieth's merciless eyes stared down into those of the dying man. She cupped Rafn's face in her gloved hand, lifting it so that he could look into her eyes.

'Amusing,' she told him, her words twisted by the cruelty of her lips. 'But I fear I do not have the patience to watch the rest of the performance. Your friends are waiting after all.'

The last thing Rafn Sharkstabber saw was the flash of Beblieth's dagger as she brought it slashing across his eyes. The witch elf did not bother to finish him off, but left him to writhe and suffer, perhaps to be found by the main body of the Baersonling warband. Perhaps to offer a lively meal for whatever scavengers were still abroad in the Norscan winter.

It made little difference to Beblieth. The fate of a dumb animal was less than nothing to her. The fate of the druchii traitor who had set the beasts on them, however, was something she would need to consider quite carefully.

An elf, after all, should be shown some dignity when he met death.

THE FLAMER HISSED, little fangs sprouting from the cusp of its beak. The daemon was not a mindless abomination. It understood the boastful words of the shouting mortal. Feeding on terror and despair, it found Urbaal repugnant, like the dung of a fly upon a slice of sweetbread. The daemon would remove the offensive blight, then resume its interrupted repast.

Crackling daemon fires engulfed Urbaal as he charged at the beast. The Chosen's steed screamed as it was enveloped in searing hellfire. Rider and mount vanished within a pillar of coruscating smoke and flame, the dying wail of the horse devoured by the hissing crackle of burning flesh. The daemon sizzled with villainous joy as it watched its victim burn.

Spidery eyes glimmered in shock as something emerged from the pillar of glowing smoke. The flamer shrank before the steady advance of the vengeful figure. Ash dripped from Urbaal's smouldering armour with each step, smoke wafted from the crusty reminder of cloak and surcoat. Runes, blazing like snakes of lightning, crawled beneath the surface of his armour, like termites burrowing into wood. Thick, carapace-like growths of cartilage and bone slowly melted back into the Chosen's armoured body.

Urbaal lifted his sword, the long fang of steel flaring into malefic life as a putrescent inner light erupted from within the blade, transforming it from an instrument of metal into a blinding sliver of starlight. Howling energy rippled from the sword, a terrifying radiance of inimical power that made even the daemon tremble.

Urbaal pounced upon the recoiling beast like a cat springing upon a mouse. He drove his blazing sword into the flamer's stalk-like body, skewering it upon the shaft of starlight. Like the tooth of Tzeentch himself, the sword slashed through the flamer's ethereal essence. The daemon withered upon the Chosen's blade, wilting like a dried-out flower, its ropy arms crumbling into twig-like sticks, its face collapsing into the husk of its body. Urbaal shook the daemonic offal from his blade, grinding the desiccated wreckage beneath his boot.

Even as he crushed the daemon's husk into dust, a purple circle of runes flickered into life beside Urbaal. The shifting figure of another daemon began to form in the second summoning circle.

THERE WAS A blinding burst of light as Urbaal slaughtered the daemon. Kormak hid his eyes from the display, then returned his attention to the chains that bound him. Impelled by the horrific energy of the daemon, his mutant limbs had grown strong, able to cheat the mutable metal of his bonds. He worked one hand free just as the first of the attacking warriors reached him. Kormak willed his hand to assume a crab-claw shape, the huge scything edge of the claw slashing through his attacker's wrist, sending his hand rolling across the broken earth. Before the stunned warrior could react, Kormak caught him between the pincers of his claw. The man struggled in the marauder's grip, fighting to break free of the pincers. Kormak sneered at the effort and willed his arm to change again, becoming an axe-head. As the pincers of the claw flowed together to form the new mutation, they slashed through the foeman's waist. The severed halves flopped about on the broken ground like fish in the bottom of a boat.

The Norscan battered the other manacles that bound him, keeping his eyes fixed upon the battle raging around him. The Kurgan attackers had fallen upon Urbaal's warband and were now thickly mixed with the knights. Urbaal's men fought well, but not well enough to overbalance the numbers of their enemy. Beyond them, Kormak could see the shadowy shape of the laughing sorcerer who commanded them. Snakes of burning red light whipped from the robed sorcerer's hands to rend and slash the knights, cleaving through flesh and armour like a hot knife through butter.

Opposing the sorcerer was Urbaal's magus, the bird-like Vakaan. Perched upon his daemonic disc, the magus sent his own spells raining down upon the ambushers. Kormak saw one Kurgan flayed alive by a wailing whip of daemonic lightning, another torn asunder by a blue bolt of mutating energy. Sometimes the two mystics would turn their attention upon each other, sending blasts of power searing at their opposite. Each time the spell would shatter against the counterspell of the other magus, leaving only an acrid smell and a residue of smoky light.

'Traitor!' Vakaan wailed at the sorcerer. 'You would break the word of Prince Tchar'zanek?'

'You are not worthy of the honour!' Odvaha raged back. 'You are not worthy to profane the Bastion Stair and free Lord Kakra from the Bloodthirster! The Raven God will smile upon me when I succeed where you could only fail! Then will Tchar'zanek know it was I he should have chosen, not worthless waste-land scum!'

Kormak saw Odvaha hurl another of his withering spells against Vakaan. This time, instead of being destroyed by the magus's counterspell, the magic seemed to take greater strength from it. Glancing from the unseen shell of protection Vakaan had woven about himself, Odvaha's spell instead smashed into the line of fighting warriors. A dozen men, Kurgan and knight alike, were caught in a shim-mering explosion of orange light and purple fires. The warriors screamed as their bodies were twisted and corroded by the sorcerer's exalted magic. Flesh melted and popped as new organs sprouted and old ones collapsed. Bones stabbed through skin, skin thickened into scaly leather. A mad infection of uncontrolled, undirected mutation swept through the fighters, ripping their bodies apart in a horrific display of the Changer's might.

The Norscan snapped his attention away from the men dying only feet from him. His eyes settled upon the hated shape of Tolkku. The tattooed zealot was beset by one of the Kurgans that had not been caught in the treacherous magic of Odvaha. The mystic was falling back, his puny dagger no match against the heavy axe of his foe. There was a pleasing expression of terror in the eyes of the zealot, yet even in his fear, Tolkku maintained a white-knuckled grip upon the painted skull he held in his left hand.

Kormak threw off the last of his chains, charging the Kurgan. The flesh of his mutant arm flowed into the shape of a bony sword. He drove the iron-hard limb into the Kurgan's back, impaling him upon a blade of bone. Kormak threw down the dying warrior, snapping his neck with a brutal kick of his boot. He stooped and tore the axe from the Kurgan's dead fingers.

'I saved you so I could kill you myself,' Kormak snarled at Tolkku.

Instead of cowering, the zealot snickered, displaying the painted skull in his hand. The weird pattern of pink swirls and jade diamonds drew Kormak's gaze and refused to release it. 'Fool! You killed that wretch because *I* commanded it! *I* am the master!' The zealot turned his head, his eyes narrowing as he saw Odvaha unleash another barrage of magic against Vakaan. 'Now, I want you to kill the sorcerer.'

Kormak struggled to resist the impulse that burned through his brain. Against his own volition, he turned towards the warring sorcerers. 'This is not over,' he growled through clenched teeth.

'Of course not,' Tolkku chided him. He pointed a bony finger at the Norscan. 'It will end when I add that pretty skull of yours to my collection!'

Kormak glared at the priest, then was forced to look away. His treacherous body, subsumed to the will of Tolkku and his hypnotic skull, had carried him into the gory mush left behind by Odvaha's change storm. Shattered limbs twitched and flopped upon the ground while broken bodies continued to pop and burst. There was an unclean life clinging to the mire as the mutating energy of the spell slowly dissipated. Kormak stepped wide around the mash of loathsome fluids and molten flesh, not trusting even his mutant constitution against the horrible residue of the spell.

Something huge and bear-like rose from the mire, bellowing at him with its tri-fold mouths. Kormak struck out at the grisly horror, the stolen axe of the Kurgan slashing through a foreleg and toppling it snout-first into the gory earth. Tentacles of raw muscle sprouted from the patches of brown hair on the spawn's back, slapping at the marauder with blind fury. One clutch of tentacles coiled about Kormak's arm, clinging to him with bone-breaking strength. The marauder brought his axe chopping down, hacking through the oozing tendrils like cordwood. His arm shifted into a new shape, slipping free from the coils that remained.

The bony claw of Kormak's arm snapped tight about the tentacles as he pulled free. The marauder drew upon every ounce of power in his mutant body to drag the ghastly Chaos spawn towards him. The bear-like thing slowly crawled at him, its dripping jaws slobbering open to bellow and growl. Kormak lifted the stolen axe, then brought it slashing across the nest of slug-like eye-horns that peppered the beast's scalp. The thing shrieked, its entire body shuddering as it tried to retreat, one club-like paw severing its own trapped tentacles in its urge to flee.

Kormak started to follow the blinded abomination, but again his body rebelled, the commanding magic of Tolkku's mind crashing over him like a tidal wave. He felt himself turn towards the sorcerer once more. The magic duel between Vakaan and Odvaha had shifted, and it was the magus who was reeling. Odvaha had summoned another of his daemons, a gruesome thing of pink light with dangling ape-like limbs and the fanged sucker of a leech acting as its face. Trying to defend against both sorcerer and daemon, Vakaan was finding it impossible to do either.

The Norscan spat into the dust. Breaking free of Tolkku's magic would wait. He had seen the way Odvaha's enemies died. It was time to show the sorcerer how a marauder killed his.

CHAPTER SIX

BEADS OF BLOOD dripped down the dusky face of Odvaha as the sorcerer struggled to maintain the withering magical assault against his foes. Trying to keep both of the daemons he had summoned from slipping free of his control was taxing his concentration to its utmost. Odvaha knew that if the daemons broke free of his control their one desire before they faded back into the Realm of Chaos would be to tear the flesh from his own bones! The servitors of the gods did not suffer servitude to mortals lightly.

Odvaha saw the horned marauder charging towards him from the corner of his eye but could not spare the attention to crush him with one of his spells. The sorcerer snarled a command to the pair of Kurgan warriors he had held back as bodyguards. The armoured reavers growled with satisfaction, eager to thrust themselves into the fray. Odvaha watched them lope off, then was forced to restore full concentration as the binding circle around the pink horror began to flicker.

He did not see the lone marauder crash into the two Kurgans with the graceless fury of an avalanche. He did not see one Kurgan head leap from its neck, chopped clean through by the Norscan's axe as neatly as a flower from its stem. Blood drenched the face of the second Kurgan, blinding him. As he staggered back, Kormak rammed his blade-like arm through the warrior's chest, ripping through lungs and heart as it burrowed up beneath his ribs. The warrior struggled to make a dying attack against his killer. Kormak's axe easily swatted aside the cruelly flanged mace the Kurgan held, then the marauder slammed his horned head into the man's face, mashing his features into a morass of blood and gristle.

Kormak threw aside the mangled Kurgan and glowered at the robed sorcerer. Bellowing ferociously, he rushed the magician, determined to still the alien command thundering inside his mind. A look of absolute horror crept into Odvaha's eyes. The sorcerer was gripped with a moment of indecision, wrestling with which danger to confront. A wail of ghastly jubilation echoed above the battlefield as he reluctantly loosed the daemons from their bindings and spun to confront Kormak.

It was too little and much too late. Kormak's mutated arm came scything down, crunching into the sorcerer's shoulder. Odvaha's arm dropped from its socket, only a greasy rope of tendon holding it against his side. The pain-wracked sorcerer sent a blast of rippling red light slamming into Kormak, hurling the marauder from his feet and sending him sprawling on the ground.

Kormak spat blood from his mouth, coughing with disgust as he saw Odvaha turn and flee. The marauder painfully rose to his feet, feeling broken ribs grind together. Disgust turned to grim laughter as he saw the sorcerer come racing back, his escaped daemons bounding after him. Whatever magic the sorcerer still commanded he sent burning into his monstrous adversaries, trying to blast them back into the spectral world of gods and ghosts. Kormak tightened the hold on his axe, then crooked his arm back. With one mighty effort, he sent the heavy broadaxe spinning through the air, across the dozen yards between marauder and sorcerer. The brutal blade slammed into Odvaha's back, crunching home in a spray of gore. The sorcerer's body folded around the butchering steel, flopping prone upon the ground.

A haze of shimmering violet winked into life between the fallen sorcerer and his daemons. The monstrous things hissed and raged at the magical obstruction, but made no effort to cross the barrier. Slowly, still growling their fury, the daemons became indistinct, shadowy. A moment later, and only their foul smell lingered to remind the world of their intrusion.

Vakaan hovered above the fallen Odvaha upon his daemonic disc. The magus waved his hand and the haze he had summoned vanished. He stared down at the crippled sorcerer, pointing at him with a

merciless finger. Not for the daemons would be the
honour of vanquishing the traitor.

In response to Vakaan's command, the mangled
bulk of the Chaos spawn came lumbering over the
battlefield. The bear-like abomination seethed and
churned with vile growths but somewhere within its
mutated mind, beneath the animalistic mindlessness
of madness, it recognised the man whose magic had
reduced it to such a vile state.

Kormak felt his gorge rise as he saw the loathsome
spawn exact its revenge. Odvaha would have fared
better being left to his spiteful daemons.

The marauder turned from the gruesome spectacle,
then slumped to his knees. Black-hued blood bubbled from his mouth; fire seemed to grip his heart. As
crimson dots danced before his eyes, Kormak's last
thought was how vile it was to die another man's
slave.

THE STANDING CIRCLE was a ring of towering megaliths
rising from the ice and snow of the mountain. Runes,
strange even to Pyra's eyes, were inscribed upon
them, marks of a race old even when the first elves
walked the shores of Ulthuan. Who the mysterious
builders had been was unknown even to the most
learned elves. There were whispers of primordial Old
Ones, legends of god-defying giants and myths of the
terrifying shaggoths. Whatever had reared the towering stones, their work had endured the savage and
not always natural elements of Norsca for aeons.
Pyra could feel the magic bound into them, seething
with power.

'You are certain this will work?' Prince Inhin demanded as his warriors began to warily approach the circle of megaliths. Cautious, the noble was letting his vassals examine the sinister ring of gigantic stones before deigning to near them himself.

Pyra gave her lover a look of condescending indulgence she knew he found infuriating. 'That is the purpose for which they were raised,' she told him, hiding her own doubts that there might be other powers within the stones that had not yet been discovered. 'The ancients who built these circles were tapping into the ley lines, the magical veins that wrap around the world. By setting each circle upon the lines, they were able to travel instantly from one to another. So long as they knew the right incantation.'

'And you know the incantation?' Inhin shook his head. 'How much did that little secret cost you, I wonder.' He glanced at the armoured shadow of Sardiss and sneered into the Black Guard's metal mask. 'You are a woman who doesn't overly care what the price may be once you see something you want.'

'I might inquire as to your own limits, my prince,' Pyra rejoined. She smiled as she watched Inhin's shades probing every snowbank and bush with paranoid efficiency. 'If I did not already know them quite intimately.' A sardonic curl of her lip accompanied the sorceress's words. 'But perhaps you are more arduous in other arenas.' She gestured a slim hand at the scowling figure of Naagan. 'What did you promise the Hag Queen to gain the loan of Naagan and his bitch?'

Inhin rounded on Pyra, clenching his fist before her face. 'You push me too far, woman. One word from me and you'll be wearing chains when I send you back to Naggarond!'

The noble's eyes widened with alarm as he felt razored steel press against his throat. With amazing speed, Sardiss had covered the ground separating the two elves and now had his dagger against the prince's neck. Inhin cast a desperate look at the standing stones where he had sent his retinue. He started to open his mouth to call for aid, but felt the Black Guard's knife prick his skin the moment he tried.

'Do not play your noble airs with me, Inhin,' Pyra's voice hissed at him, low and filled with menace. 'We are partners, you and I, and don't think to forget it. I intend to profit from this expedition, not sit idly by and accept whatever scraps you toss me.' She gently stroked Inhin's bloody neck, tugging the knife away from his throat. 'One word from me, and you will not get back to Naggarond at all. I suggest you remember that, my prince.' There was something lascivious about the way she caressed the armoured arm of Sardiss as she pulled the Black Guard away from Inhin.

The humiliated noble glared at both of them.

'I will tell Lord Uthorin of this,' he snarled.

'By all means, my prince,' Pyra laughed. 'Tell Uthorin. Let us see how well he favours you when he hears how loyally you have been serving his interest.' The sorceress looked past the fuming noble, pointing at the standing circle. 'Run after your men, my prince. I think they have decided the circle is safe enough to receive your eminent presence.'

With a snarl, Inhin turned and stalked away.

'You should not press him too far,' Naagan warned. The disciple had been leaning against one of the megaliths, close enough to observe the exchange. 'He is a dangerous enemy to make.'

'He is a preening ass in need of gutting,' Sardiss growled.

Pyra patted the Black Guard's pauldron. 'When the time comes, my love, he will be all yours. For now, he is still useful to me.' She arched an eyebrow as she looked at Naagan. 'The question is, how useful are you?'

Naagan genuflected, extending his hands to either side of his body. 'I am only a humble vessel of Khaine's will. I am useful to whoever serves the Bloody-Handed God best.' Somehow, Pyra could not shake a feeling of mockery in the disciple's eyes as he spoke to her.

'You grow diplomatic without your murderous whore skulking after you,' the sorceress said. Her thin smile was malicious and petty. 'A pity she could not rejoin us in time. Perhaps she will make some Norscan animal a good wife.'

The pallid shape of Beblieth stepped from behind the stone Naagan had been leaning upon. The witch elf's body was coated in blood, her unkempt hair wild with clotted gore. Pyra could tell at a glance that none of it was her own. The witch elf extended her hand, tossing something that rolled across the snow before sliding against Pyra's boot. The agonised face of an elven corsair stared blindly from the severed head.

'You would have made better time without the litter, my lady,' Beblieth sketched the slightest of bows. 'But there is no harm. After I did what you asked, I came here and waited for you to catch up.' The witch elf bowed again, then turned and marched off into the ring of megaliths. Naagan formed a more respectful farewell, then followed after her.

'Say the word and I snap that harlot's neck,' Sardiss snarled.

'No,' Pyra hissed at him. 'When that time comes, I want to see the last drop of life drain out of her eyes before I send her soul snivelling to her precious Khaine!'

'Come.' the sorceress said. 'Let me work my magic upon the circle before that weak-kneed schemer Inhin calls everything off.'

'THE WAY I see it, you lot got two choices.' Gorgut was reasonably sure he had the right number of fingers held up. If he didn't, he was certain none of the goblins cowering before him was cheeky enough to correct him. After sacking Kastern's tower, Gorgut's mob had turned north, following the wizard's dying words. There was magic to be found, a dying human never lied because… Well, they just didn't.

The warband's losses attacking the wizard's tower had been considerable. Fortunately, Zagbob had found sign of a small goblin settlement in some caves after they had crossed into the Kislevite oblast. Gorgut didn't like goblins from this far north, they tended to be even weedier and more cowardly than the ones in the south. Sure, they

claimed it was because any goblin that stood his
ground and tried to fight the human horse soldiers
ended up spitted on a spear, but Gorgut had no
patience for that kind of cringing philosophy. Certainly an orc would never lower himself to eking
out a life as some slinking ground rat! The fact that
there were no orcs among the oblast tribe was proof
of that.

Still, even if the craven grot-fondlers weren't worth
spit in a fight, they would be useful in other ways.
Green mutton, if it came to it. That was why Gorgut
had Nagdnuf helping him choose which of the gits
they had captured were going with them. He was
trusting his cook's eye for spotting goblins that
would taste better than his missing leg.

'You maggots can join up with Gorgut Foechewer,'
the black orc bellowed. 'Or you can stay here with
your old warboss.' The orc lifted his other hand, displaying the mangled head of the tribe's chieftain. He
had managed to push two of his thick fingers up the
stump of the goblin's neck and used them to make
the jaw flop open and closed.

'Stay with the git that couldn't even guard his own
cave,' Gorgut hissed in a reedy voice he was convinced didn't sound at all like his normal guttural
roar. 'That's the bestest idea of them all!'

The morbid puppet show swayed any goblins in
the crowd that might have been considering slinking
off the moment the warlord's back was turned. It
wasn't a question of breaking their loyalty to their
old warboss, goblins didn't have an ounce of loyalty
for anything that couldn't threaten, beat or whip

them into obedience. What Gorgut did need was to make them too afraid of him to run off.

'Make sure to pick out the fat ones,' Gorgut snarled into Nagdnuf's ear. 'Give the rest of them knives. We'll take on the winners and salt the losers.' The goblin cook giggled and rubbed his hands together as he hurried to comply with his warlord's orders.

'What about the shaman?' Dregruk asked, lumbering up to Gorgut as the black orc stalked from the cavern where they had herded the other prisoners.

Gorgut drew a deep breath, stifling the belch brewing in his gut. 'Time I had a talking to that runty little sneak.' The black orc was careful to keep any trace of intimidation out of his voice. He didn't expect Dregruk to be observant enough to notice, but he was too smart to admit even so slight a sign of weakness around another orc. Truth be told, the shaman was why they had attacked the goblin tribe in the first place. Zagbob had scouted out the caves with his squigs before the rest of the warband was even within sniffing distance of it. He had reported the presence of a shaman among the goblins. That fact had decided Gorgut's mind about attacking the subterranean lair.

Of all the losses suffered at the wizard's tower, Gorgut was feeling the absence of Oddgit even more than Pondsucker. As reassuring as a big smelly troll was, Gorgut felt a lot safer with a shaman's weird powers at his beck and call. Besides, he needed a shaman to tell him when he found the magic loot he was looking for! A goblin wasn't a substitute for an orc, but Gorgut didn't have much of a choice. If he did run across a proper orc shaman, he'd have Dregruk bash this one over the head. Until then, he'd need the ugly little grot.

The shaman was tied to a little chair made of bone and sinew sitting in the centre of a smelly cave that looked like either a latrine or a fungus farm, possibly equal parts of both. He was a thin, reedy goblin wearing a patchy leather cloak and a thick hood studded with sharp bones and a line of pig tusks sewn along its crown. A motley arrangement of dried fungus and shrivelled birds hung from little tethers woven into his clothes. Gorgut couldn't see much of the shaman's face beneath his hood, but what he could see was all dark and crinkly, like rotten fruit, with a big ugly eye painted across his chin.

Zagbob stood a few feet from the tied shaman, an arrow at the ready. One of the scout's ghastly squigs, a filthy, flatulent thing with oozing sores and over-sized fangs, hopped around the captive, nipping at his dangling feet.

'You killed my favourite squig,' Zagbob was saying as Gorgut entered the chamber. 'I'm gonna make you pay for that, shroom-face!' The scout let an arrow fly, the feathers on the shaft whistling past the shaman's sharp nose. The arrow slammed against the wall of the cave, shivering as it stuck into the packed earth. A dozen other arrows already peppered the wall.

Gorgut cuffed Zagbob, sprawling the scout on the floor. 'Fool around with one of the others, I need to talk to this one.' The scout scowled, but carefully withdrew, hiding in the shadows against the wall.

'If you're gonna stick around, get where the boss can see you,' growled Dregruk, shoving Zagbob across the room. The goblin glared daggers at the massive orc, but knew enough to do as he was told. The farting squig loped after the chastened hunter, hopping at his heels as he carefully pried arrows from the wall.

'Any good reason why I shouldn't let Zagbob have you?' Gorgut asked, crouching low to speak to the tied shaman.

'The curse of Mork will smash your skull,' the shaman threatened. 'The rage of Gork will grind your bones!'

'I saw some of that when we were fighting,' Gorgut said. 'Your magic popped some of the lads' heads like they was pimples. Pretty impressive stuff. You even slagged Zagbob's horned squig. Never did like that nasty bugger anyway.' The warlord patted his belly. 'Thing didn't even taste so good.'

'I'll taste worse,' the shaman threatened.

Gorgut laughed at the threat, slapping Dregruk until he joined in. 'Eat you? No, that wasn't what I was thinking, at all!'

'Nagdnuf don't know no recipe for shaman,' Dregruk elaborated, then crumpled as Gorgut drove his elbow into the orc's breadbasket.

'We come here looking for you,' Gorgut hurried to explain. 'I want a shaman for my warband, and I want the best one I can find. That's why we come here, to find you. Even down in the Badlands they've heard of... of–'

'Snikkit Sharpteeth,' the shaman said sourly.

'Yeah, Snikkit, the bestest shaman in the whole north,' Gorgut said. He didn't like the incredulous look in the shaman's eyes. The black orc clenched his fist and grabbed hold of the chair, lifting both it and the goblin off the ground.

'Look, you dung-licking twit!' Gorgut growled. 'I'm givin' you the same choice I give the rest of your tribe. You follow me as your new warboss or I'm gonna pick my teeth with your bones, recipe or no recipe!'

There was raw terror in the shaman's eyes now. His head seemed like it would snap off his neck such was the enthusiasm with which he nodded his agreement. 'You got yourself a shaman, boss! Best shaman in the whole north, yessir! Won't be no cause for regret with Snikkit looking out for you and keeping you right with the gods!'

Gorgut set the chair back down, grinning a toothy smile at his new shaman. 'Cut him loose, Dregruk,' he told his lieutenant. The hulking orc shuffled forward and with a few deft turns of his thick paws broke the leather thongs binding Snikkit.

The shaman stood, rubbing his bruised limbs where the ties had chafed his skin. He patted his cloak, ensuring that the contents of its hidden pockets were still safe. Zagbob's smelly squig came bounding over, snapping at the freed shaman. With a flick of his claw, Snikkit cast a greasy white powder into the squig's face. The monster stumbled back, stunned and sneezing. With each sneeze, the squig's body began to swell. By the fourth sneeze, the body burst like an over-ripe melon, splattering the squig's innards across the room.

'Oi! That was my favourite squig!' Zagbob roared, nocking a fresh arrow to his bow. Gorgut reached down and cuffed the scout.

'None of that you sneaking little sneak!' the black orc snarled. 'Show some respect for Mork and Gork and your new shaman!'

Snikkit turned, fixing Zagbob with his gleaming yellow eyes. The goblin's face pulled back in a fanged smile. 'Listen to the boss, or your new shaman's gonna turn *you* into a squig!'

Snikkit snatched his confiscated staff from where it leaned against the wall of the cave and slowly shuffled into the tunnel beyond. Dregruk and Gorgut followed after the sinister goblin. Zagbob simply stared at the mess of the popped squig and began quietly considering ideas for revenge.

It became easier for Zagbob once he started dismissing those that might entail any sort of danger to himself.

VISION RETURNED TO Kormak as a red fog. Drums sounded inside his head, drowning out his thoughts, leaving only a numb stupor. He pressed a hand to his eyes, pinching them closed again. The effort seemed to help the pounding in his brain. Slowly, he strained his powerful arms to lift his body.

The marauder found himself lying upon a reed pallet strewn with furs and skins. There was a murky smell of smoke and tanned leather, a grimy taste of blood and sweat to the air. Kormak gritted his teeth and gradually opened his eyes again. The drumming inside his head lessened, feeling like a blunt knife pressing against the inside of his skull instead of an entire sword.

'You should be dead,' the hated voice of Tolkku said.

Kormak flinched from the zealot's clammy touch as the leprous hand of the priest patted his scalp. 'The sorcery of Odvaha should have killed you. It is my magic you may thank that you are still among the living.'

'I will remember that,' Kormak growled at Tolkku, rising from the pallet. He could see now that he was inside a large tent of stitched hide. It did not resemble the yurts of the Hung or the huts of the Kurgans, but was more like the shelters erected by Norscan hunters. The familiarity gave him a reassuring sense of kinship with the place. After so long among the horrors of the Wastes and the savagery of the Inevitable City, even this echo of his homeland was invigorating to his spirit.

'Indeed,' Tolkku said. 'Every soul you send to Mighty Tzeentch will be owed in part to my magic.'

Kormak turned his head slowly, fixing the zealot with his piercing gaze. 'Then let us see how the Raven God likes yours!' The marauder's arm shot out, changing and twisting into a fleshy rope of muscle and sinew. The tentacle whipped at Tolkku, lashing towards the priest's neck.

Tolkku merely grinned at the display. Kormak felt his arm shudder before it could strike the zealot, rippling with pain as though he had punched a wall of solid stone. Sickness bubbled in his guts, doubling him over in agony. Tears clouded his sight as he stared at the weirdly painted skull the zealot held in his hand.

'Let that also be a reminder of the gifts the Raven God has given me,' Tolkku warned. 'You will live until it ceases to amuse me. Then I will add your skull to my collection.'

'I… will… kill… you…' Kormak squeezed each word through clenched teeth.

'This says otherwise,' the zealot laughed, stroking the painted pate of the weird skull he held. 'I wonder what magic will be inside your head when I claim it?' he mused, almost to himself.

Kormak retreated from the jeering zealot. Spying the Kurgan axe he had used to cripple Odvaha, the marauder seized the weapon, his hand exulting in the chill of steel beneath his fingers. Let the zealot brag of his powers while he could. Kormak would find a way to break the sorcerous shackles Tolkku had bound about him. And when he did, it would be the zealot's turn to squirm.

The marauder pulled open the flap of the tent, emerging into a small circle of similar huts clustered about a smouldering bonfire. The charred husks of several skeletons rose from the centre of the conflagration, impaled upon thick pine stakes. There was only the faintest hint of scorched flesh on the wind, so Kormak knew it had been many hours since the wretches had met their fiery fate.

The terrain about the camp was rocky and rugged, a jagged stretch of foothill almost barren of greenery. Ugly grey dust cloaked everything in a grimy coating, like clumps of cobweb spun from dirt. Kormak could even see the strange dust clinging to the armour of the warriors he could see sparring in the field above the tents, sending little clouds of spidery strands coughing into the air with each thrust or parry. Ragged banners displaying the symbols of the Raven Host and its subordinate tribes fluttered from rough posts scattered throughout the warcamp.

Kormak felt his attention drawn away from the sparring Norscans, away from the hide tents and the grim bonfire. The familiar, imposing aura of the Chosen was too compelling to ignore. He could see the armoured bulk of Urbaal the Corruptor standing at the base of one of the cliffs that loomed above the camp, the robed figure of Vakaan Daemontongue beside him. The two champions of the Raven God were speaking with a tigerish Norscan raider leaning upon an immense double-bladed great axe.

'You will need more men if you would take the Bastion Stair,' the Norscan was telling Urbaal. 'When I sent Jodis Wolfscar, she had the whole of the Bloodherd with her. A bunch of filthy gors, I grant, but enough muscle to butcher their way through anything! That was nine days past and I've not seen hide nor hair of Jodis or any of her warband. They say the Bastion Stair itself devoured them all.'

'Keep the superstitious prattle to yourself, Ljotur Arason,' Vakaan scoffed. 'The Blood God has no power over true followers of the Changer! If your wench and her brutes failed, it was because they were not worthy of serving the Raven God.'

Ljotur stiffened at the mockery of the magus. He sneered at the bird-like sorcerer, stroking his thick moustache with his thumb. 'Just as Odvaha said you were unworthy? You had better succeed warlock! Prince Tchar'zanek will not forgive you killing his favourite sorcerer. Breaking open the gate may be the only way to get him to spare your souls.' He shook his head and laughed. 'No, I do not think I would trade places with you, magus, whatever glory the war-lord has promised you.'

'There is no glory greater than serving the Raven God,' Urbaal's steely voice intoned. 'By harnessing the dumb might of the Blood God's realm we shall make the Raven Host strong! Strong enough to wipe away the weak Empire and bring the glory of Tchar'zanek to the very corners of the world!'

Ljotur nodded in grudging agreement with Urbaal's sentiment. 'My scouts have seen some of our enemies. It is strange for them to be this far north of the Troll Country. I have consulted my seer and he has seen an elven wizard clad in white and silver in his dreams. He has seen the elf take the Eternal Blade and drive it into the Mouth of Tzeentch, bringing hurt even to the true gods! He has also seen a north-man, swollen with the blessings of Tchar, take the Eternal Blade and with it throw open the gates of glory and cast down the portal of rage.'

'Which vision is true?' Urbaal demanded. Ljotur shrugged his shoulders.

'Both. Neither. It is never safe to depend upon the prophecies of the seers. The Raven God answers every question only with more questions.' The Norscan tapped the heft of his axe. 'This is what I depend on. I advise you to do the same. Still, the presence of

Empire-men this far north, and in such numbers, makes me wonder if perhaps my seer did have a true vision.'

Urbaal straightened, his armour shining darkly in the light of the gibbous moons. The Chosen beat his armoured hand against his breastplate. 'Let the coward southlanders send their cringing whelps. The Raven God will gorge upon them all!'

CHAPTER SEVEN

NARROW VALLEYS WRITHED between the craggy peaks of broken hills, their jagged faces split and weeping stagnant brown filth. Ugly plants like thorny vines clung to the valley walls, reaching at the men who dared stray so close to them, sphincter-like mouths slopping open in unclean bloodlust. The sky overhead faded gradually into a garish violet, and from it strange lights dripped, sputtering against the rocks like splashes of fire.

Urbaal crouched over something sprawled against the wall of the valley, ripping away clumps of hungry vines to expose the nature of their meal. He grunted as he saw his guess confirmed. What lay under the vines had been a man once, a weathered Norscan with rich blond hair and a beard. The body was shrivelled, the skin distorted by the pock-mark wounds where the vines had fed, but the dark boiled

leather armour and jewelled arm-rings made it clear
he was no starveling mountain brigand, but a warrior
of the Raven Host.

Vakaan moved towards Urbaal, the vines cringing
from the magus as his daemonic platform drew near.
The monkey-familiar on Vakaan's shoulder gibbered
excitedly, hopping up and down. The magus pointed
to a deep series of slashes across the man's breast.
They were old wounds, nearly scarred over and made
long before the man had died.

'The claws of a wolf,' Vakaan said.

Urbaal nodded his armoured head.

'He bears the mark of one of Wolfscar's men,' the
Chosen agreed. He glanced at the bleak pass around
them. 'Ljotur was right. They did come this way.'

Tolkku pushed his way through the burly shapes of
Urbaal's warriors to crouch beside the body. The
zealot passed his hands over the corpse, plucking at
the gore-drenched garments, exposing a gaping
wound in the body's midsection. He dipped a finger
in the sticky waste, putting it to his mouth. 'Dead a
few days,' he decided, spitting out the taste. 'Killed by
a spear from the looks of it.'

'It was a lance.'

All three of the leaders turned to regard the speaker.
The surviving warriors of Urbaal's retinue grudgingly
stepped aside for Kormak. The warband had lost
most of their horses in the battle with Odvaha and
his daemons, the rest had been left behind at Ljotur
Arason's camp. Kormak had found a grim satisfaction seeing the haughty knights reduced to marching
through the broken terrain of the valley. Now he

took renewed satisfaction from the spiteful eyes that watched him from behind the masks of their helms. The Norscan snorted with contempt. He had seen these men fight. The only one he respected was Urbaal; the others he could slaughter like sheep given the chance and an absence of sorcery.

Kormak thrust his hand into the wound, expanding his fingers until they brushed each side. He pulled his hand free, the fingers still splayed, demonstrating the size of the weapon that had killed the man. 'Bigger than the hunting spears of Kislev and the Hung,' Kormak said. 'Only the horse-soldiers of the Empire use this kind of weapon.'

'No horse could cross this ground,' Urbaal's metallic voice intoned. 'Certainly not the weakling steed of a southlander.'

'Then he wasn't struck down here,' Kormak answered. He pointed at the squirming vines. 'The man might have crawled here from wherever the fight took place. The plants would have licked up any trail his wound left behind.'

Tolkku clapped his hands together at the idea, a grisly smile spreading beneath his tattoos. 'We can follow the vines back,' he said, gesturing at the writhing plants and their puckered mouths. There was a subtle difference in colour between those that had feasted on the dead warrior and those that had not. Further down the wall of the valley, other clumps of vine could be seen with a faint pinkish hue to them.

Urbaal strode to one of the writhing clumps of pinkish weed. He stretched his hand towards the vines, not flinching as the leafy tendrils coiled around his gauntlet. With a snarl, he pulled free, ripping strands of vine from the wall. It was not sap but blood that dripped from the torn stalks. Blood lapped up from the trail of a dying man.

'We follow the vines,' Urbaal declared, tossing aside the quivering stalks. 'They will lead us to Jodis Wolfscar.'

'What if the southlanders won the fight?' asked Vakaan.

Urbaal stared hard at the magus, then glared at the bruised sky above. 'This is the land of the true gods,' the Chosen declared. 'The faithless southlanders will win nothing here except their doom.'

A FLASH OF scarlet light exploded within the snowbound ring of megaliths. Clouds of foul black vapour rose from the circle, choking the vultures flying overhead. Scrabbling things, like the profane progeny of scorpions and eels, emerged from their refuges, scuttling into the maze of cactus that sprawled all around the plateau of the megaliths. The gnaw of unholy magic made skin-trunked trees rip their roots from the milky soil and creep away from the standing circle in a grotesque exodus of swaying branches and dripping brain-fruit.

From within the light and smoke, lithe figures emerged. Even finding themselves in a landscape of horror and madness, the druchii maintained the arrogance of their step, the contempt of all things in their knife-like faces. Cloaked shades carefully stole from the ring of stones, crossbows gripped in their gloved hands, eyes watching the monstrous terrain for the first sign of aggression.

Prince Inhin brushed Norscan snow from his armour, snapping his fingers and waving his warriors to take up positions on either flank of the warband. The snow was strangely incongruous beside the scintillating powdery frost that clung to the megaliths. A sinister breeze blew a flurry of the shimmering stuff straight into the clump Inhin had cast off. The patches of disparate snow flowed into each other, melting and boiling like animate things. Inhin could not shake the image of two colonies of ants trying to exterminate one another. The noble shuddered at the strange impression and looked away.

'We are here, my prince,' Pyra said, bowing low before her master.

Inhin stared at the sorceress, eyes drifting down the pale leg the cut of her dress exposed, then lifting to appreciate the fullness of her carriage. He found the coy gleam in her eye less appealing. When this was done, he would blind the woman. She didn't need eyes to serve his needs and it would be amusing to watch her trying to cast spells without the ability to consult her grimoires and scrolls.

'Here?' Prince Inhin spat. 'Where the hell is here? This looks no different than the last three wastelands your magic has taken us!' Inhin's voice dropped into a low, sinister whisper. 'If you tell me we must march to another of your damn circles, I promise I shall strip you naked and stake you out for the harpies when we return to Naggaroth. Maybe I'll let Sardiss join you so you don't get lonely waiting for the harpies to eat you alive.'

Pyra's expression curled into a sneer. 'You may do with Sardiss as you like, once we do not need him any more. As for my magic, you would do well to remember its power.' A fiery glow entered the elf's eyes, sparks of flame that singed her brows. 'Especially here, *my prince.*' She lifted her staff, pointing with it at the sky above them. Some of Inhin's arrogance deserted him when he stared up at the angry bruise that marked the heavens. Everything else, from walking trees to fighting snow, he had been able to accept, but somehow seeing the sky changed and twisted offended him to the very core of his being.

'We are here,' Pyra repeated. 'And now the hunt can truly begin.'

Inhin recovered himself, clapping his hands together. At his summons, Beblieth sauntered over to the nobleman, an exaggerated swagger to every lascivious twist of hip and shoulder. Pyra's eyes narrowed as she saw the hungry way the witch elf looked at Inhin.

'I have need of your service,' Inhin told Beblieth. 'Scout ahead of my shades. We are looking for the asur wizard and the human animals he has brought with him. Find him and I shall reward you.'

'I am ready to obey my prince in whatever way he commands,' Beblieth told him. Inhin could not fail to notice the way her tongue lingered over her lips when she finished speaking.

'Then you must do your best to please me,' he said. 'Find the loremaster and bring me his head.' Inhin looked over at Pyra. 'Oh, and that little thing Pyra wants if you happen to find it. She tells me it might be useful.'

Beblieth sketched a salute, marching through the ring of Inhin's warriors and the perimeter of shades. Inhin watched the witch elf vanish into the creeping forest of crawling trees.

'You place too much trust in her,' Pyra warned him, unable to keep a trace of jealousy from her voice.

'I am not so mad as to take a witch elf into my bed,' Inhin laughed. 'But I am realistic enough to appreciate what she can do. There is every chance she could kill the asur all by herself.' He laughed again as he saw the flicker of disappointment on Pyra's face. 'There are bigger things to consider than petty revenge, my sweet. Things- like conquering Tchar'zanek and his stupid animals and using them against that old fool Malekith and Uthorin the pretender.'

Pyra's smile softened. Her hand slowly stroked Inhin's face, lingering so that he could kiss her fingers. 'Of course, my prince,' she whispered. 'But you would not deny your favourite her little pleasures, would you?'

Inhin pulled her hand away, tightening his fingers about it in a fierce grip. Pyra winced as a little shiver of pain went down her arm. 'So long as your pleasures do not interfere with my ambitions,' he warned. Inhin released her, relishing the marks his fingers left behind. 'If it makes you feel better, you can kill Beblieth after she brings me the loremaster's head.'

The noble's sardonic laugh was slithering through Pyra's ears as she watched him stalk away. Soon, she promised herself, it would be time to dispense with Inhin and his pretensions.

Then she would only need to worry about Sardiss. She didn't want a spy of the Witch King's lurking around after she made her move. The easiest thing would be to pit them against each other, but that was exactly what the fools would be ready for.

'Did he hurt you, my love?' Sardiss demanded as he came up behind the sorceress. Pyra turned away from him with an indignant curl of her shoulder.

'He's done worse,' she said.

'I'll serve you his heart on a silver platter,' Sardiss promised, his strong hands gripping her shoulders.

'Not yet,' Pyra hissed. 'Wait until the time is right, my champion. When Inhin has outlived my purposes, I shall help you skewer the pig. But until then you must wait and be patient.'

A black smile wormed its way onto Pyra's face, unseen by the Black Guard. 'When it is time to be rid of Inhin, you will be the first to know.'

KORMAK ROARED WITH fury and drove his mutant arm into the torso of the screaming southlander. The bony blade gored through the soldier's steel breastplate and pierced the leather hauberk beneath. Blood exploded from the man's mouth and his sabre clattered down the rocky slope as it tumbled from weakened fingers. The marauder spun the dying wretch around, using his body to block the strike of a second soldier. The southlander held back his blow at the last second, afraid to hit his dying comrade. Kormak wrenched his arm free and sent the corpse hurtling down the slope at the man. Both soldiers collided and were set careening down the jumbled heap of broken stone. The Norscan threw back his horned head in a howl of exultant savagery and lunged after his fallen foe. He found the wretch wailing, his leg broken by his fall. Feebly he lifted his sword to defy the immense marauder. Kormak batted the weapon away with a contemptuous slash of his axe. The Norscan's boot smashed into the soldier's face, knocking him prone upon the ground. Kormak stood over the wretch, then brought his axe chopping down into the soldier's head, splitting helm and skull like a rotten egg.

The marauder wiped the spray of brains and blood from his face and shouted his triumph to the staring sky. Let the Raven God watch him! Let Mighty Tchar see the way Kormak exulted in the gifts of flesh his god had given him!

Around him, Kormak could see the other warriors of Urbaal's band taking their own gory toll upon the men of the Empire. They had outnumbered Urbaal's men when the battle began. The warriors of the Raven Host had just emerged from the narrow fissure between the hills, entering a wide expanse of muddy clay, bubbling and spurting as unseen fires boiled it from below. Despite the sinister appearance, the ground was safe to cross – at least as safe as anything in the Chaos Wastes could be, and they had made good time sprinting over the forsaken muck. There was no question of Jodis Wolfscar's trail now; the bodies of her slaughtered warriors were abundant enough. Few bore the kind of wounds that marked the man in the pass. Most were brutally violated, their flesh mangled by fang and claw and horn. Many bore the unmistakable marks of predation and the way some of the bodies were contorted and disfigured with agony, it was obvious not all of them had been dead when they were eaten.

The clay mire gave no sign what had killed Wolfscar's men. The muck refused to hold footprints for any time. A horde of giants might have beset Wolfscar's warband and the treacherous earth would have concealed all trace of them.

Occasionally, a body would turn up that bore different marks. A torso ripped apart by a lance, a skull cracked by a steel-shod hoof. Kormak pointed these out to Urbaal and again repeated his warning about southlander knights.

As though his warning had evoked the capricious humour of the gods, a large body of armoured cavalry appeared far below the horizon. The flattened terrain gave no hiding place to conceal the riders, their appearance could have been no more impossible than if the boggy clay had spit them out. Tolkku had drawn one of his weird skulls from the skin bag he carried. A sinister thing with no sockets in its face, somehow the zealot used the morbid charm to descry the nature of the riders.

'Empire-folk,' he had pronounced. 'Thirty or forty to our ten. One of their heathen priests leads them.'

Kormak and the other warriors prepared to sell their lives for what havoc they could claim. There was no hope of outrunning the riders, even if there had been someplace to run. Urbaal had growled a curse upon the mischievous daemons that favoured his enemies.

But if magic had been kind to the Empire men, Vakaan had the power to force it to be kind to the Raven Host. The magus had produced three gnarled stones from a pouch sewn into his robes. Kormak could feel the chill of sorcery in his bones as Vakaan's birdlike tongue formed a raspy incantation. Emerald fires burst from the pebbles as the magus cast them to the ground.

Charging soldiers of the Empire and hardened warriors of the Raven Host alike fell to their faces in awe as Vakaan's sorcery ravaged the flatland of clay. Like a farmer sowing seeds, the magus ministered to his pebbles. There was a ferocious pulse of power, a throb of malignance that made the ground tremble. In less than the blinking of an eye, immense boulders burst from the clay, expanding and rising like foam upon a crashing wave.

The warriors of Tzeentch gave praise as the magic of Vakaan gave birth to a refuge from the southlander cavalry. As the jumble of boulders and rocks grew into a hill, they clambered up the raging slopes, jeering at the stunned knights and soldiers who gazed upon their sorcerous bastion.

The southlanders might have broken but for the presence of their false-priest. The grizzled old man had the look of a veteran warrior about him despite his flowing robes and shaven head. He clutched the tiny hammer that hung around his neck, knuckles turning white as he pressed the icon into his skin. The priest took solace from the token of his god, fear draining away, replaced with the most bitter of hate.

'Do not fear, men of Sigmar!' the priest's voice roared in the grating tones of the southlander tongue. 'This is no black miracle! It is an illusion. A falsehood. A daemon's lie!'

The conviction of the priest did not spread into his followers. It was the man who rode beside the bald cleric who decided things. A wiry, sinister figure shrouded in a black cloak, his face hidden beneath the shadow of a wide-brimmed hat, the man turned his stern gaze upon the soldiers.

'You have heard Father Wilhelm.' the officer raged. 'We outnumber the heathen scum and the protection of holy Sigmar is our shield!' He drew a strange weapon, a cylinder of steel fitted to a wooden hilt from a sheath and pointed it at the hill. There was a crash and a flash of flame. One of the Kurgan warriors screamed in pain, clutching his bleeding face before falling down the slope of the hill.

'Grey Lancers!' the officer shouted, holstering his smoking weapon. 'Dismount and send this vermin shrieking into the abyss.'

KORMAK SMILED AS he saw the same officer scrambling up the side of the hill. The two enemies locked eyes across the still expanding pile of jumbled stone, sharing a moment of hate. The marauder could smell the stink of death on this one, the foul smell of torturer and sadist. He noted the little hammer icons dangling from strings fitted to the officer's sword.

'You need your god to steady your hand, little worm?' Kormak snapped in crude Reikspiel. It was strange, speaking the language of slaves while he himself was Tolkku's thrall. The marauder's face pulled back in a sneer as he savoured the irony.

'Sigmar will judge me worthy when I spill your life on these hell-spawned rocks, cur,' the officer hissed.

Kormak spat and hefted his axe. 'Sigmar licks the dung from Tchar's back-feathers.'

The officer's eyes went crimson with wrath. He lunged at Kormak with the violence of a tempest, his sword slashing and jabbing at the marauder's twisted bulk. Kormak felt slivers of pain flash through him as the southlander's steel glanced across his flesh. His own axe seemed a clumsy weapon beside the lithe sword, the southlander managing to intercept it at every turn. Kormak grinned, allowing the officer to become fixated upon defending himself against the axe.

Abruptly, Kormak let one of his hands slip free from the handle of the axe. Fingers melted into a knob of iron-hard bone while his forearm stretched to twice its natural length. The suddenness of the mutation caught his foe by complete surprise. The officer was thrown from his feet as Kormak's mutant mace smashed into his chest. The marauder could feel his enemy's breastplate crumple beneath the blow, could hear ribs snap under the impact.

The southlander was thrown, landing in a tangle of limbs and pain. Kormak laughed at his enemy, willing his mutant arm to reshape itself into a gigantic, insect-like claw. The Empire man watched him as he advanced, hate refusing to make room for pain in the smouldering pits of his eyes.

'Mutant filth!' the southlander snarled. 'I've sent hundreds of your foul breed to the stake! Know this, monster: no mutant touches a witch hunter twice!'

Kormak ran at the southlander, draining every ounce of speed from his immense frame. It was not enough. The witch hunter reached to another holster on his belt, drawing a second pistol. There was a grimace of loathing on his face as he aimed and fired.

The marauder felt the bullet slam home, felt its searing trail stab through his chest. Unspeakable agony pulsed through him as his heart was ripped and torn. The pain brought him to his knees, then an even greater pain flooded through his body as he felt his heart binding itself together once more, as his flesh knitted itself whole again. The tang of Tolkku's grisly magic stained his thoughts, polluting his soul. The zealot, it seemed, was not finished with his slave and would redeem him even from a southlander's bullet.

The witch hunter stared in open-mouthed horror as he saw the fatal wound seep close and the marauder rise once more. He fumbled at his belt in a pathetic struggle to reload his pistol. Kormak slapped the foul-smelling powder horn from the man's hands. The marauder's teeth lengthened into wolfish fangs as he lifted the southlander off the ground. The witch hunter gave a deafening shriek as Kormak began peeling flesh and muscle from the man's arm with his claw, like a malicious child plucking petals from a flower.

'The mutant is touching you,' Kormak growled through his fangs. 'Why don't you stop him, witch hunter?'

'IMPRESSIVE SORCERY, FOR an animal.'

Prince Inhin's comment was one designed to vex Pyra. She refused to give the preening noble the satisfaction of seeing her rise to the bait. 'An illiterate ape could work such magic in this place. Perhaps you might try your hand at a spell or two, my prince.'

Inhin's face turned sour. He rounded on Beblieth. 'You were told to find the asur. I do not see any of our treasonous kin over there.' The noble's brow knitted in perplexity as he stared down at the witch elf. 'Tell me, just how simple do I need to explain things for you? I've had dogs that could obey better.'

Beblieth lowered her face as Inhin upbraided her, more to hide the anger in her eyes than out of any sense of shame. 'I will do better, my prince.'

Inhin turned away. The dark elves stood upon the plain of clay, some leagues distant from where the Grey Lancers fought against Urbaal's warband. They had been crossing the strange morass for hours before Beblieth had returned, informing them that she had found the human allies of the asur wizard. Eager to confront the loremaster and steal from him the artefact that would give him control over the Raven Host, Inhin had ordered a gruelling quick march to close upon the enemy.

'Given your performance, better will not be very hard to do,' Inhin quipped.

'Forgive me, my prince,' Beblieth asked. Inhin gave her a withering scowl.

'Tell me why I should,' he demanded.

'Because Beblieth has provided the means to find the traitor asur,' Naagan said. The morbid disciple of Khaine held his arms across his chest in a peculiarly boneless fashion. More than anything, it made the elf look like some lurking vulture. He nodded at the distant melee. 'Those are warriors of the Raven Host down there, warriors with at least one powerful sorcerer among their number. Ask yourself, my prince, why would such warriors be here?'

Inhin turned his scowl on the disciple. 'I neither know nor care what moves a pack of stupid animals.'

'You should,' Naagan advised, some of the deference slipping from his tone. 'Your father did not care about the ways of animals either. He had his heart ripped out upon the altars of the lizard-kin.'

'My father was a fool,' Inhin said, his voice cold and filled with menace. 'If you have a point to make, priest, do so. And quickly.'

Naagan bowed his head in apology. 'I think the northmen are about the same purpose that guides our own quest. They seek the Bastion Stair and the Spear Dolchir carries with him. Has it occurred to you that if the Raven Host were to gain the Spear they would have no need of alliance with Lord Uthorin... or Prince Inhin?'

The noble nodded his head slowly, grudgingly allowing the wisdom of Naagan's observation. 'Then we shall simply see to it that the animals fail.' He turned a cold smile on Pyra once more. 'You boast of your sorcery, *my sweet*,' he savoured the way she jumped to hear him use the same words as Sardiss. 'Let us put your power to the test. The barbarian's magic raised a mountain. Let us see if Pyra Night-blade is able to cast it down again.'

THE SPIKED FINGERS of Urbaal's gauntlet sank into the face of the Grey Lancer, gouging deep furrows in the southlander's flesh. The man struggled to free himself, trying desperately to pull his sword free from the Chaos champion's clutch. Urbaal's own sword held the weapon in a grip of steel, the daemon-forged metal of the Chosen's blade slowly bending the weak Imperial craftsmanship. Urbaal savoured the terror in the eyes that stared at him from between the splayed fingers of his gauntlet. An image flashed through his mind, the recollection of a wolf caught in the jaws of a trap, desperately trying to tear itself loose.

The Imperial sword broke with a shrill snap, a foot of the blade spinning away to be lost among the steadily growing rocks. Urbaal's blade lunged past the broken parry of his enemy, chewing into the soldier's side in a spray of blood. Urbaal tightened his hold upon his foe's face, feeling bone and cartilage crushed into ruin beneath his grip.

'Monster! Beast of the Pit!'

Urbaal turned slowly as the caustic words fell upon him. The face buried within the metal mask of his helm snickered as his eyes settled upon his accuser. The shaven-headed false-priest. Truly Tzeentch was being generous to his champion this day. Urbaal finished breaking the face of the screaming thing he held, letting the human wreckage flop and writhe and he stalked away to find new prey.

'Daemon-kissing scum!' the priest shouted, his voice cracking with the fury of his words. 'By the strength of Sigmar, you will answer for your heresies!'

Urbaal stood still, his burning eyes taking the measure of his enemy. The priest was old, well past his thirtieth winter, but he had done his best to stave off the ravages of age. There was muscle beneath the white robes and shining mail he wore. His hard face was grim and scarred, the leathery mask of a veteran warrior. Almost, Urbaal felt a twinge of grudging respect as he saw the priest lift the gigantic warhammer he bore. Then the Chosen's gaze fell to the little icon dangling about the southlander's neck and his contempt for his foe swelled.

'There is only one heresy,' Urbaal's iron voice hissed. 'The blasphemy of being a fool.' He tightened his grip upon his sword. The weapon blazed into life at his command, assuming the scintillating aura of divine power that had vanquished Odvaha's daemons. 'Die now, false-father, and know your god is a lie.'

The priest braced himself for the Chosen's assault, muttering prayers to his god. Golden fire slowly gathered in the bludgeoning hulk of his warhammer. Flares of righteous fury crackled from the southlander's eyes, licking out like fiery lashes of sunlight. 'Behold the power of Sigmar and despair, monster!'

Urbaal laughed. 'I see only the hand of Tchar. He would not have me grow bored with our battle, false-father.'

With astounding speed, the Chosen sprang at the priest, his shimmering blade sweeping down at the shaven pate of the priest. His foe caught the glowing weapon with the heft of his hammer. For an instant southlander and Chosen were locked in deadly struggle, both men exerting the strength of their bodies and the power of their gods to overwhelm the other. Urbaal saw doubt flicker on the priest's hard face as the Chosen's blade inched downward. Horror flashed across the man's features as he realised his lack of faith. Renewed fury blazed up in his eyes, the prayers spilling from his lips grew louder and more enraged.

Urbaal staggered as the priest forced him back, breaking the hold of the Chaos blade upon his warhammer. The Chosen was forced to retreat as the burning hammerhead came smashing down at him, pulverizing the stones at his feet. Urbaal snarled, the sound distorted and twisted by his mask. He could feel the eyes of the other combatants upon the hill watching him, eager for the first sign of weakness. The merciless gaze of the gods pressed down upon him and in his ears he could hear the mocking laughter of the Changer.

The Chosen slashed at the priest, his blade scraping across the southlander's breastplate. Metal bubbled and flowed like wax beneath the touch of his sword, but the blow failed to penetrate to the enemy within the armour. Urbaal spun to catch the priest's warhammer as the enemy drove at him again. Once more the two foes were locked in a struggle of strength and determination.

Urbaal's smouldering eyes glared into the pious fires of the priest's gaze. The Chosen pressed all of his weight, all of his anger, all of his ambition into the effort to tear the hammer from the priest's grasp. He scowled inside his helm as the priest's prayers became a thunderous echo in his ears, an accusing cacophony that quickly rose into a deafening tumult. The Chosen growled and clenched his teeth against the maddening din, refusing to be cowed.

The priest snarled back at him, struggling to maintain his hold against the brutal monster. Inch by inch, the weight and fury of Urbaal was driving him back, his feet sliding in the pebbly ground. The southlander tried to draw upon reserves of faith, but there was nothing left to throw into the contest. Inch by inch, he was pushed back, pushed to what he knew would be his death.

The monster glared back at him, inhuman eyes glowing from the skull-like face of his helm. The priest tried to find some sign of weakness, some testament that there was a man of flesh and bone within the gothic armour, beneath the plates of steel and sapphire. Anything that would tell him that his enemy was mortal. Anything that would give his failing faith new hope.

Suddenly, the hill trembled and began to collapse. Overhead, the priest could see the birdlike magus upon his hovering daemon struggling to prevent the dissolution of his spell. The sorcerer was unequal to the task. For every wild gesture of his arms, every shrieked incantation of his voice, the collapse accelerated. Screams echoed over the grinding of stone and the quaking earth. It pleased the priest to hear the harsh tones of northmen mingled with the war cries of Imperial soldiers.

The priest smiled at Urbaal.

'Sigmar's justice is upon you,' he snarled as the slope above the two combatants came crashing down upon them in an avalanche of smashing boulders and choking dust.

CHAPTER EIGHT

PYRA FOLDED HER arms across her breast and watched as pillars of dust continued to rise from the broken hill. Only a faint sheen of sweat on her body betrayed the great effort she had made to work her spell. For all of her scorn for the crudity of northmen magic, in the darkest corridors of her soul, she shuddered at the malign power she had pitted her sorcery against. The magus did not simply exploit the winds of magic, use them like fuel or even wield them like a thing of ithilmar or steel. No, in some obscene way, the Chaos wizard was part of the magic, his very essence in communion with the awful power spilling from the rent between worlds. It was a thing Pyra could regard only with equal parts of terror and envy.

'I believe Prince Inhin wanted a prisoner,' Naagan's cold voice broke through her dazed mind.

'There are survivors,' Pyra told him, hating the way her voice exposed the weakness she felt. She tried to make up for it by staring hard into the disciple's eyes. 'Unlike some, I obey the commands of my prince.'

Inhin chuckled as he saw Naagan flinch as Pyra suggested his disloyalty. The noble put his arm around the sorceress, kissing her ear. 'You have done quite admirably, *my sweet*. I only hope the effort was not too taxing.'

'My prince, there is still the matter of a prisoner,' Naagan reminded.

Inhin pointed a warning finger at the disciple. 'Do not be overeager to fatten Khaine on the blood of captives. I will provide for the Lord of Murder in good time. Right now, there are questions I want answered.' He turned his head, staring past the sinister disciple. Unheard, the cloaked figures of Inhin's shades had drawn near. The noble gestured at their leader.

'One prisoner,' Inhin ordered. 'One of the Empiremen. You can kill any others.'

The shade smiled beneath his hood as his master made the bloodthirsty suggestion. The cloaked scout nodded as he gazed at the distant pillar of dust, imagining the broken, wounded things choking beneath that cloud. There would indeed be work for his knife. He gave a whispered command and the rest of the cloaked sneaks began to file off across the bubbling plain of clay.

Pyra's eyes narrowed as she saw Beblieth's lithe figure stalk after the departing shades.

'Where do you think you're going?' the sorceress demanded.

Beblieth did not try to hide the fire in her stare when she turned upon Pyra. 'Prince Inhin needs a prisoner,' she grinned. 'He also said we were free to kill any others.' She looked over at the dark elf noble, expectant and eager. Inhin gave the slightest nod of his head and the witch elf was off, outpacing the shades with a grace and speed that made even the sure-footed scouts look clumsy sluggards by comparison.

'Murderous wench,' Pyra spat as she watched the witch elf prance across the solid patches of clay protruding through the mire.

Inhin shook his head and sighed. 'You have your playthings,' he said, glancing at the armoured bulk of Sardiss. 'Do not begrudge me mine.'

BLOOD CASCADED FROM an ugly gash on Father Wilhelm's bare head. The priest wiped at his eyes, trying to clear them of the crimson that smeared his vision. The ground continued to roil and tremble beneath him, his lungs felt scratchy with the tang of dust. His side felt as though on fire; a shard of jagged stone had torn through his mail to chew its way into the flesh beneath. The fingers of his left hand were fat and purple, a sliver of bone sticking out from his thumb. But he was alive, and for that he gave praise to Sigmar.

Father Wilhelm's eyes settled upon an object lying beside him. He bent down, almost collapsing as pain from his side pulsed through him. He fought through the agony, falling only to his knees. Timidly, almost tenderly, he shifted rubble from the object that had caught his eye. He closed his right hand about the heft of his warhammer and thanked Sigmar once more for sparing him the destruction that had been visited upon the debased northmen.

The clatter of stone against stone drew the priest's attention. Wilhelm watched as small rocks bounced down the ragged heap of ruin. At first, only a few, then the few became many. Cold dread worked its way into the priest's spine. Fear overwhelmed pain and he rose to his feet, clenching his warhammer as best he could in a single-handed grip. The prayers he offered to his god changed from gratitude to entreaty.

A sapphire claw burst from the pile. An instant later, the heap was falling forwards, broken from within by an armoured devil. There was no dust staining the Chosen's mail, as though the base elements were repulsed by the abomination inside. Unblemished, the armour of sapphire and bronze gleamed in the sickly light of a maddened sky. Only the sinister sword was changed. No longer did it burn with the malignity of a Dark God, but was instead a sickly thing of fanged steel and daemon-skin wrappings. Eyes puckered open along the length of the blade and a mouth slobbered from the weapon's pommel.

'Thank your little Sigmar for sparing me as well,' Urbaal mocked, his voice a metal vibration behind the death mask of his helm.

'Blasphemer!' Wilhelm spat, but there was no strength behind his disgust.

Urbaal laughed darkly, marching forwards like a lion on the prowl. 'Blasphemy? One cannot blaspheme against a myth, false-father. I have forgotten much, southlander. I cannot name the man and woman who gave me life. I cannot remember the land that first bore my step. Even the first soul I sent shrieking into the claws of the Raven God, even this is lost to me!' The burning eyes of Urbaal's helm flickered menacingly. Instinctively, Father Wilhelm recoiled from the display of unclean magic.

'This, I know,' Urbaal hissed, touching his gauntlet to the side of his horned helm. 'I know that your god is a lie.'

The Sigmarite roared as he heard the blasphemy spoken. Wilhelm flung himself at the gloating northman, at the monster that claimed it had once been human. Urbaal blocked the sloppy swing of the priest's warhammer. The impact of sword against hammer set the broken bones of Wilhelm's hand grinding together. The priest cried out, stumbling back as pain flooded through him. He let the warhammer fall from his grip, clutching his maimed hand. Urbaal stalked after the faltering priest.

White light gathered about Wilhelm's hands, flowing from the whole one into the injured one. The divine power raced through his tortured appendage, knitting together broken bones, binding shattered flesh. Urbaal turned his face, unable to endure the purity of the priest's magic.

'My god stands with me,' Wilhelm snarled, lifting the discarded warhammer from the ground. Once again, a fiery glow seemed to bleed up from the depths of the weapon. 'Before him, all darkness must fall!'

Urbaal growled, forcing himself to endure the hateful aura surrounding the priest. The Chosen's sword clashed against the warhammer, the two champions locking once more in a struggle for dominance. Urbaal's hellish eyes narrowed. Savagely, he brought the armoured knee of his leg smashing into the priest's wounded side. Father Wilhelm gasped, crumpling in a moaning mass as raw suffering exploded through his body. As his hammer fell from his hand, the glow surrounding him flickered and died.

The Chosen loomed over the priest, pinning him to the earth with a bronze boot. He pressed his weight down upon the southlander, crushing already splintered ribs. Wilhelm cried out, blood bubbling between his teeth.

'Sigmar, I commend my soul to you!' the priest groaned.

The corrupt sword of Urbaal stood poised above Wilhelm's shaven head. 'It is not Sigmar who will claim your soul, southlander.' The Chosen paused, his eyes glowering down at his fallen enemy. 'In the Halls of Tzeentch, you will find a real god, falsefather. Perhaps the Changer will even remake your soul into something better.' Urbaal laughed and raised his sword for the killing blow.

'But somehow, I doubt it,' the Chosen snarled as he split Wilhelm's skull like an egg.

BEBLIETH EASILY OUTDISTANCED the shades, entering the billowing column of dust and debris. A dazed southlander stumbled into her path. She swung at him with one of her daggers, freezing when it was only an inch before his terrified eyes. She smiled as she saw the horrified disbelief on the man's face. Perhaps he had never seen an elf before. In the distance, Beblieth heard a pained moan. Her smile tightened. With the first dagger poised before the man's face, she raked the second across the back of his neck. The man fell in a gurgling puddle at her feet.

He'd never see another elf, Beblieth mused as she stalked away from her kill. Inhin might want a prisoner, but he'd only get one after Beblieth had sated her own needs. She hesitated as she saw something with broken legs trying to free itself from beneath a boulder. She could not tell if it was northman or southlander. Either way, it gave a most satisfying shriek when she punched both her blades through its eyes. She wiped the sticky mess from her blades in the animal's hair and started to stalk through the fog of dust to the next moaning thing. The witch elf froze, casting an amused glance over her shoulder.

Like lightning, she spun, catching the bolt searing through the air at her. She grinned at the shocked shade who had tried to shoot her in the back.

'Prince Inhin... he wants... one alive,' the scout sputtered, trying to decide if he dared fit another bolt to his weapon.

Beblieth smiled at him, then looked thoughtfully at the bolt she held. 'He wants a southlander,' she stated. 'He didn't say anything about you.'

The shade shrieked as Beblieth flung one of her daggers at him. The poisoned weapon sheared through his hand, sending fingers spilling to the earth. The screaming elf tried to push the poison from his wound with his remaining hand, even as he turned and started to run. He had only gone a few paces before a stabbing pain in his breast brought him up short. Cold lips brushed against his ear.

'I believe this is yours,' the witch elf hissed, driving the crossbow bolt deeper into the shade's heart.

There was still some life in the scout's eyes when Beblieth seized him by the shoulders and spun him around. Whatever life was left was quickly exterminated as a half-dozen bolts thudded into the shade. Beblieth let her now dead shield fall, pushing the body forwards as she dove left for cover.

'Traitoress!' a druchii voice raged. 'Murdering fanatic!'

More bolts came clattering against the boulder behind which Beblieth had taken refuge. The witch elf smiled, her pulse racing with the thrill of battle. Inhin's shades would not relent until she was dead. Six arrogant braggarts who fancied themselves expert killers. Her smile faded as she caught a faint sound to her right. Seven, including the one trying to flank her. The one the bowmen were trying so hard to keep her from noticing.

Beblieth ran her fingernail along the edge of her dagger, covering it in a fresh paste of poison. She'd offer the one trying to circle her to Khaine. The others would just be practise.

Before she could move, however, Beblieth heard the sharp scream of the sneaking dark elf. Something huge and brawny rose from behind the rocks, the shade gripped in both of the brute's hands. With a bull-like roar, the brawny figure brought the scout smashing down into one of the boulders, splashing the elf's brains across the stones. Beblieth expected the hulk to beat his chest in triumph, like some jungle ape, but the anticipated display was spoiled by a fresh fusillade from the crossbowmen. Only the blinding effect of the dust could have kept the shades from finding their mark. The brute dove from his boulder, crashing down behind Beblieth.

The dark elf could see that the brute was a northman, a hulking mass of swollen muscle, his head sporting great horns, his flesh peppered with little fangs of bone. She felt her skin crawl as she saw the way the animal's eyes watched her. Beblieth smiled when she noted the absence of any weapon in the northman's sinewy paws. It was the cold, vindictive smile of a viper.

'The one you killed was mine,' the witch elf spat, forcing her tongue to the harsh speech of slaves. 'Now I must offer Lord Khaine something else.'

The horned brute had been reaching for her. Now he recoiled. It was not quick enough. Nothing merely human was. Blinded by a flash of leg and a curve of thigh, now the dumb northman was treated to a better view of her sinuous body as Beblieth stabbed her daggers into his chest. She twisted them in the wound, ensuring they would not close, then danced back, all in a dazzling display of violence that would have staggered the quickened senses of an elven swordmaster.

The beast was staring in disbelief at his injuries, at the dripping daggers in Beblieth's hands. He made a staggering step towards her, then took a second. It was only when he managed a third that Beblieth's face twisted with concern. A fourth step and she knew something was wrong. The poison should have spilled the man to the ground, have him screaming in pain until his lungs burst from the effort! Instead, he was coming for her!

Muscle and tissue began to melt and flow like wax, reshaping themselves into a monstrous claw. Kormak snarled through his fangs as he closed upon the witch elf.

'My turn,' the marauder spat.

THE WITCH ELF spun and dropped, slashing at Kormak with both of her poisoned daggers. The Norscan felt the burning metal rip through his flesh, one tearing through his leg, the other cutting a deep furrow in his arm. His body shuddered as the deadly taint on the blades entered his bloodstream. Growling like an enraged bear, Kormak brought his claw-arm scything at the witch elf.

Beblieth twisted at the waist, throwing herself from the path of the mutant claw, her hands slapping against the broken stones. She twisted again, using the muscles of her upper body to propel herself at the marauder. The elf's inhuman speed was blinding, her daggers nothing more than an impression of pain as they again bit into Kormak's flesh.

The marauder felt his brain darken, then the flush of purging fire roared through him again. He ground his teeth against the pain, accepting it as the cost for life. He knew the witch elf's poison would have killed him at the first touch but for Tolkku's preserving magic. Clearly the zealot still lived and intended that his thrall should do likewise.

Kormak lashed out at his foe as she tried to slink away again. It was his turn to surprise the witch elf, his mutant arm sweeping forwards as he willed flesh and bone to lengthen and stretch. This time it was the elf who felt pain stab into her body as Kormak's claw snapped tight about her waist. Thin blood spurted from the gruesome wounds, splattering Kormak's crude armour.

'Hurts, doesn't it?' Kormak snarled, tightening his grip. He felt something crack beneath the pressure and enjoyed the pain that pulled at the elf's face.

Suddenly, the marauder was struck from behind. He grunted as a pair of bolts slammed into him. The lack of concentration was enough. Beblieth tore herself free from his hold, dropping down in a crouch. Vindictively, she stabbed her dagger into Kormak's chest, digging for his heart.

Kormak slapped her away, a clumsy effort that she easily avoided. He noticed that her escape was not so seductively graceful as before and that she bled profusely from the ugly holes his claw had chewed into the milky skin around her waist.

Beblieth flung herself flat as several crossbow bolts streaked over her head. Kormak was staggered by the fresh dose of poison she had stabbed into him, unable to even think about the bolts that slammed into his body.

From the ground, Beblieth watched as Kormak ripped the bolts from his flesh. Her eyes narrowed with disgust as she saw the wounds close. She cast her gaze around her, then a cruel gleam sparkled as she saw what she expected to find.

'Forget the warrior, fools!' she shouted. 'Kill the sorcerer or we are all dead!'

To emphasise her point, she threw a stone at the pile of boulders just beyond Kormak. Almost, but not quite hidden behind the pile was the tattooed shape of Tolkku the zealot.

The fusillade of bolts stopped. Beblieth watched as the shades abandoned their vengeful attempt to kill her. They had seen the way Kormak had resisted her poisons and knew it was no natural force that preserved him against them. None of them wanted to take the chance that the sorcerer who was protecting Kormak might have more dire spells to work directly against them.

Kormak ignored the slinking shades as the elves swept past him, intent upon climbing the rubble pile to reach Tolkku. He had eyes only for the bleeding witch elf. He could see that her wounds were sapping her quickness and strength. He could see that with every breath, the odds favoured him more than his foe.

'I'll make your death quick,' he promised, his mutant limb reshaping itself into a fanged axe.

Beblieth cocked her head, looking at him with the same sort of patience that might be shown to an idiot child. 'Are you sure, barbarian?' she purred. 'I think I hear your master calling you!'

It was true. Kormak could feel the imperious, driving pain gathering in his mind. He knew the sorcerous touch of Tolkku's commanding skull. He did not need to see the zealot to know he had cast aside his healing talisman for the skull of command. As the shades drew nearer, Tolkku's summons became even more painful. The Norscan felt blood trickle from his ears and knew he could resist his hated master no longer.

Beblieth clutched her sides, watching the marauder stalk away. Desperately she wanted to drive her blades into his back, but feared that her slowed reflexes would make her easy prey for the brute. She would not die at an animal's hands.

'We will meet again,' the witch elf promised as she watched Kormak climb up towards the shades.

Naagan would heal her wounds, make her whole again. When next they met, the marauder would not surprise her with his loathsome mutations. She would be ready for him. Ready to offer him to Khaine.

Like a wounded wolf, Beblieth slunk away. There was murderous purpose in her retreat. She had counted the shades climbing the rubble. There was one missing. It was just possible one of them had found Inhin a prisoner.

It would be tragic if the wrong elf received credit for bringing the prince his prize.

PANIC STARTED TO creep into Tolkku's eyes as he watched the shadowy shapes climb towards him. Even over the broken jumble of cracked stone there was an inhuman grace to their movements, a surety of purpose and footing that was both chilling and malevolent. Tolkku drew sorcerous energy into his body, urging the commanding pressure of his talisman to bring his slave to him. The Norscan brute would save him from the dark elves.

The zealot's body shuddered as a crossbow bolt smashed into his shoulder. He struggled to remain standing. A second missile slammed into his leg, knocking him down. The priest withdrew his magical protection from Kormak, drawing the healing energies down into himself, using it to still the crawl of poison in his own veins. With another, even more desperate part of his brain, Tolkku focused upon channelling his command through the painted talisman of bone and teeth. The Norscan would come, or he would let the magic build up inside his head until it burst!

Another bolt smashed into Tolkku's body, lancing through his side like a dull sliver of fire. Tolkku grasped at the dripping wound with his free hand, trying to pull the missile free. He glared at his attackers as they approached him, staring into the almond-shaped eyes and their merciless arrogance.

One of the shades cried out, blood exploding from his face as his eyes burst beneath the malignance of Tolkku's magic. The others uttered shouts of warning, fitting fresh bolts to their weapons. Tolkku raged at the slinking shades, heaping contempt upon their courage and ancestry. The elves, if they understood, did not acknowledge the zealot's insults. Instead they peered from behind their refuge and aimed their weapons.

The wailing shriek of an elf spoiled the aim of the others. They spun to see one of their number hanging like a gutted rag doll from the chitinous claw of a roaring Kormak. The marauder shook his mutant limb, shaking the carcass free. The limp wreckage slumped against the rocks, its broken spine jutting from the ghastly gash in its back.

The three remaining shades fired at the marauder. One bolt smashed into his knee, dropping him. Another lanced through his chest, puncturing his lung as it punched out his back. The third glanced off one of his horns, a finger's length of bone splintering from the impact. The shades hissed among themselves. Two turned to finish off the crippled Tolkku, the third drew a fresh bolt for his crossbow and took careful aim at Kormak's forehead.

With a brutish bellow, Kormak pounced at the dark elf, lashing at the shade by stretching the bones of his mutant arm. Even extended, he was too far away to strike the assassin, but the unexpected horror of the mutation was enough. The shade's eyes went round with shock, his aim spoiled by his moment of fright. Instead of smashing through his skull, the hastily fired bolt tore through the meat of Kormak's arm. The wounded marauder cursed as he felt poison sizzle through his muscles, numbing them. In only a few steps, his arm felt like a dead lump of lead. Only his feral bloodlust kept him going. Even until the last moment, the shade expected the poison to drop him.

Now Kormak was close enough to reach the elf. His mutant arm snapped closed upon the crossbow as the shade struggled to reload it. The elf abandoned his weapon to the marauder's grip, dragging a slender sword from the sheath at his side. A blur of silvery metal, the thorn-like sword slashed through Kormak's arm, biting deep enough to grate against the bone.

Kormak screamed through clenched fangs and brought his other arm smashing around. The elf dropped beneath the punch and tried to pull away. His sword resisted his effort to rip it free, its edge trapped in Kormak's unnatural flesh. Distracted by the struggle, the shade's face broke when the Norscan drove his head into it.

A thin, weedy wail rose from the shade as he clutched his dripping features, trying to push teeth back into his mouth. Kormak hobbled after him, the agony of his mangled leg increasing with each step. The elf was not so pained as to ignore his enemy. The shade drew a throwing knife from the sleeve of his cloak, sending the deadly blade flickering into the Norscan's chest. Kormak staggered, unable to pursue the dark elf as he scrambled over the rocks to recover the weapon of the scout whose eyes Tolkku had burst.

The dark elf was scowling through the mask of blood that had become his face as he aimed the crossbow at Kormak. He never loosed the bolt, however. As he turned to attack, Kormak ripped the elf's blade free of his arm, throwing it like a spear at the cloaked monster. The thin, almost weightless blade of ithilmar crunched through the shade's midsection.

There was disbelief in the elf's eyes as he stared at his own sword protruding from his belly. Then the expression froze as life faded from the shade. Without a sound, he pitched from the top of the boulder, landing in a broken jumble almost at Kormak's feet.

The marauder grunted with pain as he forced himself back to his feet. He lumbered up over the rocks, compelled to answer the imperious summons of his master without regard to his own suffering. He could hear the sounds of battle, the war cries of men and elves. How he would fight, he did not know. How he would save Tolkku, he did not know. It was enough that he would be able to still the electric fire pounding inside his head.

Tolkku was sprawled on his side, bleeding from his many wounds, the painted skull still clutched tightly in his splayed fingers. Over him stood the armoured malignity of Urbaal, his sapphire mail stained with thin elvish blood. One of the shades lay dead at the Chosen's feet, brains leaking into the ground. The other backed away, slowly sheathing his sword and unslinging his crossbow.

The surviving elf was just below the level of the rocks upon which Kormak perched. The marauder drew upon the last reserves of strength in his poisoned body. Like a great tiger, his massive frame coiled and grew tense, every muscle taut with strain. Kormak launched himself from the rocks, smashing down into the slinking elf. The shade heard him, throwing his crossbow into the Norscan's face. Fangs snapped, his nose crumpled as the heavy weapon smashed into him, but there was no stopping his momentum. With the violence of a meteor, Kormak came crashing down, the cloaked elf beneath him.

The sound of splintering bones rose from the crushed body. Kormak grabbed the elf's head, twisting it full around, breaking the shade's neck like a twig.

The Norscan slumped against his last victim, his breathing growing shallow as the druchii poison took its toll. It was an effort just to keep his eyes open, to watch the grinning Tolkku as he slowly stood, amber light dancing from his fingers as he used magic upon himself. The zealot's wounds were like butter, knitting together, pushing free the elven missiles embedded in his flesh.

Urbaal stared at the zealot, then regarded the prone Kormak. The Chosen stared at the many wounds riddling the marauder's flesh, impressed that even Tolkku's magic had kept him standing for so long. Even a champion of the Raven God could appreciate the fighting prowess of such a warrior.

'Mend him,' Urbaal told the zealot.

Tolkku looked up, surprised by the warleader's command. There were still wounds in his own flesh that needed tending. The Norscan would keep. If he didn't, then there would be another skull in Tolkku's collection.

Urbaal noticed the zealot's hesitancy. Clawed fingers closed about the Kurgan's throat, lifting him off the ground. 'See to his hurts,' the Chosen growled, 'then lick your own wounds.' He dropped Tolkku to the ground. The painted skull rolled from the zealot's fingers. Tolkku made a desperate grab for it, but pulled back when Urbaal's boot came between his hand and his talisman.

The Chosen looked down at Tolkku then turned his head to stare at Kormak. Urbaal brought his boot smashing down into the painted skull, shattering it into a hundred fragments.

'Find a new pet, zealot,' Urbaal said. He locked eyes with Kormak. 'This one is too good a fighter to be your dog.'

THE ANGUISHED SCREAM rang out over the dark elf encampment. The sentries watching the perimeter shrugged, ignoring the shriek. They had been listening to the sounds for hours now and even the most sadistic of them no longer found them engaging. Instead they watched the bleak landscape of violet grass and weed-choked knolls, waiting for the monstrous scavengers that might be drawn to the screams. Already they had accumulated a pile of scaly, jackal-like things and feathered vultures that seemed equal parts centipede and bat. One grotesque creature, large as a Norscan sweat lodge and armoured like a dwarf steamship, had emerged from the long grass, defying the best efforts of the druchii to drive it off. It relented only when it had an elf warrior clenched tightly in its trifold jaws, crunching his armour like the shell of a nut. Each sentry dreaded the possibility the loathsome monster might return.

Prince Inhin was oblivious to the concerns of his warriors, focused entirely upon the mangled man stretched between two posts set in the ground. He had supervised the torture of the wretch, using an old trick employed by the now extinct feral humans of

Naggaroth. A long strip of damp leather had been wound around the man's body, like a great slimy bandage. Then the elves settled into their chairs and watched as the sickly northern sun slowly dried the binding. The stretched leather contracted and tightened as moisture was sucked from it.

The elves didn't even bother to ask any questions until the second hour. Their captive had been screaming his throat raw, begging and promising whatever he thought his captors wanted to hear. Inhin listened to the desperate babble with boredom clouding his eyes. Truly humans were nothing but low beasts, incapable of anything but fighting and rutting. An elf would have tried to find some harmony in his pleas, added an ascetic of poetry to his cries. A human just screamed and whined like a wounded dog.

Pyra leaned over the moaning captive, her dark tresses spilling down, brushing against his face, filling his nose with the lusty smell of her perfume. She smiled at him, but it was the chilling smile with which a spider might favour a fly.

'We are looking for Dolchir,' she said, astonishment working into the Grey Lancer's face as he heard the perfect Reikspiel sing from her cruel lips. 'He calls himself a loremaster of the high elves and he is responsible for bringing your... herd... into the northlands.'

Pyra pressed her finger against the man's mouth as he tried to speak. He winced as her nail stabbed into his cheek, drawing a trickle of blood. 'I know you want to show us where he is. He is our enemy. It is because of him that you have suffered so. I won't lie to you and offer you life. You would be a fool to believe me. But I can offer you revenge. You do want revenge?'

She pulled away her finger. The man spat at her. 'Daemoness!' he cursed. 'I will not betray my regiment or my Empire!'

The sorceress patted his bloodied hair. 'A few more hours and I think you will change your mind.' She gestured to Naagan. The grim disciple of Khaine came forward with a silver-chased jar. He poured the briny mixture of saltwater onto the prisoner. He shrieked as the tightened leather began to expand again, removing the constricting pressure of his bonds. The salt burned as it oozed into his cuts.

'Breathe easier, brave little beast,' Pyra told him. 'It will take time for the bindings to dry again. For them to close about you, grind your bones together like some great python.' A soft laugh escaped her as she saw the anguished horror of realisation flood the Grey Lancer's eyes.

Pyra rose, turning towards Inhin. 'I think the animal is broken now,' she said.

The prince snapped his fingers, motioning Beblieth forwards. Inhin had chosen to overlook the suspicious fact that none of his shades had returned with the witch elf. It was more politic to accept the absurdity of her story about barbarian wizards and mutants killing them all.

'Let the thong tighten around it one more time,' Inhin told her. 'Just to remind it what pain feels like. Then you may cut it free. Tell it to guide us to its camp.'

Beblieth bowed as the noble started to walk away. The witch elf fingered the ugly scars around her waist and moistened her mouth.

'Oh, and Beblieth,' Inhin called over his shoulder. 'Leave the animal at least one finger to point with.'

CHAPTER NINE

SARDISS MARCHED AT the head of Inhin's warriors, holding the leash of the mutilated human guiding them. The Black Guard was imposing in his mail, poised like a steel spider, one hand resting casually against the pommel of his blade. The dark elves around him gave Sardiss a wide berth, fearful both of his sinister skill with the blade and of the loathing with which he was held by their prince. Eventually, an accident would befall the Black Guard. When it did, no one wanted to be caught too close to him.

Prince Inhin himself was well away from the head of the column, secure at the centre of his warriors, Pyra – and her sorcery – at his side. There was a puffed-up air of arrogance in the noble's step now. Soon they would find Archmage Dolchir's camp. They would slaughter the foolish asur and his stupid

humans, seize the Spear and with it bind
Tchar'zanek's Raven Host to his every command.

Naagan watched them all, wondering if Pyra had
not overplayed her hand leading the prince along.
Inhin was no fool, even yet he might suspect treachery. The disciple patted the vials of poison secreted
beneath his robes, a venom for every purpose his
devious mind could conceive. He almost hoped
Inhin would make trouble.

The dark elf heard the slightest rustle of under-
brush beside him. After leaving the plain of clay, the
terrain had become a rolling landscape of prickly
cactus and gigantic ferns, all powdered with a scarlet
mush that was too sticky to be called snow. There
was a resemblance to clotted blood about it that
both disturbed and excited Naagan. It meant they
were nearing their goal, the landscape of the Wastes
changing itself to reflect the murderous madness of
Khorne as they drew close to the Bastion Stair.

'You are sure they know,' Naagan said. He did not
turn his head, only shifted his eyes as Beblieth drew
closer. The disciple kept one hand coiled about his
own dagger, an instinctive reaction to having the fey
witch elf so near. As far as Inhin knew, Beblieth was
out ahead of the column, scouting the terrain in case
their tortured guide was leading them into a trap. It
was as well the northmen had killed all of Inhin's
shades before they set out to find Dolchir. It made
less work for Beblieth.

'I killed three of their sentries and left a trail even a
blind ogre could follow,' Beblieth assured him.
'Dolchir is not the only asur among the humans.

Several of our degenerate kinsmen from Nagarythe were with him.'

Naagan stroked his chin, smiling his cadaverous smile. 'That is good. With the Shadow Warriors to guide them, even the humans should be able to prepare a fine ambush. Inhin's warriors will be butchered.'

Beblieth scowled. 'It would be simpler just to kill the preening peacock.' She drew one of her daggers, making a slicing motion with the blade.

The disciple shook his head. 'Pyra fears Inhin's warriors will try to avenge him if he were murdered. Or worse, they may follow Sardiss. She may treat with the Witch King yet, but if so, she would have it be her choice.' Naagan returned his attention to the warriors marching through the red slush. 'No, she is right to thin their numbers. Soldiers take strength from their comrades. Kill many of those comrades and the survivors weaken. Become pliable.'

The witch elf made a dismissive shake of her head. 'And how then does the sorceress think she will defeat Dolchir if not by using Inhin's warriors?'

Naagan laughed. 'The archmage does not have many asur with him. His troops are animals begged from the Empire, human chattel whose only value is their numbers. Pyra plans to make up the losses Inhin suffers with reinforcements. Animals of her own. Animals loyal to her, not our dear prince. Pyra's sorcery has revealed to her a warband of orcs some small distance from here. The brutes are no friends of the barbarians of this land, nor of the humans Dolchir has allied with. Her magic will bend the stupid monsters to her will and with their strength to support her, she will be able to dominate Inhin's troops.'

The disciple's eyes narrowed and he cocked his head as faint shouts reached him. The smile returned to his leering face.

'Unless I am mistaken, it seems Inhin has encountered trouble around the next bend,' he said. 'We should see what we can do to help him,' Naagan continued, slowly strolling towards the sounds of conflict. He could see the column breaking apart, swarming like an angry anthill as the dark elves were thrown into confusion by the Imperial ambush. There was a serene look of contemplation on his face and he wondered how much more vibrant the scarlet slush would look with the blood of druchii upon it.

KORMAK FOLLOWED URBAAL through the jumbled wreck of Vakaan's hill of sorcery. Freed from Tolkku's magic, the marauder knew he was bound to Urbaal by chains every bit as strong. Chains of obligation. Chains of a debt owed and unpaid. There was another reason though, a reason deeper even than the rough sense of personal honour demanded by a Norscan's beliefs. Urbaal was Chosen, the mark of Tzeentch was even more firmly upon him than it was upon Kormak's mutant flesh. He could feel the eyes of the gods upon Urbaal, he knew the magnitude of the duty entrusted to him by Tchar'zanek. Urbaal would find glory or doom. Kormak would follow him to claim his part of destiny.

Tolkku followed after the two warriors, his stained face pinched into a bitter scowl. The zealot's healing arts had given Kormak back his strength and expunged the dark elf poison from his veins, but the marauder was under no illusion that the Kurgan had done it for his benefit. His sour gaze was that of a cheated horse trader, wishing only for the speedy death of his former property. Only fear of Urbaal kept the priest's hate in check.

Kormak smiled at that thought. If the zealot imagined the only danger to him was the Chosen's displeasure, then he was sadly mistaken. He appreciated the reasons Urbaal had included the healer in his retinue. But there would come a time when the zealot's black arts were no longer vital to Urbaal's quest. Kormak would be watching most eagerly for that moment.

The three northmen prowled among the boulders looking for other survivors. Sometimes they found a broken southlander dragging his ruined body through the rubble, wretches who were easily settled with a boot crunching down upon their necks, but of Urbaal's warriors there were only shattered corpses. Kormak lingered over one black-armoured giant, tearing a curvy bronze axe with a gnarled handle of elk antler from his dead hand. He tested the balance of the weapon, finding it light and awkward. He stuffed it beneath his belt just the same. Even the delicate pony-axe of a Hung nomad could spill its share of blood.

'What will we do?' Kormak asked of Urbaal as they stalked past a heap of butchered things that had once been Empire soldiers.

'What we must do,' the Chosen answered, his enigmatic words ringing through the skull-face of his helm.

'Find the Bastion Stair and secure it for the Raven Host,' Tolkku said.

Urbaal stopped and stared at the Kurgan zealot. 'Is your magic enough to make the land show us the Bastion Stair? We serve the Raven God. That pits us against the other Great Powers.' Urbaal shook his steel head. 'No, knitter-of-wounds, it will take sorcery greater than yours to trick the Wastes. Already the land moves against us. First it brings the southlanders to us, then the slinking elf-folk. It would keep us from learning what has become of Jodis Wolfscar and from finding the Blood God's throne.'

'Then how can we do what Tchar'zanek has commanded?' Kormak wondered, his blood chilled by this talk of vindictive landscapes and the malignity of Dark Gods.

'We find Vakaan Daemontongue,' Urbaal told him.

Find the magus they did. He crouched upon the highest rise atop the collapsed rubble of his mountain. The sorcerer's robes were torn, his helm dented and singed. Sap-like ichor dribbled from gashes in his face and hands. The monkey-like foetus crawled and gibbered from its perch upon his shoulder. The breaking of his magic had nearly broken Vakaan with it. For the first time since leaving the Inevitable City, the feet of the magus rested upon solid ground.

The daemon steed of the magus hovered above him, the fanged maw set into its underside snapping and slavering as it tried to rend the flesh from the sorcerer's bones. A flickering haze of orange light burned between magus and monster, keeping the vengeful nightmare at bay. Vakaan's hands wove in desperate gestures, trying to maintain the barrier.

Kormak cursed when he saw the disc trying to devour its master. He drew the Hung pony-axe, then willed his mutant arm into a long blade of thorny bone. His braced himself for the gruelling dash over broken ground that would end pitting himself against a daemon fiend.

Vakaan saw the start of the marauder's sprint. The sorcerer's eyes were wide with despair. 'No!' he cried. 'I am bound into it as it is bound to me. Slay the daemon and you kill me with it.'

Kormak stayed himself, his mutant arm oozing back into a semblance of normality. Urbaal slowly removed his own hand from the hilt of the sword sheathed at his side.

'What would you have me do, magus?' the Chosen demanded. 'I yet have need of your powers and would not abandon you to the revenge of a daemon.'

The slavering disc surged forwards, exploiting Vakaan's distraction, nearly breaking through the weakened barrier. The monkey-familiar gave a bark of fright, its malformed paws weaving before it in perfect unison with Vakaan's sorcerous gestures.

'You must seize the disc, hold it fast while I repair the binding runes the elf witch scarred with her magic!' Vakaan gave a wail of despair as the disc's fangs shot forward of its body on a stalk-like appendage, its teeth tearing at the spectral haze. 'By the Changer, there is no other way!'

Urbaal nodded and snarled a command to Kormak. The marauder stuffed the Hung axe back under
his belt and joined the Chosen, climbing up the
rocks to where Vakaan struggled against his rebel-
lious steed. Reluctantly, Tolkku followed after them,
chanting for protection from daemons as he invoked
his own magic to oppose the frenzied disc.

Urbaal came behind the slavering disc and seized it
in his iron grip, armoured gauntlets steaming as they
clutched the daemon. Kormak hesitated, feeling the
evil aura of the thing, fearing the searing pain touching it promised to inflict. He ground his fangs
together and set aside his fear. Grabbing the disc was
like trying to hold lightning – there was no substance
to it, only burning pain. His hands slipped through
the unreal shadow of its essence, fingers vanishing
under the rainbow lights of its skin. He felt his hold
slipping, sliding through a puddle of stinging cob-
webs. The wrongness of the thing offended his body
more than the pain. A primal terror rippled through
him, begging him to free it of his clutch. Little feath-
ery growths, like weird fungus, began to creep up his
arm. *Free me*, the parasites called to him.

The feel of something solid under his fingers was
almost like a physical blow to Kormak. Desperately,
he focused upon the sensation, using it to anchor his
straying thoughts to things real and tangible. He
found that his hands had slipped through the daemon's substance to close around the band of bronze
that circled it. The metal felt red hot beneath his
touch. Compared to the stinging crawl of but a
moment before, it was a soothing release to him.

Slowly, the three northmen pulled the daemon back, wresting it away from the barrier Vakaan had woven from his magic. The disc shivered and struggled to be free of them, desperate to slaughter the man whose soul tied it to the mortal world. Thorns and talons sprouted from its sides, slashing and tearing at the men who held it. None of its captors relented, understanding only too well that if they let the daemon slip free now, it would not be content with only the blood of the magus upon its teeth.

Vakaan gradually came to his feet. He glared at the errant daemon and removed a thin strip of bronze from his tattered robes. The magus wove his hands in a complicated pattern above the metal. His mouth expanded, bones shifting and reforming to accommodate the macabre intonations of his spell. They were not words of Norscan or Kurgan, but the speech of the Dark Tongue, the voice of Chaos itself. Kormak felt blood trickle from his ears as he heard it. The monkey-thing on Vakaan's shoulder started to shriek, though whether in exultation or terror it was impossible to decide.

The disc shuddered, its efforts to break free growing even more desperate. Kormak could feel ice forming beneath his skin, could sense his lungs filling with arctic mists. That part of him he knew was his soul quivered and railed, its sharp definitions collapsing in a crust of spectral slime. It was not death the disc threatened him with, but annihilation, the complete eradication of flesh and spirit. The temptation to surrender to it goaded Kormak. He could see the same thought on the tattooed face of Tolkku, wondered if it also lurked in the eyes of Urbaal.

None of them relented however. Whatever hell the daemon threatened them with, it could only be a sweet release from the wrath of Tzeentch if they allowed their fear to upset the Changer's schemes. Instead of releasing the disc, the three men tightened their holds upon it, trying to close their minds to its rage.

An instant, and then the malevolence of the disc was gone. The daemon's struggles subsided and it became quiet once more, less creature than thing now. Briefly, Kormak could see fresh patches of metal glowing upon the bronze band that circled it, welding together its scarred magic. Vakaan's hands were empty when he glanced at the magus, though otherwise the sorcerer had not seemed to move. How the bronze had flowed from magus to daemon was a riddle Kormak decided he did not want to know.

The men released their weird captive, breathing easier once their arms were free of the stinging nothingness that formed it. Vakaan strode towards the now truculent disc. He gestured and the thing dropped down, hovering only a few inches from the rocks. The magus stepped onto its back and it rose once more, levitating ten feet above the jagged stones. Vakaan was bound to the earth no more.

'Your daemon is returned to you, magus,' Urbaal said. 'You owe your life to me.'

'What is life without power, Chosen of Tzeentch?' Vakaan asked. A green membrane snapped closed over his eyes as he considered his own question. 'The elves have worked their havoc quite thoroughly,' he stated when he opened his eyes again. 'Only the four of us are left of your entire warband, great Urbaal.'

'They will pay for their interference,' the Chosen promised, clenching his fist.

'We may make better use of them than revenge,' Vakaan said. 'The sorceress who broke my spell could not hide from me the purpose behind her magic. It was too great a spell to keep her thoughts from weaving themselves into its eldritch energies. They call themselves druchii and name themselves the enemies of our enemies. They seek the Bastion Stair and the relic borne by the southlanders.'

'Then they will fail,' Urbaal growled.

Vakaan shook his head and gestured to the oozing plain of clay beyond the jumbled heap of stones. 'The other gods stand against what we would do,' he warned. 'This land bears the stain of Nurgle the Pox-father, a quagmire to drag us down yet firm enough to give speed to the hooves of southland steeds! No, there are powers that defy the glory of Tchar'zanek and would not see the Raven Host triumphant even against the weaklings of the Empire.

'But the ways of the Changer are crafty,' Vakaan continued. 'If the other gods stand against us, perhaps there are others who are too insignificant to draw their notice, others who can find the Bastion Stair without their interference.'

'You say that the elf-folk can succeed where we cannot?' Tolkku's voice was hollow with refusal to believe what he was hearing.

'Only in small things,' Vakaan explained. 'Tzeentch will allow heathen Khaine only such glory as will lend itself to his ultimate triumph. The elves will find the Bastion Stair. We will find the elves.' The magus pointed at Kormak, at the sticky blood that coated his armour. 'There is power in blood, power that engorges Savage Khorne. Blood calls out to itself. 'Tell me, did any of the elf-folk escape your axe?'

Red rage burned in Kormak's eyes as he answered. 'One,' he growled, remembering the sensuous curves of the witch elf's body as she drove her poisoned daggers into his flesh. 'When next our paths cross, she will not be so lucky.'

Vakaan waved aside the marauder's wrath. His feathered fingers drew a pouch of coppery weeds from his belt. 'If she lives, the blood she has lost will seek to find her. With the help of my sorcery, it will succeed despite the treachery of the Wastes.'

The magus's eyes narrowed with amusement as he saw the feral rage smouldering in Kormak's gaze. 'Be content, Norscan. Soon you will have your chance for revenge.'

GORGUT'S CRAGGY BROW knitted with concentration as the shrill wail echoed in his ears. The black orc scratched his leathery scalp, trying to make sense of the sound. After a few moments, he decided it was just noise, not words. He lifted his powerful arm, ready to cuff Snikkit on the ear. A look at the grim little shaman however, made the warlord reconsider. Instead he punched Dregruk in the face, knocking the orc onto his arse.

'Stop blockin' the light,' Gorgut snapped at his lieutenant.

Dregruk blinked at him stupidly, then glanced around at the burning village around them. Carefully the orc rose to his feet and shifted well out of the warlord's way.

Gorgut watched him for a minute, then was distracted by a pack of his greenskin warriors playing a crude game of ball with the hairy head of a Kurgan. One of the orcs let up a huge whoop of triumph as he caught the severed head. An instant later he was smashed down under a huge pile of punching, biting orcs. Gorgut slapped his face when he noted that the warrior's own team-mates were the first to tackle him. Thick as two short dwarfs, most of his mob would have a hard time outwitting their own dung.

Another shrill wail made Gorgut look away from the chaotic rumpus. He glowered at Snikkit, then at the fat old woman tied to the wattle fence. He threw a rock at a pair of goblins slinking along the back of the fence, scattering the sneaks. Interrogating prisoners was serious business! Not to be interrupted by bloodthirsty cowards trying to shove splinters of wood under the captive's toenails!

'How come the humie cow doesn't talk so I can understand?' Gorgut demanded. Whether his words were directed at the prisoner or at Snikkit seemed a bit dubious, but finally the shaman decided to answer.

'You see, boss, these humies up north don't like the ones down south,' Snikkit explained. 'So they come up with their own way of talkin' so's the ones down south can't understand.'

'But I ain't one of them south humies,' Gorgut growled. 'How come I can't understand these ones?'

Snikkit blinked his eyes, a nervous smile wrinkling his face. 'Because you can understand the humies down south, boss. These humies don't talk like that.'

'Well, tell 'em to start talkin' so I can understand 'em,' Gorgut snarled back. He shook his fist under the woman's nose, the entire paw bigger around than her whole head. 'You better start tellin' me what I want to know!' he threatened.

The Kurgan shrieked again. Gorgut rolled his eyes and threw his hands up.

'See! What's that supposed to mean?' the black orc snapped. 'Is that even words?'

The shaman shook his hooded head and leaned on his staff. 'You can't scare 'em like that, boss.' Snikkit drew an ugly-looking dagger from the folds of his robe, fingering the rusty edge with his thumb. The shaman's leathery skin made a rasping noise as it slide across the metal, like a razor hissing along a strop. The woman's face went pale as the goblin leaned towards her. 'This is how you ask 'em stuff,' he giggled.

A stream of sounds bubbled from the Kurgan's mouth. Gorgut's brow knotted together in concentration. Some of it might be words, he decided. In his eagerness, he grabbed Snikkit's scrawny arm and pulled the shaman back.

'What'd the humie say?' the black orc demanded. 'She tell you where this lot is hidin' their magic?'

Snikkit shrugged his shoulders. 'I don't know, boss. I don't speak humie.' The goblin turned back around to finish questioning the woman.

Gorgut started to lift his axe, murder in his beady eyes. He sucked at his fangs as he realised he couldn't chop up the shaman into little pieces and feed them to Zagbob's squigs. The weird little fungus-freak was the only magician he had. Lose him and there wasn't anything like a good chance of getting another one. Besides, Mork and Gork didn't like it when their shamans got killed, no matter how annoying they were.

Instead, the black orc tried to count to ten in his mind and backed away. It wasn't the easiest thing to do because he wasn't sure if seven came before or after three. Before that dilemma was solved, he turned around and boxed Dregruk's ear.

'You said this village looked like a good one,' Gorgut snapped. Dregruk was grabbing his ear in pain. The opening was too good to let pass, so Gorgut punched him in the other ear for good measure.

'It wasn't me, boss!' Dregruk protested. 'Zagbob found the place and said it looked good!'

'You lettin' a grot do your thinkin' for you now?' Gorgut snarled.

Dregruk blinked at him, carefully letting one of his paws drop away from his ear. 'What'd you say, boss?'

'Don't make me hurt you, you stupid git,' Gorgut growled. Dregruk flinched as the black orc raised his fist again. 'I said where is that squig-fondlin' twerp at?'

The two orcs stared at each other for a moment, then turned to watch as a small knot of goblins came slinking past. The scrawny little sneaks gripped heavy earthen mugs in their hands, a pungent amber-liquid that smelled like cattle urine slopping from the jugs with each step. A motley assortment of casks, furs, salted meats, scraps of armour and dried fish hung from their belts or was draped over their backs. Many of the goblins sported oversized weapons that looked suspiciously like the ones the Kurgans had been carrying when Gorgut and his orcs attacked the village.

Gorgut's red eyes blazed as he saw the lone goblin the mob was carrying on their shoulders. Even with his face hidden beneath a horned Kurgan helm ten sizes too big for him, the stink of squig sweat rising from his hide armour was impossible to mistake. Gorgut bulled his way through the goblin looters, scattering them like sheep. The looters carrying Zagbob unceremoniously dropped their hero and scrambled for safety. Gorgut grabbed the scout by the horn of his new helm and started to lift him into the air. The goblin squealed, falling out of the bottom of the oversized armour. Gorgut stared angrily at the now empty helm, then tossed it aside.

'Where's my magic stuff?' Gorgut snarled, glaring down at the squig hunter.

'Didn't they have any?' Zagbob asked, his face trying to look innocent. 'Didn't Snikkit find some for you?'

Zagbob shrieked like a stuck pig as Gorgut reached down and grabbed him. This time the warboss had a firm hold on the goblin's neck. 'That weedy runt is too busy playin' with his knives,' Gorgut growled. 'So why don't you tell me where all this humie magic is!'

The scout sputtered, fighting to keep the choking pressure off. 'Honest boss, they had so much nice stuff, I thought for sure some of it was magic!' The goblin's eyes narrowed with thought. 'You sure some of it ain't?'

'Anything worth havin' they would have used on us,' Dregruk snarled at the goblin.

Gorgut spun around. Dregruk covered his ears and ducked, but his leader only looked at him with sullen realisation. The black orc let Zagbob slip through his fingers and fall back to the ground.

'You lot!' he roared at the orcs playing with the severed head. 'Knock that off and pack it up. We're movin' out!' His face lifted in a snarl as he heard another scream sound from the direction of the fence. 'Somebody tell Snikkit to cut it out! There ain't no magic here!'

The black orc glared at the smouldering village around him. It was the first settlement the warband had encountered since crossing the Troll Country, a small cluster of hide huts and wattle fences. There had been perhaps twenty or thirty warriors among the inhabitants, hardly enough to put up a decent scrap for a mob the size that Gorgut had gathered. The rest of the humans had been too little or too old to be any good in a fight – the kind of humans only a goblin would waste time with. Gorgut wrinkled his nose as the stink of smoke and burning flesh assailed his nostrils. At least there had been a lot of horses. Nagdnuf knew ways of cooking horse that made the black orc's mouth water just thinking about it.

'You, smart git,' Gorgut snarled at Dregruk. 'Make sure Nagdnuf packs plenty of horsemeat. Tell him if it ain't enough, he's got another leg to make up the difference.'

Dregruk nodded, bowing and scraping as he scrambled to pass on the warlord's orders, overjoyed to escape without being hit again. The orc lieutenant paused only long enough to give a spiteful glance at Zagbob still lying at Gorgut's feet.

Gorgut looked down at the scrawny squig hunter. He stabbed a thick finger at the goblin. 'Next time you say you found some magic, there better be some magic!'

'But there *is* magic here, monster,' a mocking, chill voice spoke.

The black orc's huge body swung about, his immense axe gripped firmly in his claws. He glared at the weird figure that stood before him, a thin, slender she-elf that was all curves beneath her tight black dress and high leather boots. Gorgut grunted in ill humour. There wasn't enough meat on the elf's bones to feed a snotling.

'Where'd you come from?' the black orc demanded, then decided he really didn't care. He didn't like elves. They were all thin and stringy, too sneaky to make a proper fight when it came down to it. Usually they hit you when you weren't looking and then slipped off before you could even cuss them out. All the spleen of a goblin and none of the taste. Even a tough old dwarf was better.

Gorgut's axe chopped out at the elf, sweeping in a murderous arc at her. The black orc put all of his frustration and anger in the blow, his enormous weight behind the axe. When his blade failed to connect with anything solid, the black orc overbalanced and crashed to the ground. A few titters rose from the crowd of greenskins that had gathered, drawn by their warlord's angry bellow. Gorgut glared at the mob, trying to decide which were the jokers so he could stretch their necks and pull out their gizzards.

Instead he pointed a claw at the smirking she-elf. 'Gut that witch and bring me her liver!'

A few of the boldest of the orc warriors lifted their grimy choppas and came charging at the slender elf. Like their warlord, the blows of their rusty weapons failed to strike anything solid. One orc crashed to the earth, his comrade's choppa buried up to the heft in his ribs. The other orc looked about guiltily, then scurried away.

'It should be obvious even to a dull brute like you that I am not here,' the she-elf said, staring down at Gorgut. She ran one gloved hand along her side. 'This is an apparition, a ghost if you like. My body is quite far away. Quite safe from your excitable temper.'

Gorgut got to his feet. As he straightened, he rammed his fist full into the smirking visage of the she-elf, almost falling over again when there was nothing for him to hit. The black orc spat, crossing his arms over his chest.

'All right, so you ain't really here. Where are you at?'

The apparition laughed. 'I think we must reach an accord before I tell you that.' She scowled as the black orc blinked at her. 'Make an agreement, an arrangement.'

Gorgut spat again. 'You speak good, for a bony little elf-sow,' he conceded. 'But never mind the fancy words. What're you doin' here?'

'I have use for you and your army, Gorgut Foechewer,' the sorceress said. 'I am in need of fierce warriors to fight my enemies.'

The orcs snickered at the comment. Gorgut joined in, his eyes twinkling with amusement as he stared back at the apparition. 'I'm not surprised. Never knew an elf was any good in a stand-up fight. Who are you tryin' to kill?'

The she-elf's face darkened into a scowl. 'Does it matter?'

Gorgut barked with laughter again. 'No. We're ready to kill anything.' The comment brought growls of approval from the gathered orcs. Several of the goblins cast anxious looks at their hulking comrades and began to slink away, clearly less keen to share in the orcs' blind eagerness for carnage. 'The real question, fairy-lady, is why we're gonna kill what you want us to kill.' He stabbed a finger at the apparition. 'Why we don't just start with you?'

The sorceress sighed. 'Because you are looking for magic.' She gestured at herself again. 'This should be proof enough of my powers. Can your crude little shaman do this?'

'No, but he's plenty mean with a knife,' Gorgut warned.

'Swear service to me and I will lead you to a trove of ancient weapons from the forges of the Blood

God.' Gorgut wasn't sure exactly what a Blood God was, but he liked the sound of it. 'With weapons such as I will give you, none will be able to stand against you.'

Gorgut nodded as he considered the apparition's offer. He tried to see some sign of a trick, but couldn't. He didn't like elves, but if this one wanted to lead him to a cache of magic weapons, he'd let her.

'All right,' the black orc grunted. 'Me and the lads will do your fightin' for you.' He lifted a warning fist, shaking it in the apparition's face. 'But you try and trick me, I'll skin you like... like... like something I'd skin all slow and long like.'

The sorceress wore a thin smile as she heard the orc's threat. Disdain was too complex an emotion for any greenskin to recognise. 'Very well, monster. Look for a purple light on the horizon. Follow it, and it will lead you to my master's camp.' Her directions given, the she-elf's apparition faded away.

Gorgut stared at the empty space where the vision had stood, waving a suspicious hand through the air. He grunted with satisfaction when he was sure there was nothing there.

Zagbob rose from the ground, shaking dust from his hide armour. 'We really going to help the she-elf?' the goblin asked nervously.

Gorgut chuckled darkly. 'Yeah, we'll do the fairy-lady's fightin' for her,' he told the squig hunter. 'And then maybe we'll do some more fightin' she ain't fig-urin' on!'

CHAPTER TEN

THEY STOOD, STILL and silent, clinging to the frost-coated walls of the mesa overlooking the snow-filled wadi. Even the crows circling above the sunken draw failed to detect them, croaking and cawing to one another in their relentless search for carrion. The wraith-like figures, with imperceptibly deliberate motions of their slender hands, drew their sombre cloaks tighter about their blackened mail of ithilmar scales. Emerald eyes studied the wadi, watching it for even the faintest whisper of motion. Hands rested against the curved yew of heavy elven warbows, ready to fit a white-feathered shaft to the weapons in a flicker of lethal precision.

There was the slightest suggestion of movement in the snowy ditch, the little wadi writhing its way through the rocky ground. One of the shadows swung into motion, raising its bow. They had spent the better part of a day fixed upon this spot, waiting for the first sign that the dark elves were still pursuing the Grey Lancers. Now, the Shadow Warriors had their answer. Their foes were coming. Many of the treacherous druchii had escaped the ambush. The Shadow Warriors anticipated this new chance to avenge their land against their faithless kindred with vicious abandon. Only when the last of the druchii was purged from the world would the stained honour of Nagarythe be cleansed.

Emerald eyes narrowed with disappointment. The distant figures were more distinct now, moving with a purposeless lumber that was not even a shabby echo of the murderous grace of the druchii. A few yards more, and the eagle eyes of the elves could tell the creatures were orcs, the little things capering about their flanks goblins. An unworthy enemy, simple brute beasts that were an insult to the martial discipline of Shadow Warriors. Still, they could pose a threat to the Grey Lancers if the humans were not warned in time. The orcs and their goblin slaves looked to outnumber the humans quite dramatically. It would be a question of tactics and preparation to settle them.

The left Shadow Warrior turned to address his comrade, to let the other sentinel know he would remain and watch while the other high elf returned to the camp of the Grey Lancers and made his report. The elf's face tightened with shock as he turned, however. His comrade's body lay upon the hoarfrost, the warm blood pumping from the stump of his neck melting the ice. The elf's head stared at him with sightless eyes, its blond locks wrapped in a leather-clad fist.

The fist belonged to a lithe, pallid shape garbed in only the scantiest suggestion of armour. She grinned at the other Shadow Warrior and shook a stray lock of hair from the savage beauty of her face. A dripping dagger hung from the fingers of her other hand. Impossible as it seemed, the dark beauty had discovered the hiding place of the Shadow Warriors and stole upon them with such stealth that neither of her foes heard her approach.

'I could have killed you as easily as your friend,' the witch elf said, her voice a lusty purr. Her eyes winked with unrestrained malice. 'But I thought we might have some fun before I feed your soul to Khaine.'

The Shadow Warrior did not waste words with the assassin. In a blur of motion, he spun and loosed an arrow from his bow. With the same blinding speed, Beblieth twisted and spun. There was the meaty thud of steel stabbing through bone. The witch elf licked her lips, lowering her hand and the decapitated head of her victim. From the forehead, the Shadow Warrior's arrow still trembled.

'Such disrespect for the dead,' Beblieth laughed. She hurled the head full into the face of the Shadow Warrior. The high elf ducked the macabre missile, but his horrified attention was fixed upon the callous display. He did not see the thorn-like dagger leap from Beblieth's other hand. The first he was aware of its presence was when he felt it lance through his lower leg, snapping muscle and tendon in its path.

The Shadow Warrior crumpled on his maimed leg, feeling the venom on the druchii blade pumping through his system. He kicked out as the witch elf dove towards him, a fresh pair of daggers in her murderous hands. Beblieth threw herself back, dancing away from the sweep of his boot. She laughed as the Shadow Warrior tore his sword from its sheath. She cast a brief look over her shoulder at the wadi below.

'The greenskins will be a long time marching through the canyon,' Beblieth said. Her smile grew coy, almost impish. 'Don't disappoint me, cousin. I have a lot of time to kill.'

SWAGGERING THROUGH THE snow, Gorgut Foechewer gnawed on the leathery husk of salted pony in his fist. Nagdnuf had done an enthusiastic job of preparing the horseflesh and without any of the usual attempts at sneaking poison into the food. Gorgut was almost annoyed by his cook's lack of petty treachery, it was irritating to give his food tasters a free meal. There was nothing so depressing as a fat goblin. Unless of course the fat goblin was squealing from the bottom of a pot.

'I don't like it, boss.'

Gorgut shook his head and glowered at the speaker. His meaty fist was half-raised to bash some courtesy into the goblin that had startled him out of his thoughts, but the black orc thought better when he found he was staring down into the painted face of Snikkit. You could never be too sure about abusing a shaman. Sometimes they turned you into a toad for doing that.

'What don't you like?' Gorgut growled, slowly lowering his clenched fist.

Snikkit lifted one of his scrawny hands, weaving it through the air, crumbly bits of dried mushroom falling from his fingers. The flakes twinkled as they fell, smouldering like bits of ember before they fell to the snow. 'There is magic in the air,' the shaman warned.

The black orc snorted with ill humour. 'That's a good thing, you twit. I want magic! It's the reason you lot are up here. To find me some magic!'

Snikkit bared his long fangs. 'Not the good sort of magic,' he hissed. 'Not like the kind Mork and Gork make. Not the kind that you trap into a sword or an axe. This is the bad kind, the kind turns your bones to jelly and your spine to puddin'.' He tapped his long, knife-edge nose. 'Smells like elf-work, boss.'

Gorgut nodded as though understanding every word. 'Well, if the fairy-lady is up to somethin' we'll just have to make her sorry she ever crawled out of her mammy.' The orc looked across at the marching mob of his warriors, all bulging muscle and foul-temper. He snorted again as he thought what his boys would do to any weedy little elf.

'They can rub us out with their magic,' Snikkit protested. 'Elves is sneaky and don't fight fair!' he added, a sliver of fear in his voice. 'Trust me, boss, this ain't good what I smell!'

Gorgut sucked a stray bit of meat from between his tusks and spat it out. He turned his beady eyes away from the shaman and studied the terrain. The wadi the orcs had been following was a shallow trench through the rocky plain. It was tough going, slugging through the thick-packed snow, especially for the goblins, but he appreciated the natural defence the draw offered. Their advance would be hidden from any casual observer lurking on the plain. He wasn't afraid of a fight, but rather that any enemies would choose to flee before the orcs could close with them. Especially if the elves were playing games with him.

He could still see the purple fire dancing up in the bruise-coloured sky. It was something that had grown increasingly annoying to Gorgut. He could see it, but none of his lads could. He'd cracked more than a few heads before he understood it was some trick of the fairy-lady's magic. Only he could see the fire, even Snikkit didn't know it was there. Gorgut scowled at the thought. He didn't like the idea of someone putting things in his brain.

Staring at the witchfire, Gorgut's wits considered the cliffs rising over the plain. For the first time he appreciated the danger they presented. If there were any spies up there, then they would be able to see his mob as it marched along the wadi. Far from protection, if somebody knew the greenskins were down in the trench, the wadi could become a bad place to be very quick. Gorgut mulled the possibility over for a few moments, then roared for Zagbob.

'Get your smelly damn squigs and go scout the high ground,' the black orc snarled.

The squig hunter looked at his warboss through squinty eyes, trying to ferret out Gorgut's intention. The black orc punctuated his order with a slap that knocked the goblin off his feet. 'Yeah, I means you, you stupid git! Now get on with it!'

Muttering through his fangs, the goblin skulked off, the bloated shapes of his squigs capering after him like a gaggle of deranged puppies. Zagbob stalked to the wall of the wadi, struggled to climb it for a moment, then barked at one of his squigs. The animal bounded over, crouching as Zagbob hit it with the butt of his spear. The goblin stepped onto the squatting monster, then hit it again. Straightening up, the squig lifted Zagbob over the lip of the hole.

'What do you expect him to find, boss?' Dregruk asked.

Gorgut didn't even look at his lieutenant. 'I'd say your brain, but I don't think you ever had one.'

Zagbob gave a shrill shriek and tumbled back down into the wadi, an arrow shivering from one of the clawed liliripes dangling from his squigskin helmet. He rolled across the snow, pawing at his body to ensure no other arrows had struck him. An over-eager squig bounced atop the goblin, snapping at him with its huge jaws. Zagbob cursed the beast, delivering a savage punch that nearly popped one of its leprous eyes. The chastened squig howled and bounded away again.

Gorgut gave only passing notice to Zagbob's antics. Instead the black orc drew his gigantic axe and lifted it over his head. An arrow whistled through the air, glancing off the rusty blade. The warlord's monstrous face split in a feral grin. 'Ambush!' he roared, a cry of delight rather than alarm. The orcs in his mob took up the brutal howl. 'Somebody wants a fight, lads! Let's give 'em one!'

A single savage bellow thundered through the wadi as the orcs lunged at the snowy walls. The muscles of the monsters bulged as they pulled their bulks up onto the rocky plain. Arrows came fast and furious, slashing into the surge of barbarian beasts. Orcs grunted with pain, some slipping back into the wadi as shafts sank into necks and hearts, but it was not enough to dim the blood-crazed roar.

'WAAAGH!!!'

Gorgut's grin grew into a fanged rictus as he saw the ranks of human soldiers cowering behind the snowdrift, hastily nocking arrows to their bows. The thunder of hooves did not diminish his feral enthusiasm, nor the sight of dozens of horsemen galloping towards them as they leapt their chargers over the bulwarks of snow. The black orc relished meeting the cavalry charge head on. If the stupid humans thought they were going to drive the orcs back into the wadi like a pack of slinking grots, then the humans were daft. Orcs died with their wounds at the front and the blood of enemies on their claws!

'Na priznaz!' Gorgut bellowed in debased Reikspiel so that the humans would understand and tremble. He was reasonably sure that their armour was like that of the southern humans, they had a south smell about them anyway. 'Na priznaz!' he repeated. 'Na mercy!'

The archers had relented in their fusillade as the horsemen came nearer. Now the only arrows flying across the battlefield were the crude shafts loosed from goblin shortbows. The smaller greenskins were peeping just over the lip of the wadi, loosing with a reckless abandon, giggling with equal glee when their arrows sank into an orc or a man's steed. A few injured orcs spun about to reprimand the goblins for their slovenly marksmanship, caving in faces with each kick of their iron-shod boots.

The horsemen were only a few lengths from Gorgut's mob when the black orc heard a shrill voice ring out from the wadi. 'Cover your eyes, boss!' Snikkit shrieked.

Gorgut turned to bark at the interloping shaman. The motion spared him the blinding glare that blossomed between cavalry and greenskins. Like a wall ripped from the sun, the brilliant light dazzled the orcs, burning their beady cave-worm eyes. What the oncoming thunder of hooves and lances could not do, the brilliant wave of light accomplished. The fighting spirit of the orcs crumbled, shattered like glass upon stone. The brutes tore at their eyes, howling with pain. They broke before the unaffected cavalry, dashing blindly for the wadi.

Gorgut raged at his fleeing warriors, then spun to decapitate the charger of a knight trying to ride him down. The headless animal smashed into him, crushing him to the earth. The black orc roared, heaving the bulk of the dead animal off him, then smashing the head of its trapped rider with his fist. Another rider came charging at him, his lance stabbing down. Gorgut seized it in his paws, twisting his body in a display of primordial strength. The armoured knight was torn from his saddle and flung through the air to land in a broken tangle of steel and flesh.

'Fight da 'umies, ya poncy grot-fondlin' sunz-a-swine!' the black orc bellowed. He bent to the ground and retrieved his axe, his blood boiling as he watched the riders push his warriors back into the wadi. He watched the humans stab down at the orcs with their lances, then start to gallop back towards the snow bank. It didn't take a tactical genius to figure out their plan. Dozens of orcs surged up out of the draw, blinking the blinding lights from their eyes, intent on exercising their rage on the carcasses of their persecutors. The knights widened the gap between themselves and the orcs, then the archers began to fire again, raining shafts into the onrushing horde.

This time Gorgut saw the enemy wizard. Standing behind the archers on a little rise, the wizard was taller and thinner than the other humans, dressed in diaphanous robes of white and wearing a conical helm of gold. The sharp features and intense eyes more than anything impressed upon Gorgut that the magician was an elf. His knuckles tightened around his axe. If there was one thing he did before he met Gork in the eternal war, it would be to shove his fist down that cheating mongrel's throat.

The black orc roared a warning to his warriors and clenched his eyes closed. He waited for three breaths, then cautiously opened one eye. The wizard's arms were flung wide apart and there was a crackle of energy about him, but it was a fading energy. Gorgut looked over at his mob, groaning when he saw that none of them had listened. The wizard had unleashed his sneaky magic again, blinding them and sending them slinking back to the wadi. He spat into the bloodstained pebbles at his feet. It was up to him then, one black orc against a few hundred humans and their elf sorcerer.

Gorgut considered it fair odds.

Gorgut also had a hard time understanding numbers bigger than twenty.

SARDISS WATCHED THE human cavalry smash into the orcs. A cruel smile spread across the Black Guard's face. The greenskins had performed their role admirably, luring out the Grey Lancers. By springing an ambush against the orcs, the humans had walked right into the trap. Beblieth had eliminated the sentinels who might have warned them, just as Pyra's magic warded off any prying sorcery the archmage Dolchir might have employed as a last ring of protection.

The Black Guard scowled as he thought about his mistress. She had lingered behind, concentrating on her magic, leaving the destruction of the humans entirely to Sardiss. This he could understand; he was less understanding about Prince Inhin's decision to keep out of the fight. The druchii noble had displayed a yellow streak during the first engagement with the asur and their human allies. His arrogant refusal to 'lower himself' to fighting animals did not deceive Sardiss. The fool was unworthy of all the honours and powers his position afforded him, but this latest abuse of that position would spell his undoing. Sardiss had been working on the resentments and misgivings of Inhin's warriors since before the *Bloodshark* landed in Norsca. Now all of his sedition was bearing a most bitter fruit. He would have another discussion with Pyra about the noble's continued usefulness. Then, with or without her blessing, he would skewer the preening traitor like an eel and leave his carcass for the vultures.

From his perch atop the snowy knoll, Sardiss watched as the knights became further enmeshed with the orcs. He could see their leader, a huge black-skinned brute, bellowing and raging, trying to form his savage rabble into some sort of organised defence. It was an almost laughable effort. Blinded and blood-crazed, the orc warriors were chopping into anything near them, be it man, horse, or greenskin.

Sardiss dismissed the melee from his mind. He had other concerns at the moment. Lifting his hand, he motioned to the warriors behind him. With cold precision, the dark elves marched to the top of the knoll, lifting their cumbersome crossbows to their shoulders. Sardiss glared at the backs of the human archers supporting the knights.

'Loose,' the Black Guard snarled.

Steel strings snapped, bolts thudded into flesh, punching through leather and chain with grisly ease. Screams, howls of pain and shock. The close-ranked files of the human archers disintegrated as the ambushers found themselves ambushed. Officers roared at their men, stemming what threatened to become a rout. Bowmen hastily nocked arrows to strings.

Sardiss brought his armoured fist chopping down again. 'Loose.'

The repeater crossbows of the dark elves took their murderous toll on the rallying archers. Men crumpled around the bolts that slammed into them, thrown back by the murderous impact. There was no answering volley, human determination was no equal to elvish speed and the hideous engineering of the druchii. Again and again the crossbows fired, reaping their bloody harvest.

Now Dolchir turned, the archmage's attention drawn away from the conflict with the orcs. He stared in dismay at the gory wreckage of the bowmen, then his face contorted with awful fury. He waved his palm through the air before his eyes. There was a brilliant flash. In its wake, the archmage fixed his wrathful stare on Sardiss and his warriors, as though only now able to see them. Sardiss knew whatever spell Pyra had worked to protect them had been broken. The humans were beneath the Black Guard's contempt, but he had a respect bordering on fear for the powers the archmage might bring to the battle.

'Front rank!' Sardiss snarled. 'Spear and sword. Second rank. Concentrate fire on the asur!'

The Black Guard saw the look of disbelief on the faces of the druchii closest to him. They had heard Pyra's command that Dolchir be taken alive. Sardiss smiled at their anxiety. 'Just kill him,' he growled. 'I will make apologies to the sorceress.'

The high elf archmage was gesturing again, weaving another spell. The hurried volley from the druchii crossbows glanced away as they shot towards him as though striking an unseen shell. Sardiss growled again at his warriors. So long as they kept up

the volley, the archmage would be too busy
protecting himself to cast any of his spells against
them. He was counting on the time that would allow
him. Time to close with the fool and twist his head
from his shoulders.

Sardiss rushed down the snowy bank, his
armoured boots gouging toeholds in the frosty rock,
Inhin's warriors all around him. The druchii raised
their voices in a terrible warcry. Not the mindless
rage of orcs, but the hiss of ancient hate and spite
that only a race founded upon betrayal and exile
could nurture. The surviving archers broke before the
charge of the dark elves, but other men rushed to
take their place, men with swords and halberds and
spears. They were clumsy, ungainly as toddlers beside
the ethereal grace of the dark elves. Limbs were cut
from shoulders, heads danced from necks as the
druchii almost effortlessly carved a gory path
through the humans.

The Black Guard delivered a mutilating swing of
his greatsword, chopping the grey-armoured hal-
berdier before him into separate halves that toppled
and bled in the snow at his feet. Sardiss smashed his
boot into the dying thing's face, then glared once
more at the little rise where the archmage stood. His
eyes narrowed with hate. The white-robed wizard
was beset on all sides, trying to defend himself from
the fusillade of the crossbows while at the same time
trying to steel the strength and courage of the knights
fighting the orcs. To fail in either enterprise would
mean doom. Sardiss chuckled darkly, ripping
through the throat of a swordsman stupid enough to

charge him. He barely heard the bloody gargle as the wretch crumpled to the ground.

The archmage would soon have bigger problems than either crossbows or greenskins.

Shouting commands to the warriors closest to him, Sardiss rushed the rise, eager to spill asur blood. He sensed rather than saw the dark elves curtly ending their uneven contest with the humans, rallying around him as they charged the archmage. He savoured the look of terror in Dolchir's eyes as the wizard saw death reaching up for him on the edge of Naggaroth steel.

The Black Guard's blow never landed. Like a flash of silver lightning, an axe intercepted his sword, nearly ripping it from his hands. Sardiss glowered at this new foe, this last defender of Dolchir the Fool. No human, this enemy, but another of the treacherous high elves. More powerfully built than Dolchir, his pantherish body was covered in scale armour fashioned from ithilmar, his narrow helm edged in gold and adorned with rubies and sapphires. A huge cloak was wrapped about his shoulders, the pristine pelt and paws of a white lion. There was an ancient disdain in the high elf's sharp features every bit as pitiless and unforgiving as that locked behind the helm of Sardiss.

'White Lion, you will never see the shores of Ulthuan again,' Sardiss snarled. Dark elf warriors circled the lone fighter, closing upon him from three sides. 'We are ten to your one. Pray for a quick death.'

The White Lion's eyes narrowed with loathing as his slinking adversaries came towards him. 'I looked forward to a fair contest. I should have expected no duel of honour from a druchii,' he spun as he spoke, ripping the jabbing spear from the clutch of one dark elf, then slashing the fingers from the hand of a second who dove in to exploit the momentary opening. 'It is only fair to tell you: I am not one, but two.'

As he spoke, a huge shape launched itself from the rise. Crouched upon the shelf of rock, it had been almost invisible. Some unspoken gesture from the White Lion had called it, commanded it to abandon its stony vigil. Now it came smashing down with force and speed that was awesome even to the elves. A druchii warrior vanished beneath the furry bulk, bones cracking as the four-hundred-pound weight crushed him. A huge paw lashed out and the face of another warrior vanished in a welter of blood and ragged flesh. The survivors staggered away from the beast. Three feet at the shoulder, broader than a bull, the brute had the same colour pelt as that which its master wore. Golden barding protected its belly and neck, while steel sheaths added to the lethality of its paws. Few druchii had experienced the horror of facing a war lion of Chrace. Fewer still had returned living and whole from such an encounter.

With a roar, the war lion was among the dark elves, ripping at them with its claws, tearing at them with its powerful fangs. Sardiss had only a moment to consider the battle before he was again beset by the beast's master. The White Lion wove a blinding curtain of steel between the two elves, his ithilmar axe sometimes licking out to scrape against the Black Guard's armour. Sardiss was unable to penetrate the blur of the high elf's defending steel, his own sword incapable of breaking through the parrying axe to stab the warrior behind it. Frustration and rage boiled within the Black Guard with each passing breath, goading him into brutal recklessness. Sardiss restrained himself only with supreme effort. Rashness was the last thing he could afford against a foe so deadly.

Sardiss's world disintegrated into a swirl of steel, only the motion of his enemy filling his existence. Only dimly did he hear the bestial, triumphant roar rising from the wadi as the knights finally broke before the mindless butchery of the orcs. Only faintly did he see armoured humans converge upon Dolchir, helping the exhausted archmage down from his perch, lowering him into the saddle of a courser and galloping off across the frosty horizon. His world boiled down to the crash of steel on ithilmar, the smell of blood and sweat, the creak of armour and the rasp of fatigued breath.

The death cry of the war lion smashed into the narrow world of Sardiss with elemental fury. It was a sound at once fierce, defiant, and pitiful, the last gasp of a titan dragged down by lesser foes. The high elf fighting him faltered, clutching at his breast as though sharing the death-agony of his beast. Sardiss lunged at the reeling White Lion, driving his blade into the gap between breast and loin. The flexible links of armour between the two sheets of scale splintered beneath the fury of his strike, blood and bile oozing over his sword as he shoved it deep into the White Lion's belly. There was a look of outrage on the high elf's face as he slumped to the ground and his axe fell from lifeless fingers.

'You and your kitten died like sheep,' Sardiss growled, pushing the blade still deeper. He enjoyed the flicker of hate that swept up into the elf's eyes and froze there as life deserted his body. Callously, he pushed the body off his sword and let it flop to the ground.

Sardiss froze as he saw the huge monster leering at him from above the mangled carcass of the war lion. He had assumed the superior numbers of his warriors had finished the beast, instead he found a gruesome orc standing over it, the brute's claws still buried in the monster's arm. The orc's arm, in turn, was wrapped around the lion's neck. In an impossible display of raw strength, the greenskinned beast had grappled with the lion and snapped its spine.

Of his own warriors, Sardiss could find no trace. The orc snarled something at him, then dropped the war lion. It took a lumbering step towards the dark elf, dragging the lion's carcass after it. The weight must have registered at last to the orc's dim wit and it paused to carefully pull out the claws still sunk in its arm.

The Black Guard was ready to face the ugly beast, it was the closing circle of other orcs that gave him pause. Where were his warriors? Why had they abandoned him? Sardiss bit his lip in disgust. He had been betrayed and abandoned. The hand of Inhin was behind this, the hand of the preening noble who dared believe Pyra was his and his alone. The maggot who had the madness to plot against the Witch King.

There would be no question this time. Sardiss would cleave the noble's skull in half for this treachery!

There was no question of the lumbering orcs catching him. They might as well have been standing still for all their clumsy antics meant to the lithe druchii. Sardiss easily dodged their clumsy attempts to confront him, sometimes lingering long enough to cut fingers from a groping hand or shatter the rusty sword clenched in a leathery fist. Feeble goblin arrows whistled through the air, but the archery of the creeping goblins was too distant to allow them any real chance of striking so quick a target. Sardiss might have laughed at their efforts, but his mind was too filled with thoughts of vengeance to entertain any humour.

The Black Guard scrambled back up the icy face of the knoll behind which his crossbowmen had been positioned. He was not surprised to find them gone. What did surprise him was the red-robed priest waiting for him. Even more surprising was the poisoned dagger Naagan deftly stabbed into Sardiss's armpit, driving it down into the dark elf's heart.

Disbelief was in the warrior's eyes as he slumped at the feet of Naagan. The disciple of Khaine stared down at him, eyes filled with disapproving contempt. 'I bring word from your mistress, Sardiss of the Black Guard. She says you have outlived your usefulness.' Naagan slowly replaced his dagger in its sheath. His lean frame bent and he recovered the Black Guard's sword from the snow. Idly, his corpse-like hands brushed ice and blood from the blade.

'Prince Inhin will, of course, want proof you will trouble him no more,' Naagan said, kicking the paralyzed Sardiss onto his back and lifting the heavy sword over his head.

The last thing Sardiss felt before the darkness claimed him was the bite of his own blade as it sank into his neck.

CHAPTER ELEVEN

'ANOTHER ONE,' KORMAK growled, letting the corpse slip slowly from his grip. The body slopped into the frozen puddle of its own entrails. Before a southling lance had opened its belly, the carrion had been a warrior of the Raven Host, its arm bearing the scar that marked it as one of Jodis Wolfscar's men. It was the third the small warband had discovered since entering the winding, snow-swept valleys beyond the plain of clay.

A green membrane slid closed over the eyes of Vakaan Daemontongue as the magus concentrated upon his conjurations. The vile monkey-like familiar gibbered and scrabbled about the sorcerer's shoulders. Abruptly the membrane slid back, revealing the magus's distant gaze.

'The dark elves mirror our steps,' Vakaan said. 'I can sense them. They are not so far now.'

Steel creaked as Urbaal tightened his fist. 'Then they should make peace with their stinking gods,' the Chosen spat. 'Nothing mortal defies Urbaal the Corruptor twice.'

Vakaan held out his staff, blocking the armoured champion as he turned to stalk off. 'There will be time enough for vengeance later,' he promised. 'It is more important that we find Jodis Wolfscar and the Bastion Stair. Even if the dark elves are seeking the relic, even if they capture it from the southlings, it will be useless to them unless they journey to the Bastion Stair and the Portal of Rage.'

Anger smouldered in the Chosen's eyes, but gradually he relented to the wisdom of the magus. 'First we run Tchar'zanek's errand, then we kill elves,' he agreed.

Kormak watched the exchange carefully. At Urbaal's promise of revenge, the Norscan stepped away from the gutted body of Wolfscar's warrior. His right arm shifted into the semblance of a fanged claw. The mutant limb clacked open with a meaty slobber. 'Just remember, the naked wench with the daggers is mine,' he snarled. The marauder's claw snapped shut with bone-snapping force.

'Now the slave makes threats?'

Kormak rounded on the tattooed Tolkku, fangs lengthening in his face as he growled at the zealot. 'More than threats, she-ling!' The marauder swung his claw at the Kurgan, but found the blow arrested before it could land. He twisted his head to find Urbaal's hand gripping his claw, the Chosen's sword at his throat.

'The Kurgan's words are wind,' Urbaal's deep voice stated. 'It is a fool who wastes his energy fighting wind. A fool is of no use to me, or the Raven Host.'

Kormak glared into the skull-face helm of the Chosen, locking his eyes with the fiery glow behind the visor. It was the Norscan who at last relented. The claw Urbaal held shifted and shortened, becoming a brawny arm once more.

'If you kill me, slave, who will see to your hurts?' the zealot's scornful voice jibed. Tolkku held another of his skulls in his hands now, a strange yellow thing with a thin coating of papery skin stretched tight about it and lips that were tightly sewn shut. The Kurgan had his dagger poised to cut the stitching. Kormak could only wonder at the kind of magic Tolkku was ready to unleash.

'Seek sport when you are your own man,' Urbaal warned the zealot. 'Until we have secured the relic and cast open the Portal of Rage, your flesh and soul belong to Urbaal the Corruptor. Forget that, and it will not be a Norscan marauder who spills your heart's blood.'

Tolkku tried to scowl at the threat, but it was impossible to keep the fear out of his eyes. Slowly he replaced the desiccated head in the manskin bag, the flanged dagger to its feathered sheath. 'It is the will of Tzeentch,' he proclaimed.

'Then you must thank the Raven God for his protection,' Urbaal said. The Chosen slammed his sword back into its scabbard. 'How near are we to the Bastion Stair?' he asked, turning towards Vakaan once more.

The foetal familiar was gibbering and wailing, tugging at the magus's robes and hair. Vakaan tried to fend off its outburst. 'Near,' he warned. 'The Wastes may deceive mortal senses, but they cannot trick their own.' Vakaan pushed the familiar's dripping mouth away from his ear. 'My imp knows that we are near the realm of the Blood God.'

'It seems frightened, sorcerer,' Kormak said.

Vakaan's weird face grew grim. 'The world of the Blood God is fear, Norscan. All the terror of the spheres, all the nightmares and horrors of worlds within worlds, drawn to the Brass Throne and the Temple of Skulls. The Bastion Stair is the gateway to the kingdom of Khorne himself, Master of Battle, Lord of Slaughter!' The sorcerer's thin frame trembled as he evoked the dread name. 'Yes, my familiar fears. It fears because it knows what is near. We will share its fear soon enough.'

The magus brought the butt of his staff cracking against the side of his daemonic mount. The disc growled in protest but relented, drifting where Vakaan guided it. The antics of the imp became still more desperate. The disc had floated only a few yards away when the imp's body suddenly became bloated, like a bladder filling with wine. It swelled until it burst in a spray of purple light and shrieking fire. Blue ichor splattered magus and steed. Vakaan's eyes turned skyward, then shifted to stare in horror at the thing now perched on his shoulder.

The monkey-imp was gone. In its place was a dwarfish thing of claws and fangs no bigger than a man's finger. The blood-black daemon cackled and hissed at the magus, then threw itself into Vakaan's face. The sorcerer shrieked as the malice tore at him, its burning hands sizzling through his cheek to rip teeth from his mouth. He lifted his hand, an incantation dribbling from his mangled face. Jade lightning burst from his fingers, enveloping the malice, casting the imp of Khorne from his shoulder. The thing crashed to the snow, smouldering and writhing until its unnatural substance collapsed into a scarlet foam.

'By the Raven God!' Tolkku muttered, fumbling at his charms and talismans. Cautiously, Urbaal and Kormak approached the maimed Vakaan. As they approached him, they soon shared Tolkku's awed fright.

It was only a matter of a few steps, but it was enough. The world they saw, the snowy valley that an instant before they had seen Vakaan cross, melted before their stunned eyes. Now they stood upon a plain of ice, great craggy mountains rising into the distance. Even more shocking was the change in the sky. Gone was the weird luminance of the clay marsh. Now the sky was a sullen red, as though painted by all the fires of hell. The sun was disfigured and sullen, ugly spots leering down at them like the empty sockets of a celestial skull. They could feel the baleful influence of this land clawing at them, whispering to them with words of blood and battle.

'The realm of Khorne,' Vakaan said, daubing at his mangled face. 'The power of the Blood God was too great for my familiar. Its essence was usurped by a malice. We may thank Tzeentch its essence was not enough to sustain a more powerful daemon.'

Urbaal nodded, then gestured at Tolkku. The zealot rummaged among his talismans for a potion to fix Vakaan's injuries. The magus commanded his steed to descend so he could be treated.

Kormak gave the ministrations of the zealot small notice. His eyes were riveted to the great wall stretching between two mountains. Its steps were enormous, looking as though they could have been torn from the earth only by the gods themselves. Immense spikes of iron projected from the top of the wall, and upon each Kormak could faintly discern the rotting things impaled upon them. One body spitted upon the stakes was more distinct than the others. Kormak felt his stomach quiver when he understood why. It was clearer because it was so much larger. Not the impaled body of a man, but that of a giant.

At the top of the steps an archway split the wall, two great horns of brass that curved towards one another. Their facades were a black that was not simply devoid of light, but seemed to devour light into itself. Kormak could see faces writhing and screaming beneath the darkness, wailing their eternal suffering to the Wastes. A great flock of vultures circled the ramparts, sometimes descending to investigate the spitted trophies on the walls, but never daring to peck at them. Even the lowest beasts knew not to steal from the Blood God's table.

'The Bastion Stair,' Kormak whispered.

Vakaan fixed a chilling smile on him and shook his head. 'No, only the gateway to the land where it will be found.' The magus spat a shattered tooth into the snow.

'The Bastion Stair is far less pleasing to the eye.'

PRINCE INHIN'S WARRIORS held their crossbows at the ready, keeping the weapons trained upon the mob of monsters scavenging the encampment of the Grey Lancers. The elves watched as the brutes squabbled over the equipment Dolchir's allies had abandoned. Goblins greedily defended kegs of beer and ale while grotesque orcs barked and snarled at one another as they looted armour and salted meat from the Imperial stores.

'I say it is a mistake to allow these beasts the pick of the plunder,' Inhin snapped. 'There will be nothing left by the time they are through.'

Pyra laughed at the noble's concern. 'There is nothing down there of value to us. Dolchir has escaped, and with him he has taken the Spear of Myrmidia. Let the orcs take what they want. It will convince them of our sincerity and goodwill.'

Inhin looked away from the shambles of the Imperial camp and pointed a commanding finger at the sorceress. 'This had better work, my dear. I do not trust these animals.' He wrinkled his nose in distaste, blinking his eyes. 'Their smell is offensive.'

'We lost many warriors in the ambush, my prince,' Pyra's voice purred. 'We need allies if we are to capture the artefact now.' She gestured to the jagged, snow-capped mountains all around them. 'The warriors of the Raven Host will not thank us for our presence here, nor is Tchar'zanek's rabble the only barbarians in this accursed land. Enemies are all around us. We must exploit whatever help we can find.'

Inhin might have said something more, but a stiffening of his closest crossbowmen made him turn around. He coughed as the stench of greenskin assailed his senses. Sauntering towards the dark elves with the swaggering bravado of a drunken corsair was the black-skinned beast that led the orc mob. At his heels hobbled a spindly goblin cloaked in a patchwork robe.

'Warlord Gorgut Foechewer,' Pyra addressed the orc, her tongue curling around the feral speech of the greenskins.

Gorgut snorted at her subservient words, missing the ironic inflection behind them and the mocking smile on the mouth that spoke them. He coughed as he passed the druchii guards, sneering at their weapons, laughing at the thin arms and delicate frames of the bowmen. The black orc paused before one guard, flexing his arm into a knot of muscle bigger than the elf's head. Gorgut laughed again, then swaggered towards the sorceress and her patron.

'The fairy-lady and the prince,' the orc's guttural voice rumbled. He punctuated his insolent greeting with an amused snort. 'I decided my boys did most of the fighting. I want all of the loot.'

'Insolent cur!' Inhin snarled, his hand flying to his sword. Pyra gripped his arm, thankful that her patron's outburst had been voiced in their own language, a tongue unknown by the greenskins. The noble resisted her restraint, then slowly relented.

Gorgut's ugly visage split in an even wider smile when he saw Inhin relent. A part of him was disappointed; he would have enjoyed splitting the elf's head like an egg. He made a point of turning away from the red-faced prince and focusing his attention on the sorceress. She was clearly the one in charge here. That meant she was the only one he needed to bother about.

'Think that ain't fair?' Gorgut demanded.

Pyra shook her head. 'No, mighty Gorgut. Indeed, you are right. Your warriors did fight magnificently. Prince Inhin's soldiers were late adding their effort to the fray.'

'They fought like a bunch of gits,' Gorgut declared, spitting a blob of phlegm into the snow. 'Let my lads take all the risks and do all the dying!'

'We had to see how well you animals could fight,' Inhin snarled. This time he spoke in words the orc could understand, the mongrel slave patois of the quarries of Naggaroth. Pyra rolled her eyes as she watched Gorgut's brow knot with concentration as he tried to work out the meaning of the insult. To her surprise, it seemed the orc failed to take it as such.

Gorgut slapped his knee and barked with laughter. 'Trying to learn how to grow a spine, eh? Watch how real warriors do in a scrap?' He shook his apish head. 'Won't do no good. This poncy lot is too scrawny to do any real fighting!'

Pyra's knuckles turned white as she tightened her grip on Inhin's sword-arm. 'That is why we need your warriors, Warlord Gorgut. We hunt a traitor, one of our kinsmen.'

'The fancy twit who makes the sparkly lights?' Gorgut growled. 'You better find him before I do.'

'That is my point,' Pyra said quickly, seizing Gorgut's words before the thought behind them had a chance to dissipate inside his thick skull. 'Together we can find him much faster.'

Gorgut shook his head. 'No. You promised me magic. That's what I want.'

'And you shall have it,' Pyra assured the black orc. 'The traitor has much magic with him. Help us, and you shall take your share of the spoils.'

Gorgut leaned forwards, displaying his fangs before the face of the sorceress. 'Fine and nice, fairy-lady. We'll help you lot find this git. Just remember the way we split the loot.' He jabbed a thick thumb at his armoured chest. 'Me and the lads take the dragon's share. You lot get what's left. You don't like it, you can bugger off.'

Pyra could feel Inhin's body trembling with rage beneath her hand. 'Agreed, Warlord Gorgut.'

The black orc snorted his contempt as he turned and started to stroll back to his scavenging warriors. He turned back around suddenly, shaking a threatening fist at the sorceress. 'Don't think to cheat me, neither!' Gorgut stabbed a finger at the cloaked goblin following him. 'This git is a shaman. He's got magic of his own. He'll tell me if you try anything.'

Pyra's eyes narrowed as she stared at Snikkit. The shaman made every effort not to meet her gaze. She could sense the paltry magical power of the shaman in the aura that swirled about him. Even more, she could sense the fear bordering on panic that gripped the petty conjurer. Terror of elf-kind was something, it appeared, that was shared by goblins even beyond the shores of Naggaroth.

'We would not dream of betraying you,' Pyra assured the warboss. Gorgut gave her a last smirk of disdain, then marched back towards his own kind, Snikkit hurrying after him with indecent haste.

'I will peel every inch of skin off that animal's bones,' Inhin swore as he watched Gorgut lumber off.

'Patience, my prince,' Pyra said, releasing her hand from the noble's arm. 'The orc is useful to us. When he is not, I ask only that you allow me to watch the beast suffer.' She turned her eyes from the departing warlord as she noticed the red-robed figure of Naagan approaching. A cruel smile worked onto her angry features as she saw the bundle the priest bore. 'In the meantime, I have something here that will improve your humour.'

Naagan bowed before the sorceress and her prince, extending his hands towards them. Cupped in the palms of his hands was an object wrapped in reptilian leather. Inhin stared at the offering, an edge of suspicion in his eyes. Pyra noticed his hesitancy and bent down to unwrap the present.

'I know this will please you, my love,' she said.

The folds of flayed cold one hide peeled back to expose the shrivelled features of a decapitated head, the shrunken skull of a dark elf. Even after Naagan's profane rites of preservation, there was a look of shock in the dead features of Sardiss.

'I am afraid he outlived his usefulness,' Pyra explained, stroking the shrivelled lips of her murdered lover.

THE BODIES OF Wolfscar's men continued to form a morbid trail through the snowy wasteland. No longer did they bear the marks of lance and sword. Now they were torn and mangled, gored by horns, hacked by crude axes and run through by primitive spears. Many showed the marks of bestial teeth upon them, flesh stripped from their bodies even as they fought against their killers.

Kormak rose from inspecting the husk of one brawny warrior who might once have been a Kurgan warchief from the quality of the armour that clung to his gnawed bones. The wolf-claw symbol of the warband of Jodis Wolfscar was carved into what remained of his forearm. The marauder turned and regarded his comrades. 'Whatever killed them, it was not the southlings.'

Urbaal nodded his armoured head. The Chosen strode to Kormak's side, glaring down at the frozen carrion. 'These are the marks of beasts. Even the lowest Hung does not fight in so debased a manner.'

'They may have fallen prey to flesh hounds, or even worse daemons of the Blood God,' Vakaan cautioned. The magus hovered above the scattered corpses, his attention drawn to the horizon rather than the bodies, keeping a careful vigil for the malignant forces his sorcerous sight told him were near. 'This place exists between worlds, half mortal, half the realm of the Blood God. In such a place, daemons become things of flesh and with appetites of flesh.'

'They can die like flesh?' Urbaal mused.

'As much as such things can ever die,' Vakaan said.

Kormak stiffened as he listened to the magus. The Norscan's steely gaze swept over the heaps of butchered humanity. He could see Tolkku picking among the dead, looking for interesting skulls to add to his collection. The marauder also saw a faint hint of movement close to the zealot. A fanged grin split his face. One of the dead was not quite as dead as the zealot believed. Kormak continued to watch as Tolkku's hunt brought him ever closer to the non-corpse.

The Kurgan cried out in surprise as the body sprang at him. Before the priest could bring either dagger or magic into play, a powerful arm was wrapped around his neck, locked in a choking embrace. Tolkku's assailant spun him around, using the zealot as a shield against his comrades.

Kormak could see now that the attacker was a woman, strongly built with dusky, sun-beaten skin and the broad features of a Sarl. Thick brown locks dangled over the left side of her face while a tiny horn protruded from the right side of her brow. Her eye was a malignant gash of amber that blazed from her darkened flesh. Only a brief halter of leather, sealskin leggings and mammoth-hide boots guarded the woman against the elements. Below the halter, running from rib to belly, were the grey slashes of a wolf's paw, monstrous furrows that were gouged deep into the meat of the woman's body.

'Go ahead and kill him,' Kormak grunted at the Sarl. 'He's no friend of mine.'

Urbaal glowered at the marauder, then raised his hand in a placating gesture. 'Peace, Jodis Wolfscar. We are warriors of the Raven Host. Sent by Prince Tchar'zanek to secure the Bastion Stair against our enemies.'

The woman continued to glare suspiciously at the survivors of Urbaal's warband. At length she reached a decision. With a none too gentle shove, she released Tolkku. Instantly she retrieved a heavy axe with a blade of blackened bone from the snow. She continued to study the men, especially keeping her attention on the venom-eyed Tolkku.

'You are Jodis Wolfscar?' Vakaan asked. 'Ljotur Arason said we might find you.'

The woman shrugged. 'If you were sent by Tchar'zanek, where is your army?'

'Tchar'zanek already sent an army,' Urbaal said. There was challenge in the Chosen's voice. His next words left no doubt of his meaning. 'Where is *your* army?'

Jodis shook her head and laughed bitterly. 'They are all around you, and in a hundred nameless ravines and gorges. The Bloodherd betrayed us when we found the Bastion Stair. They swore allegiance to Khorne and fell upon my warriors like wolves.' She spat the hateful words, trembling with anger at the memory. 'They have made Thar'Ignan their beastlord and made the Trail of Carnage their lair. The minotaur sent some of his beasts in pursuit of those who escaped. They followed us this far before we beat them back. I sent the survivors back to Arason to inform the Raven Host of the Bloodherd's betrayal.'

'None made it back,' Urbaal said. 'They were ridden down by southlings who also seek the Bastion Stair.' The Chosen stared hard into Jodis's half-hidden face. 'They must not find it first.'

Jodis nodded as she considered Urbaal's words. 'There is some dark force that feeds the Bloodherd, the same force that turned them from the Raven God. It gives them strength, strength beyond that of mere beastmen.'

'If they are mortal, they will die,' Kormak boasted, fingering the edge of his axe. He had gone through too much to be frightened by the words of a Sarl.

The woman studied him with a sceptical look. 'I will enjoy watching them chew on your bones, hero,' she told him. A last cautious glance at Tolkku, and Jodis started to walk through the scattered remains of her warband. 'Follow me,' she told the men. She pointed with the head of her axe at the black mouth of a distant gorge.

'The Bastion Stair is beyond that ravine.'

PRINCE INHIN HAD his pavilion erected well up-wind of the orcs and goblins. Even with a half-mile between them, the drunken roars of the brutes was an ear-rattling din. Not for the first time, the noble contemplated sending one of his soldiers down to poison the captured beer.

Inhin leaned back in his sable-covered campaign chair and regarded the lithe shape of Beblieth. It was a pity such a comely form was tainted by the Temple of Khaine. She would have been so much more enjoyable as something other than a witch elf. There was a gleam in her dusky eyes as she felt him studying her. It was the slightest thing, but more than enough to sober Inhin's fantasies. The image of a serpent slithering towards its mesmerised prey flashed through his thoughts.

The noble shifted his gaze from Beblieth to the heap of bloodied rags and dripping wounds cringing at her feet. All humans looked alike to Inhin, but he could recognise the livery of the Grey Lancers beneath all the gore.

'This creature knows what I want?' Inhin asked.

'Yes, my prince,' Beblieth answered. The witch elf knotted her hand in the prisoner's hair, forcing his face up from the floor. The battered knight moaned in dread as she stared at him, her pink tongue licking her full lips.

'I will not demean myself speaking a slave tongue,' Inhin stated. His look grew sour. 'There was been too much of that today,' he added.

Beblieth bowed her head in understanding. A savage tug on the man's head brought him whimpering upwards, onto his knees. 'Tell the prince what you told me. The way I taught you.'

There was a moment of sobbing, tears rolling down the man's slashed face. Beblieth quickly grew tired of the inarticulate babble. She dug her fingers deeper into the man's blond hair, nails scraping into his scalp. Blood joined the tears oozing down his face.

'Exalted lord and master of all the world! Prince of the druchii... and... and.' Horror filled the man's eyes as his mind tried to remember the unfamiliar titles, the musical names Beblieth had taught him with the edge of her dagger.

Beblieth sighed. 'They are not overly clever, these brutes,' she apologised. Looking down at her prisoner, her expression hardened. 'Tell my prince about the asur traitor.'

A last gasp at defiance flickered over the knight's features, but the merciless gaze of the witch elf quickly stifled it. A moan of unspeakable guilt and wretchedness wracked the captive and his body sagged in Beblieth's grip. She pulled him upright once more, not a trace of pity for him in her eyes.

'The... traitor... has the Spear,' the man cried. 'There are... are twenty... maybe thirty of us left. Too few to fight our way back to Kislev.'

'Tell my prince what you are going to do instead,' Beblieth commanded.

'We... we ride to... the Bastion Stair,' the prisoner sobbed. 'Archmage Dolchir...' He shrieked as the witch elf raked her nails through his scalp again. 'The traitor is going to try to seal the portal by himself. He would see the Spear of Myrmidia destroyed rather than fall into... than to be returned to those who have rightful claim upon it from their sovereignty over all the lesser beasts of the land!'

Beblieth released her hold, allowing the wretch to collapse onto the floor.

'You have not told any of this to Pyra or Naagan?' Prince Inhin asked.

'My loyalty is to you and Lord Uthorin,' Beblieth answered.

'The Spear must be mine alone,' Inhin said. 'We cannot trust them with it. Their magic puts a strange madness in their minds. Only a cold, practical use of the Spear will further Lord Uthorin's ambitions.'

Beblieth smiled at the seated noble. 'And your own ambitions, my king.'

An inner glow seemed to shine from Inhin's face as he heard the witch elf address him. 'We will speak of this again,' he decided. He looked again at the sobbing pile of rags and meat on the floor of his tent. He waved at it with his gauntlet. 'You may dispose of that now.'

'Give it to the goblins,' Beblieth said, shaking her head. 'I begin to find the screams of humans tedious.'

CHAPTER TWELVE

IT STRETCHED AS far as the eye could see, as though it might straddle the entire world. Monstrous and gigantic, the wall reared up into a fiery sky, its cyclopean mass rising like a mountain of blood and death. It was a thing of steel and brass and bone, of fang-like spikes and razor-sharp sheets of twisted bronze and pitted iron. Skulls grinned everywhere, skulls of obsidian and jet, skulls of metal and chain, the shrieking bones of humans and the grinning heads of daemons. Some stretched for what seemed miles of the wall's impossible length, their goat-like horns contorted into the axe-blade rune of the Blood God. Others were merely a few dozen yards in size, their grinning fangs only a little bigger than a man's leg. These skeletal gargoyles nested between the obsidian horns that jutted from the base of the wall, gleaming darkly in the hellish light of a dead sun.

C. L. Werner

Atop the wall were great totems of bronze, immense pillars that seized the sky with jagged fingers. Chains and cages swung from the towers and upon the top of each, picked out in blood-caked brass, was again repeated the skull-rune of Khorne. Carrion birds circled each totem, their croaks and caws forming a deafening cacophony. A grisly psalm to soothe the fury of a mad god.

The centre face of the wall was broken into still another representation of the Blood God's rune. This was formed from immense sheets of blackened steel, each a dozen yards across that had been hammered into the eerie crimson granite that supported them. The gigantic symbol was itself broken at the centre, split by a series of megalithic steps, steps that seemed to flow like molten lava down the face of the titanic wall. They shimmered and steamed, but never did they abandon the substance of their shape. Each was a rectangular plateau, half a mile wide and nearly as tall. Even the biggest giant to ever stalk the Wastes could not have lifted his foot from one step to another. Smaller creatures were less than insects before such enormity.

Daemon faces leered from the front of each step and a great balustrade of spiked, skeletal towers flanked each side of the stair. At its very top, bound within a set of curled bronze horns the size of small hills, was a fiery glow. It was not light that made the head of the stair glow, but the raw hate of existence itself, the murderous bloodlust of the most primitive beast and the cultured hate of the most learned mind, all mixing into a knot of unadulterated carnage as the emotion was sucked into the spectral world beyond the mortal plane.

Beblieth could feel the malignancy pressing down on her, trying to crush her soul into the scarlet snow, trying to grind her body into so much paste against the scab-hued sky smouldering in the heavens. She felt every act of cruelty and malice shrieking at her from the pits of memory, condemning her as soft and weak, a thing of mortal limits. The witch elf steeled herself, whispering the catechisms of Khaine, trying to draw strength from her god. The effort only made the unseen malignancy laugh in its million hissing voices.

Snikkit clutched at his ears, screwed shut his eyes, and wiggled his way into the centre of the biggest bunch of Gorgut's orcs he could find. The shaman moaned and gibbered, foam dribbling from his mouth, snot falling from his nose. He could feel his heart trembling beneath his ribs, trying to burst itself with sheer terror. This, the shaman knew, was a place of magic such as he could scarcely begin to comprehend. It was not the magic of sorcery and witchcraft, but magic enslaved into iron and steel, bound within bone and brass. It was magic distilled and tortured into a single purpose, recast into a single awful form. This was the magic of hate.

Naagan clutched his side and stumbled, his dagger sliding through his bared skin, carving letters into his bleeding flesh. The disciple averted his eyes from the wall, where something looked back at him. He could feel the hunger of the thing, could hear its tongue licking its monstrous jaws, smell its corpse-breath, sense the growl of its belly as a rumble in the ground. Meat. For all of his magic, for all of his intrigue and power and status, for all the debts owed to him and the alliances he shared, all he was to the thing on the wall was so much meat. And the thing on the wall, he knew, *was* the wall.

Zagbob crawled on his belly through the snow, trying to force the spear from his claws. Again and again came the impulse to stab the blade into his belly, to watch the sticky green blood spurt from his own body, to paint obscene words on his face with the last drops of his life, to surrender his soul and let something else into his flesh. The squig hunter had finally fallen to the ground in an attempt to deny the weird thoughts. His squigs hopped and slobbered around him, sometimes snapping at him as he squirmed in the snow, oblivious to the mortal horror of their master.

Pyra pulled her cloak tighter around her, for once allowing her enticing curves to vanish within heavy folds of wolf-fur and sealskin. The sorceress could feel something pawing at her, groping that part of her that was beyond flesh and bone. Her soul bruised under the sadistic touch, cringing like a small child when it sees the whip. The ugly growl of the thing shuddered through her spirit and she knew it was angry, that it had tasted that part of her that had opened itself to the dark arts. The thing's anger gave her hope, and some of the arrogance she had felt when first exposed to the mighty forces of the north flickered to life inside her. But it quickly faded. Even magic swollen by the forces of the north winds were nothing beside the raw, primordial power of the thing. It slobbered and snuffled, continuing its spectral violation, chewing at her soul like a dog with a new bone.

Gorgut breathed deep, staring up at the gigantic wall, at the snarling daemon faces, at the flocks of vultures and the numberless legion of skulls. The smell of rotten meat, rancid blood and rusting steel washed down inside his body. The black orc grunted and turned his head to Dregruk.

'So this is the Bastion Stair?' Gorgut growled, nodding his head. 'Looks like a good place for a scrap!'

By degrees, the others gradually broke free from the spell of terror that had beset them. Few had succumbed to the daemonic force, mostly goblins that had expired through sheer fright. The survivors were already looting their former comrades, conspiring to carry as much of the plunder on the corpses as they could manage. Several orcs were trying to break up the confused mass of squabbling goblins, while others began to lope off towards the Bastion Stair, finding courage rather than terror in the malignity exuding from the structure. As their warlord had said, anything that angry would make for a good fight once they tracked it down.

The dark elves watched the greenskins, making no move to join them. Their sophisticated minds understood better than the orcs what had just happened and the enormous power it implied. They understood now the nature of the place they had thought to storm and seize.

Pyra was the first to recover her wits. The sorceress was dripping with sweat, her cloak clinging to her body in a wet mess. She cast its weight aside, smoothing the black robes beneath. She looked at the fear and doubt on the faces of the other druchii, an infection that had claimed even Naagan. She saw them looking away from the wall, as though not seeing it would blot it from their memory. The expedition teetered at the edge of disaster. The terror evoked by the wall had settled into their brains in a way it never could with brutes like the orcs. Now it threatened to consume them.

'My prince,' Pyra hissed, striding to Inhin's side. She was weak from her ordeal, leaning on her staff like a wizened crone. Inhin turned eyes that were wide with fear towards her, the face around them was almost colourless from fright.

'All for nothing,' the noble whimpered. 'I will die in there, killed by something without name or title. My bones will be unburied, my death unwritten! I, the greatest prince of all Naggaroth will leave nothing after me. Even my enemies will forget I ever existed!'

Pyra's hand cracked hard against Inhin's cheek. The slap brought outrage flooding into the noble's face. Inhin pressed a hand to his reddened face. He glared at the sorceress, noting her weakness. Inhin's gauntlet came smacking across her beautiful countenance, knocking her down into the snow. Blood streamed from Pyra's broken lip.

'You dare touch me! You snivelling harlot,' Inhin raged. He pointed an armoured finger at the prone sorceress. 'I know your kind, like all you courtesans, sniffing around my power like a bitch in heat!'

'My prince,' Pyra gasped through her bleeding lip. 'The warriors are afraid. You must rally them or all is lost!'

Inhin's rage flickered, a shiver of fear dancing down his spine. He glanced at the Bastion Stair and shuddered. 'No,' he snarled. 'We're not going in there! It's death to go in there. Death, and things worse than death!' He stabbed his finger down at Pyra. 'You go in there. It's your plan. You do it!'

Pyra scowled at the noble. 'You would give me your warriors?'

The prince shook his head in disbelief. 'Of course not!' he shouted. 'Take your animals with you. They seem eager enough!' Inhin's face darkened. 'But that's it, isn't it? You want me separated from my loyal warriors. This was never about the Spear or the barbarians, was it? This was all about killing me!' Inhin drew his sword, glaring down at the staggered sorceress.

'Which of them was it, whore? Uthorin? Or maybe that insane maggot we call a king?'

'My prince!' Pyra pleaded. 'What I told you is the truth. With the Spear we can bring Tchar'zanek to his knees, and with the Raven Host at your command, all of your enemies will be destroyed!'

Inhin pressed his sword to Pyra's throat. 'What good does that do me if I'm dead?' he hissed.

Pyra braced herself for the killing blow. She stared in disbelief as Inhin calmly sheathed his sword. The prince turned, staring with some amusement at something behind her. Faintly, Pyra could hear the soft sound of footsteps in the snow.

'Beblieth,' the prince chuckled as he addressed the approaching witch elf. 'How timely. I was going to finish this traitor myself, but I think you will be so much more adept at it than I.'

Beblieth smiled down at Pyra, her gloved hand running through the thick locks of her hair. Slowly the witch elf drew one of the barbed daggers from her belt.

So fast did she move that Inhin only understood what was happening when he found himself face-down on the ground, struggling to draw breath into his quivering body.

Beblieth wiped the noble's blood from her poisoned blade with Inhin's cloak, then bent down to help Pyra from the ground. The sorceress stared coldly into Inhin's gaping eyes.

'I am told the poison of the waruli is slow to kill,' she hissed. 'It numbs the body into a trance-like state. The victim slips into a dreaming slumber from which he never awakens.' Pyra shook her head, a teasing gleam in her expression. 'If that is so, my prince, I wish you only unpleasant dreams.'

The two elves turned away from the dying noble and made their way back to the druchii soldiers. Inhin had been useful only so long as he could rally his warriors to Pyra's needs. Unwilling to go further, his usefulness was at an end. He had feared an ignoble death, to be lost and forgotten. Now, as Pyra led the remaining dark elves towards the Bastion Stair, the corpse of the noble sat alone in the scarlet snow, to rot lost and forgotten beneath the molten sky.

It was a thought that warmed Pyra's heart and cheered her spirits.

FROM THE ROCKS, Kormak watched as the motley alliance of orcs and dark elves marched towards the Bastion Stair. The marauder felt a hot knife of hate blaze through his heart as he saw the pale shape of the witch elf gliding between the armoured ranks of her kinfolk. The Norscan could almost imagine himself leaping down, charging through the grim ranks of elves and monsters, cutting his way to certain destruction if only he could wring the neck of the sadistic killer. He had fought many battles and all manner of foes over his bloody life, but never had he been toyed with the way he had at the hands of the witch elf. It was a shame that continued to chafe at his warrior pride. The only wergild that would satisfy him was the death rattle rising from her throat as he choked the life from her.

Urbaal's steel hand closed about Kormak's shoulder, tightening, pulling him back behind the jumbled heap of stone. 'Be still, marauder. I know you lust for revenge. First we accomplish our quest. Then there will be time enough for a reckoning.'

Kormak struggled to free himself of the Chosen's clutch. 'I will not be cheated by the daemons of the Stair,' he snarled. 'The witch is mine!'

Urbaal swung the Norscan around. 'None can defy the will of the gods. If it is your fate to kill the elf, then not all of the Blood God's daemons can cheat you. If it is not, then all of your anger will not change her doom.'

There was still rage on Kormak's face, but Urbaal could tell that he had made an impression with his words. The blood-mad impulse had passed, the marauder would not throw himself into some reckless bid for revenge. He would wait now, bide his time and watch for a better opportunity.

'They will reach the Stair before us,' Tolkku said, his voice sour. The zealot sneered at Jodis Wolfscar. 'Perhaps we would have fared better without a guide.'

'Let them gain the Stair first,' Urbaal said. 'They will attract the attention of the Bloodherd, leaving us free to act as we will.'

Vakaan nodded, pointing down at the dark elves. 'They still follow the southlings,' the magus said. 'That means they have not captured the Spear. We cannot waste time fighting the druchii and the orcs they have joined with. While the southlings have the Spear, they pose a greater danger.'

'How so?' wondered Jodis, staring intently into the stern features of Vakaan.

'Consecrated to weak southling gods, the Spear might be used to seal the Portal of Rage and stem the flow of Chaos, reducing the winds to nothing more consequential than a breeze. The sorcerers of the Raven Host would lose their power and the daemons bound into the service of Tchar'zanek will be unable to retain a form of shape and substance but instead will fade back into the realm of the gods.'

'And if the Spear were re-consecrated to the Raven God?' asked Tolkku, a greedy light in his eyes.

The membranes slid closed over Vakaan's eyes as the magus thought about the possibility. 'If the Spear were consecrated to Tzeentch, it could be used to tear wide the gate between worlds. From the Portal of Rage would pour the might of Chaos, not the miserly trickle that is enough to empower the psychotic slaves of the Blood God, but a great flood that would magnify the sorcery of the Raven Host, allow us to summon entire hosts of daemons from the void and bind them to our will. The Spear could challenge the great Skull Lord Var'Ithrok and steal from him the imprisoned spirit of Kakra the Timeless, greatest of the Raven God's Lords of Change.'

'But first we must gain the Bastion Stair,' interrupted Kormak. He gestured with his axe at the now distant shapes of the elves and their allies, dwarfed to the size of ants by their approach to the colossal stair.

'There is another way,' Jodis said. The woman motioned for her companions to follow her through the rocks. They stole through the jumble of broken stones for several minutes. When they reached a point from which they could see the Stair once more, they saw it from a new angle. Invisible from the front of the Stair was a smaller stairway, a man-sized construction that zigzagged its way into a great archway set into the side of the bottom-most step.

'Another way in?' Urbaal asked.

Jodis nodded her head. 'This is how my warband entered the Stair,' she said. 'It is invisible unless one knows where to look for it. While our enemies scale the front of the Stair to gain entrance, you can avoid them by entering from the side.'

Urbaal nodded. 'A good plan,' he agreed. 'We can leave the elves and the orcs behind. That will leave us only the daemons of the Stair to face.'

'And the Bloodherd,' Jodis warned. 'Do not forget about them. I doubt you will be able to leave the first step while Thar'Ignan lives. And do not think all of the Blood God's slaves are daemons. Before the Bloodherd turned upon us, we fought many black-armoured warriors of the Skulltaker tribe. I suspect they have their stronghold higher upon the Stair.'

'You speak as one who is staying behind,' challenged Kormak.

Jodis gave the big marauder an amused smile. 'When you fail, Tchar'zanek will send others. I will stay here to show them the way.'

Urbaal pressed his hand against the marauder's chest as Kormak bristled under the snide words. The Chosen turned and glared at Jodis. 'Stay behind, Wolfscar,' his voice growled. 'When we return in triumph, you will have cause to regret your cowardice.'

The Chosen drew his sword, its steel burning with coruscating flames, sending weird shadows dancing among the rocks. The eyes of Urbaal burned no less fiercely as he regarded Jodis Wolfscar.

'I promise you will regret it.'

THE FRONT OF the first step was a great table of bronze edged in leering metal faces. Situated in the mouth of the largest of these, a horned daemon skull fifty yards across set into the back of the step, was a great doorway. A hellish glow smouldered within the opening, casting its gruesome pall over the entire plateau.

Even the orcs seemed finally overcome by the sinister aspect of this place, some of them casting furtive looks at the flanking stairways descending back to the fields of scarlet snow, others swatting the nearest goblins in an effort to ease their nerves.

Gorgut swaggered through his men. He grunted and scratched his nose, then hawked a blob of spit against the bronze wall, watching it sizzle against the metal. At length, he turned and directed a suspicious squint towards the black ranks of the dark elves.

'You certain there's magic in there?' he demanded, staring at Pyra.

'Ask your shaman if you don't believe me,' the sorceress answered with a dismissive flick of her hand.

The black orc nodded, turning to glare at Snikkit. 'What about it? You smell any magic in there?'

Snikkit's eyes had grown round as saucers, his hood was damp with perspiration. There was a rancid stench of fear rising from his grimy robes. It was almost on his tongue to lie to the warlord, but Snikkit knew however bad things might get inside, he couldn't imagine it being much worse than what Gorgut would do to him if he thought the goblin was lying. In a frightened whisper, the shaman croaked his answer. 'Yeah, boss, there's all kinds of nasty stuff in there! You shouldn't touch none of it!'

Gorgut bellowed with laughter, his grim humour soon spreading to the other orcs. 'Just like a grot! Scared of his own shadow.' The warlord's meaty paw smacked against his breastplate. 'I ain't afraid. There's magic in there, then I'm going to get it. I'll go back to the Badlands the biggest thing since

Ironfang!' He turned around to bark at his mob, shifting his gaze from each orc and goblin in the warband. 'We're going in there! If it moves, stab it until it stops moving! If it doesn't move, keep your grubby paws off it until Snikkit checks it out! Any git trying to sneak off with anything magic is going to be sorry!' Gorgut patted the ugly axe slung over his shoulder. 'But he ain't going to be sorry long.'

'Mighty Gorgut,' interrupted Pyra. She stepped forward from the ranks of her warriors, still leaning slightly on her staff. It was a ruse to make the greenskins think she was still weak. She wasn't sure if the deception would fool their shaman, but the crude little creature did not seem overly bright. She knew as long as the orcs considered the druchii to be unworthy of their attention they were reasonably safe from the monsters. That would be of great benefit once the time came to deal with the brutes once and for all. For now, Pyra allowed a mocking air of deference into her posture and voice.

'You agreed that we should share in the spoils,' she said. 'I promise that we will ask very little of your indulgence.'

'Ask all you want, fairy-lady,' Gorgut laughed. The black orc was still chuckling at his joke as he organised his motley troops.

'How long will you put up with that animal?' Naagan asked as Pyra stole back to the ranks of her troops.

'Until I don't need him,' the sorceress answered. She turned back to study the black orc. Gorgut was conferring with his equally ugly lieutenant and a nasty little goblin she had seen the warlord use as a scout before. Gorgut appeared to be explaining some complex matter to the goblin. Whatever it was, the goblin was clearly upset by what he was hearing. The lieutenant finally tired of the scout's protests and wrapped his paws about the little creature's scrawny neck, lifting him from the ground and shaking him like a rag doll. When he set the goblin back down, he seemed much more agreeable to whatever was being asked of him. Soon, the goblin was snapping commands to the grotesque two-legged hunting animals the orcs kept. The manic beasts jabbered and slobbered, then with erratic leaps hurried off through the doorway like a demented herd of mountain goats. A last anxious look at his warlord, and the goblin hunter was hurrying after his beasts.

'Beblieth,' Pyra called from the corner of her mouth. The witch elf was quickly at her side. 'Our friend has sent his scout on some sort of mission. Follow the goblin. Watch the creature. I don't want any surprises. Not from a pack of dumb animals.'

WITHIN THE BASTION Stair, Pyra discovered wide corridors with narrow ceilings that vanished into the black murk far overhead. The walls were of bronze and steel, everywhere adorned with skeletal gargoyles of brass and spikes of iron. Chains and hooks and cages of every description hung from the unseen ceiling, swaying in time to some unfelt breeze. The air was hot, like cinders as it was drawn into the lungs, and it reeked of blood. The rattle of metal pounding against metal, the grinding of steel against steel, the roar of molten iron rushing through a forge, these were the sounds that thundered through the halls, almost deafening in their violence.

The Bastion Stair, gateway to the very throne of the Blood God. Pyra felt another tremor of fear shiver through her. Again she wondered at the madness of pursuing Dolchir into this place. Perhaps Inhin had been right, perhaps all that she would find here was death. But was there anything else waiting for her in Naggaroth? She had promised this prize to both Malekith and Lord Uthorin. To fail to deliver the Spear and Tchar'zanek's Raven Host to one of them would end in nothing less than a brutal, slow death.

'It seems the animals have found something,' Naagan told her, a trace of amusement in his voice. Pyra wondered how much of her inner thoughts the disciple had guessed. The priests had weird powers, powers even those schooled in the Convent did not understand. She would not put mind reading beyond them.

Pyra smoothed her thoughts and looked past the cadaverous Naagan. The greenskins had foolishly allowed the dark elves to form ranks behind their own, stupidly ignoring the menace of three dozen crossbows at their backs. It would be disgustingly easy when the time came to dispose of them. For now, however, Pyra was more interested in the antics of the greenskins ahead of her in the hall. They had stopped before a huge doorway bordered in skulls. The brutes were slowly barging through the door, into whatever chamber lay beyond.

The sorceress listened intently for a few moments, but could not detect any sound of battle beyond the usual noise of goblins bickering. 'We should see what they found,' Pyra decided, motioning for her warriors to follow her forwards. The druchii warriors formed a double column and marched to the side of their allies.

The room the orcs had discovered was enormous. Pyra might almost have described it as palatial if not for the overall horror of the place. Red walls surrounded them, fiery runes of Khorne burning in their faces. A broad flight of steps climbed up to a level landing surrounded on two sides by iron stakes, each stake spitted with dozens of fresh skulls. Blood and hair still dripped from many of the gruesome trophies, forming gory pools on the gravel floor. In each wall of the landing, the immense skull of a giant leered, its brow gashed with the skull-rune, angry fires burning in each socket. Below the broken jaw of each gigantic skull was an archway, but whatever lay beyond the arches was lost in a swirling mass of crimson mist.

Behind the landing, a second flight of steps swept upwards from either side, forming separate landings before converging upon still another tier set high upon the rear wall of the chamber. Here, the carved face of a mammoth daemon grinned, the fangs of its lower jaw forming the opening of yet another doorway. Below this upper tier, suspended from the ceiling, was a great cauldron of steel and bronze, its surface marked with the arrows of Chaos. Hanging from great chains, the cauldron vomited an endless stream of molten slag, the fiery metal pouring into a great basin that never seemed to fill. Scattered braziers fought with the infernal forge to light the enormous hall, but it was the eerie glow of the walls themselves that lent everything its ruddy hue.

The orcs were already climbing the stairs, pushing goblins ahead of them. Pyra could hear Gorgut's savage voice raised in barks of command. He seemed to be urging the orcs up to the middle tier of steps. More worrying was the way he also seemed to be encouraging his mob to make as much noise as possible.

'What are those animals up to?' Naagan wondered.

Pyra's eyes narrowed with suspicion. She looked around for any sign of the sneaky goblin scout or Beblieth, but could see neither. Just how clever was this animal?

'We should close the distance with our friends,' Pyra said, keeping any hint of alarm from her tone.

'I thought the idea was to let the animals take all the risks?' Naagan protested. 'Let them do all the fighting for us.'

'Maybe he has the same idea,' Pyra snapped at the disciple.

All at once, from the mouths of the archways, a braying, snorting horde erupted into the chamber. Ugly, twisted creatures, their fur hanging from them in dripping mats, their fangs and claws dark with blood, they came in their dozens. Some were wiry and nearly furless, their manlike heads sporting stumpy horns, their feet warped into cloven hooves. Others were utterly inhuman things, capering upon four legs like beasts of the field. Many had the heads of oxen and goats, their huge horns painted with gore, their bestial faces scarred with the skull-rune. One and all, the brutes bore an array of clubs and axes, spears and flails in their hairy hands. Somewhere within the maddening discord of their bleats and howls was a suggestion of feral intelligence and ancient hate.

Pyra did not know if the beastmen had been drawn by the racket of the orcs or if they had simply followed their scent. All she did know was that battle had descended upon her ragged force, a battle she was unprepared for. Quickly she snapped orders to her warriors. The dark elves formed a circle upon the first landing, facing the enemies converging upon them from either side. The front ranks held spears, the rear ranks their crossbows. It was a tactic of supporting arms that had served the druchii well in their conquests. So long as their ammunition held out.

The beastmen came, roaring and raging. The foremost seemed to fling themselves upon the druchii spears, as though eager to die upon them and in their death rip the weapons from their foes. If such was the thought, then the monsters had not reasoned with the keenness of Naggaroth steel. The dark elves simply twisted the blades in the meat of their dying enemies, then dragged the spears from the ruptured flesh. The ranks behind them loosed bolts into the oncoming herd, the repeating weapons taking a butcher's toll. Soon the landing was littered with dead and crippled beasts, their ugly heads raised in cries of agony and fury. Still the others came, crushing their own fallen beneath their hooves, oblivious to all except the destruction of their adversaries.

From the centre of her ring of warriors, Pyra unleashed her magic. A ram-headed monster wearing strips of chainmail over its crimson fur whinnied in terror as its eyes became chips of ice. The spell spread swiftly, freezing the horror on its face, stiffening its arms into frosty lumps. The frozen monster tottered and lost balance, shattering into chunks of dripping meat as it crashed against the floor. The sorceress selected a hulking thing with the face of a pig that rushed through the wreckage of her first victim. The beastman scarcely had time to feel the pain as its body exploded in a burst of raw dark magic.

Pyra lifted her gaze, watching the orcs as they fought their own horde of beastmen high overhead on the left-hand segment of the second tier. There was little in the way of tactics in the orc's behaviour. The brutes just charged into the biggest beastmen they could find, chopping and slashing at them until they were dead. Here and there, a goblin poked its head between the legs of the orcs to stab a beastman in the groin with a spear or to send a poisoned arrow speeding across the hall. For all the crudity of their tactics, the orcs were in a more defensible position than the dark elves, forcing the beastmen to either rush them from below or charge at them from above. Either way, their enemies were caught upon the uneven surface of the stairs. Many lost their footing as their hooves slipped on the blood-slick steps. The goblins were quick to bring their weapons slashing into the necks of these defenceless foes.

The sorceress still could not shake the terrible suspicion that Gorgut had planned for this, somehow. She was convinced the black orc was up to something. She smiled grimly. Whatever he was about, it was unlikely the rest of his mob would stick to the plan once he was gone. Pyra studied the packed mass of orcs, looking for the dark-skinned bulk of their warlord. One spell, and she would no longer need to worry about Gorgut Foechewer.

Pyra had just sighted Gorgut when a deathshriek broke her concentration. One of her warriors was flung into her, almost knocking her to the floor. The warrior had been savagely gored, his throat flopping hideously from the rent in his neck. Pyra glared at the mass of beasts now pressing hard against the line of her defenders. She could see their leader, a towering monster covered in dark fur, its head that of a goat, knobbly horns framing his face. It wore the ripped remains of human armour tied across its broad chest and in its paw was a huge flanged mace studded with spikes. As she glared at the monster, she saw it tilt its head back and give voice to a piercing howl. In response to its cry, dozens of beastmen poured from the archways, rushing to join the battle.

The sorceress sneered at the champion. The spell she had been shaping to deal death to Gorgut she now unleashed upon the beastman. Her smile died when she saw her magic evaporate as it struck the monster. The harsh skull-rune glowed hatefully from the champion's breastplate as it absorbed her magic.

The beastman's dull black eyes gleamed back at her and there seemed a note of amusement in its tone as it howled for more monsters to join the battle.

'We cannot stand!' Naagan gasped. The disciple was frantically trying to employ his magic to heal the hurts of the warriors, but he could not keep up with the horrifying turn the battle had taken.

Pyra looked again at the greenskins. Any hope that the monsters might be drawn down to support the druchii was dashed. Instead of fighting their way down, the orcs were resolutely butchering their way up to the top tier. It was no simple turn of battle that made them turn that way, of such she was certain.

Any question was removed when she saw something leap through the archway behind her. It was one of the fang-faced squigs and quickly a second followed it. Clinging to the horns of a third was the goblin scout himself. The squigs hopped and leaped through the raging mass of beastmen, biting at the monsters then jumping away again before the savage brutes could retaliate. Pyra watched with grim fascination as the squigs swiftly crossed the hall and bounded up the stairs, joining Gorgut's mob just as the orcs cleared a path to the top landing.

Gorgut quickly decapitated the beastman he was facing, shoving the brute's body into the fiery cauldron with one hand while pushing one of his orcs to take his spot with the other. The warlord bent and listened as Zagbob made a hurried report to his chieftain. A wicked grin split the orc's face. Cupping one meaty hand to his mouth, the orc turned and bellowed down to Pyra.

'Oi! Fairy-lady!' Gorgut barked. 'Now let's see how you lot can fight!'

Pyra did not have time to wonder at the meaning of the orc's bellow. The entire hall shook as something enormous crashed against the right archway, the archway from which the squigs had reappeared. Even the beastmen turned about in fear as the chamber shook again.

'Mercy, Lord Khaine!' Naagan cried as the wall exploded into a twisted mass of torn metal and shattered bone.

As she saw the huge shape lumber through the rent in the wall, Pyra felt the urge to pray too. Blasphemously, she wondered if even Khaine could protect her from the thing that now reared its misshapen head and trumpeted its fury until even the ears of the gods must ring with its feral malevolence.

CHAPTER THIRTEEN

FROM THE VERY top of the hall, Gorgut grinned as he watched the metal wall rupture like a swollen belly. The shriek of twisted metal was soon drowned out by the deafening roar of the beast that had caused it. The orc's beady eyes gleamed with black amusement. Zagbob had outdone himself. Gorgut had told his scout to find the biggest, baddest beast he could and then provoke it enough to follow him back to the dark elves.

Gorgut resented the way the elves had used his lads as bait to draw out their own enemies. Maybe none of his warriors had wit enough to understand what the scrawny elves were about, but Gorgut did. He didn't like being the rat at the end of someone's squig-stick. Now the elves were going to know what it felt like.

The monster Zagbob had lured back was beyond anything Gorgut had seen before. It was like a big red mountain, easily able to swallow an ogre whole with one snap of its immense jaws. In shape, it was something like a mammoth hog-wolf-spider thing. It had one leg that was a big paw while the other was more like a bunch of twisted scorpion-claws. Its hind legs both ended in hooves and from its back bristled a forest of black horns that quivered and shook like the legs of a crushed spider. Its thick bull-neck and the top of its head were sheathed in plates of bronze barding. A huge nub of bronze jutted over its snout, like the nose-spike of a rhinox. Thick horns spiralled away from just above either ear. From its snout, a great ring of brass dangled and the underside of its monstrous chin supported a tuft-like beard of horn. The great beast's eyes burned with pained madness, not the dull rage of an animal, but the lunatic frenzy of a thinking thing. It was a look that gave even Gorgut pause.

'We going down there to kill it, boss?' Dregruk asked.

Gorgut chuckled and shook his head. 'No. We'll let the skinnies play with it awhile. The same way they let us have all the fun with them knights and the wizard.' The warlord raised his voice into a louder bellow so that all of his ragged mob could hear him.

'Let's go see what kind of loot's lying around this place,' the black orc barked, gesturing with his axe at the archway beneath the fangs of the carved daemon. He stared down at the shivering, exhausted huddle of Zagbob. The warlord kicked the panting scout. 'Lead the way,' he growled. Zagbob stared murder at

Gorgut, but one display of the orc's tusks had the goblin back on his feet.

Gorgut gave one last look at the battle raging below. The behemoth was attacking everything, dark elf or beastman. His huge frame shook as a regretful sigh rumbled through him. It was a shame to miss out on such a scrap, but he could console himself that there wasn't anything small enough on the beast to take home as a trophy anyway.

THE METAL WALLS of the fortress pressed close around the four northmen. The heated surface sent a weird crimson glow oozing against them, leeching the strength from their limbs with its sweltering aura. Burnt meat dangled from the chains swaying from the ceiling, fat sizzling as the motion of the intruders knocked the chains into the heated walls.

Kormak was once more in the lead. Of them all, he was the most skilled in the arts of tracking and hunting. Perhaps some of Vakaan's spells might have made the marauder's talents superfluous, but the magus had displayed a marked reluctance to call upon his dark arts since entering the Bastion Stair. In subdued tones he had warned Tolkku against drawing too heavily upon his own magic. 'This is the Blood God's domain,' he cautioned. 'All sorcery is repugnant to him. Draw upon your magic only as a last resort. It is not wise to tease the dragon in its own lair.'

Kormak doubted if even the Kurgan zealot needed to be reminded to be wary. The oppressive heat, the grisly surroundings, the pools of fresh, sticky gore they passed with alarming frequency, any of these would have put even the most inexperienced Hung horse-thief on his guard. But there was something more, a constant feeling of being watched, of an unseen force, powerful and malignant, watching their every move. Kormak's skin crawled whenever he allowed himself to concentrate upon the feeling. Whatever was watching them, he knew it only had to rouse itself to action to obliterate them all. He felt like an ant that lifts its head and recognises the boot descending to crush it.

The marauder ground his teeth and spat against the heated wall. The spittle sizzled against the skull-strewn bronze. He watched it for a moment, then noticed something lying upon the floor, almost lost in the shadow cast by a spiked cornice. Kormak knelt and retrieved the object from the shadows, shifting it from one hand to the other in an effort to lessen the contact of the hot metal with his hands.

'What have you found?' Urbaal asked. The Chosen came forward, staring at the silvery mesh of chain Kormak had discovered. The marauder handed the tiny fragment to Urbaal, impressed when his armoured gauntlet closed about it without any notice of its blistering heat. The Chosen studied it a moment, then dropped it to the floor again. 'South-ling steel,' he pronounced with a low growl.

'You believe it is the southlings who have the Spear?' asked Tolkku. Urbaal nodded.

Kormak stared at the long narrow hall, studying each shadow for any sign of other debris left behind by the southlings. He smiled to himself. No, he

wasn't looking for southlings. He was looking for the
elves, and in particular the prancing witch who had
disgraced him. They were looking for the Spear too.
He wondered how near they might be, indeed if they
had discovered the same trail the warband itself was
on. The question made him touch the faint smudges
of the dark elf's blood on his armour. He looked
back at Vakaan hovering above the floor on his daemonic steed.

'Can you tell how near the elves are?' he asked.

The membranes flicked closed over Vakaan's eyes.
The magus bent his head in concentration for a
moment, then waved his hand towards the left.
'Somewhere down there,' he answered. 'If the trail
keeps upon the path it has taken, we will be able to
avoid them.'

Kormak nodded his horned head. 'If we have the
lead, then we must make certain to keep it,' he said.
He turned to Urbaal. 'I will scout ahead, see if any of
the Bloodherd are there. If there are, they will follow
my scent and I can lead them away.'

'Jodis Wolfscar warned it is death to face the beastmen,' Urbaal replied.

'Then it is death,' Kormak growled back. 'If my
death allows you to find the Spear and open the Portal of Rage, then Tchar will smile on my spirit and I
shall be exalted in the halls of my ancestors.'

'Your bones will be chew-toys for goat-kin pups,'
Tolkku laughed derisively.

Urbaal stared hard into Kormak's eyes, then slowly
nodded his agreement. 'Clear the path, Norscan.
Find glory or death, as you will, but clear the path.'

Kormak pulled the heavy axe from its fastenings on his back and sprinted off into the shadowy gloom of the bronze labyrinth. It was not thoughts of either glory or death that burned behind his eyes, however. It was thoughts of pale, laughing flesh and poisoned daggers.

When Kormak found an opening in the left-hand wall, he turned down it. He did not know how far he would need to travel to find the dark elf; he only knew what he would do when he did.

So lost in his bloody thoughts of vengeance was he, that Kormak was almost on top of the monster crouching in the darkness of the side-corridor before he saw it.

The beast had been distracted as well, intent upon the splattered mess of limbs it had been gnawing on. In the crimson glow, Kormak could see hands and feet protruding grotesquely from the gore-mound. A wet skull, its scalp still covered by a chainmail coif of southling manufacture stared silently at him from the top of the pile, as though welcoming another lost soul to the monster's larder.

THE BEASTMAN TOWERED over even Kormak's huge frame. It was easily nine-feet tall, its head a ghastly mixture of human and goat, its naked torso scarred with skull-runes and recent sword wounds. It wiped a hand-like paw across its fanged muzzle, blood and bits of meat dripping from its fur. The gor's lips pulled back in an eager snarl and it dropped the gnawed human leg it held.

Kormak braced himself to meet the monster's charge, but the brute displayed a human level of cunning. Instead of rushing the man, it feinted towards him, then spun and dove for the wall behind it. Kormak roared with fury, lunging after the beastman. His axe slashed down in a cleaving arc, aimed at the gor's shoulder. The beastman spun before the blow could hit it, intercepting Kormak's axe with the handle of its own double-axe. The impact trembled through Kormak's arms, throwing him back, nearly ripping the weapon from his hands.

The beastman grunted, its nostrils flaring. Warily, it began to circle the marauder, rolling the huge double-axe clenched in its claws. The black eyes of the gor bored into those of the man. Its fanged mouth pulled back in a savage grin.

'You die, Norscan,' the beastman snarled as it pounced.

Kormak had prepared himself for the monster's attack, but so shocking was it to him to hear words rasp past its fangs that the gor's axe was almost against his skull before he recovered himself and blocked the descending blow. The marauder's body shook with the fury of the impact, the brutal strength of the goat-headed beast almost enough to batter aside his desperate defence. The gor brayed angrily, twisting the axe about in its grip to hook the handle of Kormak's weapon. The marauder was pulled forwards as the beastman tried to tear the axe from his hands. He twisted his head, raking his horn against one of the monster's paws. The brute recoiled in pain, licking blood from its paw.

'Grakthar feast on manflesh,' the monster promised, displaying its fangs. 'Norscan scream when Grakthar chew his bones!'

Kormak grinned back at Grakthar, his own fangs stretching, pushing clear of his lips as they lengthened. 'I hear no screams, beastkin,' the marauder growled back. 'Only an animal that is tired of living.'

The beastman roared, spittle flying from its fangs. It charged back at the marauder, driving its axe down in a butchering chop. Kormak dodged the blow, bringing his own axe swinging around, cleaving through the tendons of Grakthar's leg. The monster bellowed in pain, smashing the butt of its double-axe into the Norscan's chest. Kormak felt ribs grind together beneath the blow, blood boiling into his mouth. It was his turn to recoil in pain.

Grakthar pursued the staggered human, all of its animal hate consuming its primitive mind. More than the ancient loathing of its kind for men, it was the savage instinct of hunter and prey that filled its brain. Wounded, the smell of fresh blood spilling from his mouth, Kormak had made the transition from adversary to meat.

Kormak glared at the monster as it sprang at him once more. He caught the descending double-axe with the head of his own weapon. He cried out in agony as he felt his muscles burning, as he struggled to defy the greater strength and mass of Grakthar's misshapen body. The beastman brayed and bleated, all trace of speech lost in its hungry snarls. Slowly, inch by inch, the gor forced Kormak's body down. The marauder howled in fury as his knees buckled and he was pressed to the ground. The edge of the double-axe gleamed down at him as Grakthar pushed it towards his face.

Summoning the last reserves of his strength, Kormak ripped his axe free. It spun away, clattering against the heated wall. Grakthar's weapon was nearly wrenched from the beastman's claws and the gor's body spun with the violence of Kormak's move. In the end, however, the brute retained hold of its weapon while the human did not.

The advantage was lost even as it was realised. Kormak's arm shifted, melting into the gruesome shape of an axe-head, a fanged mouth running down its middle. The mutant jaws gaped wide and snapped closed on one of Grakthar's paws, severing the appendage at the wrist. Grakthar whinnied in shock, stumbling back, staring in disbelief at the spurting stump.

Kormak did not allow the monster time to recover. His mutant limb slashed after the reeling beastman, chewing through its midsection, spilling the half-digested muck in Grakthar's belly. The beastman shrieked, throwing down its double-axe. The brute seized Kormak in its claws, lifting him off the floor. It pulled him towards its fanged muzzle, determined to rip out his throat before it was overcome by its own wounds.

Kormak leaned into Grakthar's face, slashing it with his long horns. The stunned beastman dropped him, clapping its paw to its mangled cheek and ruptured eye. Kormak dove at the monster from where he fell, his cleaver-arm gashing its uninjured leg, all but tearing it loose at the knee.

Grakthar crashed to the floor like fallen timber, splattering its gory collection of limbs and heads against the bronze walls. The brute struggled to lift itself again, its remaining paw groping feebly at the blood-slick floor. Kormak clutched his side and carefully made his way over to the fallen beastman.

'Khorne cares not…' Grakthar coughed when it saw Kormak standing over it.

The marauder scowled down at the man-eating monster. 'Neither do I.' His arm assumed the shape of a bony spear, shooting down into the brute's horned head, smashing through flesh and bone, punching through the gor's skull to impale the brain beneath. Grakthar quivered on the end of Kormak's arm, then its massive body slackened and became still.

Kormak slumped onto the floor beside it, breathing hard, biting his tongue against the pain from his cracked ribs. He glanced at his axe, all but shattered by the superhuman effort that had finally unbalanced the beastman. He crawled to where Grakthar's weapon lay, pulling the huge double-axe into his lap as he sat with his back against the stinking carcass of the gor. There was nothing to do but wait, wait for either death or Tolkku's healing magic.

The Norscan smiled as he saw the skull wearing the chainmail coif watching him from where it had been thrown. He looked down the silent corridor beyond the corpse of Grakthar. Somewhere down there he would find the witch elf. If he could convince the others that the southlings were there too, then there was just a chance he might live long enough to settle the score with his enemy.

BEBLIETH CLUNG TO a skull-faced cornice, trying to drag air into her scorched lungs. She cursed the vile goblin yet again, the thought of blaming her own arrogance never entering her mind. She had stalked the goblin scout, as Pyra had told her to. Indeed, she doubted if the stupid runt had ever even suspected she was there. Through the grim halls she had followed him when he broke off from the rest of the greenskin mob.

At last, the goblin found what it had been looking for. In a vast cavern gouged out from the maze-like nest of corridors and galleries, the goblin confronted a truly gigantic beast. Beblieth could not guess what the hunter was about as it fired arrow after arrow into the slumbering brute. It seemed to her that the goblin had lost its fragile grip on intelligence and its brain had collapsed into suicidal madness. It was only when the monster at last stirred and started to pursue the now fleeing goblin that she guessed the mission Gorgut had sent it upon.

The witch elf raced down side-corridors, desperately trying to draw ahead of the goblin and cut it off before he could lead the pursuing behemoth back to the main body of dark elves. She rounded a corner, confronting the scout as he raced towards her. The goblin snarled at her, pointing its clawed finger. One of the gruesome squigs hopped ahead of its master, bounding after Beblieth like a rabid toadstool. The witch elf smiled at the laughable threat. She had killed asur swordmasters and the hulking reptiles of Lustria in her time. The squig with its fangs and claws was no challenge. She smiled as the bright-green monster sprang at her. Her daggers struck it from either side, seeking to bisect its body.

As soon as Beblieth struck the squig, it exploded into a cloud of putrid gas. The witch elf recoiled from the noxious explosion, but was not quick enough to keep some of the murky vapours from searing her eyes and throat. Almost blind from tears, she was powerless to stop the cackling goblin and its surviving squigs from running past her. It was all she could do to throw herself back into the side-passage before she was trampled by the hurtling bulk of the pursuing beast.

Beblieth had considered leaving the other druchii to their fate. Only the cold realisation of her chances of making it alone stayed her flight. Alone, even a witch elf would be tempting prey for all the fiends of the Wastes. Worse, if any of the druchii survived to escape back to Naggaroth with word of her cowardice, the Temple of Khaine would set its assassins on her trail. Even a witch elf had no illusions about eluding the avenging knives of Khaine's killers.

Instead, Beblieth cleared her eyes as best she could and followed the rampaging behemoth. She could tell from the sounds of battle ringing through the corridor that she was too late to warn her kinsmen. The beast had already found them, its trumpeting roar booming off the bronze walls. She could hear the clack of crossbows, the piercing shrieks of dark elves being torn to ribbons. A last thought of retreat, then Beblieth drew her poisoned daggers once more.

Ahead, she could see the beast's hindquarters jutting from the ruptured wreckage of the wall. Beyond the flanks of the brute, she could see armoured ranks of dark elves firing on the monster, stabbing at it with long spears, slashing at its paws with swords. While she watched, she saw Pyra fling her arms wide, drawing upon her arcane powers to combat the behemoth. Nor were the dark elves alone. Dozens of dark-furred beastmen were rushing to the attack. There were still knots of the goat-headed savages fighting isolated druchii, but most of them seemed to have decided that the behemoth was a more pressing menace.

'Azuk'Thul!' the brutes brayed and growled, terror filling their mad bleatings.

The behemoth hissed as it heard its name, almost as though it were confirming its title for the horrified ears of its victims. Beastman or dark elf, the monster made no distinction, but brought its huge claws snapping down, spearing mangled bodies with each click of its pincers. A volley of crossbow bolts peppered its snout, a crude axe of steel and bone scarred the bony spur jutting from its chin, black lightning flashed against its face – each attack only adding to Azuk'Thul's berserk fury.

Beblieth opened the vial of coatl venom. Deadliest of the serpents of Lustria, it was one of the most potent poisons known to the assassins of Naggaroth. It was death for any dark elf discovered with it, testament for its killing power. The witch elf kept her blade well clear from her body as she coated it in the viscous syrup. She grinned as she stared at the hindquarters of the behemoth. It would never know why it was dying.

The witch elf sprang at Azuk'Thul, sinking her dagger up to the hilt in its hind leg, just above its monstrous hoof. For a moment, it seemed the beast was oblivious to both her attack and the poison. Then its quaking roar rumbled through the corridor. Beblieth was dashed aside as Azuk'Thul's thorny tail slammed into her. She dropped clear before she could be crushed against the heated wall, rolling across the floor, narrowly eluding the beast's stamping hooves.

Beblieth pressed back against the hot wall, feeling her bare skin blister at the contact. Azuk'Thul was still moving, trying to force its gigantic bulk free from the ruptured bronze. Impossible as it was, the behemoth was defying the venom from her dagger, poison she had used before to burst the heart of a dragon on the bleak shores of Naggarythe. She could still see her dagger embedded in the abomination's flesh, buried to the hilt in one of the beast's arteries. She could even see the black taint of the poison spreading around the wound. Yet still the bloodbeast raged.

The tail came slamming down again, denting the bronze wall as she ducked beneath its battering sweep. Beblieth slashed at the limb, digging at the leathery flesh. Wormy blood squirmed from the wound, dropping against the floor like tears of flame. Azuk'Thul shook the corridor with another of its deafening roars.

Her ears ringing with the bloodbeast's howl, Beblieth did not hear the barbarian as he charged at her.
Only her combat instincts saved her from the slashing sweep of Grakthar's axe, the double blade cutting
hair from her head as she rolled beneath it.

'We meet again, witch,' Kormak growled from
behind the axe.

Beblieth sneered at the marauder. 'You should feel
honoured,' she spat. 'There are not many animals I
need to kill twice.'

Before the witch elf could make good her threat,
the hoof of Azuk'Thul came smashing down between
the two enemies, throwing both off their feet.

'Forget the elf, Norscan!' Tolkku was shouting. 'We
have bigger problems.' The zealot gestured frantically
at Azuk'Thul. Vakaan hovered beside the priest,
weaving his hands in a complex pattern before him,
drawing upon his magic to defy the behemoth.
Urbaal simply drew his sword, marching resolutely
towards Azuk'Thul, the thousand names of the Raven
God a whispered mantra on the champion's lips.

Kormak shook his head, jumping back as
Azuk'Thul's tail came smashing down again. The
marauder chopped at it with his new axe, bringing a
spurt of sizzling blood from the monster. The bloodbeast roared, redoubling its efforts to break free from
the wall. The marauder ignored it, his eyes searching
only for the mocking elf warrior.

She was already in motion. Against Kormak alone,
she would have stood her ground, but she knew better than to face the entire warband. There was only
one path of retreat, and she took it. She turned her

dodging roll as the bloodbeast's tail lashed out at her into a graceful flip that carried her onto the behemoth's leg. She stabbed her dagger into its flesh, using the blade to anchor her position. She looked down at Kormak, pausing to blow the enraged marauder a kiss before scrambling from her precarious perch onto Azuk'Thul's back.

Kormak gnashed his teeth, racing after her before Urbaal could stop him. The marauder brought his axe smashing against Azuk'Thul's side. He was torn from the ground by the behemoth as its entire body lurched forwards. Unable to pull back through the gaping hole it had made, the bloodbeast had decided to push into the hall where the embattled dark elves and beastmen continued to fight it.

Azuk'Thul's massive hooves shook the ground, each step making the axe slip a little more in Kormak's hand. The marauder tightened his hold, bracing himself for that moment when he would inevitably fall to the floor and be pulped by the bloodbeast's smashing hooves. As he resigned himself to death, he cast his gaze upward, scowling as he saw Beblieth crawling along Azuk'Thul's back, using the thorny forest of its spines to pull herself towards its armoured neck.

Hate gave the Norscan strength when he needed it most. His arm became again the pincer of some crustacean horror, black and chitinous. He let the axe slip away and stabbed his claw into Azuk'Thul's flank. The monster turned on him, snapping its fangs at him. Kormak lunged up the brute's side, leaping onto its back, clearing the behemoth's vengeful jaws.

Azuk'Thul glared at him with its dull eyes, its thick tongue striking at him like the tail of a scorpion. The marauder parried the purple, slimy appendage, gashing it with his claw, sending milky ichor spurting across him.

Azuk'Thul relented in its persecution of Kormak, drawn away by the renewed assault of its other enemies. Kormak could see Urbaal, his sword again blazing with the power of Tzeentch, slice at the beast's leg, a fountain of blood spraying from the wound. He saw a glowing pentacle take shape beneath the beast's shoulder, and a gruesome blue thing with apelike arms manifested as Vakaan called one of his daemons from the void. He saw ranks of dark elves spraying bolts from their crossbows into the monster. Behind the elves stood one of their women, a lissom figure clad in a tight black gown slit along one side. She raised her staff and a frosty wind battered the behemoth. Everywhere beastmen of every shape and form chopped, stabbed and clawed at the monster.

The odds still seemed to favour the monster. With one smash of its claw, Azuk'Thul scattered the crossbows, pulverising three dark elves in the attack. It lowered its head, twisting the bronze horn above its snout from side to side, battering beastmen into mush with each grinding turn of its neck. Its huge pincer snapped open and closed, dealing mutilating death with each strike. Entrails and severed limbs were heaped about its feet, its body was sticky with the blood of its many victims. The damage being dealt to it was hideous, but instead of weakening it,

Azuk'Thul seemed to take strength from the havoc. Kormak thought of the croaking gasp of Grakthar. 'Khorne cares not from whence the blood flows.' Neither, it seemed, did this abomination spawned by the Blood God's madness.

Kormak dug his feet into the flesh of the beast's back, steadying himself by grabbing onto the spines. If the beast had any weakness, then it would be its head. Anything mortal would die with steel in its brain. The marauder willed his arm to become a metallic axe with a cruel spike of bone jutting above the blade. It was time for Azuk'Thul to learn that fleas bite back.

He made his way forward, his footing slipping as he found himself on the thick bronze plates smelted to Azuk'Thul's neck and head. The barding was almost red hot as he dropped and struggled to keep from falling. His hand found a purchase between two of the plates. Slowly, he began to creep forwards. His gaze darkened as he found Beblieth ahead of him. The witch elf was pressed into the space between the barding and one of Azuk'Thul's horns, using the narrow gap to brace herself as she applied poison to one of her daggers. She looked up and sneered as she saw Kormak.

'Persistent,' she hissed. She glanced at her dagger and the half-empty vial of venom. 'I should have enough for you and him.'

'Take some yourself,' Kormak growled back. His mutant arm bristled as dozens of bone spikes suddenly sprouted from the axe. 'It will hurt less, I promise you.'

Beblieth laughed, rising to face the marauder. Carefully, Kormak made his way towards her. The witch elf watched him come, then suddenly she threw the vial at him. The vessel struck the bronze barding beneath his feet, shattering. The already slippery metal became like glass under Kormak's boots. He cried out as his feet gave beneath him and he went sliding down the armoured face of Azuk'Thul.

'No time to waste on animals,' Beblieth laughed as she watched him slip away.

The marauder fought for a handhold as he slid down the behemoth's face. His hand finally locked on the gigantic bronze horn above its snout. Even as he struggled to tighten his hold, his perch shook. He clung tight as he was pushed through the air. Azuk'Thul was grinding more beastmen beneath its horn. Kormak scrambled to keep on the upturned side of the behemoth's face. As the huge head rose once more, he stared into the eyes of the monster. Azuk'Thul glared back at him, primal fury boiling in its gaze.

Suddenly, the bloodbeast's eyes turned a frosty white. Little slivers of ice began to spread over its brows, but the spell was too feeble to entomb the entire monster in ice. Its power petered out, leaving Azuk'Thul blinded but alive. The abomination's crazed brain associated its plight with the man clinging to its horn. It threw back its head, raging, trying to fling Kormak off of it, to smash him against the walls of the hall.

It was impossible to retain his precarious hold against the monster's fury. Kormak was falling once

more, sliding off the beast's head. His scrabbling
hand locked around the first thing that offered safety.
Kormak looped his arm around the bronze ring set
into Azuk'Thul's snout. He clung there, his dangling
legs kicking against the beast's fangs.

The monster's frenzy swelled, its entire body shivering with frustrated fury. Kormak could see Beblieth
crouched upon its head, leaning down from the
safety of her perch in the crook of its horn to rake her
poisoned dagger across its ear again and again. The
sight added to his own rage. He brought his axe lashing out, chopping into the massive snout.

Azuk'Thul reeled back, wailing in pain as its sen-
sitive snout was struck. It snapped and clawed at
the empty space before it. In its blindness, it could
not see what had hurt it, it only knew from whence
the blow had come. Kormak braced himself until
the beast's fury lessened. Then he struck the nose
again. Once more, Azuk'Thul railed against an
invisible enemy, lurching forwards and gnashing
its fangs.

Kormak craned his neck, taking note of the boiling
pit of metal and the fiery cascade falling from the
suspended cauldron. A dangerous plan suggested
itself to him, one made all the more pleasant by its
chance of taking the witch elf with the monster.

Kormak struck the nose a third time, only this time
waiting until Azuk'Thul was in the direction he
wanted, facing towards the cauldron. The bloodbeast
rushed forwards, gnashing its fangs. The marauder
slashed its snout again, its sizzling blood scalding his
flesh as it poured over him. He clenched his teeth

against the pain and repeated the attack. Again, Azuk'Thul lunged forwards, snapping and clawing at the invisible enemy. Now the heat of the cauldron and the pit was hot against Kormak's back. He grinned at the blind eyes of Azuk'Thul and struck one last time.

Azuk'Thul sprang forwards, the entire hall shaking with the fury of its lunge. But this time there was no hard floor beneath its claws. The behemoth gave a piercing wail as its claws sank into the molten metal, as its side was scorched by the searing cascade from the cauldron. Kormak braced his boots against the monster's snout. There was no time to judge distance, only to act and pray that he would clear the pit. The marauder launched himself from Azuk'Thul, hurtling across the fiery gap. He crashed with a grunt against the lip of the middle tier, his hands coiling around a steel stake. It was almost a shock to him when the groaning stake held his weight and he found that he was not going to join Azuk'Thul in its fiery tomb.

The beast roared and shrieked. Its forelegs already burned into ash, the rest of the monster toppled into the pit, crashing into the bronze lake. Azuk'Thul struggled to pull itself clear, but it was a hopeless fight. Like fiery tar, the metal dragged at the monster, pulling it down even as it melted its flesh.

Kormak stared down at the dying monster, a satisfied smile on his face. He started to pull himself up onto the landing. A shadow fell across him. The marauder froze. Raising his gaze, he found that there was already someone on the landing.

Beblieth stared down at Kormak and leaned against the already weak stake. The steel groaned even louder as she pressed against it.

'Impressive,' she told Kormak, nodding to the burning husk of Azuk'Thul. 'But I am afraid you missed one.'

CHAPTER FOURTEEN

'BEBLIETH!' A SHARP voice rang out. The witch elf shifted her gaze from the struggling marauder below her to the one who had cried out. She saw Naagan, the disciple's robes splattered with blood, clenching his dagger in his fist. Naagan was rushing up the steps towards her.

'Beblieth!' he called out again. 'Do not kill the barbarian.'

The witch elf scowled as she heard the cadaverous priest's words. She looked beyond Naagan, staring out over the havoc of the hall. The mangled carcasses of beastmen were strewn everywhere, but mixed in with them were the armoured bodies of druchii. Far too many druchii. Of the warriors who had followed Pyra into the Bastion Stair, perhaps six were still standing. They stood in a protective ring as Pyra conversed with a hulking armoured human. Behind the first human were two others. One was the tattooed magician she had tried to kill in the rocks. The other was a sorcerer clad in feathered robes and standing upon a strange disc that hovered several feet above the floor.

'Do not kill him!' Naagan implored again. 'Pyra seeks alliance with the humans.'

Beblieth's scowl darkened. She sneered down at Kormak. 'Fall or fly as you will, barbarian,' she hissed. With a sinuous twist of her lithe body, she pushed herself back from the steel stake. The shifting of her weight caused the already weakened metal to shudder, grinding downwards as it lost its tenuous grip.

Kormak lunged at the lip of the landing just as the protesting stake was bent out of all semblance of shape. His mutant arm stabbed into the floor, digging deep into the crimson stone. Snarling with effort, veins bulging in his neck, the marauder lifted himself from the pit.

Beblieth folded her arms across her chest, smirking as the panting Norscan pulled himself onto the ledge. She laughed as the spent warrior crashed in an exhausted huddle on the bloody steps.

An instant later her laughter was smashed from her body as the huddle suddenly pounced upon her like a raging tiger. Kormak's fatigue had been partly feigned, a deceit to lull the nimble elf, to play upon her arrogant disdain for what she considered a mere animal. The feint worked and Kormak's powerful arms wrapped about Beblieth's body, trapping her hands against her chest. Kormak's teeth lengthened into fangs as he tightened his hold, squeezing the elf, crushing her like some jungle python. He could feel each breath gasp from her body, his arms closing, pressing, smashing the slender body still more tightly.

'I am going to send you into the halls of the dead,' Kormak growled through his fangs. The face of the witch elf was turning blue, all arrogance and pride gone from her eyes as they bulged in their sockets. 'I am going to enjoy doing it,' the marauder snarled.

Cold steel pressed against his neck. From the corner of his eye, Kormak could see the red-garbed elf priest. 'If I so much as cut your skin, barbarian,' Naagan hissed, 'the poison on this blade will kill you.'

Kormak didn't answer Naagan, instead tightening his hold on Beblieth.

'I have called off my dog, Urbaal,' Naagan shouted down to the lower hall. 'Call off yours before I kill it!'

Urbaal raised his armoured head, glaring at the enraged Kormak. 'Release the she-elf, Kormak!' he growled. The Chosen clenched his fist when the marauder ignored him. 'Release her, or when the elves kill you, I will let Vakaan feed your soul to his daemons!'

The threat pressed upon the only fear left in Kormak's mind. To die was no evil, but for his soul to be fed to daemons, never to enter the halls of his ancestors, this was a horror to unman even the marauder. He knew that it was within Vakaan's power to work such evil, just as he knew Urbaal would not hesitate to allow such a fate for one who had defied him. With a snarl of frustration, Kormak threw the witch elf down. He spat on the prone murderess, then turned and stalked down the stairs to rejoin his warband.

'When he doesn't need you anymore,' Kormak growled as he marched off, 'then you will die.'

'When you feel a knife in your back, know it is mine,' Beblieth snarled back between ragged gasps.

Kormak found Urbaal in close conference with the robed she-elf he had noticed before. It quickly became apparent that Pyra was the leader of her people and that she was indeed intent upon capturing the Spear.

'Alone, neither of us is strong enough to challenge this place,' the sorceress told Urbaal. 'Our shared enemies have the relic and if allowed to remain unchallenged, who can say what havoc they can cause both our peoples.'

'Where are your orcs?' Urbaal asked, suspicion in his voice. 'We watched you from the rocks. You had quite a mob of them helping you.'

Pyra's expression flickered, darkening with both embarrassment and anger. To be tricked by a stupid, slobbering orc was an indignity that chafed her pride. 'The greenskins betrayed us. They intend to capture the Spear for themselves, even if they cannot understand its true purpose. All the more reason why we must work together.'

'You can't mean to trust these creatures?' Kormak snarled as he joined the leaders. The marauder leaned down and ripped a huge axe with a horn handle from the dead fingers of a goat-headed beastman. He swung the weapon idly in his hand, testing its awkward balance.

Urbaal shook his head, keeping his eyes fixed on Pyra. 'I am not fool enough to trust an elf,' he said. 'But there is truth in her words. Our chances are long enough without the added menace of the orcs. We can use any help we can get, no matter what shape that help wears.' The Chosen thrust out his armoured hand. Pyra stared at it for a moment, trying to remember the crude rituals of the slaves her family had kept when she was small. At last, she put her hand out and gripped the champion's gauntlet.

'A pact then,' Pyra said. She looked from Urbaal's steel mask to the sullen features of Kormak. 'Death to the first one who betrays this alliance,' she added with a cold smile.

Even in the maze of bronze halls with their piles of skulls and morbid trophies, the rank smell of the cages was nauseating. It was the stink of waste and unwashed humanity, the reek of death and despair. The stench was not helped by the butchered beastmen strewn along the corridor between the cages, entrails strewn about the floor. One look at the carnage was enough to tell Urbaal it was the work of orcs, who chop at an enemy until it was too badly mauled to defend itself. Once it reached that state, living or dead, it was no longer of any interest to them. There were signs that the goblins tagging along with the bigger greenskins had happily finished off the wounded their hulking cousins left behind.

'This is recent,' Kormak said as he inspected the still dripping intestines of a four-legged beastman. 'Maybe an hour. Probably less.'

Urbaal nodded, kicking the head of a mutilated ungor from his path. He looked over the butchery. Heaped against one wall, its flesh slowly cooking, was the slumped corpse of an orc. There were a few scrawny goblins lying scattered about the carnage, but overall it looked like the orcs had killed with impunity. The Bloodherd, it seemed, had met their equals in savagery.

Pyra walked to the Chosen's side, a pair of her warriors flanking her. The sorceress seemed to read the turn of his thoughts. 'Even if they aren't weakened, we cannot allow them to run free,' she said.

'No,' Urbaal disagreed. 'We seek the Spear, not your unruly orcs.' He gestured at the corpse-strewn corridor. 'This Gorgut must still have a few score warriors to have wreaked this kind of havoc against the beastkin. I see little evidence that his numbers have been thinned. I will tell you the same thing I have told my own warriors – this is about capturing the artefact, not revenge.'

The elf's lips twisted in a look of disgust. 'Gorgut is looking for it too,' she said. 'We can't leave that monster at our back.'

Urbaal laughed. 'The orcs will stop to fight everything they see. The Bastion Stair will finish them long before they can menace our quest.'

Pyra shook her head. 'Do not underestimate this monster's cunning,' she warned. 'I have already made that mistake once.'

The exchange was interrupted by a pained howl from one of the cages. The dark elf warriors were inspecting them, jabbing their spears between the bars, trying to see if anything was still alive. They gave amused chuckles when they heard one of the filth-caked bodies groan as they stabbed it. The elves lifted their spears for another thrust, wagering amongst themselves which would be the one to finish the captive.

Before they could strike, the spears were torn from their hands by a shimmering blast of blue fog. The weapons clattered against the floor, the warriors cursed, grabbing their stinging hands. Vakaan, his eyes still glowing from his spell, hovered close beside the cage, his staff held defensively across his body.

'This man is a warrior of the Raven Host,' the magus hissed. 'Touch him again at your peril.'

The scolded dark elves glared at Vakaan, but none of them was prepared to challenge his magic. They picked up their spears and skulked away, finding other cages to investigate.

Vakaan gestured with his fingers and a smouldering orange glow began to illuminate the steel cage. It was a cruel thing, too narrow to allow a captive to sit and too short to allow him to stand. A lone prisoner would have been cramped in its confines. The Blood-herd had crushed three people into the ugly cage. The magus could see that all of the men bore the slash-marks of Wolfscar's command. Two of them were dead and had been for some time. The third clung to life, but only barely.

'Kormak,' the magus called out. 'Your assistance please.'

The marauder walked over to the cage, quickly understanding Vakaan's intention. He seized the blood-crusted bars in his hands. The rusted metal shuddered in his grip. As he persisted, they began to bend. Finally they snapped with an ugly shriek, flakes of red rust flying in every direction. Kormak caught the prisoner as he tumbled out of the opening.

The captive was a sorry sight, the mangled shadow of a once formidable warrior. Kormak judged that he was an Aesling by the cast of his features and the stubble of blond hair clinging to his scalp. Under the torture and deprivation of the beastmen, he had withered into a scarred scarecrow. Hands that might once have held axe and shield were gone, only crusted stumps remaining. As Kormak set the captive gently on the floor, he could see the rot of infection seeping from the untreated wounds.

'The man needs healing,' Kormak said, staring at Tolkku.

The zealot merely shrugged and smiled. 'I do not waste my magic on the dead.'

Kormak felt his blood boil at the Kurgan's dismissive words. Whoever the man had been, he had been a warrior of the Raven Host. He had been mutilated fighting the enemies of Tchar'zanek. If there was anything they could do for him, then it was their obligation. Only the lowest Hung woman-snatcher would leave a comrade in such a sorry state.

'He may know things that would be useful to us,' Pyra observed. The elf's words had as much effect on Tolkku as those of the marauder.

'Nurse him yourself, then,' the Kurgan grinned. He leered suggestively at the sorceress. 'Even a dying man might like that.'

Pyra glared at the insulting zealot, then turned towards her own healer. 'Naagan,' she said, 'tending the wounded human seems to be beyond this man's feeble powers. Would you see to him?'

The disciple of Khaine bowed his head. Removing several phials from his belt, the priest strode over to the fallen man. Kormak bristled at the elf's approach, ready for any treachery. Naagan made a placating gesture, trying to reassure the marauder.

'My mistress wishes your man healed,' Naagan told Kormak. 'I am not so bloodthirsty or so foolish as to defy Lady Pyra.'

Kormak backed away, still keeping a ready hand on his axe and watching Naagan for the first false move. The disciple bent over the lying warrior, lifting his head and pressing one of the phials to his lips. The prisoner thrashed against the stinging liquid. His eyes fluttered open and he struggled to push Naagan away, his gory stumps slapping uselessly against the elf's chest.

'He will live,' Naagan pronounced as he stood. 'At least long enough to tell us what we want to know.' He fingered his knife, looking expectantly at Pyra. The sorceress gave a slight shake of her head. Naagan sighed and turned away, leaving the wounded warrior to Kormak and Vakaan.

'Who are you?' the magus asked.

The prisoner struggled to focus on the voice he heard, reassured by the familiar sound of human speech. A broken smile tried to form as he saw Vakaan's feathered robes and tall helm, but particularly when he saw the daemon disc upon which the magus hovered. He knew only the sorcerers of Tzeentch could master such steeds. Strangers or not, at least now he knew they served the same god.

'They call me Valr,' the prisoner coughed. He stared with renewed horror at the stumps of his hands. 'I was warleader of Jodis Wolfscar's huscarls.'

Whatever he might next have said, Valr's words were lost beneath the excited jabber of the dark elves. Beblieth led the warriors back to their sorceress, a bloodstained tabard in the witch elf's clutch. It was the surcoat of a Grey Lancer.

'The southlings were here,' Urbaal said, taking the torn cloth from her.

'That means Dolchir and the Spear might be here as well,' Pyra exclaimed. She started to snap commands in her own language to the other dark elves.

Valr coughed, laughter croaking from his dry throat. 'They were here,' he said. 'The Bloodherd found their flesh a rare delicacy.' He pointed at the surcoat, a gesture made hideous by the lack of hands. 'If you find more than that, then the Raven God is smiling on you indeed. The beastmen devoured them all.' Valr shook his head. 'All except the elf,' he corrected himself. 'They gave the elf as tribute to Lord Slaurith.'

'Slaurith?' Urbaal growled. 'He is dead.'

'Who is this Lord Slaurith?' Pyra demanded.

'One of the Blood God's champions, marked by Khorne. A Chosen like Urbaal,' Vakaan explained.

'He is a southling,' Urbaal spat. 'A traitor and murderer. He led an army into the north long ago to destroy the Bastion Stair. He failed. He fell to the Blood God and became Lord Slaurith.'

'He is not dead,' insisted Valr. 'I heard the beasts call his name. He is master of the Second Step, warlord of the Skulltakers. Even Thar'Ignan bows to him.'

'Then Lord Slaurith has Dolchir,' Pyra stated. 'That means he must have the Spear as well.'

Valr shook his head. 'No. Thar'Ignan kept the Spear for himself. Even the minotaur could sense the magic in the thing. The Bloodherd have been taking captives to him for hours.' He pressed his stumps against his ears, trying to block out the sound the memory evoked. 'Finn was the last of my men. I saw them take him away. I saw Thar'Ignan pierce his body with the Spear. It was glowing in the darkness, glowing like a thing on fire. Finn screamed and screamed, Tchar how he screamed. But he wouldn't die. Thar'Ignan lifted him off the ground, his body sliding down the Spear, and still he wouldn't die!'

Kormak tightened his fingers about his axe. 'This Thar'Ignan must die!' the marauder snarled. Death in battle was one thing, but to die tortured and mutilated by beasts was a fate that could not be left unavenged.

'The beast will die,' Urbaal said. He looked aside at Pyra. 'If the beast has the Spear, I doubt that he will part with it willingly.'

The sorceress nodded. 'Then we are agreed. We will hunt down Thar'Ignan.'

Vakaan listened to the exchange, then turned towards Valr. 'You say the beasts ate the southlings? You are certain that none of them were killed upon the Spear?'

'Is that important?' Pyra asked, suspicion in her voice.

'Perhaps,' the magus shrugged.

Valr's brow knitted in concentration. Eventually he shook his head. 'No, the beastmen were too greedy to eat their flesh. They did not spare any for sacrifice.'

'Interesting,' Vakaan mused. He turned his disc so that he faced Urbaal once more. 'We must hurry and strike while the Bloodherd is dealing with the orcs.'

Urbaal walked over to Valr, lifting him onto his feet, supporting his maimed body. 'You can lead us to Thar'Ignan?'

The wounded warrior shook his head. 'The beasts have taken my hands. I would be useless to you and only hold you back. But I will tell you how to find the minotaur's lair. Kill Thar'Ignan and I can enter the halls of my fathers with pride.'

'IT SEEMS WE are not the first to find the beast,' Tolkku said. It was a needless observation. All through the blood-soaked labyrinth of the Bloodherd they had passed scenes of butchery and slaughter. The orcs had rampaged through the halls, emptying the corridors of all life. There had been greenskins among the dead, but far too few according to the elves to account for Gorgut's entire warband.

Now they could see the orcs themselves. The brutes had pursued their enemies as far as they could, into the lair of their savage chieftain, Thar'Ignan the minotaur. The beastlord's stronghold was a great cavern, its nearest side sharing the bronze walls and stone floors of the rest of the labyrinth. The far side of the chamber, however, was a great crater gouged out of the living earth, pitted and torn as though by the fist of a titan. Upon a ledge rising from the raw wall of the crater stood a great monolith of black basalt, its face clawed into the grisly skull-rune. The herdstone of the Bloodherd, the monolith glowed evilly in the darkness, highlighting the butchered bodies and piled skulls strewn about its base.

All about the cavern corpses were strewn. The dead of the Raven Host were now carrion for Thar'Ignan's hounds. Dozens of the ghastly dogs howled and slavered throughout the chamber. They were huge, evil things, their bodies twisted and malformed. Spines protruded from their backs, scaly triple-tails sprouted from their haunches. The faces of some were withered into skeletal visages, those of others were bloated like a toad. Each sported a muzzle filled with dripping fangs, each had long sharp claws upon its paws. Corrupted by the touch of Chaos, the hounds, along with their brutal keepers, had fallen into the service of Khorne. Most of the dogs leaped and clawed at the orc and goblin invaders, while some, too ravenous to worry about their master's enemies, continued to worry the rotting corpses of his victims.

The orcs were thickest where the fighting was most fierce. A pair of huge beastmen, their bodies draped in ragged armour swung giant glaives as the orcs struggled to bring them down. Between them, an even bigger beast loomed, a monstrous thing with crimson fur and the horned head of a bull. The minotaur wore cruelly spiked shoulder pads and bracers, a huge bronze icon of Khorne straddling its belly, a kilt of mail dangling about its flanks. Thar'Ignan held a massive war-axe in his paw, its saw-toothed blade longer than a man's leg. In his other hand, a squirming one-legged goblin impaled upon its tip, was the glowing Spear of Myrmidia. The minotaur bellowed and roared as he swung the weapons, slashing through his attackers as though they were so much wheat.

One of Thar'Ignan's enemies was not such easy prey. Roaring his own fury at the towering beastlord, the black-skinned Gorgut caught the hurtling length of the minotaur's axe upon his own. Beast and orc strained against one another, primitive savage against raw brutality. The orc roared again, pushing the minotaur back, breaking his hold.

'The one fighting the minotaur is Gorgut,' Pyra told Urbaal. 'We need to kill him first.'

'First we need the Spear,' Urbaal corrected her. The Chosen began to sprint into the chamber. He had only gone a few steps before he found himself attacked by a pair of the monstrous hounds. Urbaal dropped into a crouch, slashing the legs out from underneath the first hound. The beast yelped, sliding along the flagstones on its stumps as its momentum carried it away. The second hound leapt for the Chosen's throat. Urbaal smashed the pommel of his sword into its head, cracking its skull. He kicked the dying beast from his path, and rushed towards the embattled minotaur.

'After him!' Pyra shouted to her warriors, then dove aside as a bolt of lightning came crackling towards her.

Dark elves and barbarians scattered as more tendrils of sizzling lightning blasted into the floor. They turned their faces towards the corridor they had just left. Lumbering down the passage was an enormous beast, easily the size of a full-grown ice-bear. Its lower body was that of some giant reptile, four clawed legs tearing into the flagstones with each step, a spiny tail lashing angrily behind it. A man-like torso rose above the foremost legs, a torso clad in blackened armour. The beast's face was a nightmarish combination of reptile and ogre, jagged teeth jutting from its lower lip, a horned helm covering its head. In its hands, the beast gripped an axe that was the equal of the weapon carried by Thar'Ignan.

As the elves and men recoiled from the charging beast, it slammed one of its clawed feet against the floor, sending another blast of lightning crackling through the air.

'Dragon-ogre!' Vakaan cursed as his disc veered away from the electrical burst.

Kormak crashed against the heated wall as he dove away from the lightning. He snarled as he felt the metal burn his skin. 'Dragon or ogre,' he spat, 'it dies on my blade!' The marauder swung away from the wall, rushing at the beast.

'Help him,' Pyra hissed, stabbing her finger at Beblieth. Reluctantly, the witch elf raced after the marauder. 'The rest of you, get the Spear.'

The other dark elves started to obey their mistress when a sickening phenomenon drew their attention. The mangled masses of the hounds Urbaal had butchered were rising again, their hideous wounds

oozing closed, new legs growing from the stumps of
the old. The warriors stared at each other in shock,
then turned horrified eyes towards the pile of dogs
the orcs had already killed. These too were rising
again, wounds flowing closed, jaws gaping in revivi-
fied hunger. Hastily they formed a skirmish line,
front ranks raising their spears, those at the rear aim-
ing their crossbows.

Pyra cursed as she saw her warriors set upon by the
dogs. She glared across the cavern. Gorgut and his
warriors were fighting at the very edge of the crater,
where the flagstones crumbled away into the raw
earth. All it would take would be a minor spell, a
little push, and the warlord would topple into the
pit. It didn't matter if the fall killed the black orc. She
had faith Thar'Ignan could finish the job.

As she wove her hands before her, shaping the dark
energies of her magic into the spell she required, Pyra
was struck by a withering blast of heat. She crumpled
under the attack, only a desperate shift of her concentration allowing her to raise a protective barrier
against the hostile magic. Smoke rose from her
singed hair and garments, blisters peppered her pale
skin. Sensing the cause of the attack, she locked eyes
with the cringing goblin shaman. The creature was
deranged if it thought its hedge magic was equal to
the black arts of Naggaroth!

Before Pyra could decide how she should obliterate
the nuisance, Snikkit pointed a clawed finger at her.
The sorceress shrieked in pain as an invisible weight
smashed her foot. The goblin did not linger, but
exploited her instant of distraction to lose himself

among the combatants scattered about the lip of the crater. Pyra could only scowl at the retreating figure and add another indignity to her suffering.

THE DRAGON-OGRE SWUNG its axe at Kormak as the marauder charged it. The beast snarled its contempt as Kormak's weapon glanced off the steel gut-plate lashed across its belly. A backhanded sweep of its weapon threw the marauder back, smashing him into the ground. The winded man looked up to see the dragon-ogre rushing at him, intent upon pulverizing him with its sheer weight.

Kormak let it come, raging and howling. The floor shuddered beneath the dragon-ogre's bulk, its every step sending crackling shivers of electricity racing through the stone. Still the Norscan waited, waited until escape seemed impossible. In that last instant before the dragon-ogre would grind him beneath its claws, he flung himself aside, rolling along the floor. As the beast swept past him, he struck out with his axe. The stolen weapon did not bite deep into the beast's scaly flesh, but it cut the brute enough to bring blood bubbling up from the split skin.

The dragon-ogre wailed more in outrage than hurt. It felt its damp flank, staring incredulously at its purplish blood on its hand. Yellow eyes narrowed into little pinpoints of hate. The monster stamped its clawed feet, bursts of lightning crackling up from the flagstones. It grunted and licked its fangs.

Kormak ran his hand down his axe until his fingers were wet with the monster's blood. He flicked it at the fuming dragon-ogre. 'Try it,' he jeered.

The dragon-ogre quivered with fury. It stamped its feet again, this time melting the stone with the intensity of its electric touch. Every hair on Kormak's body stood on end as the current crackled through him. Blue fire rippled from his armour and his axe. The smell of his own burnt flesh assailed him. The marauder cried out, falling to his knees as pain overwhelmed him.

The dragon-ogre snorted in contempt. No maddened charge this time, instead the monster slowly stomped towards Kormak, each tramp of its feet sending new slivers of agony rushing through the man's body. The dragon-ogre hefted its axe, its yellow eyes glaring down at him, the twisted face tightened into a bestial grin.

Kormak snarled up at the monster and stabbed it through the foreleg with his mutant arm. The sword-like limb punched through the beast's knee, cutting through cartilage and tendon, fracturing bone and slicing reptilian veins. The dragon-ogre reeled back in surprise, its primitive nervous system only dimly aware of the damage dealt to it. As it recoiled, Kormak swung his axe at it, the blade slamming into its side just behind the thick metal gut-plate. The pallid flesh of its torso ripped apart beneath the blade, bright arterial blood spraying from the wound.

The dragon-ogre bellowed, slashing at Kormak with its axe. The flagstone beside the marauder exploded into a stinging shower of pebbles, but the man himself danced away from the vengeful steel. He struck out again at the beast, his sword-like arm raking along the heft of its axe, slicing away two fingers as it slid across the dragon-ogre's hand.

Sparks danced before Kormak's eyes as the dragon-ogre reversed its weapon, smashing him with the butt of its axe. Again the marauder flew through the air, crashing in a ball of pain against the searing bronze wall. The beast snorted and started to lumber after him. Its crippled foreleg buckled under its weight, sending it crashing to the floor. It shook its ugly head, trying to clear its jarred senses. The dragon-ogre's eyes fixed on Kormak as the marauder tried to regain his feet. With a reptilian hiss, the beast rose, plodding towards its stunned prey, its crippled leg curled tight against its belly, one huge hand clamped against the gash in its torso.

Kormak watched the injured dragon-ogre resume its relentless march. The beast was in sorry shape, but it still had more than enough strength to finish him. The marauder tried to stand, but his ravaged body defied him. His axe felt like a leaden weight in his weakened grip, his horned head an impossible burden for his neck to raise. He bled from dozens of cuts and gashes; his skin was scarred and pitted with burns. Something in his midsection made a wet popping sound whenever he tried to move. It was all he could manage to put defiance into his gaze as he stared into the dragon-ogre's reptilian eyes, daring the beast to do its worst.

The dragon-ogre snorted mockingly as it loomed over Kormak. It swatted the marauder down with its axe, ripping through his shoulder, then its clawed foot drove down into his chest, pinning him beneath its bulk. Kormak screamed as the monster's lightning burned through his flesh. The dragon-ogre stared down at him with pitiless eyes and lifted its axe for a final decapitating blow.

The blow never fell. A lithe form suddenly appeared upon the dragon-ogre's back, leaping onto the beast from the shadows. Before the beast could react, a silvery dagger was raked across its throat, digging deep into its leathery flesh. The beast's huge axe crashed to the floor as it clutched at its spurting neck. Beblieth slashed the brute again, just above its clinging hands, sending another gout of brackish blood spraying from the beast.

Smiling, the witch elf jumped gracefully from the dying monster's back, landing in a catlike crouch only inches from Kormak's head. She watched expectantly as the dragon-ogre slumped. Kormak cried out as he felt the full weight of the beast press down against him, threatening to shatter his ribs. Then the monster crashed onto its side, its tail writhing and lashing as the last of its life drained out of it. Beblieth studied the monster's death throes with malicious interest, savouring every spasm. At last she looked down at the tortured marauder and smiled cruelly.

'When you want to kill something,' she told him, 'then kill it. Don't play around.' Her cold fingers brushed against his forehead, tracing along his cheeks, circling his lips. 'If you hurry, you might be able to crawl back to your healer before you die,' she hissed before vanishing once more into the shadows.

GORGUT SNARLED AT the minotaur as he brought his glowing spear stabbing at the black orc. The warlord knocked it aside with the heft of his axe, then twisted away as Thar'Ignan brought his own axe chopping at the orc's side. The warboss barked with laughter, feeling the joy of battle thundering through his veins. Here was a foe that was worth fighting, an enemy capable of putting up a decent scrap! Gorgut sent a brutal kick into the knee of one of his warriors as he tried to attack the minotaur from the flank. The startled warrior dropped, squealing as Thar'Ignan noticed him. The minotaur brought his axe swinging around, chopping off the helmet and top part of the warrior's skull as it swept past.

Served the git right, Gorgut thought, for trying to poach. The minotaur was his to kill and nobody else's. Let the lads fight the dogs or finish off the goat-headed guards, but Thar'Ignan was his. He wouldn't have some snot-nosed grot boasting about how he helped the warlord finish off the minotaur. If anyone was going to have bragging rights, it was Gorgut Foechewer!

The black orc's fist smacked hard into the minotaur's face, reminding it where the real fight was. The stupid brute seemed to get distracted every time it killed something, sniffing and snorting as the smell of blood struck its nose. Gorgut didn't like that. There was no sport killing something that wasn't paying attention. That sort of thing was goblin work. He wasn't someone who did goblin work.

Suddenly, the minotaur twisted about in pain. Gorgut peered past the stricken monster to see a big human in dark armour slashing at the brute with a glowing sword. The orc's temper swelled. It was bad enough trying to keep his overeager lads from poaching, he wasn't about to let some miserable human take the credit. That was the sort of thing that would make him lose face with his warband, the kind of thing that made orcs desert a leader and look for someone tougher to follow.

Gorgut smashed the flat of his axe against his chest, roaring with rage. He started to rush the interloping human. He only got a few steps before he felt Thar'Ignan's axe smash into him. The orc was thrown by the impact, his huge bulk smashing through orcs and hounds as he hurtled through the air. A flash of memory rippled through his mind, as he was reminded of being kicked by his war boar when he had only been a young runt. Something broke his fall when he landed, something that swore and snarled beneath him. He pounded his fist into its head until it shut up, then stared at the dripping mess where the minotaur's axe had struck him. He poked a finger into the mush, coughing as he decided the weird thing sticking out of his skin was a bone.

'You all right, boss?' The question came from Snikkit, the robed shaman scrambling over the groaning bodies of those thrown back by Gorgut's impromptu flight. The goblin was fumbling a bottle of something from his bag.

Gorgut scowled at the shaman, then snatched the bottle from Snikkit's hand. He sniffed at the mouth, then smashed it against his bleeding chest. The pungent fungus potion burned as it splashed into his wounds, but the black orc gave it small notice. He

idly picked a sliver of glass from his skin as it started
to scab over, then glowered at the shaman.

'No, I ain't all right!' he barked. 'That weedy
human is trying to steal my kill!' Gorgut glanced
around him, then picked up his axe from the tangle
of bodies. 'But he ain't going to get away with it!' the
black orc promised.

Snikkit nodded his head in fawning agreement.
Gorgut cuffed him on the side of the head, throwing
him to the ground. The last thing he was in the mood
for was a cheerleader.

Thar'Ignan was fully occupied by Urbaal when
Gorgut charged back to rejoin the fight. Man and
minotaur circled one another, jabbing and thrusting
with spear and sword. The beast towered over the
human, but Urbaal did not give ground before him.
Indeed, the man seemed almost the beast's equal in
strength and fury. When the minotaur struck at him,
Urbaal caught its blows against his parrying sword,
using his own prodigious strength to push Thar'Ignan back. Gorgut was forced to reluctantly admit that
the human was a tough one.

It didn't matter though. The minotaur was his to
kill. The lads wouldn't respect him if he let anyone
else kill it. Roaring, Gorgut rushed the monster,
slashing its back with his axe. It wasn't a deep cut,
just something to get the monster's attention.
Thar'Ignan swung around, bellowing his anger.

'Remember me?' Gorgut roared back. The black orc
sent his axe smashing into Thar'Ignan's arm, chewing
through its muscles to scrape against the bone. This
time when the beast threw back his head, it was pain

that coloured his cry. Gorgut grinned with brutal satisfaction and raised his axe for another strike.

Suddenly the orc found himself flailing at the empty air as he teetered on the edge of the broken flagstones. The crater yawned beneath him like the maw of some gigantic beast. Gorgut had not seen what smashed into him, but it had felt like the fist of a giant. His grasping hands coiled about the minotaur's spear as Thar'Ignan stabbed at him. Gorgut wrapped his arms around the weapon, sinking his claws into the hand that gripped it.

Then the orc was falling, dropping down into the pit, pulling Thar'Ignan after him. Both monsters crashed hard against the jagged floor of the crater, crimson dust rising in a cloud from their impact. It was Gorgut who was first on his feet. The minotaur snarled at him as it struggled to rise, one of its legs snapped below the knee. Gorgut glared down at the brute and with an overhand motion buried his axe between its horns. Such was the fury of his blow, Gorgut felt his cheek ripped open by a splinter of bone flying from the beastlord's skull.

Gorgut smashed his foot into the dead bulk's neck, standing over the trembling carcass. He beat his hands against his chest and roared his triumph. Around the lip of the crater, he saw orcs and goblins grinning down at him. His eyes narrowed as he saw the dark-armoured human starting to climb down. Gorgut tried to free his axe from the ruin of Thar'Ignan's head, but it was stuck fast. He growled and turned to rip the minotaur's axe from its dead paw. Gorgut fingered the keen edge and bared his tusks at the descending human, fatigue and injury taking a second seat to the black orc's eagerness for battle.

'Gorgut Foechewer,' a voice called down to him.

Gorgut lifted his head to see a feathered human hovering over the crater. The weird human pointed down to the warlord. 'The warriors of the Raven Host are impressed by your valour.'

'Youse lot gonna be real impress'd when I kill ya!' Gorgut bellowed back. He glowered at the descending Urbaal and made ready to charge the champion.

'Gorgut has killed many great foes,' Vakaan persisted. 'But if he joins with the Raven Host, he shall fight even greater battles.' The black orc's brow wrinkled with interest at that remark. 'If he will follow Urbaal the Corruptor, he will face enemies such as no orc has fought. The name of Gorgut will be mighty among the greenskins.' Vakaan's voice dropped into a hollow whisper. 'All that we ask in return is that Gorgut shares his triumph with us.'

The warlord scowled at the magus, keeping one eye on Urbaal as he did. 'Ya ain't takin' da axe!' he bellowed, fingering the trophy he had torn from Thar'Ignan's dead clutch.

'It is the Spear, not the axe that I want,' Urbaal growled back at the orc.

Gorgut stared at the Chosen, then looked at the still glowing Spear. He shrugged his broad shoulder. 'Ya want that fancy git-sticker, ya can take it,' the orc snarled.

Urbaal strode past the black orc, his sword at the ready, and pulled the blood-slick Spear from beneath Thar'Ignan's corpse. He lifted it and shook it at

Vakaan. The magus nodded his head, turning to smile at the dark elves as they crept to the crater and saw the relic in Urbaal's grasp. With the orcs on the side of the Raven Host, the dark elves had lost their numerical advantage. Vakaan was under no illusion that the greenskins could be trusted, but at least they were no friends of Pyra and her followers.

The sorceress turned a bitter face to the hovering magus. 'What now?' she hissed, unable to keep the smouldering fury from her tone.

'Now we find Lord Slaurith and the archmage,' Vakaan told her. He looked again at the Spear in Urbaal's fist. 'We will need them both if we are to reconsecrate the Spear and bend it to our will.'

CHAPTER FIFTEEN

KORMAK'S ARM SCYTHED through the howling, black-clad berserker, shredding his ragged armour of boiled leather and strips of chain. The man was torn apart at the waist, flopping obscenely to the floor in two dripping halves. For good measure, Kormak brought the heavy edge of his axe smashing into the berserker's skull-like helm, splitting his head open. The marauder grunted as he ripped the cumbersome axe free, bits of brain clinging to its edge. Even with his wounds healed by Tolkku's magic, the marauder found the axe he had scavenged off the dead dragon-ogre to be a formidable weapon.

All around him, Kormak saw his comrades beating back the shrieking mass of black-armoured madmen. They were ugly, hulking brutes, their faces locked behind masks of bone. Their shouts and screams were not those of Norscan or Hung or southling, but

the sibilant tones of the Dark Tongue itself. Who
these men had been, what they once were, had been
lost, consumed by the fires of the Blood God's rage.
Upon each breastplate, upon each spiked shoulder-
pad or vambrace the skull-rune was etched, engraved
or embossed. Slaves of Khorne, these men had forsaken their old lives to become warriors of the
Skulltakers, denizens of the Path of Fury, the Second
Step of the Bastion Stair.

Barbarians crumpled as dark elf crossbows ripped
into them. Berserkers were ripped apart as orc choppas pounded through their bodies. The wounded
were set upon by the goblins, giggling sadists with
long spears and cruel imaginations. Kormak saw one
Skulltaker transformed into a pillar of ice by the sorcery of Pyra, another shrieking in agony as Naagan's
witchcraft melted the bones beneath his face. Beblieth was a whirling dervish of dismemberment and
murder, her mangled adversaries tumbling away
from her like waves retreating from a desolate shore.
The poisoned arrows of Zagbob whistled through the
air, skewering throats, dropping men so they would
be easy prey for the goblin's slavering squigs.

At the forefront of the battle were Urbaal and
Gorgut, man and orc trying to outdo one another as
they made the Skulltakers pay the butcher's toll. The
black orc tore through his opponents, laughing and
growling with each mutilating sweep of his axe.
Urbaal was silent and remorseless as death, leaving
only twitching corpses each time he thrust his sword.

Urbaal carved his way through the berserkers, facing the huge brute who was their champion, a great

pale-skinned barbarian with a horned helm of bronze and wielding a monstrous double-axe. The champion appreciated the carnage Urbaal had wrought to reach him, saluting the Chosen with a tilt of his axe. Then the barbarian roared and flung himself upon his foe and battle was joined.

The big axeman was the equal of any normal warrior; even Kormak wondered if he could have bested the enraged champion. Urbaal, however, was no mere warrior, but a man who bore the mark of Tzeentch upon his soul. His sword lashed out like a tongue of flame, cutting through the steel of the axe as though it were butter. The champion stared in disbelief at his ruined weapon, then reversed it to bring the remaining edge hurtling down at Urbaal.

The Chosen brought his sword flashing under the barbarian's guard, chopping through his arm, crunching through ribs and lungs until he ripped the point from the champion's chest in a welter of blood and torn flesh. The barbarian staggered, refusing to accept the damage inflicted upon him. He tried to draw upon all the reserves of strength left in his dying body, trying to will himself to a final effort. Urbaal stabbed the point of his sword up through his chin and braided beard, impaling his brain and ending his fight.

The death of their champion broke the remaining Skulltakers. The barbarians scattered, fleeing down the brass-edged archways that opened into the bronze-walled corridor. The dark elves sent a punishing barrage after them while a few over-eager orcs pursued them into the darkness.

'Skulltakers,' Vakaan pronounced as he inspected one of the dead. The magus let the bone helm clatter to the floor beside the berserker who had worn it. 'A mongrel tribe of murderers and madmen, devotees of the Blood God. They live only to kill, to spill more blood for their god and to bring more heads for his throne. They venerate the Skulltaker, Khorne's daemon executioner. It is said that only those who have seen the Skulltaker and lived are allowed to join the tribe.'

'They die like men, not monsters,' Tolkku said, spitting on one of the bodies.

'Do not make the mistake of underestimating the warriors of the Blood God,' Naagan cautioned the zealot. 'There are many in the Shadowlands who have thought them mere mad beasts and paid for their hubris.'

Tolkku laughed at Naagan. 'Elves, perhaps, but not warriors of the Raven God. We are suckled upon guile and cunning. There is nothing the slaves of Khorne can do that will surprise a servant of Tzeentch. Howl and charge, that is as far as their thinking goes. If they cannot find an enemy to kill, they fall upon themselves. They are more like beasts than the greenskins.' Zagbob appeared to be spying upon the exchange and the goblin puffed himself up with pride as he heard Tolkku's backhanded compliment.

'They were testing us,' Urbaal said, sheathing his sword as he stepped away from the corpse of the champion. 'Slaurith's dogs, the least of his warriors. Something to put the smell of blood in the air.' He patted the Spear lashed across his back and stared hard into the face of Tolkku. 'The ones that escaped will tell him we are here and what we carry. Perhaps he did not know what Thar'Ignan had, or perhaps he was not ready to take it from him. Whatever the reason, Slaurith will come for it now.'

'You sound certain of yourself,' Pyra said. 'Since you have the Spear, why do we not leave and forget this Lord Slaurith?'

'Dat be a poncy elf fer ya!' grunted Gorgut, his tusks jutting as he thrust his chin at the sorceress. 'Run when ya shud be fightin' and stick a shiv in yer back when ya ain't lookin'!' The black orc's debased Reikspiel was more growl than speech, but its meaning was understood well enough by the dark elves.

'Mind your tongue, orc,' Beblieth warned, fingering her daggers. 'Or it will be your back with a knife in it.'

'Enough!' Vakaan's voice boomed through the corridor, cracking like thunder against the bronze walls. 'Test or not, the Skulltakers are in retreat. Now is the time to strike.' He stared down at Pyra. 'We will not leave until the Portal of Rage has been cleansed,' he told the sorceress. 'We will not leave until the winds of magic have been unchained and Kakra the Timeless is free.'

Pyra's face twisted into a sullen pout. She had expected that the humans would try something like this. She shared a hard look with Naagan, understanding passing between them. They would have to act before the humans reached the Portal of Rage. First, however, they would need to restore the balance of power and remove the menace of the orcs.

'These halls must run for miles,' the sorceress said, gesturing with her staff. There were dozens of side-passages and archways opening in the walls, each more forbidding than the next. Skull-strewn stakes jutted from the flagstones, brass effigies of daemons and the arrows of Chaos marked each doorway. Everywhere were piles of rotting heads and heaps of bones. Urns smouldered in the shadows, the horns of Khorne carved into their pedestals. 'It will take many warriors to scout the right path, more than I have. We will need to split Gorgut's mob and send his brutes hunting for Slaurith.'

'No,' Urbaal said. 'We will not split our numbers.'

Pyra's eyes blazed in her pale face. 'Then where do you propose we start?'

The Chosen did not hesitate but pointed his armoured hand towards a brass-framed archway marked by a grinning daemon's face. 'When the Skulltakers broke, they fled in every direction but one.' His voice dropped into a menacing chuckle. 'If you were a coward, would you seek mercy from Lord Slaurith, a man who has sold his soul to bear the mark of the Blood God upon his flesh?' He did not wait for Pyra to answer his question. Marching away, Urbaal swung his arm in a beckoning gesture.

'We go this way,' he said.

The orcs and men ambled after Urbaal, the goblins, many loaded down with fresh loot from the dead berserkers, staggering like drunken children. The dark elves lingered behind and watched the procession.

'We can't allow them…' Naagan began. Pyra raised her hand, motioning him to silence.

'We won't,' she assured him. 'If they throw open the Portal, the Spear is useless to us. We will have nothing to bargain with.'

'Why not kill them now?' Beblieth asked, staring coldly at Kormak as the marauder passed through the archway.

'In good time,' Pyra said. 'First we get rid of the greenskins, then the humans. The magus knows some way to corrupt the Spear's enchantment. We will let him. Then it will be time for them all to die.'

THE BRONZE HALLS wound like the coils of a vast serpent through the depths of the Bastion Stair. The marks of the Blood God were everywhere, picked out in gruesome altars of bone or taking the shape of metal gargoyles leering from steel-spiked columns. Lines of stakes flanked many of the halls, a grinning skull spitted upon each, the skull-rune burning in each forehead. These, Vakaan whispered, had been victims of the real Skulltaker, their heads regarded as sacred talismans by the tribe that bore his name. Tolkku had tried to pull one of the trophies down, thinking to add it to his collection. The dead thing had come alive at his touch, snapping at his fingers with creaking jaws.

Sometimes, the warriors of the Skulltakers would appear, giving battle to the invaders. Always they were beaten back, always the survivors scattered down every side-passage except one. Only Gorgut and his orcs didn't find the abortive attacks and extravagant retreats suspicious.

'They mean for us to follow a certain path,' Kormak warned Urbaal.

The Chosen stared at the brass embossing on the walls, tracing the complex lines of arrows with his gaze. 'They mean for us to find Slaurith,' he said.

'But it is a trap,' Kormak insisted.

'Even if it is a trap, Slaurith will be there,' Urbaal stated. 'A slave of Khorne will not stray far from a battlefield. He will be there, and that will be his undoing.'

Kormak considered Urbaal's words, but could not understand how he could be so certain the chieftain of the Skulltakers would act the way Urbaal thought he would. He wondered about the way Urbaal spoke of Slaurith, calling him traitor and southling. He asked as much of the Chosen.

'I know him from long ago,' Urbaal answered. 'Longer than you might believe. He was Grandmaster of the Knights of the Blazing Sun, General of the Order of the Griffon. He led his army to the Bastion Stair, to fight and cleanse it of the Blood God's evil. As the Blood God's endless hordes slowly bled away his command, he despaired, and in his despair he welcomed a new god into his heart. He cast aside Myrmidia and the weak southling gods and became a servant of Khorne. He betrayed his men to the denizens of the Bastion Stair, sparing only those who would join him in damnation.' Urbaal's fist tightened until Kormak thought his gauntlet would break.

'Few escaped into the Wastes,' Urbaal added with a snarl.

Kormak nodded grimly, feeling the hate in Urbaal's voice. Slaurith had made a terrible enemy in the champion of Tzeentch. He wondered dimly at who Urbaal had been before he became Chosen and at this glimpse of a history the man himself had almost forgotten.

'We will kill him,' Kormak told Urbaal.

'Yes,' the armoured champion replied. 'We will kill him. For a start.'

The two men turned as they heard the raucous barks of the orcs sounding throughout the passage. They turned to find a knot of goblins kicking and punching one another. The scrawny greenskins were arguing over a barrel of ale they had discovered against one of the walls. The orcs were shouting their encouragement, clearly enjoying the violent diversion. Urbaal marched over to Gorgut.

'Control your rabble,' he told the black orc. Even Urbaal was forced to raise his head to stare into the warlord's beady eyes.

Gorgut coughed and scratched at his ear. 'Naw, da ladz is jus' havin' a bit o' a laff.'

'There isn't time to waste on these antics,' Urbaal warned him.

The black orc threw out his chest, glaring down at Urbaal. One of his thick fingers pushed against the Chosen's breastplate. 'Don't get pushy, oomie,' Gorgut growled. 'Nagdnuf's got lotz a' wayz ta cook pushy oomies.'

Vakaan again interceded between the two warchiefs. 'This arguing accomplishes nothing!' he chastised them. 'The Skulltakers will kill us all if we start fighting among ourselves. Then where will your quest be, Urbaal? How will you return to your tribes with glorious trophies and weapons of magic, Gorgut?'

'Wez'll find 'em wid or widout oomies showin' da way!' Gorgut barked back, but with a note of doubt in his bellow. The black orc smashed a fist into the head of the warrior nearest to him. 'Break that scrap up!' he growled at Dregruk. 'Tell them gits dat the next one starts a fight I'm going to drown 'im in that booze!' Dregruk massaged his swollen ear and hurried off to do as his chief told him. Gorgut scowled at the two northmen, then loped off to find something to distract him from his troubled thoughts.

'The orcs will be a problem,' Urbaal said.

Vakaan gestured towards the dark elves, lurking against one of the walls, every eye watching the tense exchange between man and greenskin. 'They will be a bigger problem if we lose them,' he cautioned. 'Gorgut can be managed. Even I, a magus of Tzeentch, cannot fathom the crooked plots of these elves.'

Urbaal nodded his understanding. 'They can still help us,' he said.

'Unless they betray us first,' was Vakaan's reply.

THE SKULLTAKERS ATTACKED the motley warband as they entered a wide chamber that looked as though it had been converted into a drinking hall. Tables and benches crafted from redwood were strewn throughout the room, chandeliers crafted from bones and brass swung overhead. It was an attack in force this time, a small army of the black-armoured barbarians charging the intruders from every side.

The warband fell into the now familiar defence that had broken six Skulltaker attacks already. Kormak and Urbaal took the point, fighting alongside Gorgut and his orcs. The dark elves surrounded Vakaan, Tolkku and their own spellcasters. The goblins scattered, keeping well back from the front lines, sending arrows stabbing into whatever target of opportunity presented itself. Zagbob, the wiry squig hunter, circled the battleline, sending poisoned arrows into wounded enemies then setting his slobbering squigs after the crippled men. Snikkit kept close to Gorgut, using his weird magic and fungus powders to heal the warlord's wounds. Beblieth kept to the shadows, circling behind the attackers. Those who earned her attention never saw the dagger that slit their throats.

The leader of these barbarians was another armoured monster, a mammoth brute seven-feet tall encased in bronze armour, only his reddened eyes betraying the existence of the man inside the plate. Kormak wondered if the warrior might not be Chosen like Urbaal, a man who had been consumed by the mark of his god. Certainly the bronze warrior took a deadly toll from the orcs, butchering three of their number before he was himself pulled down by Gorgut's axe. The black orc ripped the helmet from his crippled foe, then smashed the champion's face into pulp with his boot. Proudly, Gorgut lifted the trophy above his head, bellowing for all of his minions to see.

The Skulltakers saw as well. They despaired when they saw their champion dead. As one they turned and retreated. This time there was no scattering of berserkers down a dozen hallways. They retreated in a suspiciously orderly fashion, careful to keep contact with the orcs eagerly pursuing them.

'They lead us into a trap!' Pyra cried out.

'They lead us to Slaurith,' Urbaal snarled back.

The warband pressed on, pursuing the Skulltakers as they fought their slow withdrawal. Down a hallway lined by columns of piled skulls, past the stone effigies of horned daemons, the barbarians drew them on. The heat grew, a shimmering haze gathering at the end of the hall. Over the heads of the Skulltakers, they could see a great archway and beyond it a vast chamber that glowed with the very flames of hell.

Their course took them through that archway and into the infernal chamber beyond. It was incredibly vast, its bronze walls chased in brass. The floor was of the familiar black basalt, but the middle of the room was gouged by a wide fissure through which a glowing stream of molten metal bubbled and churned. A narrow bridge curled over the fiery chasm, joining the near side of the chamber with the far. This was marked by a monstrous wall of granite blocks, its surface pitted by barred gates ranging from only slightly larger than a man to the truly gigantic.

At the top of the granite wall, nearly eighty feet above the chamber floor, was a wide balcony bordered in steel. A cluster of figures stood upon the balcony. Most of these were wretched, pallid things, once-men whose arms had been amputated and replaced with dangling clumps of chain. Their faces were locked behind featureless masks of leather, banished along with their sanity.

It was the other figure standing upon the balcony that drew the attention of the invaders. He was a tall man encased in crimson armour adorned with bronze and brass. Steel spikes jutted from his shoulder pads, desiccated skulls impaled upon each. The skull-rune of Khorne was embossed in gold upon his breastplate and beneath it were the gilded skull and ribs of some honoured victim. The warrior wore no helm, only an elaborate circlet fashioned into bronze antlers that towered over his head. The head itself was a ghoulish thing, a withered skull, its grey skin clinging tightly to the bone. Upon the forehead, glowing like an ember, the rune of Khorne had been branded.

This, all knew, was Lord Slaurith.

At Slaurith's gesture, grinding gears turned within the bronze walls. A spiked portcullis dropped from the roof of the archway, sealing the hall behind the invaders, cutting off their only avenue of retreat. Now the fleeing Skulltakers leapt to the attack again, howls of fury once more rising from their throats. The invaders found themselves being pushed back, driven towards the portcullis.

'I warned you!' shrieked Pyra. The sorceress lifted her hands, trying to draw upon her arcane powers. She gasped and clutched her stomach as sickness boiled up inside her.

Upon his hovering disc, Vakaan was similarly stricken. The magus lifted his head, waving his hand before his eyes. Upon the ceiling far overhead, imprinted upon the rock, was a gigantic iron skull-rune of the Blood God. The dark metal gleamed evilly in its setting, the churning fury of the chasm casting weird reflections upon it.

Lord Slaurith's diseased laughter shuddered across the chamber. 'This is the Arena of Fury!' he shouted. 'Here there is only strength and steel, the slayers and the slain. There is no room for sorcerers' tricks here!'

Urbaal glared up at the champion of Khorne. He redoubled his attack against the Skulltakers, his sword glowing with a thousand colours as he carved a bloody path through them. Even Gorgut stared in open amazement at the Chosen's fury. Barbarians dropped before him like flies, the dead and the dying smashing against those who would yet defy Urbaal. The Chosen was upon them before they could push away their own wounded, sending limbs and heads flying into the air with each slash of his blade. Kormak followed close behind Urbaal, protecting his back from the mangled men he left after him. Like a wolf ravening through a herd of elk, Urbaal drove the Skulltakers before him.

At last the carnage was too much even for the slaves of Khorne. They broke into a retreat, scrambling across the bridge, racing for the far side of the arena. Urbaal did not relent, but fell upon the fleeing barbarians with the same fury, pushing the wounded into the molten chasm in his remorseless march upon their comrades. Urbaal stopped in the middle of the bridge, staring up at Slaurith.

'You bring me a present, I see,' Slaurith observed, pointing his clawed gauntlet at the Spear lashed across Urbaal's back. 'Thar'Ignan was a fool to try to hide it from me.'

'Thar'Ignan is dead,' Urbaal growled back. 'Soon you will join him.'

Slaurith's laughter rolled down from the balcony. 'I think not,' he said.

Another gesture from Slaurith and the groan of gears shuddered through the arena once more. This time it came from the far end of the chamber. Several of the gates set into the wall were rising. From each, a black armoured figure emerged. The barbarians who had escaped Urbaal rushed towards the rising gates.

The emerging fighters did not give ground before the retreating Skulltakers. Instead they held up their arms, transforming them into a staggering array of bony bludgeons, axes and claws. They met their cowardly tribesmen with violence, splashing their guts against the wall as they ripped at their vitals. When the carnage was over, they marched through the spreading mire of gore, a dozen strong and each with the corruption of mutation twisting his flesh.

Urbaal stared at the advancing marauders, unmoving, unafraid. No man could cheat the doom laid out for him by the Raven God.

But perhaps he could help some of his enemies share in it.

CHAPTER SIXTEEN

THE FIRST OF Slaurith's marauders met Urbaal upon the bridge, his arm fused into a great club of bone and sinew, a spiked flail clenched in his fist. The marauder lashed out with the flail first, the chains coiling about Urbaal's sword. The mutant pulled the Chosen towards him, bringing his club-arm smashing down.

Urbaal's sword tore free of the chains, slashing through the marauder's arm. The Skulltaker screamed as polluted blood streamed from the trembling stump. Even as he staggered back, Urbaal wrapped his gauntlet in the broken chains of his foe's flail, using it as leverage to swing the cripple around. The marauder's eyes went wide with horror as Urbaal's sword stabbed through his chest. The champion kicked the sagging wreckage off his blade, spilling the dying Skulltaker into the molten chasm.

There was a searing gurgle, a splash of fiery brass, and then the gladiator was gone.

Roaring orcs now swept past Urbaal to crash into the charging marauders. The gladiators met the greenskins with a fury almost equal to their own. Men who lived their lives only to fight and kill, they fought the orcs on their own savage terms. It was slaughter without mercy or quarter, the primitive butchery of monsters and beasts.

Kormak joined the orcs in the bloodletting. He watched as a horn-helmed gladiator, his sword dripping with the entrails of an orc, finished his foe with a decapitating sweep of an arm that had already fused itself into the grisly blade of a serrated axe. The barbarian howled his triumph as the hulking orc crashed at his feet. His eyes locked with those of Kormak, his mutant arm rippling, sprouting spines along its back. Kormak pointed at the other marauder with his axe, then, a war cry on his lips, he charged the gladiator.

Steel ground against steel as Kormak caught the gladiator's sword in the hook of his axe. Kormak's arm, split into the snapping maw of a great claw, closed about the other marauder's axe-like arm, breaking bony spines as it pressed close. The gladiator raged and roared, trying to free his trapped arm, trying to twist his pinned sword from the axe. Kormak snarled back at the mutant, then drove his horns into the man's breast. A ripping turn of his neck and the horns gouged a gaping hole in the gladiator's chest, punctured lungs gleaming from the rent. Still the gladiator struggled to fight back, trying to lower the horns of his helm to mimic Kormak's attack. The Norscan drove his forehead into the gladiator's throat, sending the other man's head snapping back. Kormak's fangs lengthened as they sank into the gladiator's neck. In a spray of gore, he pulled back. The mangled gladiator fell limp in his grasp. Kormak waited until the last pained flicker of life faded from the eyes of his foe, then released the twitching corpse. Almost as soon as it struck the floor, a pair of goblins, a massive barrel of ale tied to each of their backs, descended upon the body, rifling through its armour in search of loot.

Kormak ignored the scavengers, casting his eyes across the arena, searching for new foes to vanquish. The Raven God would feast upon the souls of Khorne's slaves this day.

From the far side of the fiery trench, Pyra watched as the orcs and humans made battle with Slaurith's marauders. She scowled as she watched the goblin shaman Snikkit capering about his warlord, shaking his staff, waving his hands and shrieking to his gods, oblivious that the glowering skull-rune overhead made his conjurations impossible.

The sorceress had chosen a safer course, keeping her warriors near her, using their marksmanship to balance the battle. Sometimes the crossbows would send bolts slamming into gladiators, sometimes it was the back of an orc that felt their sting. Each orc that fell in battle was one less to concern herself with later. Among all that throng, the only one she needed alive was Vakaan and the magus was keeping well away from the fighting, hovering over the battle upon the back of his daemon. The magus knew things about the Spear that had escaped even her research into the relic's past. She could not let that knowledge die on the end of some barbarian's sword. She also made allowance for Urbaal. She couldn't afford for the champion to lose the Spear. At least, not unless it was to the right people.

Pyra smiled as she watched the Chosen rip apart another marauder. The man's prowess in battle was impressive, she grudgingly admitted. But once they were clear of this damnable arena and she could again use her powers, she would discover if Urbaal was as resilient against sorcery as he was against steel.

'Beblieth,' Pyra called out. 'Stay close to the champion. If he falls, take the Spear from him.' She waited a moment for the witch elf to obey, then turned irritably. There was an insolent smile on Beblieth's face. 'Did you hear me?' the sorceress demanded.

'No one listens to a toothless tigress,' Beblieth said.

Pyra's eyes narrowed with anger, her pretty features crinkling into a bestial snarl. Beblieth just smiled back at her, unmoved by the sorceress's rage.

Anger fled from Pyra's eyes as they went wide with shock and pain. Focused upon Beblieth's defiance, she had not seen the dagger that stabbed into her side, crunching between her ribs. She spun about, staring into Naagan's corpse-like face. The disciple pulled the dagger out with a savage twist.

'That burning sensation you feel is the bile of the Lustrian Death Toad,' Naagan told her, his voice as emotionless as a tombstone. 'In a few moments, it will begin to corrode your nervous system.' Naagan smiled as Pyra's numbed legs collapsed beneath her and the staff fell from her hand. He tilted his head to regard the dark elf warriors gawking at their fallen leader. He dismissed them with an imperious – and annoyed – wave of his hand.

'A sorceress without her sorcery was too great an opportunity to pass,' Naagan explained. He prodded Pyra's body with his foot, rolling her across the hot floor. 'Have no fear, we will capture the Spear,' he said and kicked Pyra's bleeding body again. Now the sorceress felt her skin blistering beneath her gown. As she rolled, her frozen eyes saw the molten trench ahead of her.

'I do not know if the Spear will go to Malekith or Uthorin,' Naagan said. His smile curled into an expression of unspeakable sadism. 'But that is a decision the Temple of Khaine would like to make for itself. I am told the toad bile makes its victim insensible to pain. I dearly hope that isn't true.'

With a last kick, Naagan pushed the paralyzed Pyra into the trench. There was no scream from her frozen lips, no flailing of her numbed arms, only an expression of hopeless terror in her eyes as she sank into the burning metal. Naagan breathed deep as a wisp of black smoke rose from the bubbling brass.

'Beblieth,' he said. 'Keep close to the human, like our unfortunate leader said. After the magus has changed the enchantment upon it, be ready to make your move.'

The witch elf nodded, hurrying across the bridge to her assignment. Naagan watched her go, then turned on the still gawking elf warriors. 'No one told you to stop shooting,' the disciple warned. The warriors hastily turned back to their duty, sending an enthusiastic salvo across the burning fissure.

LORD SLAURITH'S MUMMIFIED face twisted into an angry leer. The Chaos warlord glared down into the glowing eyes of Urbaal. Angrily, Slaurith swept his clawed gauntlet down in a chopping motion. Once again, hidden gears groaned and shrieked. This time only a single gate set into the wall rose; the largest of the portals, easily five times the height of a man. Even with such a massive opening, the thing that emerged into the arena was forced to crawl from the tunnel.

As it stood, silence descended upon the arena, even the orcs awed by the enormity of this new foe. Fifty-feet tall, the bloodgiant towered over the battlers. It was more than a grossly oversized human, though there was a gruesome resemblance. Great horns sprouted from the brow of the giant's manlike face, where it should have had feet there were immense hooves. One arm, for all its size, looked human. The other was a great black claw, the skin scaly and peeling. The giant wore a great belt about its middle, from which hung cages and baskets, little rotting things flopping grotesquely inside each. A pair of huge Skulltakers with bulging muscles gripped chains fastened to the collar about the bloodgiant's neck, leading the enormous brute into the arena.

The giant's nostrils flared as it smelled the blood of the dead. Its fanged face split into an idiot leer of amusement. It tugged at one of the chains about its neck, sending one of its keepers flying. The other handler released his chain before he could receive the same treatment. Drool splashed down from the giant's immense fangs as it studied the awestruck ants staring up at it.

'Kill them!' Slaurith snarled at the dull-witted brute. The giant swung about, his face level with the warlord's balcony. 'Kill them all!'

The bloodgiant turned away. The brute studied the arena floor, then threw back its head in a savage bellow of excitement. Mammoth arms pounded against its chest, the drumbeat of its fists making the arena walls echo with thunder.

Then it was moving. A hoof the size of a Kurgan hut came pounding down, an orc exploding beneath the impact. The giant reached down with its hand, scooping a Skulltaker gladiator from the floor, squeezing the screaming man in its fist until the dripping wreckage slid from its grip like crumpled tin. The giant's claw slashed down, hurling another orc into the far wall of the arena, the pulped corpse sticking obscenely to its own impact crater.

Terror reigned. Orcs scrambled about, jabbering excitedly to each other, jostling and pushing as they struggled to reach the bridge. Surviving gladiators clawed at the now-closed gates, pleading to be let back in. Vakaan's disc whirled away, flying across the arena and well away from the giant's reach. Goblins scrambled everywhere, shoving and punching each other in their mad race to find refuge from the gigantic brute.

Urbaal swung about, staring up at the bloodgiant. The Chosen closed his eyes, calling upon the power of his god. The sword in his hand suddenly erupted with a blinding glow, a devil's tooth in his fist. Kormak could feel the power of Tzeentch flowing through the blade, defying the wards and barriers of the arena. The marauder checked his own flight, turning from the bridge to rejoin Urbaal. There was no shame dying with courage.

The bloodgiant was oblivious to Urbaal's challenge, its dull brain struggling to decide which of the screaming, fleeing shapes to stomp next. But if the giant was oblivious, its handlers were not. The hulking Skulltakers rushed Urbaal from each side. The Chosen did not see them, focused upon his titanic foe. Kormak shouted a warning, rushed to protect Urbaal from the slinking attackers. He closed upon the rightmost of the handlers, chopping at him with his axe. The Skulltaker caught the blade with his sword and soon the two men were locked into a struggle of strength and fury, each seeking to break loose first and drive his steel into the other.

The other Skulltaker cracked the broken strip of chain in his hand at Urbaal. The chain, strong enough to hold a giant, coiled about Urbaal's sword. The links began to melt as the divine energies of the blade began to corrode it, but it stayed whole long enough for the barbarian's purpose. With a sudden tug, he ripped the sword from Urbaal's grasp, sending it skittering across the arena. It landed, teetering upon the edge of the moat. Urbaal turned to race after it, but even as he began his sprint, he was dashed to the floor as the Skulltaker tackled him. The handler smashed his spiked fists into the metal face of Urbaal's helm, as though trying to punch his way to the head within.

Above the fray, the bloodgiant howled its delight. For a moment, it watched its handlers fight, then it started to raise its hoof, staring maliciously at Urbaal and his adversary. The giant's foot didn't come smashing down, however. At that instant, a ragged barrage of bolts slammed into its skin. The giant brushed its hand against the injury, sniffing in confusion at the blood staining its finger. Then the repeating crossbows sent another volley into their huge target. Now the giant seemed to appreciate the pain. It glowered across the arena, glaring at the dark elves. Another barrage peppered its chest. Across such distance, the bolts were able to do little more than break the skin, but they had achieved their main goal. They had distracted the bloodgiant.

The giant roared, stomping across the arena. It did not use the bridge, its stride wide enough for it to step across the moat of boiling brass. The dark elves fired a last desperate volley. At close range now, the bolts punched deep into the giant's flesh. As pain flashed through the giant, distraction turned to rage.

The dark elves were scattering now, ignoring Naagan's shouts for them to fire again. The giant's claw slammed down, pulverizing two of the armoured elves. The giant lifted its dripping limb and licked the mash of shredded flesh and bone from its scaly skin. Its face split in a vengeful grin and it lumbered after Naagan and the survivors. The disciple pushed one of the warriors towards the giant, then joined the others as they fled to the portcullis. The abandoned dark elf jabbed at the giant with his spear. The brute caught hold of the weapon with his hand, snarling as the sharp point cut his palm. The giant lifted spear and elf into the air, then began to shake its hand from side to side. The elf screamed, tightening his grip on the spear. It was a desperate effort, but one the elf was doomed to lose. The giant's blood flowing down the shaft made it impossible for his armoured hands to hold. Wailing, the elf was thrown, crashing against the roof of the ceiling, then hurtling back to the floor in a tangle of broken bones.

Arrows now whistled at the giant. Desperate, unable to squirm through the bars of the portcullis with their burdens of loot, the goblins turned to fight. They had the terrified tenacity of cornered rats, and the bloodgiant presented a target so immense even their slovenly aim could not fail to hit. Poison sizzled into the giant's veins as Zagbob added his arrows to the barrage, but the goblin's venom was only a drop in the ocean. It would take quarts of poison to have any impact on the brute's system.

The bloodgiant snarled again, thundering towards the portcullis. Goblins, elves and orcs scattered as it approached, only one tiny figure holding fast. Snikkit lifted his staff, shouting at the top of his shrill voice. The shaman called down all the vengeance of Gork and Mork upon the bloodgiant, spittle flying from his fangs.

The giant paused, seeming to listen to the shaman's malediction. Then it brought its hoof smashing down, exploding the goblin's body in a spray of greasy green blood.

'Oh, that's done it!' Gorgut roared. The black orc checked his own retreat and grabbed hold of the closest warrior. 'Look what that thing done! Now we got to find a new shaman!'

Dregruk tried to pull free of his chief's grip.

'Come on!' Gorgut snarled. 'We're going to settle for that git!' Half pulling, half dragging Dergruk, the black orc stomped back towards the giant, anger over-riding common sense.

Before the orcs could reach the giant, the brute was moving again. A lone goblin, half-through the bars of the portcullis, had drawn the giant's attention. The huge hand came down, closing about the goblin's legs. With a wrenching tug, the giant tried to pull the goblin free. Instead, both the goblin and the barrel of ale on his back were ripped apart. The bloodgiant stared dumbly at the dripping legs, then its nostrils flared wildly. A huge tongue pushed between the giant's tusks and licked the gory wreckage. The giant grinned as the sting of ale struck its taste buds.

Enemies, arrows and elves were forgotten. The giant swung away from the portcullis, its eager eyes now hunting for more goblins. Its dull brain now associated the scrawny greenskins with ale. There was only one thing that could excite the giant more than battle and carnage, something all the psychotic madness of the Blood God could not drive from it. The giant wanted drink.

A goblin shrieked as the giant's hand closed about it, wresting it from the floor. The brute held the shrieking goblin over its mouth and squeezed its captive as though it were a wineskin. The keg on the goblin's back shattered, its contents mixing with the blood gushing into the giant's mouth. Laughing, the giant tossed the squished goblin away, swinging its head from side to side in search of more drink.

'Get back here you craven scum!' Gorgut raged. The black orc swung his axe at the bloodgiant just as the brute lumbered off to seize another goblin.

'Careful, boss,' Dregruk warned. 'You might catch up with him!'

Gorgut gave his underling a black look, then ran after the giant.

URBAAL GRIPPED THE horns of his enemy's helm and twisted, snapping the Skulltaker's neck. The barbarian slumped across the Chosen. Urbaal rolled the corpse aside. He stared up at the balcony and the sinister figure of Lord Slaurith, then turned to see where the giant was. The huge brute was across the fissure stuffing a goblin into its mouth, its teeth grinding greenskin and ale barrel into mush. Urbaal's eyes narrowed. Much closer at hand was his sword, the flames of Tzeentch still rippling about it. The Chosen glared back at Slaurith and made a dash for his sword.

Slaurith saw Urbaal racing to recover his sword. The Chaos warlord's eyes narrowed with hate. 'Send in my champions!' he snarled, stabbing a claw in the direction of the gates. 'Send in Chorek!'

The hidden gears groaned, lifting a half-dozen of the rusty gates. Black-armoured warriors emerged from the darkened tunnels, their eyes glowing with the madness of Khorne. They fingered their axes and clubs, turning towards Urbaal. From the centre gate, a huge beast emerged, a thing of bronze and brass. It was as much ox as it was wolf, as much panther as it was boar. It was not a living thing, but a daemon wrapped in a metal shell with molten steel for blood and raw hate for a brain.

Upon the juggernaut's back rode a monstrous warrior. Clad in bronze armour adorned with the skulls of his victims, his face lost behind the mask of his horned helm, the warrior hefted his bone-handled sword, pointing its butcher's blade at Urbaal. The skull-rune set into the forehead of Chorek's helm glowed as the champion made his silent challenge.

The other champions stood back as Chorek walked his juggernaut towards Urbaal, none of them willing to interfere in this contest between the Chosen of Khorne and the Chosen of Tzeentch.

The juggernaut pawed the bloody flagstones, its bronze paws churning the rock like mud. Chorek drove his boots into the daemon's flanks and the metal monster charged through the arena, hurtling towards Urbaal in an unstoppable avalanche of daemonic fury.

Urbaal dove from its path, snatching the discarded weapon of a gladiator from the floor. He glared at the Khorne champion, now between himself and his proper weapon. Urbaal struck at Chorek with the flail he had scavenged. The steel chains clattered against the mounted warrior's shield, an immense rectangle of bronze and brass. Chorek laughed behind his helm and drove his sword at Urbaal. He blocked the blow, but was thrown back by the force behind it. Chorek laughed again and spurred his daemon after the staggered Urbaal.

Suddenly Chorek's laughter fell silent. He looked up in alarm as the bloodgiant staggered back across the molten trench. The drunken giant's gait was sloppy, its hoof nearly slipping into the moat as it lumbered across the span. The brute swung its bleary gaze about the arena, searching for more goblins. It grinned stupidly and reached down for one of Slaurith's champions. The gladiator did not cringe before the giant's sloppy grab, but struck out, his glaive slashing through one of the immense fingers. The giant howled in pain, then brought its wounded hand slamming down, smashing the gladiator beneath its palm.

Urbaal seized the distraction offered by the bloodgiant's antics. The Chosen flung his flail into the face of Chorek, then threw himself in a long dive beneath the very belly of the juggernaut. Man and daemon were surprised by the boldness of Urbaal. Chorek wasted precious moments regathering his wits. Angrily he spurred the juggernaut about, roaring for the other champions to stop Urbaal from recovering his sword.

Poisoned steel sprouted from the eye socket of the juggernaut. The venom was incapable of harming the daemon, even the steel did no damage that the creature could not quickly heal. But the juggernaut was blinded just the same while the dagger was embedded in its bronze eye socket, preventing it from regenerating. The daemon snorted its anger, twisting its head and trying to scrape the obstruction free. Chorek glared at this new attacker, lifting his shield as Beblieth hurled a second dagger. The weapon glanced off the blocking armour. Chorek snarled at the witch elf.

Before the champion of Khorne could act, however, he felt his steed twisting beneath him. Already unbalanced by its efforts to remove the dagger from its eye, the juggernaut was rolling over, forced to turn by the man who had seized its armoured neck. Kormak turned the daemon as if it were some great steer. Every vein bulged in the marauder's body, his mutant claw sizzling as the juggernaut's molten blood spurted from where he gripped it. The effort was superhuman, only the juggernaut's already compromised position making it possible. Chorek spun in the saddle, trying to bring his sword down on the horned marauder. The shifting of his weight was the final straw. The juggernaut squealed and fell, smashing onto its side.

Kormak stared at Beblieth. The witch elf simply smiled and pointed. The marauder quickly followed her gesture. If his toppling of the juggernaut had been impossible, Chorek's feat was even more so. The champion was pushing the squealing, thrashing bulk off him, shoving it aside with a bone-jarring effort. With a final shove that actually caused the juggernaut to slide a foot or better over the flagstones, Chorek freed himself from the daemon's pinning

weight. He lifted his monstrous sword, all thoughts
of Urbaal vanquished from his mind.

Kormak shifted the weight of his axe in his hand,
watching as Chorek limped towards him. The Chosen's leg had been all but flattened by the juggernaut.
Kormak smiled as he saw the blood dripping down
Chorek's mangled limb, then frowned as he felt the
wound in his side flowing down his flank. Even with
Chorek's wound it was already an uneven contest.
Kormak only had to hope that the injury the giant's
handler had given him before he had died would not
tip the balance even further in the champion's
favour.

URBAAL DROVE HIS shoulder into the gladiator standing over his sword, pitching the shrieking warrior
into the molten brass. The Chosen had no time to
watch his foe die. His gauntlet closed about the heft
of his sword. He rolled along the floor, ending the
move in a defending crouch. The axe of a second
gladiator came smashing down, blocked by Urbaal's
lifted steel. The Skulltaker howled with rage, bringing
the axe smashing down again, trying to batter
Urbaal's defence. Urbaal strained as axe met sword.
Inch by inch, he forced himself back onto his feet,
forced the Skulltaker to give ground before him. Now
another pair of champions were rushing for him,
eager to join the first and make an easy kill.

The Chosen of Tzeentch brought his knee smashing into the gladiator's groin, the blow lifting his
enemy's feet. The Skulltaker stumbled back. Urbaal
did not give him a chance to recover. Coruscating

energy slashed through the barbarian's neck, sending his head leaping into the air. For a moment the decapitated body groped blindly before it, then it accepted death and crashed onto its side. Urbaal braced himself for the attack of the other champions.

Skulltakers roared their fury as they charged Urbaal, their rage seemingly magnified by their helms. One of the barbarians suddenly staggered, his leg cut from under him. He smashed into the floor, twisting about to grip the bleeding ruin of his knee. Even as he did so, another long elven dagger stabbed at him, driven through the narrow slit of his visor to impale his brain.

Beblieth smiled and licked the man's blood from the blade. Confronted on both sides, the other champion hesitated, his eyes turning from the sinister witch elf to Urbaal, deciding which enemy would attack first.

Urbaal nodded a salute to Beblieth. The witch elf's reply was a mocking laugh. 'I don't want anything happening to the Spear. You were just in the way.'

Chosen and witch elf began to circle the embattled gladiator. The Skulltaker glared defiantly at them. Waiting for the attack to come. He was not ready when both of his enemies abruptly broke away, scrambling back as quickly as they could. Instinctively, the gladiator sprang after his retreating enemies. He did not take more than two steps before the giant's hoof came smashing down, pulverizing him.

Dust was still rising from the Skulltaker's destruction when Urbaal leapt at the giant. His sword lashed out like a tongue of flame, rippling with the power of the Changer. It bit into the hard bone of the giant's ankle, sheering through it like a woodaxe through a sapling.

The bloodgiant bellowed in agony and shock. The brute stumbled, its drunken balance destroyed completely by Urbaal's crippling blow. The giant toppled, arms flailing desperately. It did not fall far, smashing against the edge of Slaurith's balcony. Several of the Chaos lord's monstrous entourage were crushed beneath the giant's horned skull.

The giant shuddered, writhing against the wall, its head spitted upon dozens of the balcony's steel spikes. Slowly, life drained from the ghastly bulk.

'You might have warned me you were going to do that,' Beblieth snarled at Urbaal.

The Chosen shrugged. 'No different than felling timber,' he said. 'And Slaurith didn't see fit to provide stairs.'

The witch elf didn't understand Urbaal's meaning until she saw the warrior running towards the fallen giant, gouging handholds in the brute's flesh, climbing it like a monstrous mountain. Beblieth shook her head and hurried after what she now realised was a madman.

Urbaal reached the balcony just as Lord Slaurith was recovering from the giant's brutal impact. The Chaos lord's withered face split into an expression of unspeakable malignance. He pointed his armoured talon at Urbaal. 'Kill this maggot,' he snapped. The surviving flayed ones rushed at Urbaal in a mass of wailing, flailing horror, the hooks and chains that had replaced their arms flopping hideously against their sides.

Before they could close upon him, Beblieth sprang from the head of the giant, putting herself between Urbaal and the wretched creatures. Her daggers ripped and slashed without mercy, cutting a crimson swathe through the tortured men. Urbaal strode through the carnage, his eyes locked upon Slaurith.

Lord Slaurith took several steps back, giving ground before the advancing Urbaal. The Chaos lord stopped when he reached a short throne of black marble. Shackled at its foot was the battered body of a high elf, white rags still clinging to the archmage's limbs. Slaurith gave his abused captive no notice, but reached over him to retrieve a huge double-handed sword from the stand behind his throne.

'Who are you?' Slaurith hissed as he turned back to face Urbaal.

'I do not remember,' Urbaal growled back. 'I only know that we knew each other before the gods remade us into their image.'

Lord Slaurith nodded. 'Your skull will end upon one of these spikes,' he said, gesturing to the gruesome trophies spitted upon his shoulderpads. 'You should feel honoured.'

'I will,' Urbaal snarled back, 'when I cut yours from its neck.'

CHAPTER SEVENTEEN

KORMAK'S AXE SHATTERED as Chorek's sword smashed into it, peppering the marauder's face with broken steel. The Norscan staggered, then twisted his body to avoid the champion's riposte. His mutant arm, fused into the semblance of a crustacean claw, clicked shut about Chorek's arm, trapping the monstrous sword as it came chopping down at his head. Chorek struggled to free his blade. Kormak rewarded his efforts by smashing the broken grip of his axe into the barbarian's helm.

It was an effort both brutal and desperate. Kormak could feel Chorek's greater strength beginning to prevail, could feel his muscles burning under the strain of keeping the immense sword from slashing down. As he had feared, even crippled, Chorek was proving too strong to beat down. Kormak's already sinking

C. L. Werner

hopes were dashed even further when he saw something moving behind the champion. The juggernaut was lurching back to its feet, the blinding dagger now torn free from its eye. The daemon huffed angrily, snapping its bronze jaws.

Before the juggernaut could charge Kormak and relieve its master, unexpected help came to the marauder's aid. Roaring like daemons themselves, Gorgut and his remaining warriors descended upon the juggernaut, their axes clattering against its bronze skin. The daemon turned about to confront the greenskins. As it did so, a black-feathered arrow sprouted from the socket of its eye. Zagbob cackled maliciously, pointing his scrawny finger at the daemon. Three scaly monstrosities bounded through the ranks of the orcs to chomp at the daemon's armoured body.

All of this Kormak took in with a single glance over Chorek's shoulder, then he was pressed back by the snarling champion. The marauder's feet slid along the flagstones as Chorek drove him back. He felt the heat of the moat behind him, could smell the sting of boiling brass in his nose. A few more steps and Chorek would push him into the fiery slag.

Kormak yelled his desperation and brought his boot smashing into Chorek's flattened leg. The champion buckled under the impact. Kormak swung the reeling barbarian about by his trapped arm, driving him towards the molten moat. Chorek locked his other hand about one of Kormak's horns, pulling the marauder down with him.

The two foes smashed down against the heated flagstones, their faces only inches from the bubbling brass. Chorek tried to wrestle Kormak underneath him, to pin the Norscan with his armoured weight. Kormak concentrated his efforts on something much more simple. He forced Chorek's sword arm into the moat.

Chorek screamed as the boiling metal devoured his sword and the hand that gripped it. Kormak rolled the stunned champion, copying Chorek's efforts to get above his foe. Chorek ended the roll face-down beneath the Norscan. Kormak's hands locked around the back of the champion's bronze helm.

Kormak's war cry echoed across the arena as he exerted every muscle in his body to push Chorek's head down into the bubbling brass. There was not time for the champion to even shriek before the burning metal was melting his helm and vaporizing the man within. Kormak spat on the twitching corpse, raising himself from the gruesome body and the desperate struggle that had marked the passing of Chorek.

He watched the orcs making their furious attack on the juggernaut, then turned to rummage among the dead for a new weapon.

NAAGAN WATCHED THE fall of the bloodgiant with a mixture of anxiety and relief. Relief because the rampaging brute was finished, anxiety because it drove home to the disciple the lethal prowess of Urbaal. Deceit would be needed to overcome the Chosen, he would not trust even Beblieth's murderous talents in a straight fight with the human. He scowled as he looked at the last sorry remnants of Inhin's warriors. The three elves looked as frightened as goblins, ready to bolt at the first opportunity. He could expect little help from that quarter.

'If you are wondering how to steal the Spear, I can help you.'

Naagan swung around, his hand closed about his dagger. He was surprised to see the tattooed zealot Tolkku standing there, even more surprised to hear elvish words on the tongue of an animal.

Tolkku grinned as he noticed the disciple's astonishment. He reached into his bag, removing a morbidly stained skull that was too angular and lean to be that of a man. 'My tribe entertained an exile of your land. I spent many hours… conversing… with her before she left us. That is how I know your tongue. That is why I was able to listen to you when the sorceress had her… accident.'

'Why should you help me?' Naagan demanded. 'Why would you betray your own kind?'

Tolkku's smile twisted into a grimace. 'The triumph of Urbaal will not exalt the fortunes of Tolkku,' he said. 'And there are personal reasons I want to see him fail.'

'He is a formidable enemy,' Naagan pointed out.

Tolkku laughed. 'Not for me,' he said. 'I have already prepared the spell that will end his pretensions to glory. All I need is the opportunity.'

'Do not think you will gain that opportunity with the bodies of my warriors,' Naagan said, his voice thin and full of menace.

'I will attend to Urbaal. I only need you to deal with Vakaan and the orcs,' Tolkku chuckled. 'It will be easy for me to deal with Urbaal.'

'And you want nothing for helping us?' Naagan asked, his eyes filled with suspicion.

'One thing,' Tolkku answered, holding up the elf skull. 'When it is all over, I want the head of the Norscan. It will complete my collection.'

URBAAL'S SWORD SHUDDERED in his hand as Slaurith's steel crashed against it. The face of the Chaos lord split in an ugly leer. Slaurith slashed at the Chosen a second time, the impact ringing off the clashing blades. A third strike and Urbaal was thrown back, his upper arm torn and bleeding, bits of shattered armour clattering about his feet.

'We have been reshaped by the gods,' Slaurith hissed. 'But the one I chose is stronger.'

Urbaal tightened his grip upon his blade, ignoring the blood streaming from his arm. The skull-faced helm of the Chosen glared into the withered flesh of Slaurith. 'Tell that to him when I cut you down.'

Slaurith's face twisted into a bestial snarl. The Chaos lord lunged at Urbaal, slashing at him with his giant sword in a frenzied blur of murderous metal. Urbaal's shining blade intercepted each blow, dancing about the Chosen's body to form a blinding curtain of steel. The crash of sword against sword rattled through both men's bodies as they strained to batter aside the blocking blade of the other.

A growl of savagery rasped through Slaurith's desiccated lips as his sword battered aside that of

Urbaal. The Chosen ducked beneath the hurtling steel, dodging aside as Slaurith's sword gouged a scar across the bronze wall. The Chaos lord turned as he realised his mistake, spinning to bring the heavy sword around before Urbaal could strike his unprotected back. By a hair's breath, Slaurith's blade caught the edge of Urbaal's steel.

Slaurith was thrown down by the impact, tossed to the floor as though he had been kicked by a horse. The grey skin of his face pulled back into an inhuman mask of rage. Before Urbaal could close upon him, Slaurith lunged up from the floor, crashing against Urbaal, driving the Chosen against the flagstones.

Urbaal felt Slaurith's corpse-breath against him as the Chaos lord pressed the edge of the huge sword against his neck, trying to strangle his enemy. Urbaal growled back at Slaurith, bringing his legs underneath the Chaos lord, flinging him back with a powerful thrust.

Urbaal coughed as he forced air down his savaged throat, bracing himself as Slaurith came at him again. An upward shift of his sword caught Slaurith's descending blade before it could split the Chosen's skull. Urbaal threw his whole body behind the parry, pushing Slaurith back as he regained his feet.

The Chaos lord staggered back, upsetting his throne and the sword stand behind it. Angrily he kicked the broken stand at the advancing Urbaal, trying to trip his enemy. Urbaal brought his sword slashing down, shattering the stand into bony splinters.

It was the distraction Slaurith had counted upon. A vengeful laugh hissing from his withered mouth, the Chaos lord lunged at Urbaal, the double-handed sword smashing down. Urbaal twisted his body beneath the heavy blade, slamming his helm into Slaurith's chest, forcing him back. Slaurith brought the spiked pommel of his sword crashing into Urbaal's head, trying to smash him into the floor. Urbaal's body slumped beneath the blow, slamming hard into the flagstones.

Lord Slaurith smiled malignantly and raised his heavy sword above his head, poised to bring it down in a final, butchering blow against his prone enemy. The look of triumph wilted on the mummified face as his stunned foe suddenly twisted beneath him. Urbaal's glowing blade slammed into Slaurith's gut, biting through the thick bronze plate to skewer the withered organs within.

Urbaal kicked the legs out from under his shocked enemy, spilling him to the floor. He sneered at Slaurith and wrenched his sword free from the Chaos lord's belly. 'Your god may be stronger,' Urbaal told Slaurith, 'but mine doesn't fight fair.'

Slaurith snarled, trying to raise himself to his feet. Urbaal slammed his boot against the side of the Chaos lord's head, smashing him to the floor.

A great rumbling shook the Arena of Fury, a screeching wail like the howls of the damned rippled through the blood-stink of the cavern. As the quaking became more intense, the wailing was drowned out by a deep, deafening roar. The roar raged across the Arena, venting its spectral fury against the walls.

Stones slammed to the floor of the cavern or sizzled in the molten trench. With a great groan, the symbol of the Blood God shattered, raining from the ceiling in a stream of metal slivers. The breaking of the symbol seemed to cause the blood-stink to dissipate and the phantom roar to fade into nothingness.

Urbaal's sword blazed with fire as the malign influence of Khorne was broken and the magic of the Changer again held sway. He stared grimly into Slaurith's cadaverous features. 'It seems the Blood God has abandoned you. Few gods have the stomach to tolerate a weakling.' The Chosen lifted his sword, poised to drive it into the fallen warlord's face.

'Don't kill him!' Vakaan's voice shrieked. The magus on his daemonic disc came diving from the height of the arena to hover above the balcony. The sorcerer's staff was raised, as though to bring it cracking against Urbaal's head.

'I have not forgotten,' Urbaal growled. He gave the groaning Slaurith another kick of his boot. 'But whatever magic you think to work, it had best be quick.'

Vakaan nodded in understanding. A stamp of his boot and the disc lowered, hovering only a few inches from the floor. The magus looked over at the chained figure of Dolchir the archmage. 'I will need him also.'

Beblieth came forward, wiping the blood of the flayed ones from her face. She smirked as she heard the words of the magus. The witch elf stalked towards the archmage, her dagger raised.

'Alive,' Vakaan warned her.

A flicker of disappointment passed across Bebli-eth's features. She bent down over Dolchir, pressing the point of her dagger between the links of his chains. 'Whatever the human does to you, asur, know I would have done worse,' she hissed in the high elf's ear.

A deft twist of her wrist snapped the bronze chain. She lifted the battered Dolchir to his feet. The high elf had suffered greatly at the hands and paws of the Khorne worshippers. Ugly cuts marked his face, deep trenches gouged into cheeks and forehead in crude approximation of the skull-rune. The once pristine robes of the archmage were now little more than dirty grey rags, clumps of dried blood caked into the hem. His arm, snapped and crooked, was cradled against his breast. Beblieth seized the archmage by his broken limb, wrenching it straight with a sadistic tug. Dolchir's hollow eyes gleamed with pain, a trem-ble of suffering that pulled at his gashed face. The witch elf scowled at the high elf's effort to retain his dignity then shoved him towards Vakaan. The arch-mage stumbled and sprawled just beyond the snapping fangs of the disc's underbelly.

Vakaan pointed at Urbaal, gesturing for the Spear. The Chosen stared at the magus, a last flicker of doubt in his eyes, then unslung the Spear from his back. A last moment of hesitation, and the Spear was in Vakaan's hands. If the magus noticed Urbaal's hand fall back to the hilt of his sword, he gave no sign.

The magus set down his staff and tightened his grip on the Spear of Myrmidia. His expression darkened

as he felt its aura of purity, its hostility to the powers
he served and invoked. The membranes over his eyes
slid closed. Vakaan's fingers tapped against the head
of the Spear, words slithering from his lips in a subdued whisper. Nine times he tapped his fingers
against the head of the Spear, then, with abrupt suddenness, he shifted his grip on the weapon.

'The blood of innocence!' Vakaan crowed and
drove the point of the Spear into the heart of Dolchir.
The archmage shrieked as his body was pierced. For
an instant he writhed upon the Spear, then he was
still, blood spreading across his breast. Vakaan nodded his head, studying the morbid pattern of the
seeping gore.

Vakaan stamped his boot. The disc silently floated
away from Dolchir's body. Now the magus hovered
above the wounded figure of Lord Slaurith. The
Chaos lord snarled at him, groping futilely for his
sword. Urbaal's boot smashed down upon his hand,
pinning it in place.

Again, Vakaan tapped the head of the Spear, elf
blood staining his fingers with each touch. Again, the
whispered incantation, an invocation to a power
even the aura of the arena could not subdue.

'The blood of corruption!' Vakaan shrieked, driving
the Spear into Slaurith's breast. The Chaos lord
screamed, trying to pull himself up the impaling
Spear in a last effort to spill the blood of an enemy.
It was an effort beyond his vanquished strength. A
shudder, then Slaurith crashed back to the floor.
Urbaal gave the corpse a final kick to the side of its
withered head, breaking its neck.

Vakaan did not watch Urbaal vent his anger upon the corpse. The magus had eyes only for the Spear in his hand, watching as its once vibrant glow, its golden light, darkened and collapsed. The blood of the twin sacrifices had been enough to allow a different power to invest the relic. All magic, ultimately, was Chaos. Only the slightest nudge was needed to allow it to be reclaimed by the Dark Gods, to become an instrument of the Changer.

What had been the Spear of Myrmidia now burned with a black fire as Vakaan raised it over his head. Shapes and shadows rippled about it, faces that moaned with voices heard by something more primal than simple hearing. The stench of evil billowed from the thing, bringing with it a chill that sank through the flesh to claw at the very bones of all who felt it. Vakaan's daemon steed gave utterance to a plaintive wail, a sound at once fearful and loathsomely eager.

'Now,' Vakaan said, 'we are ready to face the Portal of Rage and cast aside the chains that bind Kakra the Timeless and the winds of magic.'

THE SURVIVORS OF the Arena of Fury gathered upon Lord Slaurith's balcony. The battle had taken its toll in blood. Of the elves, only Naagan, Beblieth and three of their warriors remained. Zagbob was the only goblin to escape from the drunken rampage of the bloodgiant, only two squigs remaining from the hunter's pack. After bringing down the juggernaut, Gorgut only had four orcs and his lieutenant Dregruk left. The warriors of the Raven Host had fared better in comparison. Four had entered Slau-rith's trap. Four would leave it.

While Naagan and Tolkku tended the wounded, Vakaan and Urbaal made their plans.

'I say it is too dangerous to attempt,' Vakaan warned the Chosen. 'The Blood God despises sorcery in all its forms. Do not think that this arena will be the only place my magic might fail us.'

Urbaal watched as Tolkku ministered to him, keeping his eyes fixed on the zealot even as he spoke to Vakaan. 'We cannot hope to prevail climbing the Bastion Stair. We will be challenged at each step, and by more than mortal enemies. The Blood God's daemons will be eager for our skulls to set before the Skull Throne.'

'Then we must turn back,' Vakaan said. 'We can bring the Spear to Tchar'zanek. He can give us more warriors so we can try again.'

The Chosen shook his head. 'We might never find the Stair again,' he said. 'There is always that chance. No mortal can predict the will of the Wastes. Someplace becomes noplace at the whim of the gods.' Urbaal shifted his gaze, watching the dark elves as they repaired their armour and inspected their weapons. 'Besides, I think it would be unsafe to turn back. There are some here who are waiting for just such a chance. Remember Tchar'zanek's warning. Do not mistake the intentions of allies as being your own.'

'But to try such a thing, here, on the very doorstep of the Blood God's throne,' Vakaan muttered.

'You have worked such magic before,' Urbaal stated. The Chosen shrugged his shoulders. 'And there is no other way. If we are not to fail, we must reach the Portal of Rage.'

Vakaan trembled at the prospect. 'I dare not,' he gasped. 'The Portal opens upon the Realm of Chaos itself. We would be hurled into eternity, cast into the Winds of Chaos, doomed things neither dead or alive. I dare not!'

Tolkku pulled away from Urbaal as he heard Vakaan's protest. The zealot's eyes were wide with alarm. He stared in open-mouthed horror at the Chosen.

'Yes, Kurgan,' Urbaal told him. 'I intend to use magic to breech the Blood God's inner sanctum.'

'I dare not open a gate to the Portal of Rage!' Vakaan repeated.

'Then open a gate as near to it as you do dare, sorcerer!' Urbaal snapped.

The magus recoiled from the violence in the Chosen's growl. He tried to hold Urbaal's smouldering stare, but found himself unable to match the warrior's determination. Subdued, Vakaan reluctantly nodded his head.

'The Portal of Rage sits beyond the Fortress of Brass,' Vakaan said. 'Upon the very peak of the Bastion Stair. Even with the power of the Spear to draw upon it is too far for my sorcery. Not without a proper sacrifice.'

Urbaal waved his gauntlet in the direction of Gorgut. 'Ask him for the loan of one of his orcs,' Urbaal told Vakaan.

'I'm sure if you are persuasive, he will be agreeable.'

CHAPTER EIGHTEEN

VAKAAN'S SORCEROUS GATEWAY was a pulsating, whirling mass of purple cloud and black lightning, a tear through the substance of space and time. Through the churning mist could be seen the Arena of Fury and the dead they had left behind.

Their new surroundings were gigantic in proportion, immense walls of shining brass that rose about them in dizzying angles, tilting crazily into one another, then impossibly bending back. It was an architecture of insanity, the madness of the Blood God cast into walls of metal. The floor beneath their feet was polished bone, shifting and creaking beneath their tread. No braziers of smouldering oil, no smoky torches or macabre chandeliers, the brass corridors were illuminated by a scarlet light that seemed to emanate from nowhere and everywhere. Great columns of bronze rose from the floor to support the distant ruby-tiled ceiling, and upon each column a giant skull leered down at them, the rune of Khorne stamped upon their foreheads. Huge stakes surrounded the columns, impaled upon the spike of each was a smaller skull, a thing that had once been living unlike the brass gargoyles of the columns.

More than the morbid surroundings, the aura of the place impressed itself upon the small party of intruders. It was an air of brooding hostility, the spectral hate of an insane god. Its ghostly presence pawed at them, oozing through their flesh to defile the soul within.

Vakaan shared a look with Urbaal. The Chosen gave him a slight nod. Vakaan's membranes slid shut over his eyes. Gesturing with his staff, he banished the gate. The clouds collapsed in upon themselves until with a thunderous crack, the gate was gone.

'Bravo, barbarian,' Naagan congratulated the magus. The elf's voice was thin as a knife. 'Whatever infests these halls knows we are here now.'

Vakaan shook his head and glowered at the disciple of Khaine. 'The daemons of this place knew we were here the moment I opened the gate,' he corrected the dark elf.

'Then why were they not waiting for us?' Tolkku asked. The zealot's eyes were wide with fear, constantly shifting to the columns and the lurking daemons that might be hiding within their shadows.

'They *are* here,' Vakaan told the Kurgan. 'Do not think they are not watching us.'

Kormak studied one of the stakes, his hand brushing against the skull impaled upon it. He wondered who the dead man had been, if he had died as a warrior or been butchered as a sacrifice. Hero or carrion, his doom had been the same. Another trophy to adorn the Blood God's halls.

'Why have they not attacked us?' Kormak wondered.

Vakaan bowed his head in thought at the question. Even he did not like the only answer that came to his mind. 'Perhaps they have been warned away,' he said, his voice a shallow whisper. 'Perhaps something else has already claimed us for its own.'

Naagan stared hard at the magus, disliking the sorcerer's enigmatic words. He glanced at Beblieth, then at Tolkku. If they were going to act, it would be best to do so before Vakaan's mysterious monster presented itself.

'Too much talk!' snarled Gorgut, slapping the head of his axe into the flat of his hand. The black orc spat onto the floor, watching with keen interest as the spittle vanished down between the slender gaps. 'Wherez dis port... door yer lotz's lookin' fer?' Gorgut demanded.

Vakaan gestured with his hand towards a broad flight of brass steps that climbed upwards toward a spike-fringed archway. The black orc nodded his head and grunted at his fellows. Obediently, the other orcs started to trudge off towards the stairs, the memory of the comrade slaughtered to fuel Vakaan's magic still fresh in their minds. Gorgut glowered as he saw Zagbob lingering behind. A savage kick sent the goblin scout scurrying ahead of the larger orcs.

'Follow them,' Urbaal's steel voice growled. 'In this place, it is foolish to be separated.'

Naagan sneered at the Chosen. 'Follow the beasts if you like, human. It is just like your kind to run blindly into battle. I prefer to know what I am fighting.' The disciple gave another knowing look to Beblieth and Tolkku. With the orcs distracted, the time had come.

Before Naagan could spring his treachery, the shrieking body of an orc came hurtling down the stairs, thrown by some incredible force. The fearless bloodthirst of the others collapsed; even Gorgut's eyes were wide with terror as the greenskins retreated back down the steps. Something followed them, something that gouged huge smouldering hoofprints in the floor as it stalked after its prey. Unseen, invisible at first, soon a crimson mist began to take shape. The blood of the thrown orc was running back up the stairs, moving like some liquid serpent to merge with the mist, to help it as it coalesced into a physical form.

The cloud paused upon the top step. Now it had assumed the rough outline of a human shape, but of gigantic proportions. Twenty-feet tall, its hunched shoulders impossibly broad, its limbs thick with muscle. A brutish head jutted directly from the shoulders, only the merest stump of neck supporting it. As the cloud took on greater solidity, armour of blackened steel and burnished brass sprouted from the huge body's crimson skin, each vambrace and

sabaton sporting the leering visage of a skull. Upon
the blackened cuirass were the arrows of Chaos and
the skull-rune of Khorne, each picked out in bronze.
Iron chains dripped from the monster's arms, brass
hooks securing them into the creature's flesh.
Immense axes of bronze and steel took shape in the
thing's hands. Finally, the head assumed greater def-
inition, a bald, hound-like countenance with jutting
fangs and burning eyes, a hoop of steel piercing its
snout-like nose. From each side of the head, droop-
ing down to curl across its chest, stabbing forward
like the tusks of a mastodon, were two enormous
horns capped in steel. The monster glowered as it felt
the horrified eyes of the intruders staring at it and a
gruesome smile twisted its face.

'Kaarn the Vanquisher,' Vakaan hissed, his voice
shivering with fear. 'A warlord so bloodthirsty he
massacred his own army with his own hand. For
such carnage, the Blood God exalted him, transformed him into one of his daemon princes.'

'I only care about one thing,' Urbaal growled back
at the magus. 'How do we kill it?'

Vakaan's voice shuddered and cracked. 'I don't
think it can die,' he whispered.

MORTAL OR DEATHLESS, once they could see their
enemy, Gorgut's mob lost much of their fear.
Roaring, the orcs charged the daemon, chopping at it
with their cruel axes and butchering swords. Zagbob
crept along behind them, sending poisoned arrows
slamming into the daemon's chest, the feathered
shafts whistling only inches from the helmets of his

comrades. The goblin's squigs snapped and snarled, bounding forwards to join the attack, their tiny brains converted by the bloodlust of the orcs.

Urbaal lunged up the steps to join Gorgut's attack, Kormak close beside him. Vakaan swung his staff, commanding his daemon steed to bring him closer to the fight. The magus swept his hands before him in an arcane pattern, the words of the Dark Tongue rasping across his lips. A purple pentagram glowed into life on the floor beside the towering Kaarn. Like the daemon prince, a shape began to swiftly coalesce, a pillar of rippling light that took on an almost fungus-like appearance within the burning star. Fanged mouths slobbered open all along the daemon's headless trunk. It lifted stalk-like limbs, pointing them at Kaarn. In the twinkling of an eye, the pods upon the tips of the daemon's stalks split open and gouts of blue fire spewed from the flamer's limbs, bathing Kaarn in sheets of infernal heat.

Kaarn roared, his savage bellow booming from the brass walls, cracking columns and shattering gargoyles. The daemon prince strode through the clinging fires of the flamer, sweeping his huge axes through the surging ranks of his foes. One orc was torn in half by the hellish blade, its torso dashed against the wall, its legs rolling grotesquely down the steps. The blood that exploded from its destruction flew through the air, swirling like a ribbon of gore to gather about Kaarn's body and be absorbed into his crimson flesh.

Kormak struck at the daemon as he stood soaking up the life force of the orc. The marauder's axe clashed against Kaarn's knee, shattering the ogre-skull covering it, his mutant arm slashed through the daemon's belly, spilling putrid entrails from a fist-deep gash. A kick from the daemon's hoof sent the Norscan flying, crashing against the brass wall, denting it with the violence of his impact. Kaarn leaned back, lifting his head in a savage growl, then lumbered after the thrown marauder. With each stomp of his hooves, the daemon's wounds closed a bit tighter, his exposed organs shrinking back into his body. Kaarn snuffled loudly, relishing the smell of Kormak's blood.

Another sheet of clinging daemon fire turned Kaarn from his prey. The monster's flesh boiled beneath the eerie blue fires of the flamer, his armour bubbling and melting. Kaarn poked a thumb into the oozing mess, then thundered across the stairs to face the daemon. Gorgut was brushed aside like a gnat by the monster's pounding legs, the black orc's body glancing off the steel of a huge sabaton. The other orcs scattered as well, as frightened of Kaarn's fury as of the daemon fires of Vakaan's flamer.

The flamer shrieked from the dozens of mouths peppered across its mushroom-like body. It brought both arms upwards, sending a double-blast of fire searing into Kaarn's face. The daemon prince howled in pain, but forced itself to press through the flames. Kaarn's head was little more than a leering skull as he leaned above the flamer and brought both of his monstrous axes smashing down.

The flamer exploded in a ball of ectoplasm and fire as Kaarn's axes slashed through its body. The daemon prince ground his hoof against the muck of the flamer's essence, smashing it into the floor. The front of his body was oozing blood, charred and cut by the creature's caustic death. Kaarn glared at the sticky slime, flesh slowly reforming on his scorched skull as the daemon prince's hate boiled within him.

Stabbing pain exploded in Kaarn's leg. He swung about, snarling as Urbaal brought his shining blade slashing against the back of the daemon's knee for the second time. The sword that had cut so easily through the bloodgiant's hoof, however, was finding the murderous essence of Kaarn too tough to chop through. His sword scraped against the iron bones of the daemon, its edge blunting against the thick metal. Kaarn brought his axe chopping down, smashing into the Chosen, hurling him down the stairs. Urbaal struck and rolled with bone-snapping violence, his sword clattering from his hand.

Kaarn snorted, sucking the smell of the Chosen's blood into his lungs. The daemon's regenerating face pulled back in a hungry grin and he started after his stunned prey.

VAKAAN WATCHED AS Kaarn advanced upon the daemon he had summoned. Alone, he knew that a minor daemon such as the flamer had no chance against a beast like Kaarn, but he intended to lend his sorcery to the effort. He concentrated upon a spell, focusing his will upon the head of his staff to weave the nebulous strands of power into a force of destruction.

That was when his daemonic steed squealed and abruptly dove from where it had been hovering. Vakaan staggered upon its back, trying to hold his balance. Through the empty space where he had been only an instant before, a salvo of crossbow bolts stabbed through the air. The magus spun about, glaring as Naagan directed his warriors to shot again.

The spell the magus had been shaping burst from his staff – a boiling mass of orange flame that hurtled down into the dark elves. The druchii cooked within their black armour, their shrieks of pain rippling through Vakaan's ears as he listened to them burn. They were little more than smoking skeletons when they crashed to the floor.

Naagan, in that last instant, had cast his own spell, weaving an aethyric shell about himself that blocked the worst of Vakaan's magic. The disciple staggered away from the steaming husks of his soldiers, his red robes singed, his white hair smouldering, but otherwise unmarked.

Vakaan snarled behind his helm. He gathered the winds of magic to him, shaping another spell. The elf would not be so lucky this time.

The daemon disc was suddenly jostled as a springing weight smashed down upon it. Vakaan felt slender arms wrap about him in a murderous clutch, the edge of a dagger scraping against his feathered robes. Only the supernatural toughness of the feathers protected him, foiling the disembowelling thrust of the dagger. Torn from the wings of a chimera, the feathers Vakaan wore had surprised many would-be assassins. Now

Beblieth the witch elf could add herself to that number.

Beblieth had climbed one of the steel columns while the other dark elves took aim, a contingency should the magus escape the barrage. She sprang down upon Vakaan from the lower jaw of a gargoyle skull, intent upon killing him before he was aware she was there. Now, her dagger turned by the weird feathered armour, she tightened her hold on the sorcerer's neck and tried to press her poisoned lips against his mouth.

Vakaan brought the head of his staff cracking back against the witch elf's face. Beblieth shrieked as the hot metal sizzled against her pale skin, searing a crooked scar into her cheek. Her grip loosened as pain overwhelmed her. Vakaan stamped his foot, the daemon disc spinning around in response. The shift in motion caused the dark elf to lose her hold completely. Screaming her fury, she fell from the back of the disc, hurtling towards the floor fifty feet below.

As she fell, Beblieth swung her arm back, hurling her dagger at the magus. The envenomed blade glanced off the edge of the disc, missing the sorcerer. Vakaan lifted his staff, green fire blazing from his eyes. Before he could unleash his vengeful magic, Beblieth's flailing arms caught hold of a skeletal gargoyle. With acrobatic grace, the elf turned her plummet into a spin, arching her body so that she rolled behind the steel column as she fell. The jade lightning Vakaan sent sizzling from his staff smashed harmlessly against the metal pillar.

The magus started to urge his steed downwards to finish the witch elf when a chance turn of his head noticed the immense shape of Kaarn storming down the steps, Urbaal sprawled helpless before him.

Vakaan hesitated, debating whether to help the Chosen or leave him to his fate. There was still a chance he could escape the Fortress of Brass and indeed the whole of the Bastion Stair with the Spear. He would be welcomed as a hero by Tchar'zanek.

Urbaal's warning that the Bastion Stair might not linger in the same place long enough for the Raven Host to return echoed through Vakaan's mind. If that happened, the Spear would be useless to them. Kakra the Timeless would remain the captive of Var'Ithrok and the Winds of Chaos would remain fettered beyond the Portal of Rage.

Personal glory warred with his duty to the Raven Host for mastery of Vakaan's soul. The magus stared down, watching Urbaal stir slowly as Kaarn lumbered towards him and knew what he had to do.

Kormak rolled onto his side, feeling his battered body protest even the thought of motion. He saw Urbaal swatted aside by Kaarn's axe, watched as the champion crashed down the brass steps. The daemon prince started to lumber after him, intent on slaughtering his helpless prey. Kormak ground his fangs against the pain and forced himself up. He did not bother to find his axe, but willed his arm to become one for him.

The marauder was not the only one returning to the attack. Gorgut and his orcs were charging at the daemon, howling like mad beasts. Their weapons slashed and crashed against the back of Kaarn's cuirass. The daemon prince spun around, roaring back at the greenskin throng. For an instant, the orcs recoiled. Then Gorgut threw back his head and roared back at the monster, punctuating his fury with an overhanded swing of his axe that broke Kaarn's tusk and buried itself in his lip.

The daemon shrieked in fury. He thundered back up the steps, pushing the orcs before him. Gorgut swung from Kaarn's face, refusing to release his axe. Kaarn worked his jaw, trying to knock the greenskin free. Gorgut kicked out, cracking more of the daemon's teeth. The axe pulled free and the orc started to fall. Gorgut grabbed hold of Kaarn's horn, swinging from it like a jungle ape. Gorgut's axe came slashing at Kaarn's face with each roll of the orc warlord hanging from his horn.

Kormak moved to join the orcs in their fight, determined to die in battle. As he turned, however, he saw Tolkku rushing up the steps. A purple light glowed from the painted skull the zealot held. The Kurgan was running at the wounded Urbaal. For an instant, Kormak thought the zealot was hurrying to the Chosen's aid, but then he saw the cold gleam in Tolkku's eyes, the vindictive smile twisting his tattooed face.

In a flash, Kormak understood the murderous treachery in Tolkku's hand. The purple skull would not heal the Chosen, it would kill him!

A stabbing pain seized Kormak's heart. Renegade and wanderer, he had felt something new following Urbaal, joining his fate to that of the Chosen's quest.

He could have left after Urbaal had broken Tolkku's power over him, but Kormak had stayed. He was part of something greater than himself now. Fail or triumph, Urbaal would lead him to glory such as the marauder had never dreamed of.

The Norscan threw himself down the stairs, pouncing upon Tolkku like a raging tiger. Kormak's huge body smashed into the lean Kurgan zealot, smashing Tolkku hard against the brass steps only a few paces from the staggered Urbaal. The Chosen turned and watched as Kormak grabbed the zealot's hand, the purple skull still clenched in his fingers.

Tolkku snarled at Kormak. The zealot tried to draw his dagger from its sheath, but Kormak pressed close against him, pinning his arm against his belly. The two men strained, Kurgan trying to slide his arm free from the Norscan's implacable grip. It was a struggle that could not last long.

The zealot screamed as Kormak snapped his arm like a rotten stick. The marauder bent the shattered limb back upon itself, pressing the glowing skull against Tolkku's horrified face. He screamed again as the skin blackened beneath the skull's enchanted energies. It peeled away from his face in strips. The corruption spread, crawling with hellish speed through his entire head. When Kormak let go and the zealot crashed to the floor, only a scorched skull rose from his neck.

'My thanks, Norscan,' Urbaal said. Stiffly, the Chosen regained his feet.

'Our debt is settled,' Kormak answered with a grunt. 'You saved me from this coward once.'

Urbaal nodded his understanding. He turned his eyes to the top of the stairs. The orcs had drawn Kaarn after them, pulling the daemon prince through the archway and into a huge cage-like atrium. The scarlet hell-light of the Fortress was even more intense within the atrium, mephitic vapours billowing from metal vents in the floor. The daemon prince had butchered its way through most of the orc's crew now, only Gorgut and Dregruk remaining. Arrows from Zagbob continued to sprout uselessly from Kaarn's crimson flesh.

'The daemon will finish us all,' Urbaal sighed, 'but I promise it will know it has been in a fight before I am through!'

The Chosen began to limp up the stairs, focused upon the seemingly unkillable monster. Suddenly, he found his path blocked by the hovering form of Vakaan and his steed. The magus smiled at Urbaal. Leaning down, he handed the Chosen the blackened length of the Spear. Urbaal returned his sword to its sheath and took the relic from Vakaan's lean hands.

'Be careful,' Vakaan cautioned. 'I will need that back when you are through with it.'

Urbaal clenched his fists about the heft of the Spear. He glanced back at Kormak. 'Have you ever hunted tuskgors?'

KAARN STOMPED HIS hoof down hard against the vent, denting the bronze bars. A spurt of scalding red steam erupted about the daemon, blistering his skin. The monster ignored the stinging vapour, his crazed eyes searching for his elusive enemy. Having finally

knocked the black orc from his horn, now Kaarn
intended to grind him into paste.

The daemon prince hissed with satisfaction as he
saw the black orc hobbling away. Now there was
nowhere left for him to run. Kaarn ignored the goblin arrows whistling into his flesh, an annoyance
beneath his notice. He would let the bloodletters of
the Fortress feast on the irritating flea. But the black
orc, the black orc was his.

Kaarn threw back his head in pain as something
slammed into his back. He fumbled at his spine, ripping free the heavy axe that had chopped into his
body. The monster turned about, burning eyes hunting for the over-bold foe who had thrown the
weapon at him.

'Here, you pig-sucking child-eater!' Kormak
howled at the daemon.

The daemon's eyes seemed to boil in their sockets,
its snout curling in a loud snort of fury. Hooves denting the floor, Kaarn charged at the mocking Norscan,
thundering back across the atrium towards the stairs.

Kormak held his ground, watching the daemon
lunge at him. He waited until the last possible second and threw himself from the daemon's path,
slamming against the floor.

Kaarn hurtled onwards, even a daemon prince
unable to stop his murderous momentum. Instead
of the jeering Norscan, he found himself leaping at
the sombre figure of Urbaal, the black length of the
Spear fixed in his hands. The Chosen braced himself
for the daemon's charge, setting the butt of the Spear
against the corner of the step.

Kaarn slammed into the Spear with the force of a charging mastodon. The monster's momentum drove the relic through its cuirass. The daemon stared in disbelief at the armoured mortal below him. The huge axes fell from his claws as the fingers began to blacken, crumbling into ash. A look of agony pulsed through Kaarn's eyes. With a last effort, he tried to gore Urbaal with his horns. Even as the steel-shod horn brushed against Urbaal's shoulder, it was falling apart, breaking into little blackened clumps of cinder.

Urbaal stared in amazement at the weapon gripped in his hands, something between awe and horror racing along his spine. Kaarn the Vanquisher, daemon prince of the Blood God, a fiend that had butchered nations, a terror that had murdered every hero who stood against him was dying, his unnatural life crumbling away, devoured by the awful power of the Spear.

The daemon threw back its head, howling in outrage, incensed that all the long ages of its hideous life should end in such a manner. Kaarn's furious eyes glared at Urbaal, then collapsed into cinders. The rest of the daemon prince's physical body followed. Soon there was nothing left of Kaarn the Vanquisher except a heap of ashes and a stench of blood.

'So passes Kaarn,' Vakaan pronounced, his daemon steed drifting downwards. He shifted the ashes with the tip of his staff, letting the spectral breeze of the Fortress carry them away.

Urbaal slumped against the step, breathing hard, winded by the fierce exertions of the fight. 'You could have helped more,' he told the magus, half in jest.

'I was busy hunting elves,' Vakaan returned. 'Unfortunately, there were a few I didn't find.'

'This place will soon settle the traitors,' Urbaal said.

'I hope not,' Kormak said, making his painful way down the steps to sink down beside Urbaal. 'There is still a reckoning between me and that elf witch!'

The men turned their heads, looking up as they heard Gorgut and Dregruk stomping back from the atrium. The two orcs stared in confusion at the humans and the pile of ash.

'Where'd that ugly git bottle off ta!' Gorgut bellowed, one paw clutching a bleeding knee. 'I ain't dun wiv dat zoogin grot-fondla!'

Despite their fatigue and their wounds, despite the horror of their surroundings and the malignant presence of the Blood God, the three northmen broke into laughter.

THE BRASS HALLS quickly became a confusing maze to Naagan. He did not know which path they had taken, which way might lead them back out to the face of the Bastion Stair. How they would survive a climb down that awful structure, he did not know. He only knew that their chances were better outside than inside. He turned his head as for what seemed the thousandth time he caught a furtive movement in the shadows behind one of the skull-faced pillars. If the daemons of this place decided to attack them now, their chances would quickly drop to none.

His chances, Naagan corrected himself. He stared spitefully at the witch elf stalking through the halls beside him. She was a witness, she could bring word of his failure to the Hag Queen. The Temple of Khaine would not forgive him for losing the Spear of Myrmidia. He intended to blame the fiasco on Pyra, or perhaps even Prince Inhin. It was a lie that would sit easily on his tongue. But a lie was always safest when there was only one to tell it.

'Which way?' he asked Beblieth, careful to keep his thoughts from his face.

The witch elf turned, gesturing at the hall behind them. 'Three turns to the left, one to the right,' she hissed.

Naagan's eyes blazed with annoyance. 'We are not going back there!' he snarled. 'They will be on their guard now. I do not intend to die for your stupid vendetta!'

'Perhaps you won't have to,' Beblieth hissed back.

As quick as the witch elf was, Naagan was quicker. The disciple's dagger stabbed between her ribs, just beneath her armoured bodice. He sprang away as soon as the blade struck her, as diabolic smile on his cadaverous face. The poison on the blade would kill in seconds.

Beblieth reached to her side, pulling the dagger free. She stared at Naagan. Slowly a cold smile worked itself onto her face. The disciple retreated before her advance.

'Have you forgotten, Naagan,' she snarled. 'The Temple weans its children on such poison.'

'It will still kill you,' Naagan insisted. 'Your body might resist its effects for a few hours, but you will still die!' He took another faltering step back and pointed at the witch elf. 'Unless I use my magic to heal you, you will die!'

Beblieth pounced on the disciple, driving his own dagger deep into his heart. Her lips brushed against his ear. 'Do you think I am fool enough to trust you to cure me of your own poison?' she hissed. A twist of her hand and she ripped his dagger free. Scornfully, she wiped the blade on Naagan's robes.

Beblieth felt the wound in her side. What Naagan had said was true. Her body had built up a resistance to poison, but not immunity. The poison would do its terrible work, just too late to do the disciple any good.

A fierce smile spread over the witch elf's face as she reached a decision. She was dying, but she had a few hours of life left. A few hours to sow such havoc as she still could.

Vengefully, Beblieth turned about, gliding back down the silent corridors of brass.

Three turns to the left, one to the right.

CHAPTER NINETEEN

KORMAK FOLLOWED THE others up into the red-lit atrium at the top of the brass steps. He gave a final glance at the corpse of Tolkku. There had been enough elixirs and cordials hidden in his bag to heal the worst of the warband's hurts, a final gift from a man who had proven himself traitor. Kormak chuckled grimly as he looked at that leathery bag, bulging with the zealot's collection of skulls. As a parting gesture, Kormak had started his own collection – tying the desiccated head of the Kurgan to his belt.

The atrium's gruesome aura had not diminished with the destruction of Kaarn. It still had the reek of an abattoir, the lurking malignance of a murderer's den. Crimson mist continued to rise from the grated vents in the floor. A disembodied wail, a chorus of the slaughter, hissed through the brass latticework of the chamber's rear wall. Flickers of shadow, burning shapes of scarlet and gold shifted between the gaps in the metal plates, hinting at the hostile desolation beyond.

Vakaan turned his disc about, facing his comrades. The magus held a silver knife in his hand. The membranes slid shut across his eyes. 'Last chance to turn back,' he told Urbaal.

Urbaal did not answer, simply shook his head and tightened his grip on the Spear. Vakaan sighed and nodded. The disc rotated back around, facing the magus once more towards the rounded wall. He brought the edge of his knife slicing across his palm. With a flick of his wrist, he sent the blood pooling on his skin spattering against the brass plates.

There was a grinding shriek as the sheets of metal bubbled and shivered, corroding where Vakaan's blood struck them. Like melting wax, the wall disintegrated, flowing down the grated vents, choking the crimson steam. The magus gestured with his staff and his daemon steed drifted through the opening.

Beyond the atrium was a gigantic amphitheatre, its walls forged from bronze, ringed with the tusks of monstrous beasts. Great spear-like spires rose from the bronze walls, stabbing into the bruised sky. Immense totems, gigantic pillars of brass and bone, loomed between the spires, each totem tipped with a mammoth skull-rune cast in gold. Against the walls, repeated in endless succession, the skull-rune was etched in steel, edged in bloodstone and ringed by brass.

At the far end of the circular, arena-like space the gigantic antlers of the Bastion Stair towered above the walls. Immense faces, fanged and shrieking, pressed against its blackened surface, struggling for release. They were held by the brass settings of the angular antlers, great curls of metal that moaned and shuddered against the fury of its captives. Between the antlers, lashed to them by enormous chains of steel, three gigantic rings of ebony and gold were suspended, each ring jagged with spike-like arrows that jutted from their outer edges. There was motion in the rings, a constant struggle to rotate into some new pattern, a struggle thwarted only by the daemon-forged chains.

Beneath the straining rings stretched a great doorway. There seemed no end to its threshold, simply opening into a red oblivion without beginning or ending. The blood-crazed eternity of Khorne.

Kormak stepped out into the arena, his eyes immediately drawn to the angry sky above. Dark clouds like clotted blood stormed through a violet crimson sky. Fires smouldered behind the clouds, casting their blazing light upon the blighted land. Their fumes crashed against one another like charging armies, the roar of thunder booming with each impact, red rain dripping as they boiled into nothingness, consumed by their own violence. Kormak could feel himself being drawn into that sky, hear the beckoning shouts of warlords and kings welcoming him into their eternal war. It was only with a Herculean effort that he refused their calls and tore his eyes from the celestial battlefield.

Now, more than ever before, he understood that he had left behind the world he had known. This was the domain of the Blood God, existing only by the whim of Khorne.

The floor of the plaza was composed of black rock, splitting into a narrow ledge that circled the rim of the octagonal arena. The centre of the arena was a great platform of blackened stone bordered in brass. Between ledge and platform yawned a deep trench, its depths filled with churning magma. A few footbridges connected ledge and platform, the largest of these fronting directly beneath the immense brass antlers.

Vakaan pointed his staff at the doorway across from the entrance from the Fortress of Brass. 'You must hurl the Spear into the doorway. It is invested with the power of the Raven God. It will break the hold of the Blood God upon this place. Var'Ithrok will no longer be master here and Kakra the Timeless will be free.'

Urbaal sheathed his sword and tightened his grip on the Spear. 'Then let us end this,' the Chosen said, marching towards the Portal.

Ever since learning how Kaarn had been destroyed, Gorgut had watched Urbaal with a sullen gaze. The black orc was mulling over thoughts in his savage brain, thoughts of magic and power. He still wasn't impressed by the Spear, it wasn't the sort of thing a proper orc would carry. But he respected what it could do. Anything that could kill a monster like Kaarn would make quick work of Grumlok. Then Gorgut would be warboss of the Badlands, supreme warlord of the greenskins!

While the humans tended their wounds, Gorgut made his plans. It took some head-cracking to get

Zagbob and Dregruk working together, but at last his surviving underlings understood what was needed of them. The black orc gave a sly look to Dregruk, then a slight tilt of his head in Zagbob's direction. A gruesome smile spread over Gorgut's face.

Without warning, the black orc hurled himself at Urbaal. His axe smashed into the Chosen, cracking his armour and throwing him to the ground. Gorgut's steel-shod boot smashed into Urbaal's chin, knocking him back as he started to rise. 'I wantz dat fancy git-sticka!' the warlord growled, raising his axe to finish off the fallen human.

As soon as Gorgut started his attack, his underlings sprang into action. Vakaan was nearly thrown from his disc as Dregruk pounced on him, the orc's choppa crashing into the bottom of the steed. Magus and daemon were hurled back by the powerful blow, crashing against the wall of the arena. Zagbob loosed an arrow, scowling as the poisoned missile glanced from Kormak's helmet. The snarling goblin pointed his claw at the marauder, his two surviving squigs bounding towards their prey.

'Fools!' Vakaan roared. 'Idiot beasts!' The magus struggled to recover command of his disc, at the same time frantically pulling talismans from beneath his robes. The terror in the sorcerer's voice gave even the greenskins pause. They looked at Vakaan, trying to understand the reason for his fear.

Soon it was obvious even to the orcs. As Urbaal's blood dripped from the wound Gorgut had struck him, the angry sky darkened. A fierce wind began to surge from beyond the great doorway beneath the antlers, the faces shrieking upon the black surface falling silent. A smell of death surrounded them, seeping into their lungs.

The entire plaza shook as a gargantuan figure emerged from the Portal, scarlet energies clinging and rippling about its body. It had a semblance of human shape, with great bronze-shod hooves for feet and long talons upon the tips of its fingers. Enormous bat-like wings stretched from its shoulders, shrouding its body like a cloak. Its skin was a pale burgundy, like rancid blood. Great bull-like horns protruded from the sides of its skull while a pair of smaller, sword-like growths sprouted from its scalp. Upon its forehead, burned into the crimson skin was the skull-rune of Khorne. Beneath the brand, the daemon's skeletal face glowered, its fiery eyes glowing beneath its heavy, protruding brow. Armour as black as midnight and edged in brass circled its legs and wrists, a massive plate of steel lashed across its breast.

The thing took a thunderous step onto the central platform, the magma in the trenches shivering as the mammoth hoof sent a tremor running through the floor. It lifted an axe the size of an Aesling longship, the skull-rune smouldering upon its face of blackened steel. The monster's face, inhuman in its evil, stretched into a fanged smile.

'Kakra has waited millennia for those who would free him,' the daemon's voice growled like iron upon an anvil. 'And this is the best Tzeentch can send!'

The gigantic daemon chuckled, its laughter like the rumble of a volcano. It gestured with its axe, pointing

it at Dregruk. The orc was paralyzed as a crimson
mist surrounded him. Thicker and thicker the blood-
hued fog grew, until Dregruk disappeared behind it.
Then, in the blinking of an eye, the mist surged
inwards, rushing down the orc's mouth, nose and
ears. Dregruk's body swelled, filling like a goatskin
bladder. At last, the pressure building inside his body
was too great. In a swelter of gore, Dregruk burst
apart.

The daemon smiled down at the awestruck survivors. The folded wings suddenly snapped open,
stretching clear across the arena. The bloodthirster's
voice fell to a rumbling roar. 'There is no victory
here,' it promised, 'only death.'

URBAAL SWORE IN terror as he saw Var'Ithrok emerge
from the Portal of Rage. He lunged for the fallen
Spear, eyes locked on the Portal. Using the Spear to
reconsecrate the Portal to Tzeentch was their only
prayer of overcoming the bloodthirster. The Chosen
felt victory swell in his heart as his fingers locked
around the enchanted Spear. He started to lift himself from the ground, intent on dashing to the Portal
before the Skull Lord took notice of him.

It was not the Skull Lord who struck him. Gorgut's
axe smashed down into Urbaal's back, spilling him
back onto the floor. The black orc left his weapon
buried in the Chosen's spine. Prowling around
Urbaal's body, Gorgut ripped the Spear from his
weakened fingers. A broad grin shaped itself across
the orc's brutal features. He turned and stared up at
the immense daemon.

Gorgut did not hesitate. The black orc glared up at the enormous daemon. With a tremendous bellow of raw animal fury, he turned from Urbaal and charged the bloodthirster. Gorgut's spear stabbed deep into the bronze-shod hoof of Var'Ithrok. The orc wrenched it free with a savage tug, splinters of hoof flying across the ground. Howling like some primal force, Gorgut brought his weapon slamming a second time into the daemon's hoof, watching for the first sign that Var'Ithrok would disintegrate as Kaarn had.

The relic that had destroyed a daemon prince, however, was not strong enough to destroy the Skull Lord. Var'Ithrok stared down at Gorgut, the blood-thirster's face contorting with incredulous amusement, like a shark confronted by a fierce min-now. The mammoth axe in the daemon's hand came slashing down in a broad sweep of death. Displaying supernatural skill, Var'Ithrok brought the merest edge of its keen axe slicing across Gorgut's body. The orc's head was cloven by the blow, the warlord's body hurled across the ground. It crashed against the bronze wall of the trench then fell into the hungry embrace of the magma below.

Var'Ithrok turned away from Gorgut's destruction, the Spear still impaled in its hoof. The bloodthirster's eyes burned with amusement as it considered its few remaining foes.

Vakaan swept his staff before him, magical light-ning sizzling from its head. The blast struck the daemon in the chest, crackling against its armour. The bloodthirster glared at the magus, enraged by this heathen who would profane the Bastion Stair with sorcery. The Skull Lord took a lumbering step towards Vakaan. As it did so, a glowing pentagram appeared beneath its hoof. A long-limbed daemon composed of pink light took shape within the five-pointed circle. Its claws scraped and tore at the bloodthirster, burning with each touch of its grubby fingers.

The daemonic horror Vakaan had summoned was doing no lasting harm to the Skull Lord, but it was slowing Var'Ithrok's advance, the spectral chains of its summoning circle binding the bloodthirster to the spot. At least so long as the daemon was able to endure Var'Ithrok's savage retaliation.

The magus forced himself to tear his attention away from the bloodthirster. He found Kormak pressed against the bronze wall of the arena, Zagbob's squigs leaping and snapping at him. As soon as the marauder tried to strike one, the other would lunge in, its fangs raking his flesh. Behind the squigs, the goblin himself continued to take aim with his shortbow. Already several arrows were lodged in Kormak's body, their poison slowing and weakening him. Deciding that retreat was impossible, the cruel goblin was determined to take one last victim with him before he died.

Vakaan pointed his staff at Zagbob. A burst of swirling, rainbow light engulfed the goblin. Zagbob shrieked as the muscles of his arms sprouted claws and began to tear themselves free from his body. His legs collapsed into purple jelly, feathers bubbling up from the morass. A pallid organ oozed itself up from the goblin's throat, choking his screams, then took flight upon scintillating wings. In a matter of heartbeats, the unfocused, malignant mutations Vakaan's spell sent tearing through the goblin's body left only a greasy puddle of protean muck staining the blackened stones.

The destruction of the squig hunter sent his beasts into a panic. One turned, bounding back to investigate the disintegrating goblin. A slimy tendril shot out from the puddle, searing through its foreleg. The fungal monster writhed and wailed as it thrashed against the ground, helpless to flee as the blob-like residue of its master slid over it and began to consume it.

The other squig made the mistake of persisting in its attack on Kormak. Without the fangs of the other squig to tear at him, the marauder was able to shape his mutant arm into a great bludgeon of bone. He struck the squig as it leapt at him, the fury of the blow hurling it into the bronze wall. The fungoid creature burst like rotten fruit, its wreckage slowly dripping down the face of the wall.

'The Spear!' Vakaan shouted, pointing at the bloodthirster's hoof. The magus had no time to explain further. A piercing shriek announced the destruction of his daemon. Hastily, he raised his staff and summoned a second pink horror to slow Var'Ithrok's advance.

Kormak pulled poisoned arrows from his body, his breath a hot torment as he drew it down into his lungs. He did not know what kind of filth Zagbob had used on him, nor what its effects would be. He only knew that he was the only one left to accomplish their quest, to bring final glory to Tchar'zanek and the Raven Host.

Wearily, Kormak pushed himself away from the wall. Every part of him, body and soul, tried to hold him back as he made a painful dash for the closest bridge over the trench and the towering daemon looming beyond it. Terror roared through his heart, but Kormak kept his eyes locked on the Spear stuck in Var'Ithrok's hoof.

SWEAT CASCADED DOWN Vakaan's face as the magus hurriedly summoned another horror from the Realm of Chaos. These minor daemons had no real chance against the bloodthirster, no more chance than Gorgut and his mad attack. But the magic that bound them to their summoning circles could also hold Var'Ithrok, if only for the fleeting moment it took the bloodthirster to destroy Vakaan's daemons.

Vakaan was under no delusion that any of his powers could stop the bloodthirster for long. Arcane lightning, bolts of change, orange fires that scorched the soul, these were only pebbles against the malignance of the Skull Lord. Var'Ithrok had endured since before time, it was a beast powerful enough to imprison Kakra the Timeless, one of Tzeentch's eldest Lords of Change. It was an embodiment of Khorne's rage, of the Blood God's insatiable lust for destruction. Against such a force, any man was less than nothing.

Yet still he had to try. Vakaan could feel more than the baleful gaze of the Blood God watching him. He could feel the thousand eyes of Tzeentch judging his every thought. In his mind he could hear the crackling voice of Kakra whispering to him. *You shall defeat... have defeated the Skull Lord. The glory of Tzeentch is... will be the Raven Host's.*

The magus watched as Kormak made his desperate drive across the shuddering span of the footbridge. The marauder moved with maddening slowness. How long Vakaan could hold Var'Ithrok he did not know, but he knew he had to keep the bloodthirster's attention long enough to give Kormak a chance.

Vakaan started to draw the winds of sorcery into his mind, to shape the raw magic into a withering blast of sorcery. The incantation was just hissing through his lips when he suddenly gasped in pain. His hand fell to his chest, groping at the thick steel bolt protruding from between his ribs. Blood darkened his hand as it bubbled up between his fingers. His body jerked as another bolt slammed into it inches from the first, nailing his hand to his chest.

The magus crumpled as his strength deserted him. The ornate staff fell from his hand, evaporating into smoke before it could strike the floor. Vakaan slumped against the back of his daemon steed, then pitched over its side. He struck the ground hard, his shoulder fracturing as it absorbed the shock. He moaned in pain, membranes flicking closed over his eyes as he braced himself for the end.

It came, but not in the shape he expected. Waiting for another crossbow bolt to stab through his flesh, Vakaan finally opened his eyes to see the slavering mouth of his daemonic disc hurtling down for him.

He waved his injured arm in a futile effort to shield himself from the disc's vengeance, but there was little he could do to stop it. His scream was an avian shriek as the disc's mouth snapped close around his face and began to chew.

Beblieth watched the magus die, letting the crossbow fall from her hands. She sneered at the screaming sorcerer, then smiled as she watched the last daemon he had summoned to distract Var'Ithrok flicker and vanish. The bloodthirster swung its immense body around, its burning eyes settling on the puny shape of Kormak as he sprinted towards it.

The witch elf had hoped to kill the marauder herself, but she had contented herself with allowing the daemon to destroy him. That way he would know the full extent of his defeat and his soul would be Var'Ithrok's plaything for all eternity. It would be a pleasant image to warm her cruel soul while she waited for Naagan's poison to send her to her own god's judgement.

KORMAK FROZE AS the bloodthirster turned towards him. He felt its fiery gaze boring down, stripping away the courage from his soul. There was the promise of endless agony in that stare, the threat of more than simple destruction. Those who dared defy a daemon would find no rest in death. The marauder felt icy fear crawl down his spine. Only the sight of the Spear sticking from Var'Ithrok's hoof stayed him from flight.

The marauder fought down his terror, bracing himself for the obliterating ire of the Skull Lord. Would the daemon burst him with its malignant will, the force that had allowed its rage alone to obliterate Dregruk and defy the magic of Vakaan or would it simply butcher him with its axe as it had Gorgut? Whatever the end, Kormak would face it, not flee from it.

Motion beyond the bloodthirster caught Kormak's eye. Impossibly, Urbaal was rising to his feet, Gorgut's axe still sticking from his back. The Chosen stumbled weakly, then drew his sword. He stared at Kormak, locking eyes with the marauder. The power of Tzeentch suddenly burst from the sword, burning all around it like the very claw of the Raven God.

Var'Ithrok turned as Urbaal invoked the might of Tzeentch. The bloodthirster glared down at the Chosen, raw hate dripping from the daemon's fangs. It took a lumbering step towards the defiant mortal, smashing its axe down at him.

Somehow Urbaal found the strength to dive away from the huge axe as it hurtled towards him. He was thrown from his feet as the mammoth blade gouged into the ground. Var'Ithrok wrenched the giant weapon free and brought it smashing down once more. Again, the frustrating mortal escaped, leaping back before the axe could crush him.

In its fury, the Skull Lord forgot Kormak. The Norscan understood the desperate gambit Urbaal had taken onto himself. He was playing the part of Vakaan's now vanished daemons, holding the bloodthirster's attention so that Kormak could recover the Spear and cast it into the Portal of Rage.

Kormak summoned his last reserves of strength and the very dregs of his courage. Grinding his fangs together, the marauder charged beneath the folds of Var'Ithrok's wings, dodged between the blood-thirster's stomping hooves. His arm again took the shape of a great chitinous claw as he grabbed the Spear protruding from the daemon's hoof. Howling against the agony burning through his arms, Kormak used every muscle in his body to rip the Spear free.

The Skull Lord remained oblivious to Kormak's effort, even as the Spear was torn loose. The daemon had eyes only for the insufferable human who some-how continued to elude its axe. Var'Ithrok's enraged roars threatened to split the very heavens, rumbling off the bronze walls with the force of an earthquake. Abruptly, the frustrated daemon stopped trying to cut down Urbaal with its axe. The bloodthirster's malignant eyes blazed with unspeakable hate, thrust-ing the very horror of its essence into the Chosen's mind.

Urbaal wilted under the malefic gaze, staggering in numbed shock, his wits shattered by Var'Ithrok's assault. The gleam of his sword flickered and began to fade.

Now the bloodthirster brought its axe chopping down at its bewildered enemy, but not blind and rage-ridden as it had before. It was careful now, slash-ing its huge axe in an almost delicate sweep, taking great pains not to utterly annihilate its foe. The edge of the axe rasped across Urbaal's neck, slashing through his thick armour as though it weren't even there. The Chosen's head leapt into the air, borne aloft upon a fountain of blood. Then head and body crumpled to the floor, the last glow of the champion's sword dying with him.

The bloodthirster's grisly face crinkled into a sneer as it inhaled the scent of Urbaal's blood, savouring the smell of its vanquished foe. But another smell intruded upon its pleasure. A smell of danger. Var'Ithrok spun about and it was the daemon's turn to know doubt.

Kormak stood upon the very threshold of the Portal, below the antlers and the chained rings. He stared into the void, the nothingness beyond the physical plane. And as he stared he lifted the blackened Spear he had torn from the bloodthirster's hoof. Only it was black no longer, now the Spear blazed with light, light of every colour, light that coruscated with life and power of its own. A light that was kindred to that which had rippled about Urbaal's sword. A light that promised Change even in the endless slaughter of the Blood God's domain.

Before Var'Ithrok could start to move, Kormak hurled the Spear straight up into the chained rings. It passed through each in turn, shifting and moving, gripped by some invisible force. The imprisoned rings began to turn as they drew the light of the Spear into themselves, grinding against their chains. The thick iron links snapped and melted, their wreckage sucked into the Portal. A howling discord, like the shattering of worlds, boomed from the raging void.

Var'Ithrok turned to flee, its eyes now reduced to embers of fury. The void reached out for the daemon with spectral fingers, hungering for the bloodthirster's incorporeal essence. The Skull Lord lifted its axe again, smashing it down into the flagstones, trying to use it to anchor itself to the Bastion Stair and the physical world. Var'Ithrok roared as its hooves were pulled out from under it, as it felt its body being pulled back through the Portal. The bloodthirster tried to tighten its hold on the buried axe, struggling to save itself.

Slowly, the daemon's fingers slipped free. Var'Ithrok gave a mighty surge of its wings, a last effort to defy the void, then it was gone, drawn through the grinding rings, its enormity fading into a malignant speck against the eternity beyond.

Kormak crawled away from the howling Portal, horrified by the prospect of following the blood-thirsty into the void. Dimly, he understood that it was a spiritual whirlwind that raged around him, that it could crush only daemons and ghosts in its ethereal claws. But understanding did not lessen his fear, and so he crawled, like some scurrying insect, from the scene of his victory.

URBAAL'S BROKEN BODY lay sprawled upon its belly. Kormak stood over the corpse of the Chosen, feeling a sense of loss and shame. He was not worthy of the triumph that had been handed to him. He had been brought upon the quest as a mere slave, a thing to be ordered around like a dog. Urbaal had been the leader, holding the warband together through the force of his will and his determination to succeed. It was he who had been marked by Tzeentch for greatness, not the lowly mutant who now gazed down at his mangled body.

Kormak looked up as a sound intruded upon his guilt. His face twisted with hate as he saw a lithe shape marching towards him across the narrow foot-bridge.

'Do not mourn your friend,' Beblieth said, a cold smile on her lips. 'You will be joining him in hell soon enough.'

The marauder studied the witch elf as she stalked towards him. For all of her arrogance, there was something different about her. She moved less gracefully, her gait lacked the condescending self-assuredness that had coloured even the slightest motion of her athletic frame. He noted the ugly cut beneath her breast and smiled at the gangrenous discoloration around it.

'You are already dead on your feet,' Kormak told her.

'There was life enough in me to kill your warlock,' Beblieth snarled back. 'I will still have enough life in me to spit on your carcass.'

Kormak watched the witch elf finger her daggers, her thumbs rolling against their thorny hilts. Poison might be ravaging her body, but he knew she would have saved some for her blades. The marauder let his mutant arm return to its normal shape, not trusting his natural armour against poisoned steel.

Beblieth frowned as she saw the marauder's flesh melt and flow, as she watched Kormak retreat from her. 'You disappoint me, barbarian,' she hissed. 'I thought you would make killing you at least exciting.'

The marauder stepped around behind the body of Urbaal. He leaned down and ripped Gorgut's axe from the Chosen's back. 'Just finding the right tool,' he said, fingers tightening about the heft of the heavy axe.

Beblieth sprang at the marauder, her daggers flashing at him. It was only because of the deadening effect of Naagan's poison that her leap failed to carry her as far as she intended. She landed a few feet from the warrior and as she slashed at him, her blades carved only the empty air.

The heavy axe struck back at her, a new strength burning inside Kormak's body, a strength that burned away the fatigue dragging at his limbs. It was the strength of hate, the strength that had given Var'Ithrok its godlike power. Raw and primal, it roared through Kormak's veins.

Beblieth slid back in the pooled blood of Urbaal as she tried to dodge the brutal swing of the axe. The witch elf had yet to reconcile herself to her leaden limbs and fading agility, her mind still expecting her to move with the grace and ease she had always known. She paid for not adapting. Kormak's axe smashed into her right hand. The dagger she held went skittering across the ground, followed by several leather-clad fingers.

The witch elf shrieked in pain, but it was not pain that ruled her. Combat instincts honed over hundreds of years as a handmaiden of Khaine rose to the fore. She did not cringe away from Kormak's crippling assault. Even as the marauder recovered, pulled the heavy axe back, she was on him, the dagger in her left hand licking out like the tongue of a cobra. It scraped against the marauder's waist, trying to eviscerate him. Beblieth's face pulled back in a spiteful grin as she felt bone crack beneath the slashing steel.

Howling in fury, Kormak drove the butt of his axe into the witch elf, hurling her back. He was only too aware of the lethal venom of the dark elves, where even a single cut meant a lingering death. He had felt her dagger smash into him. Yet he did not feel the searing pain in his belly he expected. Perhaps the poison acted too quickly to be felt. Then he laughed as he felt something fall from his belt and clatter on the ground. Beblieth's dagger had not struck him, it had struck Tolkku's skull.

Beblieth saw her mistake. She lunged back at the Norscan, her maimed hand cradled at her side, her dagger raised high. This time she would cut the man's throat, as she should have done before. Naagan's poison was clouding her mind now, she did not have time to savour the slow and wretched death of her foe. She would have to be quick, kill him swiftly so that she might know she had sent one last offering to Khaine before she died.

The sweep of Beblieth's dagger was slow, sloppy for the witch elf. It was still only an amazing effort that allowed Kormak to twist away from the murderous blade, to block it with a downward tilt of his horn. The dagger scraped against the horn, scarring it deeply. Beblieth spun as she struck, turning to attack again as her momentum carried her past the hulking marauder.

She never got the chance to finish the motion.

Kormak roared a Baersonling war cry as he brought the heavy axe smashing into the spinning elf, hewing through her midsection in a single butchering motion. The torso of the witch elf was hurled away by the impact, the legs folding into each other like empty boots.

The marauder let the heavy axe slide through his fingers and crash on the blood-soaked ground. There was a swagger in his step as he walked over to the mangled witch elf. He glared down at the inhumanly cruel, inhumanly beautiful face of Beblieth, watching as death froze her cold eyes. He grunted with satisfaction.

Suddenly his victory over the Bastion Stair did not feel as hollow as it had before.

KORMAK TURNED AWAY from the carcass of Beblieth. The witch elf had tried to the very last to thwart the will of Tzeentch and the glory of Tchar'zanek, but in the end it had been the Changer who triumphed. The marauder lifted his eyes, staring at the great antlers which bound the Portal. The metal rings were still rotating, assuming new shapes with each turn, their arrow-like spines growing and shrinking to accommodate the shifting pattern. He wondered if the chill he felt pulling at his skin were the Winds of Chaos as they swept from the realm of the gods into the world of mortals. Vakaan would have known, so might Urbaal. But Kormak was only a simple warrior, unable to appreciate the fruit of his victory.

As he watched, the sullen sky was transformed, changing from bloodied hues and hidden fires to

rich blues and purples, vibrant and magnificent. Kormak thought of the maw beneath the Inevitable City,
the raging void that must one day rise from its rocky
prison to consume the fortress.

A shape emerged from the Portal, towering and
gigantic. For a hideous moment, Kormak wondered
if somehow Var'Ithrok had fought its way back from
the void to wreak vengeance upon him. The
marauder's fear only lessened slightly when he found
that it was not the bloodthirster who loomed over
him. This was a different creature, a thing of feathers
and robes, not armour and scars. The grey robes
draped about a lean shape, gaunt and haggard beside
the brawn of the Skull Lord. The wings that stretched
from its back were great pinions, feathered with
opalescence, their light casting a prismatic sheen that
rippled and danced about it. A long, vulture-like
neck protruded from its shoulders, supporting a
beaked avian head. The eyes of the daemon were
swirling pits of shimmering light, constantly pulsing
with new colours as they assumed new shapes.

Kakra the Timeless leaned upon its staff, a great spiral of wood and bone and gemstone that curled and
churned beneath its feathered hand. The Lord of
Change stared down at the little man at its feet.

'Let us depart, Kormak of Norsca,' the daemon's
voice shivered through the marauder's soul.
'Tchar'zanek has raised an army for me and I would
show him how to use it.'

ABOUT THE AUTHOR

C. L. Werner was a diseased servant of the
Horned Rat long before his first story in
Inferno! magazine. His Black Library credits
include the Chaos Wastes books *Palace of the
Plague Lord* and *Blood for the Blood God,
Mathias Thulmann: Witch Hunter, Runefang*
and *Brunner the Bounty Hunter*. Currently
living in the American south-west, he
continues to write stories of mayhem and
madness set in the Warhammer World.

Visit the author's website at
www.vermintime.com

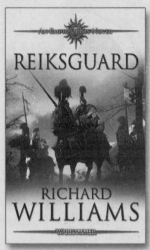
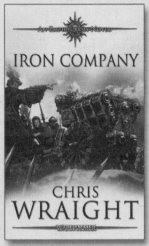

WARHAMMER

MATHIAS THULMANN
WITCH HUNTER

WITCH HUNTER · WITCH FINDER · WITCH KILLER

Buy this
omnibus or read
a free extract at
www.blacklibrary.com

C·L·WERNER

UK ISBN 978-1-84416-669-5   US ISBN 978-1-84416-554-4

TIME OF LEGENDS

‹ TIME OF LEGENDS ›

HELDENHAMMER
The Legend of Sigmar
GRAHAM McNEILL

‹ TIME OF LEGENDS ›

NAGASH THE SORCERER
The undead will rise...
‹ MIKE LEE ›

‹ TIME OF LEGENDS ›

MALEKITH
A Tale of the Sundering
GAV THORPE

This all-new series explores the tales of the legendary heroes and monumental events that shaped the very fabric of the Warhammer World.